QUARTERBACK CASANOVA

Quarterback Casanova

Lisa Rayne

FIRE SIGN
PRESS

Kansas City | Los Angeles

QUARTERBACK CASANOVA
Kansas City Griffins Series (Book 1)

Front cover design by Karol Jarvis.

Fire Sign Press
a division of Fire Sign Media Group
PO Box 9150, Kansas City, MO 64168
www.firesignpress.com

This is a work of fiction. Names, characters, places, and incidents are either the product of the author's imagination or are used fictitiously. Any resemblance to actual persons (living or dead), business establishments, events or locales is entirely coincidental and in no way reflects the nature, character, business practices or opinions of any person or entity for which a resemblance may exist. Any trademarks or trade names mentioned are the express property of their respective owners.

First Print Edition (June 2016)
ISBN: 978-0-692-69226-4 (Trade Paperback)

First eBook Edition (February 2016)
ASIN: B018X4WA48

This book is dedicated to

ALEXANDRA LARAE

Just because.

And . . .

for always saying "when" I become a famous author not "if"; for smiling when you noticed I used your signature saying about the dead fish; and for being totally awesome all the time.

QUARTERBACK CASANOVA

CHAPTER 1

Dash Janssen wanted to hit someone. White-hot heat boiled through his veins and fired his blood way past angry to downright pissed. Beneath a sun-drenched September sky, he tamped down the itch to strike out and forced himself to put one foot in front of the other.

A black microphone flew towards him, halting mere centimeters from his face. He jerked to a stop. A plague of reporters—who swarmed like locusts outside the downtown headquarters of the *Kansas City Report* newspaper—pressed close. Instead of crops, the hungry throng devoured his peace of mind and nibbled at the edges of his professional future.

"Janssen, who's the guy in the picture?" A balding newspaperman with an eager face shuffled forward.

A television broadcaster cut him off. "Janssen, how long have you two been an item?"

Dash turned away from the interrogators, but more

questions bombarded him from the other side. The commotion caused by the relentless bunch, their jockeying cameramen and shutter-happy photographers, grated against his eardrums and created bedlam on the otherwise calm city block.

No comment, Dash told himself. *Just say no comment and keep moving.*

His agent and publicist had briefed him thoroughly. He wasn't to react or respond to the press, and he certainly couldn't hit one. He'd made that mistake once, and it hadn't gone over so well. If he ended up with another fine from the Kansas City Griffins organization or the NFL Commissioner, he'd be screwed.

Another black mic swooped towards him, nearly hitting him in the mouth. Pain radiated through the molars he clenched to refrain from swearing out loud. He believed in the First Amendment, but when journalists practically mauled you while shoving one microphone after another in your face, you should have the right to defend yourself.

"Janssen, how have your teammates reacted to finding out you're gay?"

He didn't think his teammates gave a crap whom he slept with, but that was beside the point. His sleeping habits—or, more accurately, what he did in bed while not sleeping—shouldn't warrant this farce. It wasn't anybody's business.

"Janssen, why did you choose to hide your sexual orientation?"

An abrupt fist formed at Dash's right hip. He reined in the aspiring punch and tossed clipped words instead. "I'm not gay." He hated that his pro-athlete status had turned this ridiculous gossip into breaking news.

"So, you're saying you're bisexual?"

Aw, hell. Not the direction he intended to take this media circus. "No. That's not what I'm saying." So much for no comment. His agent and publicist were going to kill him.

Dash had worked hard to keep a low profile after his last *faux pas.* Now, all his efforts to stay out of the headlines amounted to naught. Just his luck, the press couldn't be content to twist the facts of real events any more. They had to start manufacturing their own.

The Griffins owner hated scandal and negative publicity of any nature. The press had already branded Dash as a hot head and featured him in several *R*-rated headlines over the last season and a half. He couldn't afford to be at the center of another story highlighting sexual behavior that would place him opposite the owner's conservative values—again. The guy already didn't like him.

He'd been warned: one more misstep and they'd bench him for so many games his season would in essence be over. He couldn't have that. With the starting quarterback temporarily out due to injury, Dash finally had the opportunity to show what he could do as more than a backup and position himself to take the first string spot permanently. He had no intention of letting this gossip-rag-worthy fiasco derail his chances.

Tilting his wrist, he checked the time on the face of the analog watch centered on a worn, brown leather band. *Ten minutes.* He had exactly ten minutes to get inside for the meeting his agent had scheduled.

How he'd manage that and keep his cool he couldn't fathom, but somehow he had to get through this mob so his personal representatives could handle business. Someone needed to start doing damage control, like yesterday. In his opinion, his people should have immediately sent out a press release and skipped this diplomatic powwow.

Screw diplomacy. He wanted the rag shut down and the job of the cretin who had phonied up that picture of him kissing another man.

Dash pushed through the buzzing paparazzi. His shoulders bunched as camera clicks exploded with the fury of machine gun fire. Tension settled into his muscles. After hours of practice, he craved a soak in his hot tub, a full body massage, and a woman wouldn't be bad. He'd showered away the sweat he'd worked up earlier on the field, but the heat from his frustration had his perspiration back on the rise. His jeans and athletic T-shirt clung to his damp skin, doing little to improve his disposition.

Dealing with this media nightmare, while trying to mind his *P*s and *Q*s, felt like torture. He'd welcome needles under the fingernails before he'd willingly walk this gauntlet again. Luckily, the *Report*'s front entrance stood only twelve short feet ahead. Once he got inside those revolving glass doors, he'd be free. The vultures couldn't follow him inside the building.

"Dash, come on. Give us something here," someone begged.

Dash shook his head and kept walking.

"Dash, you have to know your fans are curious about that photo?" a honeyed voice asked. "Especially with starting quarterback Shave Stephens out and you leading the team for the next few weeks."

Naomi. He knew that smooth as molasses Southern cadence without having to see her face. He slowly turned to his left.

Time suspended as his eyes tracked the crowd then locked on the sports journalist with whom he'd had an affair almost three years ago. She, out of anyone here, should know he was all heterosexual male. He shot her a look that telegraphed that thought, but she only smirked. He should have known. Hell hath no fury after all.

"Are you here because you're planning to sue the *Kansas City Report* for the article it ran yesterday?" Naomi finessed her way to the front of the crowd and stopped about a foot away from him.

He swallowed the lump in his throat. She looked good. She always looked good. From the moment he'd first seen her at a league party, he'd been attracted to her like steel to a high-powered magnet. That night she'd worn only a simple black cocktail dress and clear stilettos, but she'd taken his breath away. The dress's skinny straps had shown off her tempting shoulders and neckline. She'd tamed her mass of long, curly dark hair into some fancy up-do and worn no bling except a pair of diamond studs in her ears. The warm glow of her light-brown skin and her luscious curves had been all the adornment she'd needed.

His gaze moved up and settled on her face. She still took his breath away.

Today, she'd gathered her thick mane into a scrunchie placed high on her head and let her wild curls cascade down behind her ears. The large drop earrings she wore nearly brushed her shoulders. Their five uneven strands of tiny, dangling beads matched the color of the coral blouse she'd paired with tailored black slacks.

His eyes roamed over her lower half. She had a great pair of legs. Her designer pants currently shielded them from view, but he remembered what those long, shapely legs had looked like. More significant, he remembered what they had felt like wrapped around him in the heat of passion.

For a moment, longing assaulted him, stealthy longing so deep it reached beneath the years of resentment he harbored and tightened around his hardened heart. The unexpected bout of sentimentality caused unease to trickle along the hairs at the back of his neck. He was usually immune to such psychological failings.

Naomi's jewel green eyes narrowed, hinting she suspected he'd taken a stroll down Memory Lane.

He mentally shook himself and covered his emotional slip with a cold stare. "Ms. Pellier, you know the drill. Any official questions regarding legal matters should be forwarded to my lawyer."

She frowned, not happy with his response or his proper form of address. Tough. Once upon a time, he'd given her special access to his life. Then she'd betrayed him and acted such a nuisance after their breakup he'd cut her off completely.

He'd never intended for their relationship to go the long haul, but her underhanded act had accelerated the inevitable breakup. The premature end to their interlude had blindsided him. He'd thoroughly enjoyed Naomi. He'd gelled with her in ways he'd never experienced with any other woman, and they'd proved extremely compatible sexually—in bed, in the kitchen, and anywhere else he could get her primed and willing. For her to take part in this misdirected homosexual outing struck him as not only absurd but also disloyal. Leave it to her to betray him yet again.

"So, are you saying your lawyer is meeting you here now?" a masculine voice asked from behind him.

Dash ignored the follow-up question, nodded a dismissal at Naomi, and strong-armed his way towards *Report* headquarters. His brash movement knocked Naomi off balance. His hand shot out, landing on her hip. Pulling her to him, he placed his other hand on her opposite hip and steadied her. The familiar scent of her sweet Prada perfume wafted up, eliciting an olfactory Pavlovian response in his nether region.

His fingers tensed against the rayon blend of her slacks. Their close proximity made it impossible for her to miss the hardness Mother Nature wouldn't let him control. Twin emerald pools with the power to undo a man focused on his face. The look in those eyes had gone from haughty to questioning. The pulse at her neck beat erratically, and Naomi's lips parted to release light breaths, syncopated in time with her gently heaving bosom.

Dash's mind drifted once again to the erotic before he caught himself. Leaning in, he whispered for her ears alone, "You know better than this, Naomi."

With a glare, he moved her aside and entered the building. His long-time agent, Pete Daniels, paced a dull path onto the shiny black tile in front of the elevator bay.

Pete looked up. "It's about time," he fussed and steered Dash into a waiting elevator.

Right before the elevator doors closed, Dash glanced out the glass front of the building and caught Naomi's vexed stare. She challenged him with a tilt of her head, letting him know he hadn't shaken her bravado. His lips pressed into a thin line. He slid his hands into his pants pockets and wondered what her next move would be.

~ ¥ ~

Naomi willed her pulse to a normal rate as she watched Dash enter the building. Part of her wanted to throw her digital recorder at his head. The other part wanted to follow him into the building, corner him in an elevator, and strip him naked.

Okay, maybe she needed to rethink that strip him naked part. She was investigating the legitimacy of a photo showing him in a liplock with another man.

Talon "Dash" Janssen homosexual? She'd never had even a hint of suspicion. She couldn't claim to be an expert judge of a man's sexual orientation, but she'd spent enough time with her gay friends that she'd picked up a bit of their gaydar. Had she missed the signs with Dash?

The *Kansas City Report* had released the kiss picture via its online news magazine so the item had gone viral. When she'd first seen the photo, she'd immediately dismissed it as a fake. She'd waited for a statement from Dash's camp denouncing the picture as a phony or *PhotoShop* magic. When such a denouncement hadn't come, the doubts had set in—doubts about what had been real between them and what may have been cover for a man on the down-low.

Only moments ago, Dash had publicly denied being gay . . . or bisexual. Her gut wanted to trust that, but for the first time, she found herself second-guessing her reporter's intuition. The ex-girlfriend side of her, the part with a vested interest in the story being false, might be throwing her reporter sense out of whack.

Through the wall of glass fronting the newspaper building, she spied Dash greeting his agent. The footballer cut a sexy swag—tall, tan, lean, and built. When he'd glared at her with those light-brown, almost amber, eyes she loved so much, her heart had turned over in her chest despite the animosity that simmered in the chocolate-rimmed irises.

A silent curse reverberated through her mind at the injustice. *He* obviously didn't have any residual feelings from their past. The look he'd first given her, like he could see through her slacks, had suggested a contrary tale, but his words made his position clear. The Ice Prince reigned supreme—despite the evidence of the unexpected, lingering physical attraction he hadn't been able to hide.

A hormonal tingle jolted through her at the memory of his arousal. She reined in her awakening libido and sighed. No way would she go down that road again. Dash had a PhD in keeping his sex drive cordoned off from his emotions. She'd learned that the hard way.

Inside the building, Dash looked out at her. She gave a brusque nod of her head right before the elevator swallowed him and Pete. Once he'd disappeared from view, her elevated blood pressure leveled and her thoughts slid to her designated mission: get the scoop on the origin and meaning behind that picture of Dash seemingly kissing another man. She needed this story. More importantly, she needed an exclusive. Whatever it took, she had to find a way to get Dash to talk to her.

She looked around for his car. Nothing.

Shoving her recorder into her oversized tote, Naomi walked across the four-lane street to the facing coffee bar. A tall, white chocolate latte with a double shot of espresso called to her. She dug out her wallet and answered with enthusiasm. Nose hovering above the tiny oval in the travel lid, she let the sweet aroma of chocolate-laced caffeine settle over her agitated psyche. A few sips of the endorphin-producing liquid and the Dash-induced fog around her brain would be history.

Naomi took a trey of long, deep drags from the coffee cup and moaned softly in appreciation as the warm decadence slid down her throat. Equilibrium restored, she grabbed a table in a quiet, windowed corner to puzzle out her dilemma. Her boss had given her a directive—laced with a threat—before she left the office. If she didn't get first shot at this story, she could consider her career at *The Kansas City*

Sports Daily over.

A long, noisy breath escaped her. She dropped her head to the faux wood table, its surface warmed by the afternoon sun slanting through the windowpane, and rapped her forehead a few times against the toasty laminate. She should have seen this coming. Her editor had never liked having a female on his staff. Her relationship drama with Dash had only reinforced his opinion that women and professional sports don't mix, and the leave of absence she'd taken shortly after the breakup hadn't helped matters.

Her phone rang. She glanced at the screen. *Great.* Speak of the devil.

She picked up the phone and accepted the call. "This is Naomi."

"So, what'd you find out?" Her boss got right to the point. No preamble. No hello. The man had the personality of a dead fish.

"Dash is inside *Report* headquarters at the moment. He gave no comment on the way in."

"If you wait for him to give a comment, every paper in the nation will have the story. What's the point? I figured you'd have a leg up. Use your influence with him." He snickered. "Or maybe that's not so easy now that you're not sleeping with him."

Her hand tightened on the phone. *Prick.* "I've got this, Bill. I'll meet with Dash when he comes out."

"See that you do. It's been a while since you've turned in anything of substance."

And whose fault was that? she wanted to say. He'd intentionally kept her busy since her return with assignments that amounted to nothing but fluff pieces. "I'll get the story. You can count on it."

"Good. If you can't get me an exclusive on *this* story,

you're really of no use to me."

Yeah. Yeah. As if she hadn't heard him the first time he'd dropped that hint. She knew how to ferret out a story, and she didn't need the threat of unemployment to do it.

She closed her eyes, willing her voice to a tone that would disguise her budding temper. "I need to go. Dash will be out any minute." She clicked off without saying goodbye and dropped her phone on the table.

Fuming, Naomi reached into the portfolio folder peeking out of her tote to pull out a color printout of the infamous photo. She was torn. She knew how much Dash hated being in the spotlight for this type of nonsense. Despite the way they'd ended things, the last thing she wanted was to cause him any additional turmoil, but she couldn't afford to lose her only source of income with no other job prospects on the horizon. She made a nice salary so she'd managed to stash a bit of savings over the years. But with this economy and her current obligations, she'd be hard-pressed to live for very long off those savings alone.

This story was news. It wasn't going away anytime soon. If she didn't report on it, someone else would. Someone *elses* already were. They just hadn't delved beneath the surface.

Didn't she owe it to Dash to get the story right? It would be in both their interests. Surely, he'd understand that and give her the chance to play it upfront this time.

She studied the photo closely. Everyone had accepted what it showed at face value. She didn't buy it. Something wasn't right about the picture. Dash's image was off somehow. She couldn't quite put her finger on the discrepancy, but her gut gnawed at her. Trusting her instincts this time, she pushed away the uncharacteristic self-doubt that had spawned her prior wishy-washy thoughts.

Dash Janssen gay? Like he said, she knew better. A bigger story lurked behind what everyone else had accepted as obvious. She'd stake her career on it.

"And you're about to," she muttered under her breath before checking the time.

Nearly fifty minutes had passed since Dash entered the building. Time to get moving and figure out a way to get him alone. She planned to find out the truth behind that photo, and she had no intention of letting a pigheaded jock of an ex-boyfriend stand in her way.

CHAPTER 2

Butt propped on the sill of the double-wide conference room windows, Dash barely listened to the sound of Pete's voice spike in the background. Pete ranted about retractions and lawsuits and irresponsible journalism. Dash should have been paying closer attention to what was going on in the room, but his eyes kept dropping to the crowd that lingered in front of the building.

How had the press known he had a meeting here today? He hadn't told anyone, and unlike many other agents who took every possible chance—including manufacturing some of those chances—to thrust their athletes into the spotlight, Pete wasn't a publicity hound. Pete respected Dash's wish to keep a low media profile. He wouldn't leak information that could put Dash at the top of the breaking story cue for the nightly news.

Dash wondered if Naomi was still down there amongst the storymongers. The sight of her had thrown him. Why he'd been surprised to see her, he couldn't say. She was a sports reporter after all, one of the few women in the nation who covered football for the printed press on a regular basis. Logically, her presence made sense, but he hadn't seen her at a free-for-all press hunt like this in ages.

Why now?

Why had she surfaced to haunt him at this particular time, for this particular story?

The clear door to the all-glass conference room opened. Dash tore his eyes away from the view outside the window to watch a petite executive with a short, meticulously cut 'do stroll into the room. She walked over to a seated Deborah Ellison, the *Kansas City Report's* editor-in-chief, and dropped a folder on the table in front of her.

Ellison thanked her and lifted a hand in a Vanna White move. "Gentlemen, meet Laramie Mitchell."

Dash had never been a man who went for the petite type. Something about having to bend like a pretzel for favors as simple as a kiss seemed like too much work. To her credit, the confidence and poise exuded by the lady when she'd walked into the room gave her a stature beyond her mere height. Though she didn't do it for him, he suspected her own-it comportment—along with the pretty face that went with her hourglass curves—made many a man look twice.

"I'm not an idiot, Pete. I told you I had the photo authenticated before we ran it."

Ellison's comment drew Dash's attention from Mitchell's figure.

The editor flipped open the folder Mitchell had delivered and grabbed a thin stapled sheaf of papers from the open file. She tossed it towards the spot in front of Pete's chair. "Here's the expert report. The picture is legit."

Dash's body jerked upright and his butt left the windowsill before his brain processed the thought to move. "What do you mean it's legit? There's no way in hell—"

"Let me handle this, Dash." Pete lifted his hand at the same time he spoke, though his eyes never left the pages he was scanning.

The tiny messenger-woman gave Dash a dismissive smile before taking a few steps back from Ellison's shoulder. She positioned herself, hands propped beside her hips, against the credenza along the wall behind Ellison's chair at the head of the table.

"I'm warning you now, Petie, old boy. You slap me with a lawsuit, the countersuit I'll file will cost you ten years' worth of commissions . . . at least." A full-figured woman, Deborah Ellison leaned back in her chair, crossed her arms over her ample breasts, and grinned. "Might be kind of fun, actually. Laramie here—" She gestured behind her. "— hasn't had to go to court in a while. I have a feeling she might be getting bored."

Laramie gave a brief, hard laugh. "Hardly."

Dash shook his head. Ms. Hourglass Figure was a lawyer, a media lawyer. They were almost worse than the reporters they represented.

The lawyer stood. "I assure you gentlemen that our source was thoroughly vetted, the photographer checked out, and the photo's authentication followed proper procedure. Since I saw to those items personally, I know for a fact each was handled correctly. So, there will be no retraction. And unless you can provide us with some additional information other than your say-so . . ." She shrugged and gave Pete a pointed stare. "You know I don't do anything based simply on anyone's say-so, especially yours." Her eyes flashed with intense enmity.

Pete's usually charming demeanor iced. "Cut the bitchitude, Laramie."

Dash watched the exchange and wondered at the history between the two. They clearly had met before, but they didn't appear to be on the best of terms. He knew for certain Mitchell wasn't Pete's type so whatever had transpired between them in the past hadn't been romantic in nature.

Laramie straightened and glanced at Dash. Her lips pressed into a thin line. "There's no reason to believe that picture isn't just what it appears to be. You making out with your lover—your *male* lover." She strutted to the door and pulled it open. "This meeting is over, gentlemen. Have a nice day."

Neither Dash nor Pete moved. They stared at each for a moment. Dash waited to take his cue from the agent.

Pete finally unfolded his tall frame from the chair. Creasing the expert report in half vertically, he tucked the papers into the inside pocket of his designer suit. He glared at Ellison. "This isn't over, Deborah. When I find out how you managed to deal this from the bottom of the deck, Dash here will end up owning this damn paper." He buttoned his suit jacket and headed for the door.

When he reached Ms. Mitchell, she said, "Why is it so hard for your client to admit he's gay? In this day and age, it's no big deal. Maybe the truth came out before he was ready, but why not cut your losses and simply tell the truth? Everyone will respect him more."

Ellison jumped from her chair. "Wait! That's a fabulous idea. Why not give us an interview? Let the paper that broke the story tell the human side of things. Give the public a glimpse of what it's been like for you behind the scenes. Or, more accurately," she chuckled, "inside the closet." She said the last with a dramatic voice-over tone.

Dash sighed. "Even if there was such a story to tell, you people would be the last ones I'd want telling it." He moved to follow Pete, but stopped when Pete stood blocking the door.

Pete studied the lawyer. Despite wearing heels, she barely reached Pete's shoulder. Surprising Dash, Pete reached out with a hand that matched her almond-brown complexion and smoothed an imaginary strand of wayward hair. She jerked her face away from his touch, causing him to chuckle.

"Trust me, sweetheart," he leaned in, "if Dash were gay, *I*, of all people, would certainly know about it." Dropping his hand, Pete straightened. "You and your paper fucked up with this little stunt, Laramie. I hope your resume is up-to-date." He turned and strutted out the door.

~ ¥ ~

Twenty minutes later, after a brief, private pow-wow with his agent, Dash slid out the back of *Kansas City Report* headquarters. He couldn't believe the crowd of journalism piranhas out front had waited a full two hours for his meeting to finish. He moved swiftly down the block. As he approached the corner, he glanced over his shoulder. He didn't see anyone following him so he darted around the corner and set off at a jog across the middle of the street.

He weaved through the parked vehicles in the public parking lot situated on the opposite corner then crossed another street and darted into the alley between two red brick buildings at least eighteen stories high. He looked both ways to confirm no one followed him. Reassured, he slowed his pace and strode towards the nondescript white Hyundai SUV he'd tucked behind a large, hunter green trash dumpster. He kept the Hyundai for outings such as these, outings during which he preferred to remain invisible. No one looked for a QB of a top-tier team to drive around town in one of these. Plus, the heavy, smoky-black tint that dressed the windshield and windows kept him shielded from peeping eyes.

His hand shoved into his pants pocket for his car keys. The jangle echoed in the shaded silence of the alley. When he stepped around the dumpster, he froze. His fingers pricked against the sharp angles of the keys he choked with an annoyed fist and his jaw tensed.

He studied the surprise propped on the hood of his car. "Naomi." His voice came out like crushed gravel beneath the wheels of an angry eighteen-wheeler. "Just as resourceful as ever I see."

She crossed her arms against her chest and her stylish boot pumps ankle over ankle. "Hello again, Dash. How about you answer a few questions for me now?"

"No." He stepped behind the dumpster, passed her perch against the hood of his car, and slid between the brick of the east building and his driver's side door. He unlocked the car remotely with his key fob. "You'll have to find another way to get your story, just like the rest of the vultures."

When he moved to get in his car, Naomi darted to the opposite side and hopped in, too.

Dash dropped his head against the tan leather headrest and gripped his nose with his thumb and index finger. He released a sigh. "Not now, Naomi. This isn't a good time."

"When will be a good time, Dash? You give me a firm commitment to talk to me any time in the next twenty-four hours, and I'm out of here."

He stared at her silently.

"That's what I thought." She placed her tote on the floor. "I'm not getting out until you talk to me."

"Fine." He grabbed his mirrored sunglasses from the flip-down cubby above the rearview mirror and positioned them on his face. "Have it your way." He started the car and looked out the back window as he zipped away from the dumpster in reverse.

Naomi snapped on her seatbelt. "Where are we going?"

"I'm going home. You—" He looked her up and down. "You can go wherever the hell you like when I stop, but you're not coming in with me."

She stiffened beside him. "Don't do that, Dash," she said quietly.

"Do what?" He put the car in *Drive*, but didn't pull off.

"Play the asshole." She didn't look at him. "I don't deserve it. Whatever you think about what happened between us in the past, let it go. It's over. Right now, you're a professional football player in the middle of a breaking story, and I'm a reporter who wants the scoop. No more, no less." She finally turned her head his way. "How about we both act like grownups and take it from there?"

Her eyes darkened to a deep jade, a color experience had taught him to associate with her rising ire. Naomi turned fierce, and sexy as hell, when her Louisiana Creole blood got riled. That familiar tingle that started in his chest and settled in his groin whenever he got near her reasserted itself, unsettling him.

Naomi squinted when he didn't respond. She couldn't see his eyes behind the shades. She'd always made him take off his sunglasses when they talked so she could see his eyes. She'd said his eyes told her so much more than his words alone. Knowing this, he kept them on to spite her.

Eyes back on the road, he drove out of the alley.

Through the quiet left by the off radio, he felt her continued stare. Flicking his attention back to her face, he caught something soft and vulnerable in her eyes before she looked away quickly.

Thrown by the havoc her expression wreaked on all the cells that made him male, his hand flexed on the steering wheel. He stopped himself from audibly hauling in a breath over the punch of desire that hit him like a demolition ball to the gut. He still wanted her.

After Naomi, he'd had no steady woman. No matter with whom or how long he had sex, he couldn't get satisfied. Naomi had always satisfied him. In fact, sometimes being with her had made him feel too . . . everything. It had scared him a bit. A loner by nature, the thought that he might need her in his life had put him on edge in their last days together. When she'd shown her true colors, he'd almost felt relief at the knowledge that—like everyone else—she couldn't be trusted.

When he broke things off with her, he'd gone back to being alone. His meaningless, periodic sexual hookups didn't count. Naomi's presence in his car, the heady fragrance of her perfume, the thought of what lie beneath the fabric of her slacks, combined to make him want something other than his usual empty interludes. They didn't need a love match. The biology of it, he had no doubt, would still be explosive. His manhood perked at the thought.

Damn. How could he not be over this, over her, after all this time?

His gaze swung to her legs. He reached over and slid his palm down her panted thigh to her knee. She flinched. He grinned. He still got to her as well. Good.

Without looking at him, she removed his hand and

dropped it on the leather-wrapped gearshift. Her warm touch made him remember the strength and seductive power in those long fingers of hers. He wanted to feel them all over his body again if only for a brief rendezvous.

He pulled up to the two-story, black wrought iron gate that guarded the driveway to his Johnson County show home. He hit the automatic gate opener and watched as the gates groaned open. Anticipation rippled over him at the thought of entering his home with Naomi in tow. He should make the most of this opportunity. He could get the reporter in her off his back and take the edge off this oppressive sexual need in one fell swoop.

Could she feel this unresolved . . . *something* . . . between them?

He glanced her way before he put the SUV back in motion. "This is your last chance to make a gracious getaway. If you come in, you're not leaving until you get naked, horizontal, and wrapped around me for at least three hours."

She gave him a look that said *yeah right*.

He drove up the stone circle drive and parked opposite his front door. His mouth slid sideways in a crooked grin. "Okay. The horizontal part is optional. I always did love taking you standing up."

She shivered, but lifted her chin. He secretly enjoyed knowing he'd gotten her dander up. Naomi never could back away from a challenge. He waited to see what she would do, curious as to how bad she wanted this story.

"Naked, huh?" She got out of the car and looked across the top as he emerged from the driver's seat. "It'll take a better bluff than that to scare me off, Dash."

"Bluff?" He fingered his sunglasses to the edge of his nose, tilting his head down to look over the frames at her.

His eyebrow peaked. "You think I'm bluffing?"

"Yeah, I do." She turned and headed for the front door.

Dash watched the sweet outline of her butt in those high-end slacks she wore. The sway of her hips mesmerized him. His body's enthusiastic response to the sight filled the space behind his zipper until the painful press of his jeans made him want to groan out loud.

He shut the car door. *Bluffing? Like hell he was.*

CHAPTER 3

Naomi walked into Dash's home and lost herself. The memories hit hard and fast, bruising in the vicinity of her middle chest. She'd practically lived here during her last six months with Dash. She'd helped him decorate the place.

Nothing had changed. The warm colors, the elegant furnishings, the bold artwork, all remained preserved in her original design. She edged further into the entryway and glanced down the hardwood-floored hall. Her stomach tightened. Nothing had changed except for the antique hutch Dash had bought her on a surprise antiquing trip he'd taken her on to Nell Hills in Atchison, Kansas.

She'd spotted the hutch almost immediately upon walking into the nationally acclaimed antique store. She'd admired the hutch, running her hands over its fine oak-grained top in appreciation and lamenting that its large size wouldn't fit in her one-bedroom condo. To her surprise, when they'd returned to Dash's, the hutch had sat in the—

now empty—alcove at the mouth of the long hallway that led to his back office. He'd said then he'd hold it for her until she got a bigger place. Ironically, circumstances had led her to move into a small, two-bedroom house large enough to hold the piece, but he'd gotten rid of it.

Her gaze turned from the empty spot that once nestled her antique, and she choked off the sense of loss threatening to overtake her. Playful shadows danced across the entryway tile, drawing her attention to the natural light dripping through a series of skylights in the two-story-high ceiling. She'd always loved that feature. Stepping into the invading sunshine, she spun in a slow circle to survey the rest of the area and give herself time to regroup.

"I love what you've done with the place. Went crazy with the redecorating I see." The sarcasm sounded forced to her ears. She hoped he didn't notice.

"I like everything the way it is."

She stopped moving to face him. "I'd have thought you'd want to make some changes."

He shrugged. "You know my motto. If it ain't broke, don't fix it."

She did know that motto of his, and well. Living up to it had forced her into a romantic coma of sorts. They'd entered their relationship with a mutual understanding that it would be a casual fling and nothing more. Somewhere along the way, her causal heart had turned serious, but she'd done everything in her power not to let him know. Content with the way their relationship stood, Dash wouldn't have welcomed the shift. If he'd suspected the depth of her feelings for him, he'd have ended their relationship quicker than Usain Bolt could run the one-hundred-meter dash. As it turned out, he'd ended things anyway for a different reason, one even more painful than mere rejection.

Dash leaned against the door with his arms crossed. He still had those annoying sunglasses on. She couldn't see his eyes, but she could tell he watched her.

She tilted her head, contemplating his mood and her mode of approach. "So, Dash, what's it going to be? You going to give me the story behind that photo?"

His lips turned up in a lazy smile. His dimples winked at her and made her heart palpitate.

Slowly, he pushed off the door, removed his sunglasses, and dropped them on the entry sideboard next to his keys. He sauntered towards her. "Darling, I'll be happy to tell you whatever you want to know about that photo, but first we have some personal business to take care of."

Her eyes widened. She stepped back, unnerved by the realization he'd been serious about them getting naked. The memory of Dash in the buff flitted through her mind. Female parts long neglected sprang to life. She'd made a mistake allowing him to bring her here. She took another step back. "Dash, be serious."

"You know I'm not one for jokes. When it comes to getting you in my bed, I'm always serious." He continued to move towards her.

Naomi's heart pounded. She took yet another step back, but stopped when she noticed she'd almost backed herself into the living room. She glanced over her shoulder and eyed the black leather couch where he'd first kissed her below the waist. The memory incited dampening between her thighs. Her hand went to her throat, and she nixed the idea of retreating to the living room.

Dash stopped in front of her, his warm eyes lust-tinted. He reached behind her head and fisted his hand down a portion of her curly, waterfall ponytail. "You know, Naomi," his voice modulated to a low, contemplative tone, "you do things to me no other woman has ever been able to . . . before or after you. How do you manage that?"

His hand trailed down and rested on top of hers at the base of her throat. His smooth, even words washed over her. Naomi closed her eyes, fighting the urge to lean into him.

She wanted to be strong enough to pull away, but she found herself easing the other direction. "Shouldn't that be my line? You're not my type, remember?"

He chuckled. "You can't still be hung up on the fact I'm six years younger than you. I thought we'd killed that beast?"

With difficulty, she pulled away from him. "That's not what I'm talking about."

Their age difference had bothered her for a while. She'd never connected well with younger men. Their lack of maturity and inability to be dependable, responsible partners tapped into all her unresolved childhood issues. Dash had surprised her by being more mature than men she'd dated ten years his senior. As they'd gotten to know each other, and she'd learned his history, she'd understood that his upbringing had accelerated his maturation in a way no child should have to endure. Unfortunately, that same childhood had made him a trust-adverse, commitment-phobe. Which meant he lacked the dependability charac-teristic at the top of her male wish list. She couldn't rest her mind enough to put complete faith in a guy who had trust and commitment issues, especially a professional athlete.

"Ah." He nodded. "The whole pro-athlete, man-whore thing." He moved closer, brushing the front of his shirt against her blouse-covered breasts.

"I never said you were a man-whore." Her voice wavered.

His mouth curved into a half grin. He'd noticed the

tremors in her voice. "But you thought it often enough." His lips gave in to a full smile, making those annoyingly appealing dimples reappear to weaken her resolve.

Before she understood his intent, Dash backed her to the couch she'd tried to avoid earlier. She bounced off the dangerous resting place and landed against a wall of solid quarterback. Her hands flew to his chest. She pushed, trying to restore some distance between them, but he wrapped his arms around her waist and trapped her arms between them. He slid a hand down to her behind, pulling her closer and letting her feel the hard length of his arousal against her stomach. Everything in her went liquid and hungry, but she fought her traitorous hormones.

She pressed hard against his chest again to no avail. "Back off, Dash," she said in a breathless voice. "I'm not falling for your Casanova magic this time." She sidestepped away from him.

He stopped her progress with a hand to her hip and gently pulled her back against him. "Magic? Is that what it took for you to give me a chance?" He dipped his lips towards hers in slow motion. "Let's see if I can still conjure up a spell or two."

Naomi saw the kiss coming, but couldn't move. When his lips found hers, the reasons for her reluctance fled her mind. Magic? Yeah, he still had it.

His lips claimed hers without haste. He slid his tongue across one lip and then the other, taking his time as if refamiliarizing himself with her taste. Her pulse raced, and she became lightheaded. His kiss still held the potency to make her forget herself and her surroundings. Her knees faltered. She grasped his shoulders to anchor herself, melding her body closer to his.

Sensing her weakness, Dash grabbed her around the

waist with one arm and lifted her off the ground. His free hand rose to the back of her head. When he finally took entry to her mouth, he stoked the embers of their hiatal passion back to a full-on blaze. In mere seconds, the kiss slid from testing to happy-to-see-you-again to *damn*-I-want-you.

Naomi moaned, feeling her defenses melt under the seductive assault. If she didn't put the brakes on this, a trip to his bedroom would be the next order of business. She pulled away from his lips. "Dash, I didn't come here for this."

"That's okay. Now, that you're here, let's make the best of it."

His lips brushed hers again, mating seductively with the fullness of her lips then sliding across her jaw and down to that spot on her throat that when suckled by him had the power to spark her arousal almost straight to orgasm. She whimpered. She no longer doubted his seriousness. He meant to have sex with her. At this rate, they'd consummate their reunion right here in his living room.

She tried to wiggle out of his arms. "Dash, put me down."

"Okay." He perched her on the back of the couch of X-rated memories and stepped between her legs. The bulge straining the front of his pants found her pulsing core. He reached for her belt and began to unfasten it.

She grabbed his wrists tightly. "Whoa, whoa, whoa. Slow your roll, homeboy." Arousal, nervousness, and anger wracked her all at once and made her voice come out husky.

"Why? You're as turned on right now as I am. Why shouldn't we take advantage of this? I could bend you over the back of this couch and take us both to paradise."

He could. He'd done it several times before in this very spot. She trembled at the thought of him doing so again.

What had she done with her self-respect? This man had accused her of betraying him and tossed her out of his life. When she'd needed his support the most, he'd let her down. He'd proved himself cut from the same cloth as her absentee father and reinforced her belief that she should never seek romance with a professional athlete.

The realization that his suave moves could so easily entice her into wanting him again washed over her in tremors laced with humiliation. That he'd intentionally turned his seductive powers on stun to manipulate her made her lash out and bait him. "You were caught kissing another man. What makes you think I'd still want you in any way?"

Her curt tone broke his mood, but not his focus. "You mean other than your dilated pupils, your heavy breathing, and your damp panties?"

A sound of affront burst from her. "Damp panties? Don't flatter yourself." She released his wrists to dismount the couch.

He took advantage of the release to quickly undo her belt. "Do I need to prove it?"

She gasped as she slid off the couch. "You wouldn't da—"

She caught the determined look in his eyes and cut off her statement. He'd dare. Only a fool would push him to prove it by claiming disbelief.

Her hesitation gave him the time he needed to unfasten the button and slide down the zipper to her pants. "I wouldn't what?" he challenged, moving one large hand to the waistband of her pale peach panties.

The urge to run pressed hard, but she stilled the impulse. She hadn't made it in the male-dominated sports journalism world and testosterone-filled universe of professional sports by backing down from a challenge. If she showed fear, he'd devour her. *Not today. No way, no how.*

She turned sharply away from him, slapping at his hand. "Stop it, Dash! That's *enough*." Refastening her pants and belt with sharp, jerky movements, she moved to the opposite side of the couch. "You can't gloss over this by distracting me with sex. Tell me what happened in the meeting today." She pulled out her smartphone and pushed a few buttons. "I've searched for a press release from your people, but nothing's come up. Why not? What's the truth behind that photo?"

~ 4 ~

Dash clenched his jaw. Naomi's quick reversion to reporter mode served as the reminder he needed that she was a reporter first, a woman second.

He turned away and headed for the kitchen. He needed a drink, a stiff drink. Too bad he didn't drink alcohol during the season. Once summer training camp started, he strictly avoided the stuff. He'd have to settle for a really, really strong cup of coffee.

Naomi followed Dash into the kitchen, waiting patiently while he filled his coffee pot with water and measured out ground coffee beans.

The gurgle of heated water flowing through the coffee filter filled the room before he turned back to her. "You can't actually believe that picture is what it seems?"

"Why not?"

His right eyebrow went up.

She shook her head with an indulgent half smile and leaned against the frame of the doorless entry before taunting him. "It looked pretty real to me." She mimicked his earlier shrug. "People do things for strange reasons. I can think of a myriad reasons why a guy in your position would be silent or secretive in this situation—fear, intentional deception, self-denial. I'm not here to judge."

He watched her face as she said the last. A scratch of hurt settled in his throat. "Really? After everything we've been through together, you honestly believe I'm lying about this?"

This time, she raised an eyebrow. "Says the man who failed to give *me* the benefit of the doubt three years ago."

She walked over to his cupboard, pulled down a jumbo Griffins mug, and walked to the coffee pot. She waited a minute for the last of the percolated brew to trickle into the carafe before filing the mug and handing it to him. "Many women have found themselves in relationships with men they later find out are gay."

He took a sip of the black coffee she'd handed him. She was right about him doubting her before. He still did, but that was different.

She situated herself at the counter a few inches from his shoulder. "Or bisexual."

A sharp cough exploded from his airway as he choked on a swill of coffee. He sputtered through a clearing of his throat and lowered his cup abruptly. "And most of those women would admit that in hindsight there'd been clues. What about you? In hindsight, what were your clues?"

She didn't answer him.

"Right." He lifted the mug back towards his mouth, but thought better of slurping another gulp and halted the offending beverage halfway to his lips.

Naomi covered her own lips with a bent finger to suppress an impish grin.

As he watched her face, his hurt dissipated, and he got peeved. The mug in his hand plunked onto the countertop, and he spun to fully face her. "You *minx*. You don't doubt me at all."

Her lips lifted simultaneously with one shoulder. "No. I can tell there's something not right about your image in that photograph. Was it doctored?"

"No." He watched her eyes to see how she'd react to that.

"N-no. What do you mean, no?"

"According to *KC Report* Legal, they verified the authenticity of the picture before publication. They have a report from an expert certifying that the picture has not been altered."

"How is that possible?"

He stabbed rigid fingers through his hair. "I don't know. Someone's lying or bad at their job or . . . I don't know. All I do know is someone's screwing with my career. After that incident with the cheerleaders . . ." He skirted his eyes from hers and tried to stifle the sheepish pallor he felt creeping up his face.

Naomi rolled her eyes.

He gave a tiny lift of his shoulders before he continued. "DuChamps warned me after that. Third strike and I'm history." He sighed. "I want the starting position permanently. This tabloid blitz is going to screw up everything by sending DuChamps into another anti-Dash tizzy."

She perked up. "You think someone is trying to get you in hot water with DuChamps? Maybe get you back on the bench or traded off the team?"

"I don't know. Maybe. All I know is it's not me in that picture, and I don't know who the other guy is." He crossed to the pantry where he pulled pasta noodles and a stock pot from the shelves. He carried the stock pot to the sink and began filling it with water.

"Could someone have hired a lookalike? And if so, who and why?"

"I. Don't. *Know*." He turned off the faucet and sat the pot of water on the stove to boil before facing her again. "Look, Naomi, I really don't want to talk about this anymore."

"Come on, Dash." Her hands lifted and fell. "I want to find the truth. You've got to have some idea who'd do something like this."

"The truth? Ha." His facial expression turned harsh, mirroring his tone. "Don't you mean you want to find another scoop to further your career?"

Her jaw tightened with suppressed annoyance, and her eyes took on a flat stare.

"Bingo." He gloated, not shrinking from that stare.

"I'm a reporter. This is what I do. You knew that when you pursued me." The flatness in her eyes begin to lift like dawn mist assaulted by a rising sun. Solar-level heat darkened the normally jewel-green orbs into that dangerous jade that signaled her irritation level was fast approaching maximum load. "Stop acting so self-righteous and talk to me. I could use this story, and you'd do better to let me tell it than to trust someone else."

"Right. Like trust and journalism go so well together." He positioned himself in front of her. "I'd have thought the last column you did on my life would have set you up pretty well. Have you already burned out the shining star that rose over your career with *that* story?"

"How many times do I have to say it, Dash? I didn't leak that story about your childhood." She pressed her hands flat against his chest, and lowered her voice. "I would never do something like that. I tried to keep it from coming out, but I couldn't."

"You couldn't? Really? It was your byline on that article. Well, yours and Ray Jackson's. That doesn't suggest you tried very hard."

Naomi's right fist clenched against his shirt at the mention of her mentor. He'd hit a nerve.

He moved back to the stove to check his water. "I'm through talking about this for today. If you'd care to stay for dinner . . . and the night, we can speculate all you want as to the what, when, who, and why after you wake up in my bed tomorrow."

She pushed off the counter. "Stop suggesting I trade sex for your cooperation," she snapped. "It's not funny any-more."

"You slept with me before to get a story. What's so different now? At least this time, I know the score. No need to pretend there's something more going on between us than a reporter plying her assets to further her trade."

Naomi's face reddened. "You know, one of these days maybe you'll stop being such a jerk and actually let me explain what happened." A cold edge laced her voice. "I've never slept with anyone for a story, least of all you. You should know me better than that."

She stepped to him until they stood toe-to-toe. Her eyes levered up his chest to his face. The twin emeralds flashed sparks that should have set him aflame. "Besides, if I were going to seduce someone into giving me inside information, why settle for second best? I'm smart enough not to waste my time with the backup quarterback. I would have gone straight for number one and spread my legs for Shave Stephens."

His jaw twitched. He reached for her, but she spun away in a huff.

"Maybe I still will," she said over her shoulder. "After all, if you're gunning for his first-string spot, he'd have strong motive for wanting to ruin your credibility with DuChamps. That'd be one way to find out if he's a viable suspect."

"What!"

Naomi stormed from the kitchen, ignoring his angry shout.

He caught up with her in the entryway and grabbed her by the arm. "You stay away from Stephens."

Naomi's curt laugh bounced around the high ceiling. "What? Now you think you can order me around? Screw you."

"I already made that offer. You just turned me down."

"Grrrr!" She yanked her arm out of his grasp and seized his car keys from the sideboard. Snatching her tote off the floor, she headed for the front door.

"Where do you think you're going with my keys?" Shocked by her nerve, his eyes widened with disbelief.

"Home. You brought me here. You're getting me home. I'm not paying for a cab, and I'm not waiting for you to call and pay for one. You have another car. Heck, you've got two more in your garage. Drive one of those."

She gripped the doorknob and pulled open the door. It bounced off the adjoining wall with a bang. She glared at him. "I'll drop the Hyundai at the stadium tomorrow."

Leaving the door wide open, she rushed outside.

Dash followed her. "Wait just a minute, woman."

She ignored him, dashing to his car and activating the remote unlock mechanism en route.

"Dammit, Naomi. *Wait*."

She continued to the car without pause.

His anger escalated. "Don't you dare take off in my car

without my permission."

She didn't stop.

"I'll call the cops and have you arrested for theft."

After opening the car door, she eyed him over the hood. She had the audacity to laugh at him. "You do that. I'm sure DuChamps is going to love having this domestic tiff written up in the morning paper on top of all the other speculation about you. Let's see who ends up the real loser."

She slid into the car, revved it to a start, and burned out of his driveway. She never looked back.

Dash stepped back into the house and slammed the door. "Shave Stephens, my ass."

He'd make sure Naomi didn't get anywhere near another member of his team. The first man to touch her would end up with two broken legs.

After seeing her again today—after touching her again today—he understood something he hadn't suspected before. The two of them had unfinished business. They might not be a couple anymore, but she was his until he said otherwise.

If she wanted to make this a battle of wills, he'd damn well give her one.

CHAPTER 4

Naomi stopped inside the doorway of the Griffins' weight room the next morning. The clank of free weights and whoosh of pulleys accompanied muffled male voices that cursed, panted, and joked. The scenery—though not the smell—was enough to make a grown woman cry for joy. The offensive line had the room today. Half challenged their bodies beneath the free weights. The other half made their muscles groan beneath the resistance of high-tech weight machines.

She considered few sights more beautiful than a physically-fit, well-cared-for male body. Before her worked out twenty-four of the most well-preserved specimens of male physique within a one-thousand-mile radius. She stood silent, allowing herself the pleasure of ogling a firm tush here and a well-developed biceps there.

Finally, she stepped into the room. Like she had a tracking mechanism in her head and he wore a homing beacon, her eyes went unerringly to the man she'd come to find. Dash. She'd give him one more chance to be reasonable.

Dash stood under the weighted bar of the squat machine, his back to her. He'd removed his shirt, which allowed her to see the ripple of his back muscles as he situated himself into the proper position. A noticeable sheen of perspiration glistened over his torso.

She watched him squat a few reps beneath his selected weight. The nylon of his workout shorts molded to his tight, firm buns. A kick of hormones pinged through her nervous system. She stifled the urge to fan herself.

Needing a distraction to allow her body chemistry to settle, she pulled her gaze away from Dash, and let it roam around the weight room. When she spotted Jonathan "Shave" Stephens sitting at the bench press station, she smiled at the fortuitous coincidence. Shave had earned his nickname because he could shave more points off an opponent's lead, in the least amount of time, than any other quarterback in the history of the game. It stood to reason he might be able to turn the tide in this skirmish between her and Dash. Maybe she should alter her initial game plan and kill two birds with one stone.

Letting her hips sway in a movement as natural to her as breathing, Naomi glided over to Shave. She kept her focus on Shave but noticed over half the men present stopped what they were doing to watch her walk across the room. She internally shook her head at the unexpected compliment, not letting it go to her head. Men got distracted so easily.

When she got to Shave, he smiled at her. "Well, if it isn't the female Clark Kent." His words flowed out in a slow, sexy Texas drawl.

"Hello, Shave. How are you?" She leaned over and pecked him on the cheek. "And wouldn't I be the jock version of Lois Lane?"

He chuckled. "Hardly. Lois was a bit of a pansy. You've got way too much . . . um . . . gumption to be a Lois Lane knockoff."

Naomi laughed. "Why do I get the feeling you were about to refer to anatomically round male body parts rather than my 'gumption'?"

He just grinned at her, wiping his sweaty brow with a white towel.

She looked down at the leg he had strapped in a black brace from mid-thigh to ankle. If not for the injury, he'd be the current starting quarterback.

He pointed towards the leg. "Looks like your guy is finally going to get his shot at taking my job."

"Come on, Shave. Is it really that bad?"

"It's as well as can be expected under the circumstances, but I'm thirty-four years old. My body doesn't bounce back from these injuries like it used to." He dropped his towel onto the bench he straddled. "Of course, a few more sessions with the physical therapist from hell and who knows. Maybe I'll have another season or two in me yet."

"Giving you fits is he?"

"*She*. Hitler would have been a nicer taskmaster."

"Ah. Not a football fan, huh? Can't work your usual quarterback charisma on her?"

"That's just it. She *is* a football fan, the stubborn woman." He hunched forward slightly, pressing his hands against his thighs. "She keeps pushing me like I'm some high-schooler making a half-assed effort at my recovery. Knows my career and my playing style almost better than me. Heck, she knows more about the sport than most of the players here and keeps tossing my past performances at me. The only other woman I've ever met with near as much knowledge of the game is you."

Naomi considered his statements. Shave didn't give idle compliments. He focused on performance and results. Even though he'd grumbled his thoughts, he'd unconsciously given this woman high praise. A Nazi she might be in his mind, but she'd definitely gotten his attention. Naomi wondered what the woman looked like.

"Enough about Attila the Hunnette. To what do we owe the pleasure of your visit? We haven't seen you here in a while."

"Oh," she shrugged, "trying to get a certain hardheaded quarterback to work with me on the story behind the kiss that never really was." Her eyes moved to Dash, who was still preoccupied with his workout and hadn't noticed her yet.

Shave gave a hard single laugh. "Good luck with that."

Naomi glanced back at him. "Don't tell me you doubt me, big guy?" She ran a hand across his shoulder and gave him a flirtatious grin.

Shave grinned back at her. "Darling, I'd never doubt you. But you'd better have more than one ace up your sleeve if you're going to poker it out with Janssen."

He slid to the edge of the bench and placed a huge hand at the side of her waist. Letting his accent thicken, he called her bluff. "And stop trying to work me, little miss. I saw you watching him earlier. You only have eyes for one guy in this room, and he ain't me. So what's up with the flirtin'? You using me, Pellier?"

"Crap. Am I that transparent?"

"You are to me." He jerked his head in Dash's direction. "To that knucklehead you keep watching, I doubt it."

Naomi liked Shave. As a good guy and straight shooter, he could handle the truth. She needn't play games with him. She'd reserve those for the "knucklehead."

"Sorry about that, Shave." She glanced over at the squatting Dash once again. "He pissed me off the other day. Accused me of sleeping with him to get a story. I told him if I were going to sleep with someone to get a story, I wouldn't have settled for second best. I would have slept with you."

"Ouch!" Shave's deep belly laugh echoed across the room. "Really? Would've liked to been a fly on the wall for that conversation."

She took a step back, and his hand fell from her waist. "A possible theory behind the surfacing of that picture is that someone created it to get Dash in trouble with DuChamps. You know how narrow-minded that man is. He'd have a low tolerance for public homosexual displays of affection by anyone, let alone a key Griffins player no one knew was gay. Dash is already in the hot seat with DuChamps. This could be the straw that finally lands Dash at the top of the man's trade list. In which case, it would stand to reason the story was planted by someone who'd want to blow Dash's chances of remaining starting quarterback."

"Me?" His surprise was genuine.

"You'd be an obvious suspect. But I know you well enough not to waste my time exploring down that road. However, I gave him the impression I might sleep with you to find out. I just thought I'd give him reason to wonder."

"Not nice, Naomi." The natural undertones in the quarterback's shaggy, dark hair caught the light as he shook his head. "Not nice at all. Do you know what it does to a man to see a woman he's been with switch to one of his teammates?"

She grabbed her lower lip with her teeth and gave a slight shrug.

"Darling, that's just downright mean." He grinned. "And I love it. So, why don't I help you with that?" He stood. "Is he watching us?"

Naomi checked with her eyes without moving her head. Dash had finished his squats and was watching them closely.

"Actually, he is."

"Good." Shave wrapped an arm around her waist and planted his lips against her temple in a slow, drawn out kiss before he released her. "If I didn't think you'd have slugged me, I would have really kissed you."

A noise came from Dash's direction.

They both glanced his way before Shave leaned over to whisper in her ear. "Come on, it's time for you to leave so his imagination can take over."

Naomi laughed at the devious suggestion, letting Shave take her hand and guide her towards the exit.

~ 4 ~

Dash pressed down his heels and pushed up from a squatting position. He locked the squat bar back onto the machine and blew out a breath. He'd thrown in an extra set of twelve hoping it would relieve some of the sexual tension remaining in his body after his near miss with Naomi last night.

He grabbed a white towel from the side of the machine where he'd draped it earlier. Rubbing the towel down his brow and across his face, he turned towards the room and about choked on his saliva. Naomi stood with her hand on Shave's shoulder, a smile he could only classify as inviting graced her face. She'd flat-ironed her hair this morning and left it down. Parted down the middle, the long, straight strands hung to her middle back.

Shave sat at the bench press station. He had his hand on Naomi's waist. Dash's possessive instincts roared up, making him want to pound his chest then charge over and pound Shave. To stifle his urge, Dash flipped the towel over his shoulder and grabbed his water bottle from the floor at his feet. Eyes still trained on Shave and Naomi, he raised the bottle and squirted a stream of cool liquid into his mouth. When Shave rose and put his arm around Naomi to press a prolonged kiss to her temple, Dash squeezed so hard on the forgotten water bottle that water attacked his face and ran down his bare chest.

"*Dammit.*" He snatched the white towel from his shoulder and wiped his chest. When he looked up, Naomi and Shave were watching him, along with half his teammates. The amused look on Shave's face did nothing to endear him to Dash.

"You may be starting, but you're still second best, Janssen." Max Gordon, Shave's preferred wide receiver, smirked as he stopped next to Dash. "Once Shave finishes rehab, you're not going to be able to stop him from taking back his position any more than you seem to be able to stop him from taking your girl. I guess you don't put it down in bed any better than you toss a pass." Gordon laughed and walked away.

Try as he might, Dash had been unable to achieve a reasonable completion percentage when throwing to Gordon. The receiver took every opportunity he could to remind Dash of the shortcoming. The guy's jibe hit home while Dash watched Shave lean over and whisper something in Naomi's ear. Naomi laughed and nodded her head. The two turned hand-in-hand and started towards the exit.

Dash's feet started moving before he made a conscious decision to follow the couple. In four long strides, he caught up with them. "Naomi, hold on a sec."

Naomi stopped and turned towards Dash.

"Weren't you looking for me?"

She shook her head. "Nope. Actually, I'm here to see someone else this morning."

Dash glanced at Shave, who gave him a satisfied smile. He'd always liked Shave Stevens, greatly respected him on and off the field. Right now, Dash saw only a man moving in on his woman and respect no longer topped the list of feelings he had for the guy.

Naomi gave Shave a quick glance before looking Dash in the eyes. "But since I've got your attention, Dash, have you changed your mind about that interview I want?"

"No." He slid his hands towards pockets that weren't there, dropping the forgotten towel in the process. He bent to scoop it up. "I think it best if we let that matter rest."

"Rest? You know this story isn't going anywhere for a while." Her expression turned serious. "And neither am I. With or without your cooperation, I'm going to get my story. I'd rather do it with your cooperation, but I'm not opposed to forcing the matter other ways." She turned to leave with Shave.

Dash reached out and grabbed her free hand. "Before you go, don't you have something for me?"

Naomi's brow crinkled in confusion.

"My keys? You took my car when you left my place last night."

Naomi's narrowed eyes drilled into him. He'd made that statement loud enough not only for Shave to hear, but also any of his teammates within twenty feet. She didn't like what his comment implied. He smirked at her.

She tilted her head. A thick fall of hair spilled over her shoulder. "Oh, I almost forgot about that. You were such a sweetheart to loan it to me after the unfriendly way we parted." She gave him a glowing smile, a glowing fake smile, but no one but him probably knew that. "I left your keys with the receptionist in the front office. I know you're a busy guy, and I didn't want to interrupt your workout."

But she could interrupt Shave's workout?

She'd negated his implication with a simple twist of a phrase. He should have known better than to play word games with a woman who made her living crafting words.

She walked away and waggled her fingers in goodbye over her shoulder.

Shave put his hand at the small of her back. As he did, he leaned down to Naomi's ear and spoke loud enough for Dash to hear. "Sounds like you're going to need a ride. I'll be happy to take you anywhere you want to go."

"Why, thank you, Shave. I'd love to take you up on that." Naomi smiled and leaned against Shave as he escorted her from the room.

Dash cursed his stupidity at mentioning Naomi's return of his car, his annoyance at her verbally outmaneuvering him now greatly surpassed by his upset over her going home with Shave. He shook his head. She wasn't going home with Shave, he told himself. Shave was just giving her a ride.

At least, he hoped Shave only gave her a ride . . . in his car.

The disturbing vision of another kind of ride Shave could give her pushed into his mind. Fighting the impulse to go after them, he mentally wrapped his hands around Shave's neck and squeezed.

CHAPTER 5

Forty-five minutes later, Dash received a summons to DuChamps's office. He stood outside the door and ran fingers through hair damp from his shower. That he could think of, he hadn't done anything recently to warrant being called before the owner, but that didn't mean DuChamps wouldn't find something to complain about.

Steeling his nerves, Dash knocked and entered when beckoned. He stepped into the inner sanctum of the power behind the Griffins organization and pulled up in surprise. Naomi sat across from DuChamps, who leaned his massive frame against the front of his desk. He had the bulk and shoulders of a former linebacker.

A good ole boy from Texas, Martin DuChamps—like Shave Stephens—had lived his Friday-night-lights moments and carried the glory on to college. Unlike Shave, DuChamps hadn't made a standout performance during his university days and was passed over during the NFL draft.

Some players got to live football glory out on the professional field. Others, like DuChamps, had to settle for commanding it from the back office.

A couple of decades had passed since the man had last lived in Texas, but he wore his southern pride like he was flying national colors. A proud, card-carrying member of the NRA, his favorite hunting rifle hung on the wall below the mounted heads of two bucks he'd shot. The only piece in this office he treasured more was the taxidermied rattler perched next to the stuffed goose on his trophy case.

"Come on in, Dash. Take a seat." DuChamps coated the words with his heavy twang and gestured towards Naomi. "I know you know Ms. Pellier."

She looked at Dash, eyes neutral, and nodded her head.

"She came to me with a story idea. Said she'd run it by you, but you weren't interested." DuChamps rocked backwards and placed his hands on the desk beside his hips. "I thought maybe we all could discuss it."

She'd gone over his head? Dash took a deep breath and reined in his annoyance. "I don't think there's much to discuss, sir. As I informed Ms. Pellier, I'm not interested in being the center of a focus piece."

"It seems to me, son, you're already the center of a focus piece." He shook a finger at Dash. "Once again, your sexual proclivities are at the forefront of Griffins news. Hell, this business about you being homosexual is getting more press than our division standings. We're still a relatively new franchise. We can't afford for the only press about us to be gossip and innuendo."

DuChamps had located the Griffins on the southern edge of the greater Kansas City area. He'd gotten a lot of flak for doing so. This was Chiefs territory. Many people thought he should have planted the new expansion team further south in Arkansas, a state that didn't have a league team at the time DuChamps organized the Griffins three years ago.

DuChamps had opted, strategically, to plant the Griffins and their new stadium on the outskirts of the burgeoning Olathe suburb so the team was officially located in Kansas not Missouri. Still, some felt they were too close to Arrowhead Stadium where the Chiefs played. DuChamps insisted the greater Kansas City area had enough people fanatical about football to support two professional franchises, and *he* was fanatical about not giving those fans any reason to lobby against keeping the Griffins right where they were.

Standing up, DuChamps took one step away from his desk then turned back and slapped a palm loudly against the top. "Dammit, boy, I'm still fielding angry looks from the Cheerleading Coach over that business of yours with two of her girls. She's pissed because you cost her two of her best dancers."

"I didn't know they were cheerleaders when they came into the locker room. If they were concerned about the no fraternization policy, I'd think they'd have been a little more discreet about double-teaming a player while still on campus."

Dash glanced at Naomi who'd broken into a coughing fit. She was trying to suppress her urge to laugh, and he so wanted to strangle her right now.

He'd only recently straightened out the false media claim that he'd entertained two underage groupies in the locker room after the final home game last season. They'd actually both been twenty-one. Unfortunately, they'd also both been Griffins cheerleaders, which meant they hadn't readily come forward to clear up the accusation. When the truth finally came out, the women got kicked off the squad and the team slapped him with a huge fine.

Despite being cleared of any legal wrong-doing in the cheerleader case, apparently as far as DuChamps was concerned, this recent noise over the kiss photo placed Dash firmly in the middle of another sex scandal. "Sir, I've already explained that it's not me in that picture."

"True. But you haven't offered an alternative explanation so speculation's still rampant. We need to give the public the facts and put this story to bed. That's where Naomi here comes in." DuChamps gave Naomi the sweetest smile Dash had ever seen on the man.

Did the woman charm every man she met?

"Sweetheart, why don't you tell Dash here what you found out."

Sweetheart? Naomi hated when other men called her sweetheart, especially in business meetings. He waited for her to correct DuChamps, but she simply smiled at the man.

"Sure, Martin. I'd be happy to."

Sure? That was it? He glanced between DuChamps and Naomi. *Martin? She got to call him Martin?* He'd been on the man's team since the beginning and he didn't get to call him Martin. *What the hell?*

Naomi gave Dash an innocent smile. "I've traced the origin of the photo to a small journal in Ibiza."

"Ibiza? Where the hell is Ibiza?" Dash asked.

"In the Mediterranean. Off the coast of Spain." At Dash's confused looked, Naomi continued. "The managing editor of the KC *Report* told me she received a clipping of the article anonymously. With a little research, I was able to track down the freelance photographer who took the photo. The *Report* paid him handsomely to acquire an original print of the photo for analysis and for rights to run their own story." She looked back at DuChamps. "As we discussed, they claim to have had the photograph authenticated, and the photographer claimed he shot the photo on the beach outside a resort in Ibiza."

Dash snorted. "How the hell did he claim to manage that when I've never heard of Ibiza until now, and I've sure as hell never been there?"

"That's the million-dollar question," Naomi replied. "The photographer alleged you're a frequent visitor to this particular resort." She crossed her legs. "Someone's playing a pretty interesting game, and I'm curious as to whom and why."

The surrealism of the moment faded for Dash as Naomi's shapely thighs peeked from beneath her straight skirt. Her foot dangled and her calves caught his attention.

"Here's what we're going to do." DuChamps's voice broke into Dash's anatomical distraction. DuChamps leaned over his huge black desk and picked up two envelopes from the desk blotter.

Dash's eyes strayed to Naomi's face. Her eyebrows lifted and the edge of her mouth turned up.

Hell. She'd caught him checking out her legs. Could she get the upper hand in this meeting any more securely?

DuChamps handed an envelope to Naomi and one to Dash. "The two of you are headed for Ibiza this weekend. We have our Thursday night game tomorrow and a bye next week. We're going to take advantage of that scheduling to get this mess cleared up."

What? Dash scooted forward on his seat. "Sir, I can't miss that much practice. The next few games are crucial to playoff standings."

"Don't worry about practice. You focus on putting a win on the board tomorrow night and we'll have Wilson run the boys through the plays while you're gone. I suspect y'all'll have this all cleared up in a few days. You should be back by the end of next week, which will be plenty of time for you to ready yourself for the next game."

Wilson? The third string quarterback was going to take his place at practice. Was DuChamps already prepping to push him off the team? "Sir—"

"Lookie here, Dash. This isn't optional. Need I remind you your contract contains behavior standards and a morality clause? I've had enough of seeing your name in the paper." DuChamps paced a few steps in front of his desk. "I'm from the Lone Star State. Born and bred to be a one-man-one-woman kind of guy. I don't understand you young bucks swappin' out women—or, um, men—" He coughed. "—like you're changing underwear or this business about servicing multiple partners at a time." He stopped pacing and nodded at Naomi. "Excuse my frank talk, sweetheart. I mean no disrespect."

Naomi gave him a head bob of understanding.

DuChamps focused his gaze back on Dash. "But here's the thing. My wife tells me I've got to haul my a—" He coughed again. "Myself . . . haul myself into the Twenty-first Century and learn to be more tolerant. More open-minded, she says." He huffed disgustedly. "So, right now, I'm gonna put aside what I think about this current mess of yours and tell you I could care less what you or any other player does in his bedroom. That is until your shenanigans in the bedroom—or the locker room—end up a leading news story and become a negative reflection on my team."

Dash squirmed in his seat.

"I meant what I said the last time you sat in that chair, boy. Third strike." DuChamps flicked his fist at Dash with three fingers splayed. "Make no mistake. You're currently up to bat and your count is three and two. So, you can balk at this and take a final out count or you can take the opportunity to settle this matter to my satisfaction. What's it going to be?" DuChamps crossed his arms over his chest and stared challengingly at Dash.

Yep. Upper hand—check—firmly more established. Naomi had one-upped him with his boss. His career stood in the balance versus another of her bylines focused on his personal life. Dash swallowed the fury rising in his throat and nodded his consent to the owner.

"Good." DuChamps stepped behind his desk and sat down. "I've taken the liberty of booking adjoining suites for you two at the resort Naomi mentioned. I've agreed to foot the bill for this little expedition with the understanding that Naomi here will have exclusive access to you for comment purposes, and she'll give us an advance look at her piece before it's run."

Dash's gaze jerked to Naomi.

"I know what you're thinking, son, but Ms. Pellier hasn't agreed to give us any editorial power. She's simply agreed to give us a courtesy advance look so we can prepare a PR response should it be necessary." DuChamps clapped his hands together once and rubbed. "Alrighty then. Your flight leaves first thing Friday morning. Happy hunting." He picked up a stack of papers and began reading.

They'd been dismissed. Dash glanced back at Naomi, hoping she could see the promise of retribution in his eyes.

~ ㋱ ~

Dash rose from his chair and gestured for Naomi to precede him.

When they stood outside DuChamps's closed office door, he turned on her. "Really? You went to DuChamps with this? Are you kidding me?"

Naomi leaned against the wall. "Did you really think I wasn't going to do my job just because you choose not to cooperate?" She smiled. "Come on, Dash, I thought even you gave me more credit than that." She pushed off the wall and hefted her tote further up her shoulder. "Look at it this way. At least now, you'll find out what and who was behind the release of that photograph."

With a flick of her wrist, she checked the time on the diamond and emerald faced watch he'd given her on their first Christmas together.

"Nice watch," he couldn't stop himself from saying.

Her eyes narrowed. "It'll do."

I'll bet. His lips tilted left, and he peaked a brow.

With a shake of her arm, she covered the watch with the sleeve of her jacket. "I better get moving. Shave will be looking for me." She turned and began to walk away. "See you Friday morning." Without turning around, she lifted a hand in a backwards wave.

Dash watched her until she rounded the corner at the end of the hall, his annoyance over her leaving with Shave festering anew. The feel of paper crumpling in his hand made him look down. He eyed the squished envelope. Flipping open the flap, he studied the contents. His ticket indicated the first leg of the trip took them to Chicago and then London for an overnight layover. They wouldn't get to Ibiza until Saturday. The total trip would take approximately thirty-three hours. *Great. Just great.*

He glanced up. The specter of Naomi gliding down the hall to meet Shave Stephens teased his visual memory. The ticket in his hand crumpled anew. Long, determined strides launched him through the hall, down the stairs, and across the players' parking lot. Thirty minutes later, he stormed into his agent's office unannounced and slammed the door.

His eyes locked on Pete Daniels, who sat working at his desk.

Pete tossed down his pen and leaned back in his chair. "Well, come on in, Dash. I wasn't aware we had an appointment this afternoon." Pete's right eyebrow rose.

Behind Dash, Pete's secretary popped opened the office door and eased in. "Sorry, sir. He was moving so fast. I couldn't stop him."

Her look of chagrin triggered a smidgen of remorse in Dash. He hadn't meant to make the woman look incompetent.

Pete waved off her apology. "Don't worry about it, Marsha. Men three times your size can't stop this guy when he wants to get somewhere." He glanced at Dash. "Dash is sorry he caused you any inconvenience. Right, Dash?"

Dash ran a hand through his hair. The last thing he wanted was to get the secretary in trouble. "Right. Sorry, Marsha. I didn't mean to be rude."

Luckily, Pete would overlook Dash's brash behavior. Dash wasn't just one of his biggest clients. They were good friends, having known each other since college. Pete had also been a collegiate athlete. He still kept his former-baseball-player physique tip-top, joining Dash without complaint now and then for workouts that made many of his teammates beg for mercy.

Marsha looked between the two men. "Okay, as long as everything is alright." She stared at Dash an extra second. "Everything is alright with you, isn't it, Dash?"

"Not really, Marsha. Things aren't so good at all."

"Well, if anyone can get things back on track for you, it's Pete here." She stepped back through the door and put her hand on the doorknob. "Good luck," she said to Dash before shooting Pete an adoring smile and closing the door.

Dash stared pensively at the closed door. "When are you going to put that woman out of her misery?"

"You know my rule. T'aint nobody's business what I do." A wide smile spread across Pete's face, showing off a devil-may-care, bright-white smile. "She knows I'm attached."

Set inside full lips and contrasted against his brown skin, Pete's was the kind of smile that set women atwitter. Unfortunately for them, Pete preferred their opposite sex. Not that anyone could tell if they simply went by outward appearances, which meant he had as many female admirers as male. Add to that a charisma most guys would pay a year's salary to borrow for an hour, and Pete exuded a leading-man persona, the kind producers would cast in a role even if the script didn't specifically call for a black guy.

"But she doesn't know your other half has the same equipment you do. Which means she's still holding out hope that you'll see the light or, at least, eventually dump the loser so she'll have an open field."

Pete frowned. "Dash, don't start."

Dash thought Pete's partner Marcus was a tool. The man was an insecure whiney-baby who gave Pete grief every time the agent got a new male client Marcus considered attractive. "Okay." Dash waved a hand. "Not why I came." He took a step and then stopped. "Is that the problem between you and Laramie Mitchell? I sensed a not-so-stellar history between you two. What gives?"

A sigh resonated from Pete. "She was my sister's roommate and best friend their freshman year of college. We had an unfortunate misunderstanding. One I regret, but Laramie doesn't seem to be able to let it go." He waved a hand. "That's a story for another day. I doubt you stormed in here to discuss my personal life."

With a stab of his hand through his hair, the angst and anger inside Dash stewed up anew. "Right." He started pacing back and forth in front of Pete's desk.

Pete watched in silence. Eventually, he shook his head. "Are you planning to tell me what this is about? Or, do you simply intend to wear a ditch into my carpet?"

Dash stopped his back-and-forth movements. A quick grab at his back pocket lifted a wrinkled envelope. He tossed the crumple onto Pete's desk as if it contained a contagious disease. "She's at it again, and now, she's got DuChamps in on the game."

"Who's at what again?" Pete picked up the envelope and pulled out the contents.

"Naomi." Dash strode to the window. "She wants a story, and she's convinced DuChamps to send us both on an excursion to scope out the photographer who took my homosexual outing picture."

Pete chuckled at Dash's words. "You actually have to be gay to be outed, Dash."

"This isn't funny, Pete."

Pete grinned. "It's kind of funny. It's certainly a laugh a minute at my place."

Dash whirled. "Marcus?"

"Yep." Pete nodded, the amused grin giving way to a scowl.

"Ah, hell. I hadn't even thought of that." When Marcus first met Dash, he'd not been happy about Dash's closeness to Pete. The guy had been convinced more was going on between the pair than friendship and regularly accused Pete of having an affair with the quarterback. With all this recent hoopla about Dash being secretly gay, Dash could just imagine Marcus making Pete's home life hell with a constantly pointing finger and an *I-knew-it!* attitude. "Crap, man. I'm sorry."

Pete leaned back in his chair and waved a hand again. "Not your fault. I'm ignoring Marcus. He'll get over it as usual." Lacing his fingers, he propped them behind his head. "Now, what's this about Naomi?"

Dash nodded towards the envelope. "Ibiza! DuChamps is forcing me to go to Ibiza with Naomi. Can you believe that?"

"Why Ibiza?"

"Naomi traced the photographer and original story to some resort on Ibiza."

Pete sat forward. "What do you know about the island?"

"Only what the brochure showed. Posh resorts. Great nightlife . . ."

"And known as a gay-friendly travel destination."

Dash tilted his head. "You've been there?"

"Quite a few times. So, if your story originated there, it's probably not a coincidence that the scandal of choice was sexual orientation."

"Fabulous." Dash resumed his pacing. "You've got to make this go away. I'm damned if I am and damned if I'm not." He snatched the morning paper off the coffee table and opened to the sports section. He read the headline out loud, *"LGBT Activists Incensed Over Star Quarterback's Disgust at Being Labeled Gay."* He shook his head. "If I'm gay, I'm some sort of pariah because I hid it from my teammates and fans. If I tell the truth that I'm not gay, and therefore had nothing to hide, I'm homophobic. Either way, pundits keep finding a way to keep this news. DuChamps is furious. And I get the distinct impression that no matter what's to be found in Ibiza, DuChamps will find a way to use it against me."

Dash tossed the paper back at the coffee table. The

sections flew apart and scattered over the table and onto the accent rug beneath.

"I'm not going! I'll be damned if I let Naomi Pellier profit from me being in the hot seat . . . again."

"Calm down, Dash." Pete pushed his chair away from the desk. "You have a contract. An excellent contract, in fact. I should know. I negotiated it." Although Pete had a law degree, he'd opted to allow his state bar license to go inactive once he decided to become a full-time sports agent. "DuChamps's hands are tied absent a clear contract violation."

"I can't calm down. That bastard as much as said this was a contract issue. A contract issue? Can you believe that? He wants to make this about the morality clause in my agreement." Dash stopped moving. "Since when does sexual orientation become a morality issue? He's twisting this to suit his purposes. The man's wanted me gone since the cheerleader incident last season."

"Actually, he's wanted you gone since long before then. I'd say it dates back to that first Griffins party you attended, where you danced more with his wife than he did."

"What!" Dash's jaw dropped open.

"Or the fundraiser for Mrs. DuChamps's pet charity your second season when the two had an argument and DuChamps found her crying on your shoulder in the hotel gardens."

"That man can't seriously think I'm romancing his wife. She's nearly old enough to be my grandmother."

"But she doesn't look it. And let's face it, Dash. You're not known for being discriminating where women are concerned."

He shot a glare Pete's way, wishing he could shoot laser beams from his eyes and scorch the high-priced fade right off his head.

Pete put his hands up and laughed. "Don't look at me that way. *I* know you would never go there. But DuChamps?" He shrugged. "Like I said, he wants you gone. Maybe that's why. Maybe not. Either way, he simply hasn't been able to find a way around our contract . . . or Coach Waterman, who's intent on keeping you."

Crossing his right ankle over his left knee, Pete continued, "You and I both know this latest scandal isn't a morality clause issue, but DuChamps will do what he always does. He'll play a little fast and loose, get his expensive lawyers to poke through the paperwork and try to give him what he wants. He's got nothing. Be smart. Follow his edict and go to Ibiza with Naomi and see what you can find. Your best defense lies in knowing who your opponent is and why he went on the offensive in the first place. I'm working from my end on the photo authentication angle, but Naomi's probably twice the sleuth I am. Why not let her help you figure this thing out? Just play along."

"I am not 'playing along.' I'm not getting on that damn plane. And I'm definitely *not* letting that woman push my buttons again." Dash slapped his hands against Pete's desk, the volume of his voice rising to just above a yell.

Pete rose slowly from his chair and leaned with palms on his desk until he was nearly nose-to-nose with Dash. "I've got news for you, pal. Judging by your behavior, clearly she already has."

Dash frowned, incomprehension shadowing his face.

"She's got those buttons of yours pushed so firmly you're on the verge of short-circuiting." Pete straightened. "Quit acting like a prima donna. It's beneath you. Get your head on straight and focus. You've got a game to win tomorrow night. I need you in the zone against Atlanta. You can't afford to lose this game." His fists found his hips. "Then after you kick some Falcon ass, get up Friday morning and get your butt on that plane."

Dash huffed and whirled towards the door. Grabbing the doorknob, he glared at his agent. "Make this go away, Pete. Make her go away. Without me having to fly thirty-three hours to gay-pride playland. That's why I pay you the big bucks."

Pete growled and grabbed a crystal paperweight off his desk. Dash darted through the door and pulled it closed. He doubted Pete would actually heave the weight, but he wasn't taking any chance. The former pitcher could still throw a fast ball at least ninety miles per hour with extreme accuracy. Dash wasn't interested in feeling that connect with his head.

"I'm not some flunky, Janssen," Pete yelled through the door. "Get your ass on that plane Friday. Give me something else to work with here." The crack of something heavy smacking a wood desk resounded through the door. "Damn professional-athlete prima donna!"

Dash grinned. If he couldn't be at peace about this situation, then neither should Pete. Sauntering passed Marsha's desk, he winked at the slack-jawed secretary. He'd give Pete something else to work with alright, starting with the hide of a certain overly-ambitious female journalist.

CHAPTER 6

The thunk of her tote hitting her bottom desk drawer had barely receded when the smell of *Aqua di Gio* cologne hit Naomi's nostrils. The lithe, athletic body of Ray Jackson lodged itself into her work space. He was eighteen years her senior, but it did nothing to detract from the charismatic allure exuded from playful hazel eyes and a sexy swagger envied by men a decade or two younger. "Hello, Queenie."

She smiled at his use of the pet name he'd given her the moment he'd found out her ancestry. Her great grand-mother had been a revered voodoo priestess. Ray had told her that made her the descendant of royalty, a Creole Queen, and had referred to her as "Queenie" ever since.

"How'd the ambush go?" He smiled at the wide grin that spread across her face. "That good, huh?"

"He's all mine for the next week, and all expenses are being covered courtesy of the Kansas City Griffins." Naomi swirled in her desk chair, the grin too explosive to fade.

"Wow. You actually got tightwad DuChamps to spring for sending you and Janssen to Ibiza? How'd you manage that?"

She wordlessly continued to swivel and batted her eyelashes at him.

A loud guffaw burst from his lips, before they spread over straight white teeth in a seductive smile that kept him ever-popular with the ladies despite being eons past his pro football days. "The man didn't stand a chance." He adjusted to a more comfortable position and crossed his arms over his chest, his expression turning serious. "How'd Janssen take the news?"

The swiveling of the chair stopped. The fingers of her right hand rubbed absently against the chair arm. "He protested at first, but he ultimately agreed. DuChamps didn't give him much of a choice."

"Which may not be good for you. You sure you want to do this?"

"I'm sure." She pulled open her file drawer.

"Be careful, Queenie. Janssen's a scrapper. He may be blond and fair, but that boy has 'hood written all over him." He adjusted his pant leg and propped a hip on her desk. "He came up through the school of hard knocks, and he knows how to give as good as he gets. This is his career he thinks you're messing with, even though you had nothing to do with that picture. You don't back a man like that into a corner and not expect him to come out swinging."

"Dash would never hurt me."

"You mean not physically."

She looked away with cheeks burning. She gathered several manila folders from the file drawer and placed them on her desk. "That's ancient history, Ray."

His fingers found her jaw and turned her face towards

him. "Is it?" What he saw in her face must have worried him. He shook his head. "Dangit, girl." His arms flopped to his lap, wrists crossed. "You're still in love with the man."

She pulled her tote back out of the drawer and began jamming folders in. She no longer felt like working at the office. "No. I'm. Not." She whirled towards him. "I need this story."

Her situation with the editor had been coming for a long time. She'd had to work twice as hard as the rest of the personnel to become the number two sports reporter at the *Daily*. No easy feat when all the other sports reporters were male and the bias against females covering male sports still thrived in earnest.

She'd managed to out scoop, out write, and out commentate all but Ray year after year. Nevertheless, it hadn't been until she'd started dating Dash a few years back that she'd managed to advance at the paper. Even then, she knew bias was at work. Her boss had tossed her a bone or two to make sure she didn't take her direct line to a professional quarterback to one of his competitors. He'd gambled that information she might garner during pillow talk would lead to better headlines for the *Daily*.

The special concessions had annoyed her and made her a running joke with the guys. They'd guffawed in her presence about which player they could sleep with to keep her from stealing their jobs.

Dammit. She'd earned that promotion long before Dash had come into the picture. The good ole boys network just hadn't seen fit to give it to her until they'd seen something in it for them. She shouldn't have been perceived as playing the sex card to advance at her job. She loved sports, especially football. She knew the game better than just about every guy on the job, except maybe Ray, which is why she'd only risen second to his best.

Ray was a stand-up guy and true reporter. Despite his long-held, and well-deserved, position as the number one sports guy, he'd mentored her without hesitation or bias when she'd first arrived at the paper. He'd warned her from the outset that her relationship with Dash might ultimately hurt her more than it would help her. She should have listened. Unfortunately, her heart had overruled her head.

"You need this story, but you alone with Janssen across the ocean without backup may not be a good thing." Ray watched her intently.

She held his gaze without flinching. "You know as well as I do I'll get better content with Dash on site to up the ante."

Ray sighed. "I know. Just be careful, Naomi." He stood, a fierce look in his eyes. "I stayed out of your drama with Dash last time because you begged me to. If he steps out of line this time, I'm going to hunt that boy down and beat his ass. Understood?"

Naomi stood and hugged him. He was more than a mentor, sometimes he felt like a surrogate father. "Understood. Thanks, Ray. But I got this."

He hugged her back. "Famous last words."

~ Ϥ ~

Early Friday morning, Dash leaned with both hands on the bathroom sink, staring blankly at the steam-fogged counter-to-ceiling mirror behind the faucet. Fresh from the shower, he stood naked and half wet. A towel draped from one hand down the side of the bathroom cabinet. His body hurt from the pounding he'd taken last night. They'd beaten Atlanta, but just barely.

He knew he had no physical issues. The team doctors and trainers had looked him over thoroughly last night before he left the stadium. His teammates would be filing in later this morning for their physical evaluations, but he was excused because he was supposed to be getting on a plane and heading for the lovely island of Ibiza. At least, he guessed it was lovely. He'd never heard of it until two days ago and had no idea where it was until Naomi'd told him. Through a search on the Internet, he'd found details about the island's highlights and points of interest.

His head reeled; his splintered emotions worked him over harder than any defender ever had. The idea of going to a tropical isle with Naomi to flush out a story with him at the center didn't thrill him. The idea of going to a tropical isle with her for sundry other pleasures thrilled him to no end, and therein lied the problem.

That he could want her despite not trusting her confused him.

He wanted to get her alone. He wanted to get her alone with her sole interest focused on him and not the story he represented, but fat chance on that. His weakness disgusted him. She'd run her game on him once. He wasn't some idealistic chump who didn't know the score. He knew better than to fall for feminine wiles. What was that old expression? Fool me once, shame on you. Fool me twice . . .

Dammit. He tossed the damp towel onto the counter. He still wasn't feeling a trip to Ibiza. If Naomi wanted to play Diane Sawyer, let her. He didn't need to fly to the Mediterranean to figure this out.

He was in Kansas City. The team was in Kansas City. DuChamps was Kansas City. Whoever was messing with him had a connection to here. He just needed to figure out what. He wasn't letting some passive-aggressive punk fool with his life using anonymous, false press tips. He'd worked hard for everything he had, and he intended to keep it.

No one had ever given him anything, not even a real set of parents. His birth parents had died together in a car accident when he was an infant. Only a few months old, he'd ended up a ward of the state of Nebraska. By all rights, he shouldn't have a professional football career. A foster kid with a chip on his shoulder and a juvenile record, he'd done just about everything he could to ruin his life as an adolescent. If not for one fateful day the summer after his freshman year of high school, he suspected he'd be in jail now.

His cell phone rang. He reached for the phone on the counter. Glancing at the caller ID, he smiled at the coincidence and answered his foster sister's call. "Peyton, this is a surprise. I was just thinking about you."

She laughed. "Oh, really? And to what do I owe such an honor?"

He hesitated before answering.

"Ah. So not necessarily good thoughts. Thinking about that day in high school?"

"Something like that." Dash folded the previously discarded bath towel and laid it bunched along the edge of the bathroom counter. He propped his naked butt against it to avoid the cool granite and the hard counter edge.

"When I think about what would have happened to me that day if you hadn't intervened, I still shudder." The heavy breath Peyton expelled carried through the phone.

"Which is exactly why it's the last thing I want to talk about." He didn't want her reliving those memories.

She always argued they'd both been blessed that day. He had a bit more perspective about the incident now, but that day neither of them had had much to feel blessed about.

He'd changed the trajectory of his life, and hers, with an act of anger many construed as an act of chivalry.

Chivalry had had nothing to do with it. He'd been pissed, a common emotion for him back in the day. He'd gotten fed up with a man, his foster father at the time, who took advantage of someone smaller and too afraid to fight back. Dash had lost the tight lid on the contempt he'd harbored for the man for months. He'd blown the top that day, and everything else had been a fluke, a bizarre twist of fate that had freed him and his foster sister from an abusive home and put him on the path to a professional football career.

"If Coach Johnson hadn't been there to step in, I'm not sure what I did would have mattered."

"That's just it, Dash. If you hadn't acted, I wouldn't have been there long enough for the coach to get involved."

Dash remembered the incident as if it had happened yesterday. He'd been on the school track in mid-June. A few weeks before, he'd run in the Nebraska state high school track championships. He'd qualified to run in two events, but he hadn't made the final top eight to achieve All-State honors. He'd been determined to change that outcome his sophomore year and had been on the track running sprints.

The sound of an angry male voice had interrupted his self-imposed drills. He'd looked up to see his—and Peyton's—foster father pulling her across the school courtyard towards the parking lot. The man had stopped long enough to shake her and say something in anger Dash couldn't understand, but the look of complete horror on Peyton's face had made Dash's gut twist.

He'd glanced at his watch and noted it wasn't even two o'clock in the afternoon. That meant his foster mother wouldn't be home from work yet, but his foster father had chosen to pick Peyton up early from her summer enrichment classes. When Peyton had looked up at Dash, he could tell— even from a distance—that she had tears in her eyes, and that feeling in his gut had intensified.

Their foster father had yanked her by the arm towards the car. With Dash watching, Peyton had resisted but not enough to make a scene. Her look of hopelessness, and worse, of resignation as she turned away from him in embarrassment had enraged him.

He'd interrupted the old man tussling with her three nights prior. He had rushed into Peyton's bedroom at the sound of a commotion and caught the old man in her room. The man had jumped away from Peyton when Dash entered and claimed he'd just been disciplining her for some alleged infraction of the kitchen rules. The way Peyton had been clutching her robe together and the bulge in front of the old man's pants had suggested otherwise.

Dash had refused to leave the room. He'd ended up with a black eye when the old man had tried to make him. Despite a few painfully well-placed adult fists, Dash hadn't budged. They'd made so much noise that eventually his foster mother had come to investigate and dragged his foster father from the room. Dash had spent that night, and the next two nights, sleeping on the floor in Peyton's bedroom.

Not deterred, their foster father had shown up at school to try and get Peyton alone with no one home. Dash knew exactly what the pervert had in mind, and the frustration that he stood too far away to stop the man had nearly burned his insides to ash. Then, he'd spied a stray football on the field. He hadn't stopped to think about what he was doing. He'd grabbed the football and hurled it with everything he had.

The ball had flown in a perfect spiral over the athletic

fence into the parking lot and nailed his foster father in the back of the head, making the man crack his forehead against the top of his expensive, luxury car. During the man's stunned aftermath, Peyton had the sense of preservation to run from him to Dash. When his foster father had attempted to follow, the high school football coach had intervened. After figuring out what was going on, Coach Johnson had made sure neither Peyton nor Dash ever stepped foot in that foster home again.

Later, the coaching staff had calculated that, from where Dash had stood on the field to his foster father's parked car, Dash had heaved the football nearly seventy yards. The head coach had told him to bring his arm—and all his anger—to football conditioning the next morning. The rest, as they say, is history.

Lost in the memory, Dash caught only the tail end of something his foster sister said. "What?"

"I asked, what got you thinking about our darker days?"

He turned and wiped the residual steam from the bathroom mirror with his hand. "Naomi."

"You've seen her?"

He squirted shaving cream on the counter then lathered half his face. "Yeah." He picked up his razor and began to shave.

"Did you finally give her a chance to explain?"

The razor stopped mid-stroke. "About the story leak?"

"Yes, about the leak. What else?"

He'd told Naomi the story of what had transpired during high school to bond him and Peyton so close. Over time, he'd told her about his myriad foster homes, his juvenile transgressions, and the wild life that should have precluded him from going on to become a starter on a championship NCAA Division I football team and later a second round draft pick in the NFL. He'd told her those stories in confidence, never expecting them to pepper a column in the *Sports Daily*.

"Dash?"

"No, I didn't."

Peyton signed loudly. "Maybe it's time you did."

Water splashed as he rinsed the razor. "You're much too forgiving. You always try to see the good in people. For a woman who grew up in foster care, and *shitty* foster care at that, you're much too idealistic, counselor."

Adoption hadn't happened for either of them. Although he was older, they'd stayed close after he turned eighteen. She'd aged out of the system two years behind him and worked her way through college and law school. To this day, they served as each other's lifeline. If she ever needed anything, he'd move heaven and earth—without hesitation or resentment—to be there for her, and he knew she'd do the same for him.

"And for a man who grew out of foster care into a better life, you're much too intractable, football star." She dropped her voice to a scolding a whisper. "You should be able to tell the good guys from the bad by now, Dash."

"Once upon a time, I would have agreed with you. Anymore, I'm not so sure." He switched the phone to his other hand, squirted more shaving cream on the counter, and lathered the other side of his face.

"I know you probably don't want to hear this, but I liked Naomi. Still do. The fact that you're tied up in knots over this mess after all this time tells me you still do as well. You're not completely over her or what she did—or what you *think* she did—wouldn't continue to bother you so much. You're not going to be able to move on until you two clear the air. It's time you gave her a chance to explain."

Move on? They didn't need to hold hands and sing *Kumbaya.* He wasn't interested in any of that emotional catharsis crap. Naomi still got to him, yes, but he had no intention of letting it go beyond the bedroom. He wanted her sexually. That was all. Enough with the mamby-pamby thoughts he'd been having before his foster sister called. He wouldn't let Peyton—or his idle brain—confuse the matter.

Finishing the other side of his face, he skillfully turned the telephone conversation to another subject. He shot the breeze with his foster sister for thirty more minutes before getting to the real reason for her call—a desire for an update on what was going on with that photo.

She laughed when he told her about Naomi going over his head to DuChamps and the forced tropical island excursion. "I think you just got lucky, bro. This is your chance. Don't blow it."

After they ended the call, Dash looked in the mirror, running a hand over his clean-shaven jaw. *His chance? At what exactly?*

The alarm on his phone buzzed, warning him of the approaching departure time for the first flight set to take Naomi to Ibiza. He strolled into his bedroom and stopped when he glimpsed the discarded plane tickets on his dresser.

Peyton's voice echoed in his head: *This is your chance. Don't blow it.*

Pete's irate voice promptly followed: *Get your ass on that plane!*

He glanced at the bedside clock then back at the tickets. "Shit." He scrubbed his hands down his face. He had a decision to make.

CHAPTER 7

Flight 2350 to Chicago began boarding. Naomi looked around the gate area for Dash. She'd thought with a dictate from Martin DuChamps, he wouldn't dare blow her off on this. Maybe she'd miscalculated.

Someone bumped her shoulder, drawing her attention back to the boarding process. She shuffled along behind the dozen other passengers headed for First Class, a well-dressed pack of uppercrust day travelers and mostly non-communicative executives with their faces stuck in their smartphones.

Her upgraded seat status should have excited her. The newspaper always made her fly coach. With Dash still MIA, the perk wasn't giving her the rush it normally would.

Stubborn bastard. Why couldn't anything ever be easy with Dash? Just once she'd like things to go the way she expected them to go. No detours. No side trips. No extra baggage.

Sometimes she wondered how she'd gotten here. She'd never wanted a relationship with a jock. Her personal history had made her avoid professional athletes like the plague. Dash had been no exception. She'd shot him down from first flirt, figuring a young white guy couldn't be serious about her other than as a quick lay.

He'd surprised her with his tenacity, pursuing her relentlessly until she'd finally given in simply to get him to leave her alone. She'd figured she'd go out with him once then kick him to the curb. No such luck.

She should have known better. His reputation as a ladies' man had preceded him. Women flocked to Dash like bears to honey, and she'd fallen right in line. On their first date, he'd charmed her so thoroughly she hadn't been able to say no to the second or the third or the fourth date. She'd not only gone against her personal rule and gotten involved with a professional athlete, she'd gone and picked one who attracted drama like he carried the Bermuda Triangle vortex in his front pocket.

What did she have to show for her lack of fortitude? She had a career that had taken a turn for the worse because her boss believed her perceived pipeline to firsthand football information had disappeared with her break from Dash. No one seemed to remember that she'd been a great sports reporter before she'd started dating Dash.

This didn't surprise her, though. The industry considered a reporter only as good as her last story. With no substantial stories to show from her past two and a half years of reporting, people dismissed her earlier bylines as the result of her bedroom chatter with one of the most promising up-and-coming quarterbacks in the league. Even as a backup, Dash shined as a spectacular player. He didn't get to hit the field full-time, but when he did, he made a noticeable impact.

Naomi peeked over her shoulder before stepping onto the plane, hoping to see Dash at the back of the crowd. Her eyes moved over a good-looking man in a stylish navy suit. Unlike his compatriots, he wasn't clicking through his phone. His handsome golden-brown, almost bronze, face looked straight ahead. He seemed to be watching her scan the crowd. Her eyes flicked past him, but didn't find Dash.

As she turned back to boarding, she caught the gentleman's eye again. He nodded appreciatively, and his mouth turned up in a slow smile. Naomi nodded back, trying to suppress a grin. It had been a while since anyone had flirted with her. Or maybe, it had just been a while since she'd noticed. She wasn't sure.

A flight attendant sporting "Angie" in black across her white name badge greeted Naomi as she walked onto the plane. When Naomi headed towards First Class seating, another flight attendant reached for Naomi's ticket. "May I help you find your seat?"

Naomi suspected the woman actually wanted to verify she truly held a First Class boarding pass.

After checking the pass, the attendant motioned with her hand. "You'll find your window seat on the right-hand side, about half way down." She handed back the boarding pass. "Enjoy your flight."

"Thank you." Naomi wondered if the attendant would have been as diligent if Dash had been with her. *The jerk.*

True to his word, he clearly had no intention of helping her pursue this story. His mistrust of her was probably the predominant reason, but she suspected his unresolved childhood baggage fed equally into his resistance. The two of them made quite a pair.

Dash's neuroses stemmed from lack of attachment

during infancy and a failure to bond with any parental figure or find acceptance in a substitute family. He worked hard to stay detached from those around him even though she could tell he craved a human connection.

She, on the other hand, lived with insecurities stemming from rejection by her biological father. She judged every relationship against the likelihood a man could be counted on to stay. Yet, she found herself attracted to a guy who admitted staying wasn't on his agenda.

Codependent much?

She dropped her laptop bag and cardigan into the aisle seat reserved for Dash. A seat it appeared would go unoccupied. She went up on tiptoe to heave her carryon into the overhead compartment. The heavy tote dangled precariously on the edge before human heat suffused her back. Naomi glanced over her shoulder to see the man in the navy suit reach over her head and push the carryon firmly into the compartment.

Once the luggage was stowed, he looked down at her.

His intense dark-chocolate eyes took her off guard. "Um. Thanks. I appreciate it."

"No problem." His voice seeped out in a smooth, rich baritone. "I couldn't let that land on such a beautiful head." He winked before continuing up the aisle.

He looked as good from the rear as he did from the front.

But not as good as a certain pro quarterback. She nearly groaned out loud at the wayward thought. Just when she had evidence her double X chromosomes might no longer be immune to other attractive men, Dash Janssen had to traipse through her mind and derail all hope for a liberated libido. *Dammit.*

She snatched a fresh blanket out of the overhead. She

freed the rough, gray fabric from its hygienic sealed, plastic bag and discarded the plastic into the seatback pouch before taking one last glance towards her tall, dark, and gorgeous Good Samaritan. Tossing the blanket and her cardigan into the window seat, she grabbed her laptop bag and stashed it under the aisle seat one row forward. She plopped into Dash's seat, clicked her seatbelt into place, and pulled the blanket across her lap. She'd have to figure out how to work this investigative trip now that her star lead hadn't seen fit to show.

A female voice came over the plane speakers. "Ladies and gentlemen, please prepare for takeoff by making sure your seats are in the upright position and your seatbelt is securely fastened low across your lap. All carryon luggage should now be stowed in the overhead bin or under the seat in front of you, and all electronic devices should now be turned off and stowed until such time as the captain indicates it is safe to turn them back on. If you will direct your attention to the front of the plane, Angie will review our safety procedures."

Naomi checked her phone one last time in case Dash had tried to contact her. When she didn't find any messages from Dash, she put the phone on airplane mode and bent to put it in her laptop bag. A duffle bag plopped down in the aisle beside her feet, causing her to jump. She looked up from her bent position to see Dash shrug his jacket off broad shoulders. He folded the jacket, secured it under the duffle bag handles, which he strapped together with the Velcro closure attached to one side, and then easily hefted the bag into the overhead compartment.

"Move it, Pellier. You're in my seat." He watched her from behind his Oakley sunglasses.

"Cut it a little close didn't you, Janssen?"

He leaned in, purposefully invading her personal space, and smiled. "Did you miss me? Thought I wasn't coming?"

"No." She turned away from that smile to unnecessarily adjust the tightness of her fastened seatbelt. "I didn't miss you. But, yes, I wouldn't have put it past you to bail on this whole operation."

"No such luck, sweetheart." Arm along the back of her chair, he leaned even closer and placed an index finger under her chin to turn her face back to him. "I've decided we need this time together. Now scoot. This is my seat."

She snatched her chin off his finger. "You snooze you lose, Janssen. You can have the window seat." She twisted her legs towards the aisle. "Climb through."

He scoffed. "You've got to be kidding me." He flicked open the seatbelt and scooped her up. Dropping into the seat, he planted her firmly in his lap.

A loud squeak escaped her lips. Horrified, she looked around to see if anyone noticed the spectacle he was making of her. She lowered her voice to a whisper. "What the hell do you think you're doing, Dash? Let me go." She rocked forward in an attempt to get free.

His hand tightened on her waist. "If you want the aisle seat, Pellier, we'll have to share." He adjusted, turning her to fit snuggly against him in the widened seat. "I plan to make the best of the current situation. Might as well start with the plane ride over." He glanced down at her lips before focusing his eyes on hers.

What was there about a brown-eyed blond that was so smolderingly sexy? Those light, yellowish-brown eyes of his made a woman tingle inside when he focused on her. Melt in your mouth delicious, that's how she used to describe him, and he still pushed all her hormonal buttons.

He also made her nervous.

What did he mean they needed this time together?

He'd been the one to end things, and he'd kept his distance over the last two and a half years despite her many attempts to contact him. With what they had unresolved between them, how could he continue to flirt with her without conscience or remorse?

This was a game to him, plain and simple. He had a competitive spirit. She'd won the last two rounds. She'd gotten out of his house without getting in his bed, and she'd secured his exclusive cooperation for her story by getting his team owner to intervene. She had no doubt Dash was formulating his next play.

Understanding his game, she leaned into him and patted his chest. "Make the best of it. Sounds like a wise decision."

She tried to keep the mood light and flirtatious, but the closer position allowed her a full whiff of his cologne. He wore Mont Blanc Legend, that woodsy cologne he'd had on the night they'd met and the night they'd first made love. He usually reserved the cologne for evening outings. He had to have worn the scent purposely to get to her. The sandal-wood in the fragrance seduced her with memories of being twirled by him on the dance floor, being curled against him on the couch, being held by him naked body to naked body. Her flesh heated for him instinctively.

Something in her face must have revealed her mood shift because his eyes darkened and then narrowed. Before she could move, he kissed her hard and quick on the lips. When he pulled back, he looked into her eyes and ran his thumb over her bottom lip. "A wise decision indeed."

She stifled the urge to touch her hand to her mouth. The kiss had been quick, but no less potent because of its short duration. She needed to pack on thicker body armor for this battle.

"Ah-hem." They glanced up to see the stern face of Angie the Flight Attendant. "Please take your seat miss and fasten your seatbelt. We're preparing for takeoff."

Naomi scrambled to her seat and glared at Dash from under an embarrassed pallor. Leaning down, she retrieved her laptop from the bag she'd stowed beneath the seat in front of Dash. She had a deadline to meet. As happy as the cooperation of the Griffins organization had made her boss, she still had another story to submit by the time they landed in Ibiza. She'd focus on her article instead of how yummy Dash smelled or how luscious his lips had felt.

She tucked the laptop in the seatback pouch in front of her until after takeoff and glanced sideways at Dash. He watched her, his desire unhidden. She had a feeling he suspected her plan to use the computer as a shield to avoid interaction with him, but it didn't matter. Hopefully, he'd leave her alone during the flight.

Naomi wondered how safe she'd be alone on this trip with Dash after all. Maybe Ray had been right. Getting from Kansas City to Chicago shouldn't be a problem. But then she had to get from Chicago to London before they made it to Ibiza. Sitting this close to him smelling scrumptious all the way to London would tax her willpower.

A bell dinged and the captain announced they were next to depart. Once they reached cruising altitude, Naomi pulled out her laptop and went to work. She managed to ignore most of Dash's activities, but when the same flight attendant came to check on him for the third time, her concentration completely faltered.

Dash thanked the attendant for the extra bottle of orange juice she'd brought him unbidden. Under her eyelashes, Naomi watched the woman blush as she slid a hand across Dash's shoulder. Naomi tensed.

"You're welcome, sir. Just let me know if you need anything else."

"I'll do that. Thanks again . . ." He glanced at her name badge. "Darla."

The sexy purr of Dash's voice got under Naomi's skin. Annoyed with herself, she put away her laptop, pulled the blanket over her, and turned towards the window. If Dash wanted to flirt, fine, but she didn't have to watch.

When the attendant walked away, Dash leaned towards her. "I'll be back. I need to visit the little boys' room."

Still turned towards the window, she quipped, "Humph. All those free drinks finally catching up with you?"

He slid his hand under the rough gray fabric of the airline blanket. She stiffened, surprised by the move and the tingle the heat from his palm sent woman low. She feigned aplomb. Slowly turning her head, she peaked a brow and stared pointedly at the hand buried too close to the apex of her thighs.

His hand slid further up, causing her breath to catch.

"Don't worry, sweetheart. When I come back, I'll be all yours for the rest of the trip."

She shoved his hand away. His knowing look irked her, but she refused to let it show.

What was wrong with her? How could she have forgotten who she was traveling with?

Dash and women — bears to honey.

He was a womanizer, and she'd do well to remember that. If she melted for him like these other women, he'd take advantage of her offer, but it would change nothing between them.

She watched him walk away and forced her cowering willpower out of hiding. She'd be sharing an adjoining suite with the man when they got to London and again in Ibiza.

The first thing she planned to do when they got to those destinations was make sure the adjoining suite doors stayed locked, double locked even.

Did they have double locks in hotel rooms?

~ 4 ~

Adjusting his sunglasses, Dash headed back to First Class. The glasses weren't necessary inside the plane. He wore them primarily to discourage fans from approaching during the flight. He'd learned that when he wore sunglasses indoors, people took it as a leave-me-alone sign. He relied on the celebrity cliché periodically, finding it the easiest way to garner privacy when he wasn't in the mood to entertain autograph seekers. Plus, today, the shades had the added benefit of annoying Naomi. He suppressed a grin at the thought then his steps halted abruptly.

A man sat in his seat, a well-dressed man.

The stranger's words drifted to Dash. "Here's my card. If you every need assistance when you're back in Kansas City, give me a call."

Naomi reached for the business card and gave the man a charming smile. "Thanks. I'll do that."

Dash moved beside the seat, casting a shadow over the uninvited guest.

The gentleman looked up. "You'll be wanting your seat." He turned back to Naomi and kissed her hand. "Ms. Naomi, it was a pleasure. Sorry you won't be staying in Chicago. Hopefully, we'll meet up again when you return to Kansas City."

He stood, forcing Dash to step back to allow him to exit into the aisle.

Despite the scowl on Dash's face, the man offered a

hand. "Janssen, nice game last night. A few more wins would help us fans rest a little easier."

"I'll keep that in mind." Dash grasped his hand firmly and shook. He took in the guy's tailored navy suit, the easy smile, and the close-cropped wavy black hair.

The cocky SOB knew who Dash was, and he'd still had the balls to approach the woman Dash was traveling with. Dash wanted to toss his stylish, black ass out a window. He settled for an extra squeeze on the handshake, and fumed internally when the gentleman simply winked at Naomi before releasing Dash's hand and walking away.

Dash turned to the little Creole flirt and propped a fist on the hip that canted with his peeved stance.

She grunted out a chuckled. "You're kidding, right?" She reached for his abandoned orange juice and waggled it in his direction as a reminder of his earlier dallying. "Here. Your drink is getting warm."

He ignored the sarcastic offer and sat down. "Who was that?"

"Just someone I met during boarding." She gestured with the man's business card. "He noticed my press credentials when he helped me with my bag earlier and thought maybe he could be of service to me in the future."

"Like hell," Dash grumbled under his breath, snatching the card from her hand. He read the gentleman's private investigator credentials and name off the embossed, cardstock rectangle. The guy's last name was Rodriguez. *Fabulous.* He was part Latino. Just the kind of Romeo Naomi would probably go for.

Naomi snatched the card back. "I'll take that."

The announcement of the approach to Chicago came over the airplane speakers. Naomi tucked the business card away and pulled out her phone, ostensibly to check the time.

He noted her wrists. Today she wasn't wearing the diamond and emerald watch he'd given her. Intentional? Since he'd vocally made note of the watch, had she decided to stop wearing it?

He silently stewed while she prepared for landing and preened over the private investigator's antics. He'd bated Dash over her, and she'd obviously enjoyed it. Fastening his seatbelt, Dash pondered the good fortune the PI was staying in Chicago and not taking their connecting flight to London. If the man spoke to Naomi—or dared wink at her—one more time, Dash wouldn't be responsible for his actions.

Dash escorted Naomi from the plane at O'Hare International Airport and stayed close until they boarded their connecting flight. The trip to London was long, but uneventful. Naomi alternated between working on her article and sleeping. Dash spent most of the flight watching game film on his electronic tablet. By the time they checked into their London hotel, they were both off their sleep pattern enough that neither was able to sleep.

In the plush accommodations, Dash leaned shirtless and shoeless against the doorjamb of the entry that joined his suite with Naomi's bedroom. He held the tourism trifold that had accompanied his airline ticket forgotten in his hand. He'd skimmed the brochure after they arrived and learned more about Ibiza's nightlife and plentiful resort amenities. He'd decided before he left Kansas City that he needed to reevaluate this situation. Naomi had forced him into this, but that didn't mean he couldn't take advantage of the trip to settle more than DuChamps's satisfaction.

Let her work her investigative magic. As much as he wanted to uncover the origin of that photo, he also had a side agenda. With a week off at a Mediterranean resort and the hottest woman he'd ever laid hands on in an adjoining suite, the time had come to press this unfinished business of theirs. He was going to take Peyton's suggestion and use this as an opportunity to move on, move right on in to Naomi's bed. She wouldn't be thinking about Shave for long . . . or any other man. He glanced over at her laptop bag, eyeing the outside pocket where she'd tucked the card for the private investigator.

He turned his eyes back to her. She'd changed into a pajama tank and loose sleep shorts. Her thick mass of long, wavy reddish-brown hair flowed loose around her shoulders. Even without makeup, prepped for bed, she was easily the sexiest woman he'd every laid eyes on.

Head bowed over her keyboard, she typed at a feverish pace. He never failed to be amazed by how fast she could type. She knew he stood at the door, but she chose to ignore him. For now, he'd ignore her ignoring him. As much as he'd like to get their business-finishing tryst started, if he made a move now, he'd blow his chances later in Ibiza. He would suppress his body's immediate urges and wait for the romantic backdrop of the island resort.

"Are you hungry?" He finally broke the silence.

Eyes still fixed on her computer, she replied, "I could eat."

His lips turned up. The statement struck him as funny. "Of course, you could."

Something in his tone made her look up at him. "Got something to say, Janssen?"

"Nope."

The woman had an appetite. When they'd first started dating, he'd been amazed how a woman with her svelte figure could eat so often and so much. He'd never met a woman, other than his foster sister, who actually ate around him.

In Peyton's case, they'd known each other since childhood so he figured she couldn't care less what he thought of her eating habits. With Naomi, eating was one of her favorite pastimes. She'd said if a man was going to pay for her to have a meal, she felt obligated to make sure he got his money's worth. He later learned that in addition to being a food fanatic, she was hypoglycemic. If she didn't eat every two to three hours, her blood sugar dropped. At worst, this caused scary physical complications. At best, it made her cranky as hell.

"How about I order us something to eat?"

Her eyes narrowed and her gaze roamed over his bare chest. "You do that."

He nodded and turned to leave.

"And Dash?"

He turned back.

"Make sure you have all your clothes on the next time you come to my room."

He chuckled. "No problem, Your Highness."

She grinned at him before turning eyes and hands back to her laptop. His reference to their inside joke had gotten to her even though she was obviously trying to stay immune to his charms. Years ago, he'd heard Ray call her Queenie and wondered why. When she'd told him, he'd made it clear she was his Creole Queen and not Ray's. He'd referred to her on and off as Your Highness ever since.

He stepped back into his room and ordered room service. They had some time to wait so he jumped in the shower to wash off the hours of travel and rinse in cool water to calm his jittery libido. By the time he'd finished and covered himself with a T-shirt and sweatpants, a knock on his external suite door signaled the arrival of room service.

Dash tipped the attendant and wheeled the food cart to

Naomi's room. She hit a few buttons on her laptop then snapped it closed. She moved to get up.

He waved her back to the bed. "No no, Your Highness. I'm here to serve you." He pulled the lids off the platters on the cart and looked over at her. "Dinner in bed?"

She laughed. "Sure. Why not."

He served her then settled with his plate opposite her at the bottom of her bed. When he looked up, she was staring at her plate.

"Something wrong? Should I have gotten you something else?"

"No," she said quietly. "No, this is good." She looked up at him, but she didn't look happy. She looked . . . confused?

He reached for her plate. "You're not happy with that. Here. Let's switch."

She grabbed the side of her plate and pulled it away. "Absolutely not. The last thing I want is that humongous steak."

"Apparently, the last thing you want is also that grilled fish with asparagus and rice."

"Actually, it's exactly what I want." Her voice was hushed. She met his eyes. "You just surprised me that's all."

Naomi wasn't much of a hamburger and fries kind of woman. When she wanted food, she tended to want real food. Did she think he had forgotten that in so short a time?

"Don't think I've forgotten the little things, Naomi." He sat too far away to touch her, but he floated his voice out like a slow caress. "I remember everything about you."

She flushed. No doubt her thoughts slid to some of the physical things he might remember about her. She'd be right.

Her lips parted slightly and her breath whispered out. Her demeanor sent him an invitation he couldn't let his body accept. He dropped his gaze to his plate, picked up his utensils and willed his body to focus on the nutritional meal and not the dish of a woman sitting across from him.

CHAPTER 8

Not wanting to risk the easy manner he'd gained with Naomi this evening, Dash dove into his dinner and changed the subject. "What are you working on?"

She got a cat-that-swallowed-the-canary look. "Oh, just a piece about the likely success of a couple of second string quarterbacks who recently got moved up due to injuries to starters."

His interest peaked. *He* was a second string quarterback who'd recently become a starter due to Shave Stephens's injury.

"As you know, Johnson of the Jaguars went down last Sunday. This morning—" She glanced at her wrist, looking for a watch that wasn't there. "Or maybe it was yesterday morning. This time change has me all screwed up. Anyway, they added Johnson to their injured reserve list. He's out for the rest of the season. They're putting Miller in as starter next week for the Monday Night Football game."

"What's that got to do with your story?" He lounged sideways across the foot of the bed, propping himself on one elbow.

"Analyst are laying odds as to the likelihood the Griffins or the Jaguars will be playoff contenders this year without their experienced quarterbacks at the helm."

"So, they don't think I can get the job done."

"The consensus seems to be that Miller doesn't have enough time on the field or the nerves of steel he needs to lead the Jaguars to the playoffs. Where you're concerned, the opinions are split. You certainly have the on-field experience. Coach Waterman has worked you in whenever he didn't need his starter on the field. However, the current Griffins starting offensive line is more suited to Shave's strengths than yours. Many believe that makes the Griffins' chances a crap shoot."

He chewed. Around a mouth full of steak, he said, "Thanks for the vote of confidence."

"I didn't say I agreed with them." She forked an asparagus spear.

He dropped his fork on his plate. "Don't you?"

"Yes and no." She nibbled the asparagus spear down to the fork tines.

To take his mind off the commotion watching her lips caused with his awakening lower half, he reached for the cup of water on the cart he'd left beside the bed. He took a sip. "Explain that."

"I know you could easily put the Griffins in the playoffs if you stop acting like a backup Shave and start playing like a first string Dash."

He took offense. "I'm not acting like a backup Shave."

She reached for her own glass of water. "That's bull, Dash."

"We have an offense the mandates the plays—"

"You have an offense with set plays. The style in which they're implemented depends upon the guy who takes the snap."

He frowned.

Naomi replaced her glass on the tray and moved her empty plate there as well. She scooted back and propped herself on pillows against the headboard. "You forget I used to watch you play college ball before we ever met. You were quick and versatile in the pocket. You had the best play-action pass of any quarterback in Division I football at the time. Your slight of hand?" She shook her head. Her green eyes sparkled with admiration. She loved to talk football, and her passion for the sport lit up her face. "Simply amazing. Add that defenders couldn't predict whether you would throw a long or short pass or run the ball yourself, and you were downright dangerous. You were the only quarterback in the Division—and now in the National League—that could run forty meters as fast as any running back or receiver."

He'd finally gotten those All-State track honors his last three years of high school, cinching State Champion in the one-hundred meter and two-hundred meter dash his junior and senior years. He'd been the fastest sprinter on his high school team, which had earned him his nickname.

He positioned himself closer to Naomi's feet, allowing the familiarity of the moment to lure him into a comfortable ease. They'd spent many a night stretched out on the bed together talking, football being one of their favorite subjects. Out of habit, he reached for her foot and began to rub. She attempted to pull her foot from his grasp, but he didn't let her. His urge to touch her was too strong to be denied.

He pressed his thumb into her instep, massaging her

foot while he mulled over her words. "College was different. The coach built that offense specifically around me."

"Isn't that what Coach Waterman has in mind?" she countered.

"When Shave's no longer playing."

"Shave isn't playing now, Dash." She tugged her foot again.

He held tight. "But—"

"But nothing." She blew out a sharp breath and gave up trying to get free. "I keep waiting for the day you run for three touchdowns in one game like you did your sophomore year at Nebraska. Or, throw a touchdown pass over sixty yards in the air like you did more than once your senior year. Basically, I keep waiting for the day you stop playing it safe and realize that who you are is good enough."

Were they still talking about football?

Their gazes met. His thumb stopped moving. The air crackled with the undercurrent sizzling between them.

Taking advantage of his distraction, she slid her foot from his grasp in a slow, steady movement. She broke the palpable connection between them by turning away from his gaze and grabbing the laptop from the bed. She stood to put the computer in its case.

Computer secured, she turned back to him. "It's late. We should both get some sleep before our flight tomorrow."

Dash unfolded from the bed. He stood over her, letting his eyes roam over the pajama tank top and sleep shorts she wore. His gaze stopped on the way back up at her braless breasts, perky beneath the soft fabric. Under his gaze, their peaks rose to attention.

Naomi crossed her arms over her chest and said something to him. He had no idea what. Finally, she got his attention with a curt "Hello?" and a wave of her hand in front of his face.

He looked into her eyes. "Huh?"

"Stop gawking at me and take the room service cart." She leaned over the bed to retrieve his empty plate.

Her sleep shorts flapped with her movement, giving him a peek at a shapely butt cheek. The appendage below his waist was definitely awake now. He stepped behind the cart to hide the evidence of the physical effect she had on him. He'd adjusted his gaze to a respectable location on her body by the time she turned back to place the plate on the cart.

Naomi shooed him out of the room with the cart. When she moved to close the internal door behind him, he put his hand up to stop its progress.

"Did you forget something?" Her head turned to survey the bed behind her.

When she turned back, he stepped up to her. "Yes, I did."

Her brow creased. "What?"

He slid both his hands into her hair behind her ears. "This." His lips found hers in a sure, forceful kiss. He claimed her, letting all the pent up sexual attraction he'd been nursing since she first came back into his life flow through him and pass from his lips to hers.

She moaned. Her hands flew to his waist. "Dash," she breathed as she pushed against him.

He dropped his arms behind her back and pulled her closer, letting her feel everything he'd hid from her only moments before. His kiss grew more insistent and for a time, she didn't fight him. She fell into him and absorbed everything he gave.

Slowly, she finally disengaged, eyes haunted with the unaddressed history between them. "Dash, please. I—"

"I know. I know." He pulled her into a hug. "You didn't

come here for this." He inhaled, breathing in the familiar coconut scent of her shampoo. When he pulled back, he planted his hands once again in her hair on either side of her head. Focusing intently on her, he said, "Would you believe me if I told you I had no idea I was going to do that?"

She stepped back from him. "I believe you," she said quietly. "But it can't happen again. I'm not interested in being some sexual diversion for you." She put a hand on his chest when he started to speak. "It's over between us, Dash. You made that decision not me." She pushed him through the door.

The click of the lock turning on her side sounded then the sliver of light under the door went dark. He placed his forearm on the door and dropped his head against it. Her face when she'd talked about his college legacy flashed through his mind. He hadn't realized she believed that much in him—or rather, in his abilities. It was heady stuff, this feeling that someone had unflappable faith in you. He'd forgotten what it felt like . . . until tonight.

Yes, he'd made the decision to end things between them. For the first time, he regretted that decision. "No," he whispered aloud. He wouldn't let regret take hold; he couldn't let himself fall under her spell again.

Tomorrow, they'd arrive in Ibiza and he'd commence his plan to purge himself of her demons for good. She'd put him off tonight, but it would be the last time.

~ 4 ~

The next day, Naomi took Dash's hand and let him pull her from the taxi in front of the posh Ibiza resort at which they had a reservation. A wall of glass marked the entrance and slid open automatically at the center when approached.

The overhead awning offered the only shade in the sun-infused location. The orange and blues and greens of the tropical flora gracing the front landscape preened in Technicolor brilliance.

A valet came forward and scooped up the luggage planted by the cabbie side-by-side on the ground. "Welcome back, sir," the valet said to Dash. "Always good to see you again."

The valet headed into the hotel with their luggage.

Naomi looked at Dash.

"Don't look at me. I've never seen that guy before." He stared after the valet in disbelief.

"Well, he sure seemed to know you." She walked past him, and followed the valet and their luggage to the check-in counter.

Dash joined her at the counter. Completely ignoring Naomi's presence, the woman behind the counter smiled at Dash. Her welcoming look offered more than good customer service. "Hello, sir. Are you staying in your usual suite?"

"Um . . ." Dash glanced at Naomi. He looked like he'd stepped into *The Twilight Zone*.

The receptionist's hands flew over the keyboard for the reservation system. She frowned. "I'm sorry, sir. I don't seem to have a reservation for you starting tonight."

Naomi presented their confirmation ticket. "Here. I don't believe the reservation was made through the usual channels."

The woman took the sheet and read. Her eyebrows rose, and she gave Naomi an assessing once over. "I see."

The hostess's fingers flew over the keyboard again then she programmed two electronic keys and slid them across the counter. "Here are the keys to your adjoining suites." Her eyes flicked to Naomi's as she said the words *adjoining suites*, not even pretending to give a fake smile. Her eyes warmed when she turned her gaze back to Dash. "As always, please let me know if there's anything I can do for you during your stay." She managed to give him another smile that looked more like an invitation. "Anything at all."

Hello! Naomi thought. *Am I not standing here?*

While she and Dash weren't actually a couple, this twit didn't know that. The need to put the brazen hussy in her place made Naomi put her left arm around Dash's waist. She leaned into him and placed her right hand on his chest. "I'm sure he appreciates the offer." The look she gave the heifer behind the desk was the furthest thing from a smile. "But I've got him covered. Thanks anyway."

Naomi grabbed both keycards off the counter. When she glanced up, Dash's amused expression made her want to smack him. She stormed over to the elevator bay and stabbed the call button.

Dash followed her, wearing a smirk of satisfaction. "So you've got me covered, huh?"

"Don't let it go to your head. It wasn't personal."

His satisfied look got bigger. "Seemed pretty personal to me. Jealous?"

She scoffed. "Don't flatter yourself. It's the principle of the thing. I can't stand women who flirt with a man when the woman he's with is standing right there."

The elevator dinged and its doors opened.

"But *we're* not together, Naomi." Dash held the door at bay so she could enter.

Her glower pierced him as she slid past. "She didn't know that." She stabbed the button to their floor. "The twit."

He chuckled at her indignation, and she turned on him. "Don't make me hurt you, Janssen. I don't appreciate being laughed at."

He raised his hands palms out. "I'd never laugh at you, sweetheart." He leaned in. "If the situation were reversed, I'd have been jealous, too."

His words skittered over her and jacked up her pulse. They rode in silence all the way to their floor. By the time the elevator bounced to a stop and Dash exited in front of her, she had a warning voice whispering in her head: *You are in so much trouble, Naomi Pellier. What were you thinking?*

When she caught up with Dash at the doors to their suites, a bellman waited with him. Dash took his keycard from her and opened his door.

The bellman followed them into the room and unloaded Dash's luggage. "Shall I take the lady's things next door, sir, or shall I leave them here with you."

"Leave them. I'll take care of it," Dash said.

The man placed Naomi's luggage on the floor and accepted the tip Dash handed him. He bowed and gave a big grin. "Thank you, sir. And welcome back."

After the man departed the room, Dash turned to her. "What the hell is wrong with all these people?"

She studied him, looking for signs of prevarication. "Are you sure you've never been here before?"

He ran a hand through his hair. "You're joking right?"

"Dash, that guy was happy with your generous tip, but he wasn't surprised by it. You don't just look like someone they know, you're also acting like him."

He stepped up to her and placed his hands on her shoulders. "Listen to me." He leaned till they were eye to eye. "I've never been here before. I'd never heard of Ibiza before three days ago in DuChamps's office. I've never kissed a man. Or let a man kiss me." His voice rose. "I'm not gay. I'm not bisexual. Right now, what I am is confused as hell." He shook her once. "And if you continue to doubt me,

I'm going to completely lose it and go find the nearest bar where I can pick a fight and proceed to beat the crap out of someone." He released her, and threaded both hands into his hair. "At this point, it won't matter who. Anyone will do."

His eyes bored into hers with a frustration that matched his voice. He waited for her to respond in some manner.

"I'm sorry, Dash." She moved closer to him. "I believe you. I had to ask though. You understand that, right?"

He huffed out a sigh. "I understand, but it doesn't make this any easier."

He walked over to the bed and sat. After a few seconds, he flopped backwards onto the bed and spread his arms as if about to make a snow angel. "If the intent of whomever is behind this was to drive me batshit crazy, it's working." Both his hands came up and raked over his face.

She moved to the edge of the bed and looked down at him. "Then what are you lying there for?"

He dropped his hands to look at her.

"How about we change out of these clothes and go figure out what's going on? That way, you can at least beat the crap out of someone who deserves it."

"I like the sound of that." He sat up, reaching for her hand. "Have I ever told you how much I love the tough girl side of you?"

She laughed and tried to pull away from him. "No. You haven't."

He tugged her hand, making her fall across his lap. "I do." He steadied her and looked into her eyes, those amberish orbs piercing her. "A man like me appreciates a woman with a little scrap in her. You're one in a million, Naomi Pellier. Thanks for believing in me." His head dipped towards her.

Naomi averted her head before his lips reached hers and jumped out his lap. "You're welcome." She rushed to her suitcase and grabbed up the telescoping handle. "I'm going to change and make a few phone calls. I'll meet you back here in about an hour." She didn't wait for his response. She hurried through the adjoining door to her suite, making sure to lock the door behind her.

~ ५ ~

After a shower, Dash changed into a Ralph Lauren T-shirt and linen pants with cuffs that rolled up to mid-calf. Brown leather sandals on his feet, he stood staring out the window waiting for Naomi's return. He thought about her easy acceptance of his declaration that he hadn't been here before. Faced with all these people who seemed to know him, she'd shown remarkable faith for a woman he'd dismissed when she'd asked him to do the same for her.

Guilt gnawed at him.

Initially, he'd looked at this trip as simply a way to get her in bed. His body still wanted her. He had chocked that up to basic chemistry, a simple case of lust, but this pull he felt came from someplace other than pure hormonal overload.

Twice now, he'd gone to kiss her without conscious thought. The urge hadn't been a precursor to getting laid. He'd wanted to feel his lips against hers, plain and simple. He'd wanted the connection. He'd wanted that connection specifically with her. Yet, she hadn't welcomed his advances. In fact, fifty minutes ago, she'd fled from him like he carried the bubonic plague.

He glanced over at the locked door between their suites. He'd told himself his goal was to make sure that door stayed open between them so he could seduce her. Now, he questioned whether he truly wanted events to play out that way.

He'd never thought he'd want her back—not all of her. Want more than just her body. Want her heart and her loyalty and her soul. After the jealousy that had tap danced all over his ego the day he'd seen her with Shave Stephens, he wasn't so sure any longer.

He paced to the center of the room and then back to the window.

Peyton had warned him he wouldn't be able to move on if he didn't hear Naomi out about the article she wrote with her colleague about Dash's life in foster care. Maybe it was time he listened to his foster sister's advice.

What if he'd wrongly accused Naomi? Had he gone through this distance from her for nothing?

After he'd pushed her out of his life, he'd felt a depth of loneliness he hadn't experienced since before he'd aged out of the foster care system and bonded with his college teammates. It had shaken him. He wasn't interested in anything permanent with a woman. He accepted that much about himself. Having never had a real family, he had no illusions that he'd make any kind of family man.

Even after he'd made it to the pro league, his mindset hadn't changed. Women came after him all the time, but they were after the image, the glamour, the bank account. None of them really saw *him*: mediocre student, guy with a temper, at home as much in the middle of a brawl as on the gridiron.

What did he know about commitment? About being the kind of guy a woman could count on and would be proud to walk beside even if he weren't wearing a league uniform?

The only woman who'd ever made him feel like he was

more than his quarterback position was currently changing her clothes on the other side of a door she'd locked to keep him out. She didn't trust him not to use her for sex, and he didn't trust he was more to her than a story.

The door opened behind him, and he turned to watch Naomi stride back into the room wearing a sundress filled with orange and yellow flowers on a white background. Everything in him stood at attention. The orange-painted toes displayed by her braided, gold leather sandals gave him wicked ideas involving honey and her laid out on a bed with those toes in his mouth.

Maybe for the time being, he could pretend they had more between them than a photographic mystery. If he could have her back in his life for a while, maybe he could knock off the chip that had crept back onto his shoulder over the last few years. She used to silence the voices that niggled at him. He had to find out if she could silence them again.

To get that opportunity, he'd have to address more than the lock status of the adjoining suite door. He'd have to brave the conversation he'd been avoiding. She'd given him the benefit of the doubt in this photo matter. He couldn't be so petty as to refuse to do the same for her.

He escorted her from the room. They had some footwork to do at the moment. As soon as he got the chance, he was going to find a secluded spot for them to sit down and talk.

CHAPTER 9

Face raised towards the sun, Naomi waltzed out the hotel's front entrance as Dash held the door for her. "What a beautiful day for a walk on the beach." She spun in a circle. "I may never leave here."

When she stopped spinning, Dash gave her an odd look.

"What?"

The corner of his mouth lifted, causing one of his dimples to pop. "Your hem rises when you do that. It kinda gets to a man."

She smoothed down the skirt of her dress and looked around. Several men watched her with amused looks on their faces.

She blushed. "Now you tell me."

He leaned towards her. "Sweetheart, you have the best thighs on the island. Why on earth would I deny myself that view?"

She turned towards the promenade and mumbled under

her breath, "How could people possibly think a man who hounddogs women the way you do is gay?"

He chuckled, slid on his sunglasses, and fell in beside her. "So, what's first on your agenda?"

"I did a little research. I have an approximate location for where that photo was taken. Let's head that way and see what we can find."

"Sounds good." He stuck his hands in his pockets and strolled quietly beside her. His lips flattened and the serious expression that overtook his face made him appear unapproachable.

"You know, we'll probably get more cooperation if we act like a couple of tourists rather than a reporter and a guy with an axe to grind." She glanced at his preoccupied face. "So try to look like you're happy to be here with me."

"I am happy to be here with you. The circumstances that brought us here, however, are less than desirable." Dash grabbed her hand and pulled her against him, placing a quick kiss—she didn't see coming—on her lips. "How's this?"

She pushed him back a space. "Don't oversell it."

He smiled. As they strolled towards the promenade, he continued to hold her hand. The warmth of his touch seeped through her palm, and sent a mellow contentment through all layers of her skin. Disengagement from his touch should have been her first thought, but the urge succumbed to the amicable bliss she hadn't felt in three long years.

Hand-in-hand, they hit the shoreline and cruised through several shops. They didn't run into any more people who thought they knew Dash nor find anything helpful to their search. The afternoon sun moved along the sky, and they meandered at an unhurried pace. They fell into a pattern of easy existence reminiscent of old times.

Naomi noticed lots of men watching Dash as the two of them progressed. True to form, if it didn't wear a skirt, Dash didn't bother looking. By the time they hit the fifth shop, Dash finally caught on to the attention. His expression when he realized men were checking him out nearly made Naomi break into a fit of laughter. She squashed the urge. Dash wouldn't have appreciated the sentiment.

When they exited the last shop, a man on the way in winked at Dash. Naomi covered her mouth when Dash's head whipped around in a double take. The man had turned as well to get an eyeful of Dash's behind. Catching Dash's look, he said, "Lookin' good, big guy," and winked at Dash a second time.

The giggle that slipped out beneath Naomi's hand drew Dash's attention back to her.

"That is not funny." He grabbed her arm and pulled her the rest of the way out of the store.

"I thought it was pretty funny." Her giggles continued to trickle out.

Dash pulled his sunglasses off the front of his shirt and put them on. "That guy was staring at my *ass*."

"Why not? It's a pretty spectacular ass. Women stare at it all the time."

"*What?* Hardly."

She snorted. "It was certainly one of the first things *I* noticed about you. You think football draws female fans simply because we enjoy the athleticism?"

He stared at her, lines forming in the middle of his forehead.

"Don't be obtuse, Dash." She shook her head. "Definitely not. Even those of us who love the sport as much as men greatly appreciate the bonus of getting to stare at players' asses in those tight pants."

She flounced away with a switch of her hips, and Dash burst out laughing. He followed quickly and slid an arm around her waist. "Well, it's nice to know I'm appreciated for everything I bring to the sport."

"Trust me." She spun into his hold and gave him an appreciative once over with her eyes. Patting his chest, she said, "Everything you bring to the game is *much* appreciated . . . big guy."

"Is that right?" Dash's grip on her tightened.

Naomi realized her mistake almost too late. The sunglasses didn't hide the predatory look that slunk onto his face. She could literally see him gearing up for a kiss.

She extricated herself from his embrace only a second before he made his move. She took slow steps backwards. "Oh no you don't. Not again."

He took slow steps forward. His husky voice taunted her. "Where do you think you're going? It's not like you can get away from me if I decide I want you."

Her eyebrows rose in open defiance, but her internal sage analyzed the busy concrete promenade in conjunction with her sandals and figured he was right.

But on the beach . . .

Her head turned to survey the sand.

With a head start . . .

In an unpredictable burst of optimism, she whipped off her sandals and sprinted for the beach.

Momentarily stunned by her actions, Dash lost a quarter of a minute before he initiated pursuit.

Naomi flew across the sand. She was fast. She'd been a college athlete, and she still kept in excellent shape. Of course, even with a head start, she was no match for a man who spent five and a half months out of the year trying to avoid two-hundred-plus-pound defensive lineman who wanted to flatten him onto turf.

When she looked over her shoulder, he was right behind her. Barefoot as well, he bore down on her and scooped her up. She shrieked. He spun her in a circle then headed for the foaming surf.

"Dash, no!" she yelled, but he just laughed at her. She dropped her sandals on the sand when he continued towards the churning water. She gripped him tightly around the neck with both arms. "Dash, *please,* don't!" she begged.

He waded into the surf and released his grip with a dip. Her louder shriek made him laugh harder, but he didn't dump her in the water. Instead, he dropped her legs, and holding her tightly around the waist, spun her again. She threw back her head and laughed, her legs rising in an arc behind her.

It felt good to laugh like this. It felt even better to laugh like this with Dash. She'd thought they'd never be able to relax around each other again. Yet, here they were laughing, playing, like old times.

He let her slide down his front until her feet touched the wet sand.

As if synchronized, she went up on her toes and he leaned down to meet her. Inhibitions unleashed by the lull of their lazy afternoon together, they met in a kiss as wild as the surf that splashed around their ankles. They drank of each other.

His hands roamed free, touching her through the fabric of her dress. His palms glanced over the peaks of her breasts, rubbed against the side of her thighs, and passed over the mounds of her butt.

Her hands roamed too, first up through his hair then down to squeeze his backside. One hand snuck under the back of his shirt, feeling the ripple of muscles along his spine.

Neither held back. Once ignited, the flames inside them cut loose like a California brush fire. Oblivious to their surroundings, their passion flared in a vertical *From Here To Eternity* moment.

A wolf whistle sounded behind Dash, finally piercing their euphoria.

Dash's hands threaded her hair. He touched his forehead to hers. "God, I missed you."

"I missed you, too," she whispered.

"We were so good together." He pulled back. "Why did you do it?"

"W-What?"

His eyes widened.

She didn't think he'd intended to ask that question.

Now that it was out, however, he continued. "Why did you publish information I'd told you in confidence?"

She searched his face. A sense of apprehension laced with a sliver of hope filled her at the thought they'd finally get to clear the air. "You really want to talk about this?" Her hand went to his forearm.

His eyes shifted. She saw him shut down, taking the open and accepting Dash with him.

"No." He released her. "Never mind." He spun and headed back up the beach.

She jogged a few steps and called after him. "Dash, wait."

He kept moving.

Idiot, she chastised herself. What an idiotic move. She shouldn't have questioned his intent. He'd given her the opening she'd wanted for years. She should have taken it without hesitation, but she'd been so surprised, she couldn't believe he was really giving her the opportunity to explain.

Idiot. Idiot. Idiot.

She continued to move after him, feet shifting in the sand.

A little further up the beach, Dash snatched up his abandoned sandals and kept moving. A few steps from the promenade, he came along two men standing together. When Dash got close, one of them called to him. "Honey, if she didn't do the job right, why don't you let me give it a try?"

Dash gave him a casual nod. "Thanks for the offer, doll. Maybe next time."

"Ooh-wee," the bold stranger squealed and fanned himself. He turned to his companion. "Oh. My. *Gawd*. Did you hear that voice? Mister is *all* kinds of sexy."

The two men laughed and high-fived each other.

"You are so brazen," the second man said.

A few steps past the duo, Dash shook his head and continued without looking back.

The flirt cocked a hip and waved a hand in the air as he addressed his companion. "Honey, life is short. You've got to seize the moment."

Naomi agreed with him, but she'd missed her opportunity to seize the moment. Dash disappeared up the promenade, and sand tossed over her toes as her feet halted. She wiggled her digits free of the twin holes formed by the abrupt stop. She'd chased after that man once and made a fool of herself. Such a scenario wouldn't play out again. Let him hold on to his pride. She certainly intended to hold on to hers this time.

The sun's rays beat her shoulders. Turning back towards the surf, her mind tossed no less than the bluish-green liquid foaming along the beach. Maybe it was for the best. Curiosity had gotten the better of him; nothing had truly changed between them. He still didn't have enough respect for her to listen to her side of the story. His slipup could be expected amidst the ambiance of the Balearic villa. If they weren't careful, breathing the air of this cross between modern-day Eden and lover's paradise would tempt them into dangerous behaviors.

Fists balled tight at the end of arms spread wide over a tightly gripped hem, she groaned deep in her throat and began to twirl erratically. Who was she kidding? She'd fallen smack dab in the middle of dangerous behaviors with one impromptu kiss on the beach. Intoxicated by the sun, scenery, and people, she'd succumbed to the equivalent of a geographic roofie.

Her head fell back, throwing her off balance. The twirling stopped. She walked back to the surf. Fists akimbo, she dropped her head to watch the sea kiss her feet. The sandy granules between her toes loosened and flowed out with the backwash. Her temporary foolishness eased away with them. Eyes closed, she tucked away the vulnerable woman who'd almost succumbed to the romantic déjà vu that was her and Dash's prior life and drew on the mantle of tough-as-nails investigative reporter.

A tear she couldn't fight rolled down her left cheek. She'd survived losing Dash once. She wasn't prepared for feeling as if she were losing him all over again. The pain surrounding her heart snuck beneath the resolve but didn't lessen it. She was through letting Dash get under her skin.

She headed back up the beach, snagging her sandals along the way. Time to stop holding hands and playing remember-when and start doing what she came here to do. She was going on a hunt. Time to find out who took that kiss picture and why.

~ 4 ~

Naomi looked over the dimly lit hotel bar room. Shadows danced slowly around mahogany wood tables, discreetly masking the patrons yet avoiding the pathways that made navigating the floor safe. She'd been looking for Dash for hours. Their reconnaissance yesterday hadn't yielded any answers.

He'd ended the day frustrated. She suspected the frustration stemmed from their moment on the beach as much as from the lack of new information about the photo or its photographer. She'd tried to reclaim the opportunity to clear the air between them, but he'd turned her down.

Her eyes continued to trail through the bar for a glimpse of the man she hadn't seen since they went to bed—separately—last night. She'd looked for him upon awakening this morning, but gave up when she'd realized he was out of the hotel. She'd used the time to do more investigating. She had news to share if only she could find him.

She'd learned that Ibiza actively promoted itself as a gay-friendly destination. The large numbers of openly gay men they'd encountered yesterday made perfect sense now. Ibiza made a logical location to stage a story of a public figure's secret life as a closeted gay man. Why someone would target Dash for such a setup, however, still didn't make sense. Motivation to end his career with the Griffins hadn't panned out. She hadn't uncovered a suspect with enough to gain from such a result.

About to give up her search for Dash, she headed for the bar. Out of the corner of her eye, she caught a glimpse of a familiar face. He sat at a table in the back corner. She sauntered towards him.

Stepping up to the table, Naomi dropped her purse in front of an empty chair. "So this is where you've been hiding." Her hand stuttered on its way to pull out a chair. "What *on earth* have you done to your hair?" She took in the slightly shorter, trendy cut, perfectly gelled and styled.

He looked up. His eyes travelled down her frame, stopping noticeably at her chest and hips. "Who wants to know?" His voice was smooth and even, edged with a little boredom. He shifted back in his seat, his large hand surrounding a tumbler with arm extended as if to keep his drink from getting too far away.

"Who wants to—" Her head tilted sideways. Something tittered at the edge of her brain, but she pushed it aside. "Ha. Funny." She looked around the room. "Hiding out?"

She took in the near capacity crowd, noting that more male-male couples filled the room than male-female. Dash sat alone, but at the moment, he didn't look entirely out of place with this crowd.

His comment to the gentleman on the beach yesterday floated through her memory. *Thanks for the offer, doll. Maybe next time.* She'd assumed he was being glib, using his natural charm to make light of the situation without being rude to the flirt.

Had she missed the obvious? Maybe he hadn't been kidding.

Her stomach dropped. Had he been using that natural charm of his on her this whole time? Wouldn't be too hard for him to do. She was still in love with the guy. Her objectivity had flown out the window the moment he'd kissed her at his house.

Naomi looked back at him. Should she consider herself amongst that illustrious club of women who had fallen for a secretly gay man? Was that why none of her theories about possible motive for planting the photo had panned out? Maybe it wasn't a fake.

She needed to approach this story as if she weren't holding a secret torch for the guy. Time to find out if he already knew more than he let on about the gay-friendly atmosphere of Ibiza. "Have you been snowing me this whole time, Dash?"

"Who's Dash? And what exactly do you think he's been snowing you about, dollface?"

"Cut it out. The high-brow haircut and the *Queer Eye* makeover may make you feel like a different person, but the face is a dead giveaway."

His right brow peaked. "*Queer Eye* makeover?" He looked down at his Gucci dinner jacket, layered over a pale khaki cotton shirt and linen pants. A size twelve brown Italian leather loafer—worn *sans* sock—rose to hang over his knee. He placed a large manicured hand at the ankle of his now-crossed leg and let his warm brown eyes drill into her. "I'll ignore the insulting implication that I need a gay man— or anyone for that matter—to dress me since you clearly have me mistaken for someone else. Or, maybe you're just a raving lunatic. Which would be a shame since you're absolutely divine."

He motioned towards the chair she stood behind. "Why don't you sit down and tell me why my obvious style and amazing good looks have brought out your bitchy side."

The amused smirk that graced his face was one she'd seen a thousand times. Yet, this time, something different lingered at the edges. Dash's smirk rarely held much true mirth. He laced it with open sarcasm and barely-concealed distain. An obvious *joie de vivre* filled this smug upturn of lips. The man before her was genuinely amused by this turn of events, not in the least upset about being outed.

She hesitated, looking around the room again before settling her eyes back on him. "Drop the charade, Dash. You need to stick with football and give up on acting. It's time to admit that you're gay and that photo was real."

He stood, reached for his wallet, and pulled out some bills. "Sweetheart, why don't you accompany me upstairs so I can demonstrate why that comment is wrong on so many levels?"

Naomi looked closer at the liquid brown eyes openly showing their attraction to her. The corners crinkled a bit, a familiar attribute in a face she'd loved for years, but, again, somehow different. This time his body language, the pattern of his speech, and the nuances of a face that was the same but different registered all at once with Naomi.

"Good Lord." A chill rolled up her spine, making a lightheaded contrast to the wave of heat building from her temples down. "You're *not* Dash, are you?" The question whispered from her lips as she reached for the back of the chair and missed. The room tilted.

A large hand grabbed hers and pulled her against a hard chest. He wrapped an arm around her waist. "Easy, sweetheart."

"Naomi."

"Excuse me?"

"My name is Naomi." She spoke into his chest. "Not sweetheart. Not dollface." She looked up at him. "Na-o-mi."

He smiled, making Dash's dimples peek out at her. "It suits you. Okay, *Naomi*, I think you need to sit for a minute."

He lowered her gently into a chair and motioned for a waiter to bring her a drink.

When the beverage arrived, he pressed the short-stemmed goblet into her hand. "Drink."

She looked at the pinkish liquid in the glass then eyed

him, leery of the unknown libation.

He wrapped his hand around hers on the stem of the glass and lifted it towards her lips. "I thought you might need something a little stronger than water. It's sangria."

She took a sip. The sweet liquid contained pieces of chopped fruit. She took a longer swig, enjoying the superb taste. Lowering the glass, she studied the Dash lookalike. "Why didn't he tell me?"

"Why didn't who tell you what, sweet—" Her chafing look made him reconsider his words. "Um, why didn't who tell you what, Naomi?" He returned to his seat.

"Your brother. Why didn't he tell me he had a twin? Was he trying to protect you?"

"Um, first of all, since my only brother is not biologically related to me, he can't be my twin. And, second of all, what exactly would he need to protect me from?"

She reached into her purse and pulled out a folded piece of newsprint. She opened it halfway and placed it in front of him to display the photograph of two men kissing.

His face tightened. He pulled back. "Ah. I was wondering when someone would make a proactive move on that. Sorry, sweetheart. If this is about blackmail, you're a day late and a dollar short. That little charade," he nodded towards the paper, "blew my deal to hell two weeks ago. Not that I would have been susceptible to blackmail even then."

He downed the rest of the liquid in the highball he'd previously abandoned and stood again. "I must admit I approve of the rep they sent to work me over. We might have had more fun, though, if you'd've allowed me to escort you to my room before you tipped your hand."

He stepped away from the table.

She grabbed his wrist. "Wait." She pointed at the paper.

"So that is you?"

"As if you didn't know."

Her grip tightened on his wrist, and she flipped the paper the rest of the way open with her other hand.

He stared down at the headline and frowned. Sliding his wrist from her grasp, he picked up the clipping and read aloud, "*Griffins QB Has Secret Homosexual Lover.*"

He stared at her, his curiosity piqued. "Is this your Dash?"

She nodded her head, watching his expressions closely.

He skimmed the article. "He's a professional quarter-back?"

"Yes."

He sat back down. "So, I take it he's not after my money."

She laughed. "He's not after you at all. I'm the one who pursued this lead."

"Why?"

She extended her hand. "Naomi Pellier, reporter with *The Kansas City Sports Daily*. Pleased to meet you."

He didn't take her hand. The look on his face suggested he lumped her in the same category as paparazzi and pedophiles.

She dropped her hand. "It's not what you think."

"Isn't it?"

"No." She sat back in her chair. "What did you mean your only brother isn't biologically related to you?"

"I'm adopted."

She stared at him. "You're adopted," she said under her breath, more to herself than him. She took a long, slow drink from her wine glass.

"Yes. And you're after a story. You came here to get the dish on this guy's alleged homosexual lover. Right?"

"I came here to get the truth."

"The truth. The truth with a heavy dose of journalistic spin."

"Dash is a professional quarterback. If he's been hiding that he's gay, it's news."

"Why does he have to be *hiding* anything? If he's gay, why does he—or any gay man—have to go around announcing their sexual preference? No one insists that heterosexuals do that."

"I'm not saying it's right, but it's how American society works—"

He scoffed. "*Ri-ight.* Which is exactly why I spend most of my time outside the States."

"I take it you don't watch football much?"

"No. I was raised a soccer jock. Played my way through college. I watch American football occasionally when I'm home, but because I've been living in Europe for the last five years, I tend to follow world soccer."

She nodded. "Which means you missed the tabloid spread on Dash." She took a deep breath. "Look, I'm not here to stir up trouble. If Dash is gay, I'll break the true facts about the story and give Dash a chance to tell the story his way. No tabloid sensationalism. If he's not—which is what he's claimed all along—I intend to be the one to expose that photo as a fraud."

She picked up her wineglass then put it down without a sip. "Although . . . I guess . . . since you've admitted that's you in the picture, the picture's not a fraud. It's just misleading."

The stranger picked up the news clipping. The shot didn't have him full on, but you could see enough of each man's face to identify them. "This is clearly me in the picture." His brow creased.

The rough edge to his voice caused by his confusion sent a shiver up Naomi's spine. "Geez. You even sound like him. This is so strange." Her hand lifted and eased towards his face.

"Does this Dash look that much like me?"

As if on cue, an angry, familiar male voice sounded behind her. "What's *this* all about?"

Naomi jumped, dropping her hand before turning her head to see Dash glaring, not at her, but at her table companion. "Dash."

His scowl copied exactly the one she'd received from Mr. Lookalike earlier when he'd thought she was setting him up for a shakedown.

"*Shit!*" The unnamed stranger shot out of his chair and stared at Dash like he was seeing poltergeists.

Dash glanced at her then immediately back at his mirror image. "Who. The *hell*. Is *he*?"

His obvious confusion slashed at her heart.

The stranger offered a hand to Dash. "Tatum Gentry."

"Tatum?" Dash ignored his hand and focused on Naomi, that perplexed look still in place.

She wished she'd had more time to figure out the logistics of this matter before Dash had had to face such a life-altering discovery.

"I think he may be . . ." Naomi looked briefly at the man who'd identified himself as Tatum then back at Dash. "I think he's your brother."

CHAPTER 10

Dash's mouth dropped open and his chest tightened. His heart rate accelerated then tripled when Naomi stood and swayed. Tatum reached for her at the same time he did.

"I've got her," Dash said to Tatum. Easing Naomi back into the chair, Dash squatted before her. "You alright?" he asked her.

"I'm fine. I just stood up too quick."

"That's the second time in ten minutes you've almost fainted. That doesn't sound like you're alright to me," Tatum said.

Dash studied her, his worry seeping through his tone and expression. "Naomi?"

She sighed. "Cut me some slack, okay. A few minutes ago I started talking to a guy I thought was you only to realize he's your long lost twin." She lifted the sangria and sipped. "I stood up too fast. That's all."

Dash grabbed the glass from her hand. "What's this?" he

asked.

"Sangria," Tatum answered.

Dash sat the glass on the table and pushed it out of her reach. Still squatting in front of her, he placed his hands on her knees. "When's the last time you had something to eat?"

"I'm fine, Dash. Really." She glanced over Dash's shoulder at Tatum. She reached for Dash's hands and tried to remove them from her knees.

He resisted her efforts. "Answer my question," he insisted in a stern voice.

Her right hand went up to push through her hair. "I don't know . . . Breakfast. I guess."

Checking his watch, he cursed under his breath. "It's almost one o'clock. No wonder you're lightheaded. Dammit, Naomi, you know better than that." Dash stood, looking around for a member of the wait staff.

"What do you need?" Tatum asked him.

"A glass of orange juice right away and a meal with a large serving of protein."

"I've got it." Tatum walked away.

Dash sat down beside her. Placing his arm across the back of her chair, he leaned into her ear. "What were you thinking?"

"I was thinking I needed to find the stubborn jerk I came here with. I wasted half the morning before I decided he'd simply dropped off the face of the island. Then, I went and did some additional legwork on the story we're supposed to be working on *together*."

He dropped his head and released a slow breath. "Sorry about that. I went for a run on the beach this morning. I needed to clear my head."

Tatum came back and placed a glass of orange juice in front of Naomi.

"Thank you," she said to Tatum.

Taking the seat across from them, Tatum pushed the untouched glass of juice towards her with his index finger. "As much as I'm curious about what's going on here. I'd feel better if you drink this before you do anything else."

Dash picked up the glass and put it in her hand. "Good idea."

"Great. It's more than just the looks," she mumbled.

The guys looked at each other then back at her.

She pointed at Tatum. "Bossy." Then pointed at Dash. "Bossier."

Tatum's lips curved up. Dash's lips thinned.

She lifted the glass of orange juice and downed half its contents. She sat the glass down and addressed Tatum. "You said you were adopted."

"Yes."

"How old were you?"

"Nine months."

"By?"

"My parents are Gerald and Caroline Gentry. My father's a doctor and my mother's a homemaker. I also have a younger brother and sister. Classic story. Couple struggles getting pregnant, adopts a child, and finds themselves pregnant a few months later then again after that."

"Your brother and sister are your parents' biological children?" she asked him.

Tatum nodded his head. "But I've never felt they treated us any differently. If anything, my brother and sister claim, I was the one who got special treatment."

A wistful look came over Naomi's face. "You were their first. No matter how much love a parent spreads around, there's something about the first born child—however he or she comes into a family—that claims a special place in a parent's heart." Naomi glanced Dash's way tentatively then cleared her throat.

Dash ignored her sentimental comment. He watched Tatum quietly, too wigged out by the resemblance to speak.

Naomi continued to carry the conversation. "When's your birthday?"

"August 12th."

Dash's arm tensed behind her back.

"Year?"

Dash answered for him.

"Yes," Tatum said quietly. A waiter came and placed a plate of fish and poultry tapas in front of Tatum. He slid the plate in front of Naomi. "Eat."

She picked up a tapa and took a bite. "Mmm. Oh wow. These are heavenly." She popped the rest in her mouth and reached for another. She ate several before she realized the men were silent. She glanced up.

They both watched her. Dash looked amused.

Tatum's look made her feel like a steak placed before a starving man. "Do you always make those sounds when you eat?"

"What sounds?"

Tatum looked at Dash for help.

Dash grinned. "Only when she's really enjoying something."

Her head spun towards Dash. "What are you talking about? I don't make any sounds when I eat."

"Sure you do." He leaned in and whispered an explanation of the erotic sounds she made.

Her face flushed. She snapped at Dash. "Why didn't you tell me before now?"

He smiled. "Because we're usually alone when it happens, and I really don't mind."

"Great. Just great." She picked up a napkin and wiped her mouth. Hoping to turn the attention away from herself, she suggested, "Not that I have any doubt at this point gents, but would you mind sliding out your IDs."

Dash tilted his hip to reach in his back pocket for his wallet. He removed his arm from the back of her chair and slid out his driver's license. He placed it on the table in front of Naomi. Tatum did the same.

She picked up both cards and tipped them towards Dash. They displayed identical birthdates, heights, and only a small difference in weight. Dash's football girth made him heavier.

Naomi looked up at Tatum. "You're from San Diego?"

Tatum nodded. "We moved there when I started high school." He looked at Dash. "Where are you from?"

"I grew up in Nebraska, but I currently live in the Kansas City area."

Tatum ran a hand through his hair, messing up his stylish hairdo. "I was born in Nebraska." His voice was low, pensive.

"I kinda figured." Dash's voice was light. "Do you know the names of your birth parents?"

"Janssen. David and Mary Janssen," Tatum replied.

Dash jerked, surprised he knew the answer. "So, your adoptive parents told you the names of your birth parents, but didn't tell you you had a twin?" The edge in his voice had gotten worse.

Naomi glanced at Dash's face as if trying to read his thoughts.

Tatum frowned. "They couldn't have known. They would have told me."

"Sure." Dash's hand balled into a fist on the table as he uttered the curt response.

Naomi placed her hand over his fist. When he didn't say anything else, she spoke for him. "Dash was raised in foster care."

"Foster care? For how long?" Tatum asked.

"Until he aged out at eighteen," she replied.

A muscle twitched under Tatum's left eye, but he didn't say anything.

The two men observed each other. The twitch under Tatum's eye eventually settled, but his jaw held tension that should have made his teeth ache. "What kind of name is Dash?" he finally asked.

"Nickname. Real name's Talon."

"Talon." Tatum ran the fingers of his left hand through his hair. "Tatum and Talon. Janssen. Twins." Elbows on the table, he dropped his head into both hands. "Holy crap. I think I need a drink."

Dash signaled for the waitress.

Tatum placed his order then simply stared at Dash again. "I guess I should have paid more attention to my sister."

"Your sister?" Dash frowned.

Tatum nodded. "She called me weeks ago. She'd been watching highlights of the NFL games that weekend and seen a guy she said looked just like me. I guess some play you'd made had been the NFL Play of the Week or some such." He paused to accept his drink from the returning waitress and took a long swig.

Dash knew exactly which week and which play Tatum's sister had seen.

"In the back of my mind, I was curious. Thought I'd check it out at some point, but never got around to it on my last trip home. In truth, I didn't think much of it." Tatum shrugged. "You know what they say. We all have a twin somewhere."

"Somehow, I don't think this is exactly what they had in mind," Dash said.

"Probably not." Tatum polished off his drink and motioned for another.

Naomi looked between the two. "Perhaps I should give you two some time alone." She moved to stand.

Dash covered her wrist, trapping it on the table. "Stay."

"Dash, I really think you and Tatum need some time to talk. Alone. And I need to lie down for a while."

He looked at her with a suspicious eye.

She placed her hand over her heart. "Really. I promise. I'm going straight upstairs to the room and lie down."

"You haven't finished your food."

"I'll take it with me." She picked up her plate. "I'll get someone to put it in a container for me." She placed a hand on his shoulder and squeezed. Looking at Tatum, she asked, "Did you get a check?"

"Don't worry about it. I had them charge it to my room. I hope you feel better."

"Thanks." She turned and left them.

~ ᖇ ~

Tatum watched Dash's eyes follow Naomi out of the restaurant. Dash's gaze lingered on the exit even after she'd disappeared.

When Dash finally turned back to the table, he caught Tatum watching him closely. "What?"

"I take it there's more going on between you two than just the story she's writing."

"No." Dash picked up Naomi's abandoned half-full glass of orange juice and downed its contents.

When he put down the glass, Tatum lifted a brow and stared at the now-empty glass purposefully. "No?"

Dash had drunk from Naomi's glass without conscious thought.

"No." Dash met Tatum's gaze directly.

Bull, Tatum thought and took a sip of the bourbon the waitress had delivered. He sat back in his chair and gave in to the wicked grin he felt coming on. "Oh, goody then. That means the beauty is single."

The creases in his newly-found brother's forehead gave Tatum all the intel he needed to make this call. He would have to keep his hands off the sexy lady. She and Dash had a thing going. It must not be going well at the moment, but Dash telegraphed his territorial interest like a lighthouse operator flashing a beacon through a storm.

"Actually, I don't know." Dash glanced towards the door again. "We were an item a while back. We only recently reconnected when she tried to track down the story behind your photo." Dash sat back in his chair and crossed an ankle over the opposite knee. He eyed Tatum intently for a minute before he finally asked, "Aren't you gay?"

Tatum's grin morphed into a smirk, and he gave Dash the same brisk answer Dash had originally given him. "No." He volunteered no additional information.

"No?"

"No. Would it matter if I was?" Tatum watched Dash's eyes closely, but Dash's face remained unexpressive. The question wasn't rhetorical. Dash's answer mattered. Tatum had no tolerance for homophobes or bigots. While Tatum himself wasn't gay, his brother was. He'd have a challenge accepting a twin brother into his life if that twin couldn't accept the brother he already had.

"No, it wouldn't. But then, what's with the photo?"

Tatum relaxed. "I'm not sure. I've never been directly approached by anyone. I assumed it was a setup to ruin a business deal I was trying to close with a conservative investment group."

"A setup?"

"As far as I can tell." Tatum finished off his drink. "A few weeks ago, I entertained a group of investment partners I'd been courting for a while to help me acquire a piece of property on the island I needed for a development project. I had the group hooked. They were all for taking advantage of the financial benefits of the large gay clientele that frequents Ibiza, but apparently, they had a problem turning over millions of dollars to and actually doing direct business with a gay man. Something I'm betting my competitor figured out and decided to use to his advantage by paying a guy to make a move on me when a journalist *just happened*," he made air quotes, "to be around to snap a picture."

"And you *just happened* to let a man get close enough to kiss you?" Dash gave his own smirk this time.

"It's a little complicated." Tatum took another sip of his drink. "The guy was a family friend. I know him through my brother. He said he needed to talk to me about something. He seemed upset so I agreed to meet with him. He managed to catch me by surprise."

"And your investors backed out of the deal when the photograph hit the papers?"

"Yes. Giving my competitor the opportunity to snap up the piece of property I had my eye on."

"So, you're a real estate developer?"

"Of sorts. I happen to invest in various business interests that catch my fancy, but real estate developments are among my favorites."

"If the deal in Ibiza fell through, what are you doing

back here?"

"I've got a score to settle. Michelson, my competitor, may have captured a key piece of property I needed for my intended development, but other surrounding properties are needed before he can break ground on the major hotel project he—we both—had in mind." Tatum motioned the waitress for another drink. "I don't like dirty pool. If I'd been bested by quicker fundraising or simply a better offer on the table, I'd have accepted his victory and walked away. Now?"

Dash nodded, listening intently.

"Now, Michelson's going to have to fight me for every piece of property, every contractor, and every key employee he needs to make this deal work."

"You're going to build a competing hotel in a different spot?"

"No, I'm going to buy up the surrounding properties he needs so he can't build on the land he just acquired. At least, not the scale of project he currently has in mind. In fact, I have a meeting," he glanced at his watch, "in about thirty minutes. Any way you'd agree to meet me back here in a couple of hours? I'm guessing you're as curious about me as I am about you."

"That'd be a good guess." Dash stood. "Okay."

They agreed on a time and place to meet and shook hands before parting ways.

~ 4 ~

Dash headed back up to his hotel suite. He wanted to check on Naomi and make sure she'd actually gone upstairs to rest as she'd promised. She'd find it interesting that she'd been right about the motivation for publication of the now-infamous kiss photo. Someone had indeed been set up. It just hadn't been him.

Tatum's response to the underhanded shenanigans had been a revelation into part of his personality. Basically, don't get mad. Get even. Dash wholeheartedly agreed with the philosophy. He'd lived by it himself a time or two.

This long lost brother of his appeared to have a ruthless streak. He could admire that. He wondered if his brother had other traits he'd admire or if the two of them would prove too different to get along. His hand clenched. The knots that had tied around his gut at his first sight of Tatum slid back into place and tightened.

A brother. He had a brother. And not just any old sibling, but a *twin*. He couldn't fully wrap his mind around the notion.

When he'd stepped into the hotel bar earlier and seen Naomi sitting with another man, an inexplicable wave of jealousy had hit him . . . again. He'd relived the feelings he'd felt the day she'd flirted with Shave. That this particular man wore Dash's face hadn't made the feeling any easier to handle. He didn't have the right to claim her anymore, but the proverbial green monster didn't seem to care.

This trip was supposed to be about finding the culprit who'd targeted him and finding out why. He'd intended to get a little physical pleasure out of the deal, but posses-siveness shouldn't factor into the equation. He hadn't had time to analyze the frequent twinge of jealousy that kept rearing its ugly head. When he'd noticed the guy Naomi sat with had his face, all rational—and irrational—thoughts had fled his mind. All these years he'd gone it alone, thinking he had no family, no blood. Now, he needed to factor a twin brother into the mix.

Dash rubbed at the tightness at the back of his neck and

quietly slid into Naomi's room through the adjoining suite door that this time she hadn't bothered to lock. The room stood in darkness except for the faint glow of natural light around the edge of the drawn curtains. He stepped over to the bed. She slept on her side with her back to him. She'd stuffed herself deep into the covers so that only the portion of her face above her nose peeped from beneath the covers amidst a halo of loose hair.

He slid his hands into his pockets and watched her sleep. After a few minutes, he toed off his shoes and slid under the covers with her. He scooted close and spooned himself around her, draping an arm over her waist.

She shifted. Her sleepy voice croaked at him. "Dash?" She pulled at his hand, trying to dislodge it.

"Shh." He resisted the pull of her hand and pressed his palm against her abdomen. "I just want to hold you for a little bit. Go back to sleep."

She relaxed in his arms. "Are you alright?"

"I'll be fine."

Naomi rolled over to look at him. He placed an index finger against her lips. "You can grill me later, madam journalist. Right now, you need some rest and so do I."

She sighed audibly then snuggled closer to his shoulder. "You're fully clothed."

"Mmm. Makes it easier for me to keep my word."

She glanced up at him, a question in her eyes.

"That I'm only going to hold you while you sleep."

She closed her eyes, but not before a smile graced her lips. He pulled her snug against his hip with the hand of the arm she laid under and used the other to tuck her wild hair away from her face. He played with that hair for several minutes, listening to her breath. By the time her breaths evened out, his pulse rate had dropped considerably.

The scent of her hair wafted into his nostrils. The lump in his chest unwound slowly. He'd talked with Tatum for about forty minutes. It was strange having a brother after all these years and even stranger knowing that another human being shared the exact same DNA as him.

He'd never thought he'd have a family. To have this guy show up who had lived a charmed life with what Dash assumed was a textbook perfect family made him feel gypped. It could have been him except for what? A simple twist of fate? He had no way of knowing. No one knew how it had gone down but Tatum's adoptive parents, and Dash had no interest in getting to know the couple who hadn't wanted him. He'd skip having salt rubbed into a very old and very deep wound.

Tatum had been adamant that his adoptive parents couldn't have known about them being twins. Dash didn't believe that. His skepticism brought with it a bit of resentment. Tatum had grown up with two loving parents plus a brother and a sister. Dash hadn't dreamed of such an Ozzie and Harriet nuclear family in decades.

From the time he'd turned eight, he'd let go of the dream. He'd accepted he'd have no other family besides himself. He'd been good with that. He'd thrived on the challenge of being on his own, and he could think of no reason to change that now. *Except* . . . Except a curiosity niggled at him, a curiosity about Tatum and what manner of man he'd turn out to be.

"Dammit."

Naomi stirred in his arms. He hadn't meant to say the expletive out loud. He looked down to see if he'd awakened her, but she still slept.

She had been the only person he'd allowed to get truly close to him in his adult life. He was glad she'd been here with him when he discovered Tatum. Somehow, he felt she was keeping all the pieces of him from blowing apart. At a time when he should be focused on advancing to the next stage of his career, he had her pushing back into his life at the same time he found a sibling he'd never known he had.

An odd sense of displacement settled over him. As his mind puzzled with the emotional turmoil stirring in his heart, he began to doze. He fell asleep before he could find any peace within himself.

~ Ψ ~

Naomi awoke ninety minutes later to find the bed empty beside her. The sheets smelled of the crisp cleanness of Dash's favorite cologne, a scent he'd started wearing daily after she bought him his first bottle for his birthday the year after they met. She rolled over to the side of the bed he'd laid on and caressed her hand along the indentation he'd made in the sheet.

Lying in his arms had been wonderful and torture at the same time. She'd stirred several times long enough to be conscience of the feel of his arms and heat surrounding her. She wished circumstances were different enough that they could let go of these walls between them and be the couple they once were. She missed them together—the *them* that used to be confidants, the *them* that used to be best friends, and definitely the *them* that used to be lovers.

She hadn't taken another lover after Dash. She liked to tell herself her life had been too busy to allow it, but she knew the truth. She wasn't one of those women who could have sex with one man when she was in love with another.

Life sucked.

She should be over him by now. She had plenty of

reason to despise him—the way he'd broken up with her, his refusal to hear her side of the story about the infamous article, his ability to ignore their unfinished personal business. She kept willing herself to move on so she could make room in her personal life, in her heart, for someone else—for the kind of man she deserved. Unfortunately, her heart didn't seem to want to move on. Being here with Dash had only made things worse. The more time she spent with him, the more she wanted to be with him—in every way possible, including naked and horizontal.

Rolling out of bed, she got up to check his adjoining suite. He always left his side of the door unlocked. She knew it was because he hoped she'd give in to his seduction so they could rekindle things beneath the sheets. When she walked through the door to search him out, he was nowhere to be found.

Needing to catch up on a byline, Naomi went back to her suite and showered. Then, she settled onto the semi-made sheets she'd quickly tossed over the pillows and went to work on her laptop. Several hours passed and she came out of her work trance to discover she now sat typing in the dark. She stretched and clicked on the lamp. A quick check of the clock revealed the late hour. Dash should have made it back by now.

Barefoot, she dismounted the bed and padded to her side of the door adjoining their suites. When she opened the door, silence surrounded Dash's room. The only light spilt from the lamp lit behind her. She took in the flawlessly made bed and lack of movement in the room. She hadn't heard Dash return, but she sensed his presence. Creeping further into the room, she glanced through the open bathroom door. No Dash.

"Out here," his deep, rich voice called lazily to her. He

stood on the balcony with his back to her.

She spun towards the sound of his voice. "Are you okay?"

He didn't answer.

She moved outside and stood behind him. "Dash?"

More silence followed before he started speaking. "When I was twelve, I developed pain in my right leg so bad I couldn't walk on it. I hadn't done anything in particular. One minute, I was playing with my foster brothers in the backyard and the next, I was rolling on the ground moaning in pain. My foster mother at the time questioned me repeatedly about what had happened, but I couldn't tell her because I had no clue. She got angry with me. Accused me of making a scene to get attention."

Naomi stepped closer to him, but didn't say a word. She sensed what he had to say held great significance for him.

"It happened two days before my thirteenth birthday. I remember the date clearly because I was looking forward to that birthday. See, this foster mom was a bit of a tyrant. Not a new experience for me. But, birthdays? Birthdays she made special. She baked a whole cake just for the birthday kid, and we got a present. The other boys had gotten new sweatshirts on their birthdays. Not hand-me-downs or something from the thrift store, but brand new sweatshirts no one had ever worn before.

"I'd never been in a foster home that gave you new clothes or a birthday cake all to yourself so I was really excited that my birthday was only days away. Turns out my excitement was wasted. When I couldn't give my foster mother a reasonable explanation for why my leg hurt so bad and didn't stop complaining about the pain, she decided I should be punished."

Naomi put a hand on his back. "Oh, Dash."

He still didn't turn. "She punished me by taking away my birthday celebration. No cake. No present. So, no new sweatshirt.

"The next day, the pain had dulled, but it took two full days before the pain went away. I never understood what had happened. Just considered it part of the crap that was my life. A way for the universe to remind me that I'd been dealt a bad hand in life and that nothing good ever happened to a kid nobody wanted." His torso expanded as he pulled in a deep breath then contracted with its release. "Tonight, I finally understood."

She rubbed light touches across his back. "What happened tonight to change things?"

"Tatum."

She didn't say anything, simply continued to rub his back.

"He told me tonight that when he was twelve, he broke his leg. They set it the first day, but he had trouble with the painkillers they gave him. They made him sick so it wasn't until the next day under a different painkiller that he got any relief. When I asked him if it had happened two days before his birthday, he was startled but admitted that it had."

Dash gave a harsh laugh. "It's funny. Every time I used to see one of those documentaries about the weird connection between identical twins, I'd dismiss the absurdity of it all. I thought it nothing but a bunch of psychobabble mumbo jumbo not far off from those people who talk to the dead or make psychic predictions. I guess the joke was on me. All these years, I could have been a case study for one of those stories. I just didn't know it."

He dropped his head and gripped the balcony rail. Even in the dark, she could see his knuckles blanch. His posture was so taunt she was afraid he'd blow a blood vessel or pull an aneurysm.

"God, Naomi, I'm a grown man. How can I be hurt by something that happened when I was nine months old?"

She wrapped her arms around his waist from behind. "Because that nine-month old is still in here." Her palms flattened against his chest. "And he's only now learned what he's missed out on all these years."

He didn't respond for a long while. "I don't wish the childhood I had on anyone, but I have to wonder how they decided."

"How they decided what?"

"How they decided which baby to keep. Why'd they pick him instead of me?"

"Don't do this to yourself, Dash." She stepped around him and pulled one of his hands loose to slide between his body and the railing. "It wasn't about you personally. You were just a baby."

"But it was personal. What? Did I lose a coin toss? Did I cry too much?" He stepped back from her.

She could feel the pain radiating from him. It hurt to see him this way. She wanted to take the pain away. She wanted to make him feel complete and okay again, not the lesser choice, but he was retreating into himself. He was good at that. When the emotions got to be too much for him, he closed himself off and went to a place no one could reach.

She grabbed his wrist. "Don't pull away. Talk to me. Or, don't talk to me if you prefer. Just don't pull away." Her grip tightened. "You don't have to go through this alone. I'm here for you, Talon."

CHAPTER 11

The sound of his given name crossing Naomi's lips stirred Dash. She was the only woman he'd ever been with who called him by his real first name.

The first time she'd done it, she'd surprised him. He'd tried to get her to stop, but she'd been adamant. They'd been on their second date. She'd said Dash was his stage name, and she wanted to get to know the man beneath the professional football persona.

No woman but her had ever cared about the man beneath the football player. He'd fallen half in love with her that night and hadn't truly wanted any other woman since.

She didn't use his given name all the time, and never when they were in public, but she pulled it out when she wanted to put their roles aside. When they'd finally become a couple, she'd explained that sometimes she didn't want them to be the pro quarterback dating the sports reporter, but rather just a man and a woman.

Just a man and a woman. He desperately wanted that right now. "Naomi, I . . ." He broke off. The emotion glutting his voice made him self-conscious.

She pressed herself against him, reached up and palmed the side of his face. "Don't pull away from me, Talon. Let me be here for you."

He rubbed his evening-stubbled jaw against her palm. He closed his eyes and his voice shook as he said, "You don't know how much I want to lose myself in you right now." Pushing her hand more firmly against his jaw, he turned his lips to press a kiss into the center of her palm.

She turned his head back so he could look into her eyes. "I'm here for you."

Her voice slid warm and soft through him. She was offering him a soft place to fall. At a moment when his life had shifted off-kilter, he sensed only she could keep him from teetering off the edge. He wanted—needed—her and that.

He scooped her into his arms and strode back into the hotel suite. His bed greeted them at close proximity, but he wanted her all night and he didn't want to give her a convenient reason to leave him in the middle of the night. So, he decided to bypass his bed for hers. First, he approached the nightstand in his room and dipped her so she could open the drawer.

She looked up at him perplexed.

"There's something we need in there unless you're prepared to forego protection."

Naomi hesitated a moment before reaching down and sliding open the drawer. A box of condoms peeked up at her. She picked up the box. He noticed the wave of relief that flooded her when she realized the box had never been opened.

She tucked the box of condoms to her chest, and Dash pulled her back up. He followed the faint trail of light spilling from her suite. Funny. When he'd originally made plans to get through that door for just this purpose, the circumstances had been different. The reasoning had been different. He no longer wanted her simply to prove a point or to exorcise her from his system. He wanted her to fill him up. The hollowness inside him needed her, and only her, to fill him. He understood that now. He couldn't go on without knowing the true heart of her. Where her loyalties truly lied.

He'd thought she'd betrayed him once. *But had she?*

He'd never given her a chance to explain. He needed to know so he could carve out the uncertainty cluttering his heart. But what if Naomi's explanation didn't change things? Maybe he'd been right all along and she'd betrayed him like he'd always thought she had.

Then again, what if he'd been wrong? And maybe that's what scared him the most.

He'd find out.

After.

After he killed all his demons by losing himself in, on, and under her naked body.

He placed her on the bed. The skirt of the simple blue sundress she wore slid up, revealing her long sexy legs. His hand went to her thigh, fingertips brushing lightly over her beautiful brown skin. He reached up with his other hand and removed the scrunchie from the messy bun-thingie she'd improvised on top of her head. He loosed the waves with his fingers, spreading the thick mass around her shoulders. He loved the feel and smell of her hair. He'd missed that smell after they'd parted. He pulled a loose lock to his face, inhaling the scent of coconut and shea butter from the shampoo she used. His groin tightened.

She pulled away from him to turn off the lamp.

He reached for her hand to stop her. "I want to see you."

"Open the curtains," she said as she switched off the light.

"Naomi—"

She pressed the fingers of one hand against his mouth. "Shh, Dash. Don't talk. Just open the curtains for me . . . please."

He nodded in the darkness before walking to the window and sliding the curtains wide. The moonlight over the water reached into the oceanside suite, making a soft glow reminiscent of blacklight blue.

He turned back towards the bed and his breath stalled. She positively glowed in this pale ethereal light. She rose from the bed like a sea nymph enticing a sailor. On her knees before him in the sinking mattress, she reached up to slide down the top of her sundress.

"Don't." The gruff whisper rattled from his throat, but didn't sound like his own voice.

Her hand paused. She watched him confused.

"I want to do that."

On slow footsteps, he approached the sea nymph with reverence. A wayward sailor on his way to Delphi, he sensed this creature might prophecy his future. Blood rushed through his ears, a sanguine musical accompaniment to an arousal that would play from his soul until he made her body dance.

She'd offered herself to him as comfort. Part of his mind wondered if this was strictly a case of mercy sex, but he pushed back that darkness. He refused to let those demons coax his brain from the beauty before him into a disjointed world of insecurity and mistrust. He vanquished the doubt, not letting himself care about her motive for bringing them to this moment. He only cared about how they ignited each other from this second forward.

He stripped her slowly, teasing himself with each new reveal of skin and curves. She relieved him of his clothes in tandem. An item of his clothing dropped on top of one of hers. An item of hers topped that one. And so the play alternated until both rested naked before the other.

His fingers caressed her flesh, sliding over a peaked breast, glancing over a firm stomach. The feel of her skin beneath his hands tightened his flesh, and his heart accelerated like a NASCAR front-runner when she moved her hands over his chest, stopping at erogenous places along the way. The play fueled him, leading him from grateful taker to quiet giver.

He kissed her long and thoroughly, one hand behind her head, the other cupping a buttock he pressed to draw her to him. The pleasure of her mouth urged him to linger, and he lingered until she grabbed his shoulders and pulled him closer. His hands returned to her breasts, rubbed and massaged until the taunt peaks became too tempting not to taste. He finally slid his mouth from hers to communicate intimately with a nipple. He rolled the peak against the flat of his tongue until she purred in ecstasy then he grasped the nodule between his teeth and applied gentle pressure until she squealed.

Her verbal excitement drove him to test her internal heat. He found her swollen and damp in that wondrous place males dream about from the moment they hit puberty. He strummed her. First, he stroked and rubbed her outer folds. Then, he filled her with a long finger.

She pushed against his hand, revved to near breaking. He increased the pressure—and her pleasure—by adding a second finger. Her moans rose in a steady crescendo as he toyed and worked her.

Deep pants and whispered pleas soon replaced the throaty moans. "Dash," she whispered.

He ignored her first call.

"Dash."

"Umm." He acknowledged her need, but didn't deliver her.

"Dash, please."

"Not yet." He turned his mouth's attention back to her breasts and began to suckle in concert with his finger play.

He tortured her in bursts that brought her to the edge but backed off before she could fling herself over and fly. He amped her thusly thrice until her voice broke on a sob of his real name. Relenting, he added another finger and pressed his thumb to the nerve bundle at the apex of her core. She released hard, shuddering around his fingers. One of her hands clasped his head firmly to her breast. The other grasped at his back. The violence of her spasming body revealed the depth of her orgasm, but not her cries. She flung them full but soft into the darkness, blanketing the moment in the erotic stillness of enchanted moonglow.

Feeling the perfection of the moment, a greedy beast took him over. He wanted to experience her fulfillment again in isolation from his own. Before her body recovered, he slid down, pushed her knees up and open, and kissed her in that central spot between her thighs. Her feet rested flat on the mattress and she pressed up startled as if lightning flashed through his tongue. He languished there, feeding her and drinking from her simultaneously until a ripple started in her thighs then blossomed through her legs into a full-blown quake.

Hearing her cry out her second release eased all the remaining anguish inside him. Every muscle in him relaxed except the one at attention between his legs. He crawled up her torso, kissing as he went, until he could slip his tongue inside her mouth again.

She tongued him back aggressively and tugged his body farther up hers. She reached for the rod pulsing against her abdomen and stroked. Dash pumped into her caressing fingers until his control hit the breaking point. Reaching for protection, he tore a packet open then slid it on with one hand.

Impatient, Naomi reached between them to guide him into her. A slow controlled thrust sealed the connection, pulling a duet of sound from their throats. Seated deep inside her, Dash wrapped his arms around her and held on. Neither moved. He tucked his face into her neck and breathed deeply of the perfume and musk combination that was uniquely her.

She gripped him tightly. When his lips began to peck along her neckline, she moved beneath him. He joined her with slow controlled thrusts. Their tempo built gradually to an intense steady rhythm as did their breathing. Dash drew their joined hands up above her head and concentrated his strokes at an angle he knew would guarantee her pleasure. When the contractions deep inside her started squeezing against him, his hips accelerated, driving them both higher and higher into a mutual starburst of energy that pulsed and flared. Together, they erupted.

Heated and spent, they took care of their post-coital needs then wrapped themselves around each other. For the moment, nothing could destroy Dash's emotional peace. His current physical lethargy transcended all his earthly concerns. As he drifted off to sleep, he thought, *Tomorrow might be another story.*

~ Ψ ~

Naomi shifted in Dash's arms. The warmth from their entwined naked bodies made her feel cozy and languid. Making love with Dash had always been an emotional experience for her, but last night had been amazing even for them.

After the slow, heart-searing coupling they'd explored in almost complete silence, they'd slept for hours. But sometime in the early dawn, Dash had awakened her with a fierce driving need that led to a tempestuous, almost frantic lovemaking. She hadn't minded. Once she'd come fully awake, her need for him had surprised her with its matching intensity.

She wondered now how much of last night's passion was simply a residual effect from the emotional turmoil Dash had faced upon learning he had a brother. She'd like to think that some of the magic had been about her. That maybe he'd missed the physical expression of their feelings for each other as much as she had.

"What are you thinking about so hard?" His husky, morning voice intruded on her thoughts.

She looked up to find his eyes focused intently on her face and shifted so she could face him comfortably. Moving her hand back and forth over the light hair dusting his chest, she contemplated whether or not to tell him the truth. Opting to be brave, she said, "How much I've missed being in your arms while you do wicked things to my body."

His eyes darkened to a smoldering caramel. "That goes double for me," he whispered then bent his head and claimed her mouth with his. When he finally lifted his head, he ran his thumb across her bottom lip. "I'm wondering how much of our being apart is my fault."

"What do you mean?"

He scooted up and adjusted his pillow so that he could rest upright against the headboard. He pulled her up beside him and adjusted her pillow for her. "I'm ready to hear your explanation about why that story got published."

A tension mounted in her chest. He'd asked her about that two days ago then bolted before she could give him an answer. It seemed cruel for the subject to come up again after they'd spent long hours into the night and early morning getting lost in each other. She wanted to hold on to the closeness they had right now, not go back to an awkward cordialness.

Her eyes skirted his then looked down. She pulled the sheet up over her nakedness. Somehow, this didn't seem like a conversation she could get through in her birthday suit.

He placed a bent finger under her chin and pushed up. "Naomi." His voice was gentle. "I'm not going to run off this time. I'm sorry about the other day. I wasn't ready to face the truth even though I desperately wanted you to answer me."

Her shoulders lifted and fell.

He dropped his hand to cover the hand she had in her lap. "Somehow, I get the feeling my anger towards you wasn't completely justified."

"Maybe it was . . . in a way. I was careless, Dash. And for that, I'm really sorry." She tucked the sheet under her arms so that she wouldn't have to hold on to it.

"Careless how?"

"I was upset about something one day." She had planned to talk to him back then about that something—that she'd slipped up and fallen in love with him—but the foster care story had blown up before she could. Her focus had shifted to doing damage control. Once the story went live, he'd refused to talk to her at all, and he didn't respond to any of the correspondence she'd sent him later when she realized her problem was so much bigger than she'd originally suspected.

Clearly, her other little issue hadn't concerned him much, which pricked at her old personal wounds. It wasn't a wound she wanted to reopen right now so she'd stick to the story he wanted to hear. "My mom called me at the *Daily* that day, and I spilled my guts."

"I don't understand what Peyton's and my story had to do with you being upset."

"Mom encouraged me to talk to you about what was bothering me, but I was afraid. I knew your childhood experiences colored your opinion about many things, but she didn't understand my hesitancy so I tried to explain. She kept asking me questions about you and I answered. Before I knew it, I'd told her the whole story."

She glanced at his face. "I took the call in a conference room thinking I'd have more privacy there, but it didn't work out that way. One of my coworkers, David Anderson, picked up the line in another room and listened in on my call. I later found out that he'd done it before. He did it to get a bead on my stories and undercut me when he could."

He wore a blank mask. "So, you told your mother, but this guy was listening in the whole time?"

"Yes."

His brow creased. "But Anderson didn't write the story. It had your and Ray Jackson's bylines on it."

"A few hours later, I overheard Anderson talking to the editor about the story he was working on. He put a decidedly perverse twist on it. I tried to convince him not to publish the story, but he was too excited about the possible boost to his career with the buzz he knew he'd generate with the story.

"I went to Jackson for help. He did some checking regarding Anderson's alleged sources for the story and figured out how Anderson really got his information. I went to the editor. He reprimanded Anderson for his behavior, but the editor wouldn't can the story. In fact, he was peeved to learn I knew unpublished details about your foster care background and had kept quiet.

"I was beside myself. Freaking out because I knew you'd hate me for what I'd let happen. Then, Jackson came to me with an idea for how to neutralize the effect of the piece."

"Neutralize it?"

She nodded. "He figured if we broke the story first, with a more conscientious tone and human interest spin, then Anderson's story would become old news and lose its punch. Jackson wrote the story and passed it by the editor, who not surprisingly didn't care who wrote the piece as long as he got his exclusive scoop."

"How did your name end up on the piece?"

"Jackson wouldn't publish it any other way. He said it was my information and he wouldn't take sole credit for the story or uncovering those facts. The editor was supposed to give me twenty-four hours to warn you the story was about to break. I came looking for you, but your team commitments that day kept you occupied until late evening. Unfortunately for me, the editor lied and posted the story on the *Daily's* web site early. So, by the time you got home, the story was out, and to my horror, you'd already heard about it."

"And I wouldn't let you explain." His hand reached for a stray curl, but his eyes weren't focused on her as he became lost in thought.

She bunched the sheet around her with one hand and let

her head fall back against the headboard. "Yeah."

Suppressed anger twitched along his jaw when he finally looked at her again. "Did Anderson pull that underhanded crap with the other guys at the *Daily*?"

"No. Not that I'm aware of."

"Probably because he knew they'd kick his ass if he tried. Jackson, in particular, would have beat the crap out of him."

"Probably so." Ray had played running back for Dallas during his younger years. After he retired from pro football, he put his journalism degree to work. He'd gotten on in years but still kept in shape. Though fifteen years Anderson's senior, Jackson would most likely crush the younger reporter like a bug.

"I should have broken Anderson's nose when I had the chance."

"I think you did quite enough with the split lip, black eye, and two bruised ribs you gave him."

David Anderson had been the reporter Dash had hit after finding him on Peyton's front doorstep harassing her and calling her all kinds of sleazy names in an attempt to browbeat her into revealing something shady about her past relationship with Dash. When he couldn't claim the exclusive on Dash's side of the story, the man had gone after Peyton's story. Dash's foster sister was an extremely beautiful woman. Anderson had hoped to use innuendo to spin the relationship between Dash and Peyton into something more torrid than simply two foster care kids who'd had each other's backs. He'd hoped to uncover some juicy tidbit like sexual experimentation between the two teens or possibly statutory rape since Dash was two years older than Peyton.

"When I found out what he was putting Peyton through,

I could have killed the SOB."

She reached over and turned his face towards her. "I'm glad you didn't. Then, you wouldn't be here with me now."

He placed a hand over hers against his face. "I'm sorry. I should have let you explain a long time ago. Forgive me?"

Fighting dampness behind her eyelids, she nodded. "Forgive me?"

"There's nothing to forgive you for." He grabbed her by the waist and pulled her down onto the mattress back side up.

"But if I hadn't told mom—"

"You have a right to talk to your mom when you're upset. He had no right to intrude on that."

"But I told her your story."

"Naomi, I trust your mother. She would have never sold my story to the tabloids or used it against me. I know that. And you knew that when you confided in her." He pulled the sheet from around her and covered her with his body. "By the way, what were you so upset about that day?" He slid a thumb over a plump nipple.

Naomi gasped. "That's none of your business." Actually, it was, but she wasn't ready to reveal that particular secret just yet. If ever. This was a temporary interlude. A chance to save her career with a key story and a chance to make peace with Dash. He didn't need to know that he'd had her heart back then or that, much to her chagrin, he still had it.

"I say it is my business." He tickled her stomach.

She laughed and swatted at his hands. "I'm not telling and you're not going to be able to tickle it out of me this time."

His smile took on a predatory edge. "Then, I guess I'll just have to seduce it out of you."

CHAPTER 12

Dash revved Naomi's body with intimate touches and wayward kisses. The lighthearted play turned hot and heavy in a flash. By the time she screamed his name and he shuttered out his release, he had no recollection that he'd supposedly been after a confession. They drifted off in each other's arms, uncaring that others were stirring for the day.

The buzz of Dash's cell phone woke him a short while later from a sound sleep. He rolled over, grabbed his phone off the night table and checked the time before answering the call. The display glared noon. "Hello."

"It sounds as if I woke you. Given the hour, I hope you're not alone in that bed."

Dash glanced down at Naomi who shifted but didn't wake. "If I weren't, I wouldn't tell."

"Ah, a lady you respect. The lovely reporter perhaps?"

The humor in Tatum's voice annoyed Dash even as it amused him. The guy had called him out about Naomi the first moment he'd met him. Dash might be able to shield his feelings from Naomi, but apparently he wasn't hiding them well from his new brother.

"What can I do for you this morn—afternoon, Tatum?"

"I have to head back to the States tomorrow so I was hoping to spend the day together. I could show you and Naomi around the island. Show you some of the non-touristy places to eat and what not."

Dash liked the idea. His curiosity about his brother overrode the emotional uncertainty he'd felt last night. He looked back down at Naomi and ran a hand over her hair. He had a feeling she had a lot to do with that. "That sounds like a good idea. I'll have to check with Naomi, but it shouldn't be a problem."

Tatum cleared his throat. "Why don't you just reach over and wake her, I can wait."

"*Tatum*," Dash warned.

"Fine. Fine. But if you have to indulge before getting dressed, make it a quickie. I'm already downstairs." The sound of Tatum's laughter floated through the phone right before the click of his disconnection.

Dash shook his head and returned the phone to the night table.

Naomi's head turned. "Who was that?" she said in a deep, raspy voice filled with sleep.

"Tatum. He wants to show us around the non-touristy parts of the island. He's downstairs. You game?"

She rolled over and smiled. "I'm definitely game."

Despite his brother's lovely idea of a quickie, they showered and got dressed without a dalliance and headed downstairs within twenty minutes.

Naomi positively glowed. Nothing like a few orgasms to make a woman's natural beauty shine. That he'd been the one to give her those orgasms lent an added strut to his walk.

When they reached the lobby, Tatum gave him a knowing smile. Dash wanted to slap him against the back of his head, but their relationship hadn't progressed to that point yet. If Tatum said anything to embarrass Naomi, however, their physical relationship would evolve real quick.

Tatum grabbed Naomi's hand and pulled her close for a squeeze and a kiss on the cheek. "Naomi, you look absolutely radiant this morning. I'll be the envy of every straight man on the island with you on my arm." Tatum tucked Naomi's hand into the crook of his elbow and walked her towards the hotel exit.

Naomi's laughter floated through the lobby and tickled along Dash's spine right to the tip of his manhood. He'd had her repeatedly over the last twelve hours. How could she still tie him in sexual knots with just a laugh?

And what the hell was Tatum doing flirting with her?

He'd told the man they weren't an item, but everything Tatum said to Dash yesterday and this morning on the phone made it clear the guy didn't believe him. So, if he knew Dash was hung up on the lady, what was he up to? If Tatum thought he'd take advantage of Dash's slow foray out of the doghouse to make a play for Naomi, this family reunion would be over before it started.

Dash lengthened his stride to catch up with the exiting couple. As he got closer, he heard Tatum ask Naomi if she'd been shopping since she arrived on the island.

"Yes. We walked along the promenade the day we arrived."

"That's not shopping. Checking out the tourist traps doesn't count. I'm going to take you to where the locals shop. I've got a place in mind I know you'll love."

Tatum escorted Naomi to his rental car and helped her into the front seat. He skirted the front of the car and opened the driver's side door. He gave Dash a look over the hood before he got in.

Dash interpreted the look for the challenge it was. Fine by him. His lips curved into a grin and he folded himself into the back seat.

Game on.

The shop Tatum selected was filled with dresses, scarves and wraps in flowing fabrics. Outfits in colors of beautiful island neutrals mixed with those of vibrant hues. Naomi fell into shopping heaven. She slid out of the dressing room for the dozenth time, this time wearing an ankle length sleeveless, fire-red dress that fitted her curves down through the hips and moved elegantly around her legs and feet as she walked. She did a spin for the gentlemen.

Their mouths dropped open. "Wow," they both gasped in unison.

Naomi laughed.

"That's definitely a keeper," Dash said when he could finally get his throat to work.

Naomi grabbed the skirt of the dress and swished it around her ankles as she swayed from side to side. "You think?"

"Definitely," the guys said again in unison.

She laughed again. "Okay, this is getting weird."

"Ignore him," Dash said, pushing Tatum out of the way amidst his brother's own laughter. "I'm the only one who matters. You need to buy that dress." He walked slowly around her.

"I don't know, Dash. I've already picked out three dresses. This is getting a bit excessive."

"Fine. Then I'm buying the dress." Dash whipped out his wallet and handed his platinum card to the sales associate.

"Don't be crazy." Naomi reached for his card.

He snatched the card out of her reach and leaned in to whisper in her ear. "Which means you can only wear it for me."

Tatum chuckled at Naomi's expression. "I don't think you're going to win this one, sweetheart." Her frown at his endearment made him chuckle even harder. "In fact, why don't you just keep it on? It'll look great in the nightclub I want to take you all to later."

Tatum grabbed her around the waist and steered her back towards the dressing room. "Go get your stuff."

While Tatum attended to Naomi, Dash had the associate put all the items Naomi had selected on his card.

When Naomi came out of the dressing room carrying the outfit she'd entered the store wearing, the associate offered her the shopping bag full of purchases.

Naomi frowned. "But I haven't checked out yet."

The lady smiled at her. "It's all been taken care of, Miss." She handed Dash back his credit card.

Starting to protest, Naomi turned to Dash. "Dash—"

He leaned down and gave her a quick kiss on the lips, cutting her off. "You're welcome." He took the shopping bag from the sales associate and headed for the door.

As he walked away, he heard the sales lady whisper to Naomi, "I take it that one's yours. Is the other one single?"

"What?" Still stunned by Dash's actions, Naomi was a little slow on the uptake and frowned.

Dash turned to see the lady raise her hands in apology. "Sorry, I didn't realize you were with both of them."

A deep flush rose under Naomi's light complexion. "I'm

. . . Are you . . . ? You can't be serious?"

Tatum put a hand around the waist of the flustered Naomi and placed a kiss on her cheek before steering her towards the exit. "Come along, sweetheart. I think it's time to feed you. You're tripping over your words."

Naomi sputtered at Tatum and dragged her feet. Once outside, he let her go and she turned on him. "Why on earth did you do that? Do you know what she thought?"

Tatum just grinned at her and headed for the car. "Of course. And you should be so lucky."

Dash burst out laughing. He was beginning to understand this wicked sense of humor of his new brother. Tatum was completely irreverent, and Dash found it refreshing. The guy didn't seem to have an uptight bone in his body, and he clearly didn't know a stranger. The two of them were an odd set of contrasts — completely alike except for the ways they were complete opposites.

Maybe this having family thing wouldn't be so bad. Time would tell.

Dash climbed into the car, situating himself once again in the back seat.

They headed for a restaurant Tatum selected and enjoyed a light dinner. The food was fabulous and the conversation centered on casual topics that allowed them to get to know one another. Evening fell and Tatum suggested they finally get in some dancing. Knowing how much Naomi loved to dance, Dash thought it a great way to end the night.

When they got to the club, loud vibrant music pulsed over a throng of people. Naomi grabbed Dash by the hand and immediately pulled him towards the dance floor. Half way there, she stopped abruptly, forcing Dash to grab her around the waist to keep from knocking her over. She whipped her head to the left and scanned the crowd.

His eyes mimicked her perusal. "Something wrong?'

"I don't know. I just saw . . ." She shook her head. "I'm not sure. I thought I saw someone I knew."

"On Ibiza? What are the chances of that?"

She smirked. "Oh, I don't know. Maybe about as likely as coming here and finding one's long lost identical twin?"

He laughed. "Touché." He tugged her hand. "Come on. Let's dance."

Only a few songs had to play before the sexy sounds of the percussion-heavy music and the sway of Naomi's body intermittently against his drove Dash's thoughts to the bedroom. She danced like a timeless enchantress around an ancient fire—free and sensual. The music moved through her seamlessly.

His pants got tight in the groin area. He tugged the enchantress off the dance floor at the commencement of the next song.

"Hey, what's the deal? We just got started," she complained.

"Sorry, I need something to drink." *And to do you again.* He kept the crude thought to himself.

He should have known better. The first time he'd made love to her had been after a night of dancing. Her body had teased him with her every dance move, and he'd had to have her. She hadn't been one of those easy women. She'd had no intention of falling into his bed after only a few dates—if at all. But by the time the DJ spun his last tune, the chemistry between them had seduced her into a need as strong as his.

That same overwhelming desire pulsed through him now, but he didn't want her to know she still had that kind of power over him. He needed to downshift, and he'd start by staying off the dance floor for a while.

After several songs finished without Dash agreeing to head back to the dance floor, Naomi got restless. "If you're not going to dance with me anymore, I'm going to find another partner."

Before Dash could respond, Tatum stepped up and grabbed her hand. "I've got you, pretty lady. Let's see what else you've got."

"You're on." She flounced onto the dance floor, holding tightly to Tatum's hand.

The recurring bouts of jealousy Dash had been fighting since he'd reconnected with Naomi rose to taunt him again. Intellectually, he knew Naomi wasn't a woman to sleep with one man one night then move to another man the next. However, Tatum did look exactly like him. Would one twin be as good as the other as far as she was concerned?

The longer the two spent on the dance floor, the more uptight Dash got. He watched Tatum grip her waist during one groove then pull her tight during another for a *Dirty Dancing* kind of sway. By the time Tatum and Naomi headed back to the bar for a break, Dash was ready to deck the guy.

Naomi dismissed herself for a trip to the ladies' room. Tatum stepped up to the bar and ordered a mixed drink.

Dash met him and spun him around. "What the hell do you think you're doing?"

"Dancing. With Naomi." The bartender handed Tatum his drink, and he paid with a single bill.

"That looked like more than dancing to me."

"Did it?" Tatum placed his change in the tip jar.

"Don't make me hurt you, Tatum. Now is not a good time for your smart-aleck mouth."

Tatum placed an elbow on the bar and cocked himself into an arrogant lean. "I thought there was nothing going on between you two?"

Dash just glared at him.

"Fine." Tatum took a sip of his drink. "Here it is. You're lucky you're my brother or I'd be doing everything in my power to entice that lady into going back to my room when this night is over. But you might want to take a look around. The other men here don't care about your ego or your pride. Your lady is gathering a fan club."

They both looked around for Naomi, whom they found waylaid on her way back from the restroom by a trio of male admirers.

Tatum continued, "She's beautiful. She's sexy. And not that they know it—yet—but she also happens to be extremely smart. The lady's a keeper and either she's with you or she's not. I suggest you step up or step aside."

The tension in Dash's body mounted. *Smart-ass bastard.* Tatum had been testing him. All damn day. Not only had Tatum been aware of the affect what he was doing had on Dash, but the bastard's behavior had been intentional, calculated to get a rise out of him.

Dash released the vice-like grip he'd fisted his hand into and slid his eyes back to Naomi. The men eyeing her weren't few in number. Although she wasn't flirting back with anyone, she wasn't exactly ignoring the attention she was getting either, which was his real problem. Not Tatum.

He had to stop kidding himself. He had no intention of letting her go when they got back home. He'd gotten a taste of her again, and he wanted to keep that all for himself. Releasing her hold on him so she could go share everything she'd shared with him over the last few days with some other man just wasn't tenable.

A Latino man grabbed Naomi's hand and led her onto the dance floor. Dash watched him pull her into his arms. He was a smooth dancer. They moved into an impressive salsa.

They looked good together. Too good.

It was time for him to stop holding back. If he'd learned anything over the last week, it was that he didn't like sharing Naomi with other men. She was his. And, ready or not, the time had come to make that clear.

He grabbed the drink from his brother's hand, downed it, and then said in a low growl, *"Damn you."* He handed the empty glass back to Tatum then spun around with storm clouds in his normally placid eyes. He strode purposely across the dance floor.

"You're welcome," Tatum said with a grin in his voice and a lift of his empty glass, but he wasn't referring to the drink.

The dancing throng parted like the Red Sea in the wake of an intense Dash. For the rest of the night, Naomi would be dancing solely him.

~ 4 ~

By the time Dash and Naomi reached the door to their suite in the wee morning hours, they were both wound so tight with sexual tension it took every ounce of their will not to undress each other in the hallway. Dash slid his keycard into the card reader and pulled Naomi into his arms as he pushed open the door. They kissed frantically, pulling at each other's clothes. He had the presence of mind to move them out of the doorway before Naomi freed herself of her top, but just barely.

This time, his bed was closer, and he didn't care about strategy. His only interest was getting her in bed and opened to him as soon as possible. He'd tie her to the bed afterwards if that's what it took to keep her in his arms until sunrise.

He flicked on the lights and grabbed her up. Clad now

only in her lacy, lime green matching bra and panties, she watched him through glowing emerald eyes that scorched him with their intensity. He dropped her unceremoniously onto the bed. She grinned as she bounced into an unsexy sprawl. She resituated herself onto her knees and sat back on her haunches.

Without removing his eyes from hers, he stepped away from the bed and peeled his clothing off one piece at a time. Naomi's eyes watched his every move intently, darkening further and further with each item he removed. She reached behind her back and unclasped her bra. Freeing her full, round mounds, she tossed the silky cups over the edge of the mattress. The erection beneath his boxer briefs lengthened.

Naomi's eyes stayed focused on his. She unconsciously parted her lips. Her hands went to her bare breasts and squeezed. Her nipples puckered noticeably beneath the self-stimulation. His hands froze at the waistband of his underwear and his brain short-circuited, what he was supposed to be doing forgotten amidst his mouth's growing desire to replace her hands.

"You planning to keep those on all night?" She shifted onto one hip and adjusted her legs to slide her panties all the way off. "It'd be easier to do this without them, but I'm sure I could work around them." She dropped the scrap of lime green lace to the floor, reuniting it with its matching bra. Lounging on one arm, she held her body upright with a flat hand on the bedspread. She lifted her other hand and motioned with a crooked index finger for Dash to come to her.

He swallowed, heart thudding for the goddess teasing his vision. As he approached, Naomi lazed herself onto her stomach lengthwise across the center of the bed until her toes dangled off the other side of the mattress. Propping herself up on her elbows, she let her hands hang over the edge and tease the comforter cover.

Everything in Dash tightened, hopeful anticipation mixed with a slight sense of dread. If she fulfilled the promise she had in her eyes, his evening might be short-lived. He stopped a few inches from the bed. She reached out with one hand, tugged at the waistband of his boxer briefs, and pulled him closer.

Her hooded eyes seared him with a burning desire that fully matched his. "It's been a while," she whispered. "Let's see if your likes have changed." She slipped his briefs gently over his fully loaded manhood and down to his knees.

When she gripped the back of his legs beneath his buttocks and guided him into her mouth, he couldn't control the deep throaty moan that burst from him. "Naomi, you're going to kill me."

She licked over the tip of him and smiled up. "Maybe. But, like they say, what a way to go."

Placing one hand at the base of his shaft, she slid him back between her lips and pleasured him with long, slow up-and-down passes. The suction of her mouth alone nearly undid him, but when she placed her free hand beneath his balls and massaged, he nearly spilled himself too soon. He grabbed her chin with one hand and yanked himself from her mouth, fighting back a release that would signal the end of this night before he'd gotten to the best part.

In one fluid motion, he tossed her on her back and grabbed a condom. He covered himself quickly then covered her. Anxious but not careless of her comfort, he seated himself into the deepest part of her with one thrust. The sexy moan that filtered from her vocal cords was a sound he could hear for the rest of his life.

She lifted her legs and wound them around his back. She moved beneath him, trying to coax him into a faster rhythm while he fought to slow things down. "Don't go slow, Talon. Not tonight. Take me. Take me hard. *Please.*"

Her pleas broke his resolve. He obeyed with a tempo governed by her body's nonverbal cues. They fled past burning desire towards ecstasy as they fired each other's flesh. When they finally pushed each other over the edge, the explosion that rocked them blew with an intensity that left them both shaking.

The intimacy they'd inadvertently regenerated—but not acknowledged—slithered over Dash's psyche. They grabbed each other and held on silently. Mixed with the contented bliss he felt floated a subconscious memory of the vulnerability inexorably linked with the passion he'd been missing since the day he'd split with Naomi, a vulnerability they'd just unleashed and which gave her the power to hurt him in ways others could not.

He kept his own counsel about the emotions spiraling unchecked within him and fought himself over the strength of his feelings. Everything Naomi made him feel blossomed bigger and more intense than he could intuitively understand. He didn't believe in the propaganda of love, the forever-afters or the till-death-do-us-parts. Life in foster care had cured him of such foolish notions early and permanently. Still, when he touched her, held her, made love to her, intellect took a back seat to a feeling so overwhelming he couldn't even name it.

He pulled the limp, sleeping treasure tighter against him, at peace in a way he hadn't been in a long time. He reveled in the feel of her steady heartbeat. She adjusted, snuggling close beneath the high thread count hotel sheets. He smiled. He clearly would not have to tie her to the bed to keep her in his suite. When she snuggled like this, burrowing deep into the covers, she was usually out for the remainder of the night.

His hand slid through her hair. He'd shown his territorialness at the club tonight. He'd claimed her with abandon only minutes ago. He'd done everything but say the words, the words he needed to say, the ones that spiraled so close to the tip of his tongue he could barely hold them in: *I want you back*.

Tomorrow, he'd fix that. Tomorrow, he wouldn't just show her in deed, but put it all on the line so she'd no longer have to guess at what he was thinking. Tomorrow, he'd say the words and reclaim what he'd been missing for the last three years.

Tomorrow . . .

CHAPTER 13

The next morning, Dash stepped through the adjoining suite door to see if Naomi was dressed yet. They were meeting Tatum for breakfast before he had to catch his midday flight back to the States.

She had her back to him with her cell phone tucked under her ear. "Okay, sweetie. I miss you, too," she said to someone on the other end.

He frowned. *Sweetie?*

She turned, phone still to her ear, and startled when she saw him standing at the door. "See you soon," she said before disconnecting the call.

She was quiet a moment, watching him. A nervous energy surrounded her. "Did you need something, Dash?"

A sense of foreboding hit him. "We're supposed to meet Tatum in five minutes to say goodbye, but if you need to continue your call, don't stop on my account."

She glanced at the phone, a strange look passing over

the face he'd made glow with pleasure only a short while ago. "No. I'm finished."

"Sure you are." His jaw ticked and his eyes went cold. "I didn't mean to interrupt. Go ahead and call him back. I'll meet Tatum alone."

She took a step forward. "Him? Dash what are you talking about?"

She played the confused woman well, he thought. "Don't play games with me, Naomi. Did you really think sleeping with me would make me agree to your story more easily? Does your boyfriend know that's what you planned to do when you got here?"

She flinched at the verbal slap. "You think I'd sleep with you while seeing someone else?" Her green eyes iced over. "I wasn't talking to another man, you ass."

"Who the hell else would you call 'sweetie'?"

Her mouth opened and closed twice before she firmly shut her lips without saying anything. He watched her anger flit to incredulity then turn into confusion. "Are you serious?" Her voice was so soft and hurt, he instantly felt like the ass she'd just called him.

Had he jumped to the wrong conclusion again?

He'd made the mistake once before of not asking her to explain when a situation got tense. It had cost him years without the only women who'd ever gotten under his skin. He wouldn't make the same mistake twice. This time, he'd ask for an explanation. "Who was on the phone, Naomi?"

She held the phone to her chest with both hands. At his question, she tilted it out and stared at it. "I . . . ," she began, still looking at the phone. She looked up.

The look in her eyes made the awful feeling in his spine expand into his gut.

When she finally spoke, her voice was controlled but

tight. "Did you not get any of the letters I sent you?"

The sudden turn in the conversation threw him. "Yes, I got them. But I didn't read them. What does that have to do with anything?"

"You didn't read *any* of them?"

"No." Her delay in responding, frustrated him. Watching her stand there in nothing but panties and a bra had him tense and aroused, which frustrated him even more. He hated that she did this to him. Even in anger, he wanted her. Here he was ready to ask her to come back to him, and she was hiding something or someone from him.

Last time, he'd made the mistake of not letting her explain their misunderstanding. This time he'd asked straight out what was going on, and he'd be damned if he'd let her skirt the issue. "Naomi, answer my question. Who were you talking to on the phone?"

A knock sounded on the outer door to his suite before she could respond.

"You'd better get that. It'll be Tatum."

Dash glanced over his shoulder at the door then glanced back. "He can wait."

"No. Go ahead. I'll join you guys downstairs in a minute."

"You need to answer my question."

"Yes, I do. But now is not the time." She sat down on the bed, oblivious to having sat on top of the dress she'd laid out to put on. With a hint of sadness in her voice, she said, "Go on, Dash. I promise I'll explain later. Trust me. This isn't a conversation we can have with Tatum waiting in the wings."

Dash wanted to push the matter, but a more insistent knock sounded behind him. He spun and slammed shut the adjoining suite door so she could finish dressing in private.

Anger oozed through the layers of his skin. He couldn't

believe what he'd been thinking last night. What was he, some flighty, pubescent girl who couldn't distinguish the endorphin rush of sex from romantic love?

Here he'd been ready to make them a couple again, and she'd been in it simply for a roll in the hay. She had some *sweetie* back home waiting for her. How ironic that he'd been the one with the plan to seduce her and move on. Yet, she'd been the one to seduce him into letting her manipulate his emotions again.

He snatched open the door to his suite, causing Tatum to step back quickly.

Dash stormed out into the hallway and slammed the door behind him. "Let's go."

Tatum looked at the closed door. "Naomi's not joining us?"

"She'll meet us downstairs."

With narrowed eyes, Tatum slid a hand into his left pants pocket and examined Dash. He looked as though he wanted to say something, but he kept quiet. *Smart man.* Dash was in a killing mood. He didn't want to start with his newly found brother. He might, however, start with a green-eyed temptress after she made her way downstairs. In the meantime, he'd head to the hotel café to find his calm and a distraction to keep his mind off the possible joy of strangling a certain sports reporter.

~ ၦ ~

Naomi sat on the bed listening to the sound of the outer door slam in the other suite.

Dash didn't know her secret.

She'd spent all this time resenting him for his failure to contact her after he'd learned her news to now find out he was clueless. He'd not only avoided her in person but also all her correspondence to him. Two and a half years of angst and resentment wasted.

Well, maybe not wasted. Who was he to drop his head in the sand and completely wash her out of his life at the first sign of hardship?

She'd understood from the beginning that he had a problem with commitment. She'd gone into the relationship with eyes wide open, expecting nothing long-term. That understanding had been reinforced when she'd learned about his past and figured out he had deep-seated trust issues.

A woman would be foolish to expect a fairy-tale romance from a man who couldn't trust. She'd given herself a firm mandate. Enjoy each moment for what it was. Don't fall in love. Don't look back when it was over.

She'd started out with such good intentions, bucking herself up to have a limited affair, which wasn't like her at all and ultimately hadn't worked. She'd slipped on the falling in love part, probably even before she'd figured out how dangerous it would be to her heart. She should have stuck with her principles—no casual affairs and definitely no sexcapades with professional athletes.

She wasn't cut out for today's sexual revolution. She didn't have the psychological fortitude to engage in intimate relations without emotional entanglement. She hadn't been able to help herself with Dash, and as she should have expected, their relationship had ended with heartbreak—at least for her. Now, she had to relive the parting and the unease all over again.

Why couldn't this trip to Ibiza have been as simple as she'd initially told herself it would be? She should have focused on nothing but the story. Letting Dash's personal pain get to her and falling back into bed with him had been a mistake. She'd been kidding herself that she could comfort him and give in to her physical need for him and not fall prey to old emotions. She'd been determined to take these few days as a way to purge herself of what-if memories, ignoring his epic fail to step up when she'd needed him most.

She stood. She needed to get dressed, no sense wallowing in the hurt and frustration of how easily he'd previously wiped her from his life. He hadn't even bothered to read her letters? *The pompous jerk!*

How little she must have meant to him that he hadn't even been curious as to why she'd kept trying to contact him. The realization didn't bode well for the ending of whatever this was going on between them now. He'd already taken a step back. His accusing her of sleeping with him while having a man back home spoke volumes for how little he still trusted her. He'd accepted her explanation of the past article and been big enough to apologize for his small-mindedness, but he hadn't really changed—neither his mindset nor his perception of her.

He'd probably never change. His past held too tight a grip on his soul. Betrayal, animosity, loneliness were his emotional fuel. He wouldn't ever let that go. Maybe he *couldn't* ever let it go. The thought crushed a part of her spirit. If that were truly the case, she needed to move on and let go of Dash emotionally and not just physically.

In hindsight, perhaps it had been best he'd not been a part of her life over the last few years. The life she wanted for herself didn't include living in an emotional black hole, not even tangentially as part of a couple. She picked up the dress she'd laid out, now wrinkled from her having sat on it. She didn't care. She shook it out and pulled it on. No sense worrying about her appearance. Things with Dash were about to take a turn for the worse, especially after she explained her phone call.

Naomi dropped her face into her hands. She'd come to grips with this once already. She'd faced the problem alone and accepted that she couldn't count on Dash. Now, that dark place of worry and anxiousness pulled her back into its arms, hugging her tightly until she couldn't breathe. What she had to tell him would change his life dramatically—change *their* lives dramatically.

She pressed the tips of the fingers on her right hand into the middle of her chest. She forced herself to breathe. As the pressure loosened, a small ray of hope sliced through her anxiety. Maybe when she told him, he'd surprise her. She could hope that he'd accept her news graciously. She didn't want to feel that hope again only to be plunged back into disappointment, but knowing he hadn't known the truth all these years caused that hope to bubble up despite herself.

Could things change? Or was she just fooling herself?

She slipped into her sandals and stepped over to the mirror to brush through the humidity-induced waves sprouting through her hair. She needed to get downstairs and out of her head. Dash and Tatum had probably ordered by now.

Tatum. Dash was still reeling from the discovery of his previously unknown twin brother. Could he handle two emotional curve balls in less than a week? Maybe now wasn't the best time to add to his internal upheaval. Her revelation would only add to the sense of loss he still hadn't come to grips with.

On the one hand, it was his fault. She'd done everything except dance naked in public to get his attention. On the other hand, her news would hit him hard regardless of the reason for the delay in his finding out. How could she in good conscience add to his sense of imbalance right now?

Maybe she needed to put this particular discussion off until they got back home. Forcing Dash to deal with her surprise and with Tatum simultaneously didn't seem like a good idea. She'd go downstairs, have some breakfast, and try to be supportive despite Dash having just insulted her. She'd deal with his anger and frustration over the misconstrued phone call as best she could later, when they could talk without other distractions or concerns getting in the way.

Mind made up, she put down the paddle brush, whipped her hair up into a high, bushy ponytail, and threw on her crossbody bag. She headed downstairs. When she reached the hotel café, a waiter escorted her to the square table Dash and Tatum occupied. They had beverages and a plate of fruit in front of them, but no meals.

The guys sat opposite each other so she took a chair in between them. Dash glanced at her, his eyes missing the warmth they'd held the last few days when he'd looked at her.

She missed him already.

~ 4 ~

Tatum watched Naomi seat herself at the table, the air between her and Dash decidedly cooler than it had been the past few days. Dash gave her a cool look and her eyes shadowed. The lady's sadness practically leapt from her pores.

Without asking her what she wanted, Dash ordered her a glass of fresh squeezed juice. She thanked him and accepted the libation from the waitress, who made a point to drop her hand on Dash's shoulder after delivering the drink. Dash gave the waitress a once over with his eyes and an inviting smile. Tatum frowned as he watched his brother flirt with the waitress.

Naomi simply picked up her glass of juice and sipped. She ignored the couple, which made the waitress bolder. Assured that the lady at the table wasn't staking a claim on her target, the waitress made her interest clear.

When Dash didn't discourage her, Tatum decided he would. "Darling, we're trying to have breakfast here. How about taking our orders?"

She stood up from her lean against Dash's chair. "Why certainly, sir. What would you like?"

Tatum ordered breakfasts for each of them. Then, he sat back and looked from Dash to Naomi and back again. "What happened between you two since last night?"

Naomi gave him a false smile. "Oh, same old story. He pursues me, beds me, then decides I manipulated him to get a story."

"What was there to manipulate him over? I thought you already had the story. *Alleged Homosexual Lover Turns Out To Be Kissing Famous Quarterback's Long Lost Twin.*" Tatum punctuated his sarcastic headline with a smirk.

"She won't be publishing that story," Dash growled.

"No. I'll be publishing a story with a lot less scandal and a lot more human interest."

"No, you won't," Dash contradicted her.

"What are you talking about, Dash? The whole reason we came here was to clear up the story behind that photograph. Now that we have the answers, my editor will be expecting a story. I need something to show for my time away. And DuChamps has already agreed to an exclusive."

"It's not DuChamps's life. It's mine. I don't want the

story of finding my brother to be some media circus."

She looked at him with incredulity. "It wouldn't be that and you know it. That's not my style."

"Well, there are lots of things I didn't think were your style, but I'm finding out otherwise. Aren't I?"

She jumped up from her seat. "Excuse me," she said to Tatum and left the table for the ladies' room.

"What am I missing?" Tatum asked Dash after she disappeared. "Last night, you all but branded your initials on her ass. Now, you're doing everything you possibly can to alienate her. What gives?"

"What gives is that this morning I caught her talking secretly on the phone. Apparently, her *sweetie* misses her and is anxious to get her back home." He made a face when he said the word "sweetie."

"She's seeing someone else?"

"She says not. That she wasn't talking to another man."

"But you don't believe her," Tatum stated emphatically.

Dash shrugged.

"From what you've told me, isn't this how the rift between you two started in the first place? You jumping to conclusions?"

"Yes, but this time I asked her for an explanation. She blew me off. Said she didn't have time to explain this morning. She'd explain everything to me later."

"Then why are you treating her like you caught her in the act with the pool boy? Give her a chance to explain." Tatum sat forward and crossed his arms on the table. "Look, I realize I've only been your brother for a few days, but let me give you some brotherly advice anyway. Women like her don't stay single. One day, you may look up, realize you've made a mistake, only to find out she's marrying someone else. Trust me. I know that of which I speak."

"I know her well enough to tell when she's hiding something. Whatever she has to tell me, I'm not going to like it."

"Why borrow trouble? Wait until she actually drops the hammer on your head before you decide you've been assaulted."

The look on Dash's face said it all.

"Holy crap." Tatum flopped back in his chair. "You're afraid."

Dash scoffed. "Afraid? Don't be stupid."

"You're so in love with that woman you're scared out of your damn mind. You'd rather push her away than face your fears."

"I'm not in the mood for this." Dash pushed his chair back, pulled out his wallet, and threw several bills on the table. "Have a good trip, *bro*. Call me sometime." Without another word, Dash headed for the café entrance.

The sulking quarterback allowed himself to be waylaid at the hostess station by their waitress. She draped herself on his shoulder. By the time Naomi emerged from the restroom, the waitress had gotten bold enough to touch Dash's chest and arms frequently. Naomi had to pass them to get to the table, but to her credit, she didn't flinch or falter of step when Dash burst into laughter and placed his arm around the waitress's waist.

Tatum rose out of courtesy when Naomi reseated herself at the table.

"I see we're down to a party of two," she said.

"It looks that way. Seems my brother didn't like the turn in the conversation."

Naomi eyed him with a tilt of her head. "I hope it wasn't on my account. The last thing I need is for him to push you away over something between him and me. He needs someone he can count on in his corner for a change."

"I would think having a woman who loves you in your corner would be enough for most men."

Her eyes snapped back to his from her plate. "I'm not . . . You've got the wrong . . ." His look of sympathy stopped her filibustering. She dropped her hands into her lap. "Great. Why are my feelings so easy for everyone else to read, but that idiot can't figure out I would never do anything to hurt him?"

"Guys are notoriously dense when we're the ones at the center of attention."

She glanced towards Dash and his new lady friend. The waitress handed Dash a folded piece of paper which he accepted before kissing her on the cheek.

Tatum also observed the exchange.

Dash left the café without a glance at either of them.

"So, you're headed back to the States." Naomi's voice cut into Tatum's musings about Dash's current behavior.

He decided to allow her the change in subject. "Yes. I need to speak with my parents about Dash. That's why I'm cutting my trip short. I figure this is a conversation best held face-to-face."

"You're probably right."

The waitress interrupted their talk by bringing their breakfast order. She hadn't brought a plate for Dash, but she did scoop up the money he'd left on the table.

Sidling over to Tatum, she placed her hand on his shoulder and asked in a suggestive, sultry voice, "Anything else I can get you, hon?"

"I'm about to eat here, darling. Don't make me ill."

The waitress looked down at the plate she'd placed in front of him. Her brows creased.

Tatum explained. "Having you flirt with me after trying

to make time with my brother, makes my stomach churn. I prefer not to go with promiscuous when I pick my females."

Her face reddened. She gave Naomi an evil glare before she stalked away.

Naomi smiled at Tatum. "I wouldn't order anything else from the kitchen if I were you."

He chuckled. "Believe me. I won't be putting anything in my mouth that isn't already on this table. I suggest you do the same."

They ate their breakfast and talked for a long while. Before long, Tatum steered the conversation back to Dash.

Cutting him off, Naomi asked, "Have you ever heard a song called *Cowboy Casanova* by Carrie Underwood?"

Not understanding where she was going with this sudden topic change, he shrugged. "Sure."

"Well, change the eyes referenced in the song from blue to brown and that's Dash to a tee—the devil in disguise. All that sex appeal and charisma definitely inspire a woman to feelings she doesn't want to fight, but I'll be damned if I shouldn't have run for my life.

"Loving your brother has been the most painful experience of my life when it hasn't been the most euphoric. How's that for foolishness?" Naomi reached inside her purse to pull out her wallet.

Tatum stopped her with a hand to her wrist. "Don't worry about it. It's on me."

"Thanks." She smiled sadly. "Too bad I didn't meet you first. Maybe I could have fallen for the non-evil twin."

Tatum chuckled. "It's not too late. Maybe I could help you get over him."

She shook her head, fighting the pools of liquid gathering in her emerald eyes. She knew he was joking, but her breaking heart gave him a real response. "If only it worked that way." She stood, leaned over and kissed him on the cheek. "Have a safe trip."

Tatum watched her walk away. "Hang in there, beautiful lady," he said quietly, out of earshot of her retreating back. "My brother loves you, too. He's just too hardheaded to admit it to himself."

It looked as if Dash was going to have to actually lose Naomi before he accepted the truth. Unfortunately, from the look on Naomi's face, the moment of loss had just arrived.

CHAPTER 14

Dash and Naomi left Ibiza the day after Tatum. The adjoining suite door between them had remained locked on both sides during their last twenty-four hours at the resort. They'd eaten separately and avoided conversing with each other except to coordinate transportation to the airport.

On the last leg of their multi-prong return trip, Naomi sat next to a snoozing Dash. Their flight would touch down in Kansas City in about an hour. They hadn't done much talking on the way home either. Dash had ignored her, choosing to read periodically and flirt shamelessly with the female flight attendants.

Naomi tried to work diligently on her computer, but her mind wandered from the notes and draft of the story she wanted to publish about Dash and Tatum. Dash opposed her writing the story. That was about the only thing he had talked to her about since their blow up two days ago—her dropping the story.

She couldn't afford to drop this story. Her job hinged on delivering an exclusive, newsworthy piece to her editor. Turning the brouhaha over the infamous photo from secret homosexual lover to twins separated as infants could be the kind of story picked up and taken nationally. Tatum understood that and had given her great personal statements to include in the piece. She'd hoped Dash would do the same, but they'd argued about it when she'd asked him.

The article wouldn't be the same without his cooperation. She sensed his desire for her to drop the story was a test. A way for her to prove her loyalty to him. She hadn't been able to keep the last personal story about him from going public, but she could with this one. At least, that's what he thought. That wasn't really the issue—or the case.

He didn't seem to get that. Or maybe he didn't care. She glanced at his sleeping profile. Sooner or later, someone would see him and Tatum together and connect the dots. Why should she step aside and let someone else break this story? The story she'd uncovered by looking beyond the obvious.

They'd have to revisit the conversation when he awoke. Plus, she still had to explain about the phone call he'd overheard. She'd intentionally avoided that subject with him since he hadn't brought it up himself. It was a discussion she didn't want to have amidst strangers in airports or on crowded flights. It was a discussion, in truth, she didn't want to have at all.

This time, she'd like to be the one who got to bury her head in the sand. She rationalized there was no sense muddying the waters before she had to, especially when she already had her hands full with convincing him to lend his authorization to the story she needed to write. It would give the story more weight if she could include quotations from Dash along with those she'd already gotten from Tatum.

Fat chance that, at least not without intervention. Maybe she should go back to DuChamps and tell him Dash wasn't cooperating. Yeah, and that would surely piss Dash off more than he already was.

She almost wished she did have another guy waiting at home. It would serve Dash right, the flirt. The next attendant who dipped a bosom in his face was getting the remnants of Naomi's melted ice and orange juice thrown in her face. Just out of principle.

The captain announced their approach to the Kansas City International Airport. She packed away her laptop and gathered her belongings in anticipation of landing.

Dash stirred. "My car's at the airport. I'll drop you at home."

The sound of his voice made her jump. "I've made arrangements to take the shuttle."

"Unmake them. We need to talk. And we need to take care of it tonight."

"Dash, I have to make a stop on the way home. We can talk tomorrow."

"No chance, Naomi. You can run your errand tomorrow or I can swing you by on our way. Your choice."

Swing her by on their way? No chance that. She'd take care of her business after their talk. She needed to stop stalling. She needed to put on her big girl panties and get this over. Why not let Dash drive her home where they could handle this in private? It wasn't as if it was out of his way. She wasn't that far south of the airport, and he had to go way south to get to his home in the Olathe suburbs.

"Fine, Dash. You can drive me home. I'll take care of my business later."

Now, she had to find the words to tell him something he should already know.

~ ᴙ ~

The sound of light giggles floated towards Dash and Naomi when Naomi opened her front door. Dash looked up to see a toddler come barreling down the hall and duck behind the couch. The little girl was naked except for a pullup diaper.

"Tallie! You come back here," a woman's stern voice called from the vicinity of the bathroom.

More giggles filled the air as the toddler peeked around the couch. A riot of blondish-brown curls exploded around her head in a frizzy halo. The mischievous imp grinned as she looked towards the hallway, searching for the person that went with the voice. She caught sight of Naomi instead.

Her large eyes got impossibly larger. "Mom-*meeee*," she screamed and sprinted towards Naomi.

Dash's heart twisted up from his chest and lodged in the vicinity of his throat. *Mommy?* Naomi had a child?

He found it hard to breath. The thought of Naomi making a baby with another man sent his head spinning. That wasn't supposed to happen.

Get a grip, man. You weren't going to give her a family. He knew that in his head, but for some reason, seeing the evidence that she'd put aside her feelings for him enough to get serious with another man made him sick to his stomach.

"Hi, sweetie." Naomi scooped up the beautiful little girl and kissed her on the cheek. Naomi gave Dash an anxious glance.

Well, he had his explanation. Naomi had been talking to her little girl on the telephone, not a man. Once again, seeing himself fall into the asshole category, Dash could kick his own butt. Could he not learn a lesson about jumping to conclusions?

He stared at the little doll whose fat, golden thighs bracketed her mother's right hip. Chubby cheeks filled her face, but there was no mistaking her mother's exquisite bone structure beneath the childish beauty. The girl would grow up to be a stunner.

The little girl hugged her mom, head tight against Naomi's shoulder. All the while, the child's eyes never left his face. She appeared fascinated by him.

"Hey, honey, you're home." Naomi's mother materialized from the back hallway, holding a pair of pink footie pajamas.

Dash and Naomi looked up.

"How was your . . . ," Ms. Pellier's voice trailed off when she spied him standing next to Naomi. "Hello, Dash," she said in a guarded voice.

"Hello, Adele." He cleared his throat. The words got stuck in his throat and came out raspy.

"Mom, why aren't you guys at your place?" More than surprise laced Naomi's voice. He noted an edge of slight panic.

Adele's eyes flicked briefly to the child and then to Naomi.

Naomi focused on her mother and moved her head in quick, understated shakes, then gave him that anxious look again.

What was that all about? What? Did they think he was going to do or say something horrid in front of the child? He may have been an ass to Naomi in the past, but he wasn't a complete moron. He wouldn't cause a scene in front of an impressionable child.

He held Adele's gaze for a few moments, trying to gage her reaction to seeing him here. She couldn't be his biggest fan, if she was a fan of his at all anymore, after the way he and Naomi had broken up. Despite his concern about his standing with Ms. Pellier, his eyes slid back to the gorgeous little girl in her mother's arms.

Ms. Pellier walked over and reached for the child. The child twisted in her mother's arms to avoid being grabbed. Pressing a hand to the girl's back, Naomi kept her from falling.

Adele stepped back and lowered her hands. "When you texted you were coming home early, I figured you'd want to see little bit as soon as possible. So, I thought I'd put her to bed here tonight so she'd be here when you got in." She glanced back at Dash. "I didn't realize you'd have company with you."

Naomi's eyes closed. She let out a long, deep sigh that sounded like she had the weight of the world on her shoulders. "Dash and I have some things to discuss. He insisted we get it out of the way tonight."

"Well, why don't I take Tallie to her room so you two can talk?"

Dash studied the little girl, considering her unusual name. "Tallie?" The little girl smiled at him when he said her name. Dimples popped alive in her cheeks, and she reached for him, arms outstretched.

Naomi's eyes flew wide at her daughter's gesture.

Dash dropped the suitcases still in his hands and snatched up the little girl before Naomi could pull her away. The little girl giggled when he settled her against his chest, one hand clasped beneath her leg as he balanced her on his forearm and the other hand locked under her shoulder to keep her steady. She smelled good, like baby powder and sweet, scented lotion. He wanted to snuggle her close and breathe in that smell of innocence.

He held Naomi's child. The thought that the child should have been his caused an irrational longing. He knew who he was. Despite the hoard of wealth he'd amassed during his professional athletic career, he was still the kid nobody had wanted. He'd learned a lot of things being bounced from dysfunctional foster home to really dysfunctional foster home, but how to be a father or a family man a woman could depend on wasn't any of them.

"I'll take her, Dash." Naomi reached for Tallie. "Sorry about that."

Tallie shook her head and threw her arms around Dash's neck, holding on for dear life. Dash rubbed his hand up and down her back. He turned slightly away from Naomi, not ready to give up the child. It was crazy, but he wanted to hold on to her for a little longer. The thought that the child had bewitched him at first glance just like her mother made him want to smile even though the hole in his soul had opened a little wider when the little girl had grabbed his neck. "She's fine, Naomi."

Naomi looked at him uncertainly then glanced at her mother. Dash also glanced at Adele, whose face sent her daughter a message he couldn't decipher. Those looks again. He was beginning to feel like a less-than-desirable interloper.

"Geez, ladies. I'm not going to drop her. I've had enough photo-ops to know how to hold a baby."

Tallie lifted her head. She looked at her mother as if trying to gage whether she'd earned a reprieve. When her mother didn't reach for her again, she turned back to Dash and studied his face.

He studied her right back. "Hi, pretty girl. Where'd your

momma come up with a name like Tallie?"

"It's short for Taliana," Adele said.

"*Mom.*" Naomi stepped towards her mother and shook her head. "Could you give us a minute, please?"

"Taliana?" Dash chuckled. "Leave it to your mother to come up with something creative but beautiful," he said to Tallie. He ran a bent index finger down her smooth cheek. "It suits you."

Tallie pressed her palm to his cheek. "*Tal*un."

Dash stiffened. He looked at Naomi. "She knows who I am?"

Ignoring Naomi's request, Adele answered Dash. "She has a picture of you in her room."

Tallie threw both arms in the air and yelled, "Football!"

Adele grinned. "Wearing your Griffins jersey." Adele glanced at her daughter's horrified face. "It's a picture Naomi used to keep on her nightstand. Tallie kept taking it so Naomi finally gave it to her."

Beside herself and looking a little embarrassed, Naomi grabbed her mother by the arm. "Mom, *please*. Give us a minute."

"Sure." Adele nodded. Turning towards the hallway, she added with another grin, "I'll just leave Tallie with you guys." Adele dropped Tallie's pajamas on the couch and waved at Dash. "Dash, it was nice to finally see you again. It's about time you made it by. Goodnight, all."

"Goodnight, Adele."

Naomi didn't respond to her mother. She stood transfixed, one hand at the base of her throat, the other fisted at her side. That inexplicable unease still covered her face.

Tallie waved night-night to her grandmother using the open-and-close fist motion common for children her age. When she was done waving, she said his name again. This time, she said it so fast it almost sounded like three syllables. It came out "Talion."

The longing in the pit of his stomach morphed into a flock of giant geese. *Talion. Taliana. Talon.*

He looked closer at the child, who favored her mother except for her large, amberish eyes rimmed thickly in dark chocolate.

"Good, Lord," he whispered. Those were his eyes staring back at him.

He ran his hand over Tallie's head, feeling the soft, bright locks, the color of which now registered as what you got when you mixed dark blond with chestnut brown.

Dash felt a burning behind his eyes, and he choked down the boulder clogging in his throat. He looked at Naomi. Her expression answered the question he hadn't yet asked. "Naomi, what's going on?"

~ ꜔ ~

Naomi swallowed. She'd been trying to find the words to explain Tallie ever since Dash had caught her on the phone in Ibiza. This wasn't how she'd anticipated him finding out he was a father.

The shock on Dash's face wasn't a surprise, nor was his building anger, but she felt the need to defend herself. She lifted both her hands and made a hold-on-a-minute gesture. "Before you get upset, remember those letters of mine you said you never read?"

He closed his eyes and nodded.

"I tried to tell you, Dash. I did."

"The letters," he whispered. "You sent me letters to tell me I was going to be a father and just gave up and walked away when I didn't respond?"

"It wasn't just the letters, Dash." She inhaled a long breath through her nose and expelled it slowly through her mouth before pacing to the other side of the room. Arms wrapped tightly across her waist, she held herself, staring into an unlit fireplace. When she turned back to him, the haunted look in his eyes matched the feeling resurfacing inside her as she recalled her attempts to contact him. "I called you repeatedly when I found out I was pregnant. You wouldn't take my calls or call me back. This wasn't something I wanted to leave on a voicemail or send in an email or text message. Heaven forbid someone else retrieve the information."

She dropped her head and swiped her palm up her forehead to her hairline. "I even tried to see you in person, and you refused to talk to me alone." Her hand dropped and fisted at her side. The old anger at his treatment of her brewing anew. "The last time I tried to talk to you, in a room full of people, you accused me of being clingy and needy. You humiliated me in front of people we both knew and made me out to be some sports groupie who couldn't take no for an answer.

"That night, I'd had enough. I decided you were an ass and our baby would be better off without you. And you *were* an ass, but ultimately, I knew she *wouldn't* be better off without you. I know firsthand what it's like not to have your father take part in your life. So, I tried again and sent correspondence directly to your house. More than once. But you never responded."

"Why didn't you come and see me again later? The minute I saw you were pregnant, I would have known why you wanted to talk to me."

"So would have everyone else, Dash. That's the last thing I wanted. You'd been very public about your hatred of me and your belief that I had intentionally leaked that story about you and Peyton to boost my career. My getting knocked up by you would have created a whole new media free-for-all."

Dash checked the baby in his arms. She'd dropped her head on his shoulder and was falling asleep. He continued to rub her back.

He looked at Naomi and said in a quiet voice, "You've been a part of that media circus from the other side before. You couldn't have toughed it out and risked being on the receiving end for a change?"

"No." She shook her head vehemently. "No, I couldn't." She noted the hurt and frustration in his eyes. She added quietly, "I almost lost her, Dash. I couldn't risk that again."

Dash squeezed Tallie. She squirmed in his arms.

Naomi grabbed the footie pajamas her mom had dropped on the edge of the couch. "Here. I'll take her."

Dash deposited Tallie gently on the couch. Naomi sat beside her and slid on the pajamas. The girl mumbled in her sleep, but didn't wake. Naomi pulled a knitted throw from the back of the couch and draped it over the child.

Dash watched Naomi cover the baby—*his* baby. "What do you mean you almost lost her?"

Naomi's hand gently caressed the child's head. "At ten weeks, I had complications. I nearly miscarried. I ended up in the hospital for several days. I called you from the hospital." Her hand paused. "Stupid me. I'd hoped . . ."

She interlaced the fingers of her hands and slid them between her closed legs. It took her a minute before she could continue.

Tears glistening in her eyes, she looked up at him. "I needed you, Dash. I lay in that hospital bed listening to the beep of the machines hooked up to me, waiting for someone to tell me whether my baby would live or die, and I needed you." Her voice broke. "But you weren't there, and I had to accept that you would never be there for me again."

He squatted beside her and reached for her cheek. "Naomi—"

"Don't." She jumped up and moved away from him. "It won't help now."

She gave her wet cheeks a rough swipe. "I called my mom. She flew up from New Orleans to take care of me. When the doctor released me, he told her I needed to avoid any additional stress or there was a high likelihood I wouldn't carry the baby to term. She packed me up and took me home with her. I took a leave of absence from work and left town without telling anyone I was pregnant."

"You left town." His head bobbed as if he were putting the pieces of some puzzle together in his mind. "That's why I never saw you pregnant."

She nodded at him. "You'd only recently come off the publicity about you decking Anderson for harassing your foster sister. I could imagine what would've happened when the headlines about the baby started."

She slashed a hand in the air as if reading a marquee. *"Dash Janssen Dumps Reporter Mother of His Love Child."* Her hand dropped. "Or worse." She began to pace. "Just what I wouldn't have needed."

Still squatting beside the couch, Dash reached over and softly touched Tallie's hair. He leaned in and kissed the baby on the forehead before he stood. Slipping his hands in his pockets, he stared down at the child for several minutes. "Exactly how old is she?"

The pain in his voice made Naomi's heart lurch, but she wasn't going to let him make her feel guilty about this. "Twenty-six months."

The sad timbre of his voice didn't change. "So she just had a birthday."

"Yes."

"How long have you been back in town?"

"We moved back about eleven months ago. Mom came with us so I wouldn't have to put Tallie in daycare right away. Mom has her own apartment so she doesn't have to deal with our craziness all the time. She keeps Tallie at her place during the day."

"Tallie has a picture of me. She knows my name and that I play football. Does she know that I'm her father?"

He looked up when he didn't get a response. "Naomi?"

She shook her head. "No, she doesn't."

He turned back to his daughter. "I see." After a few minutes, he turned and headed for the door.

Naomi took an unconscious step towards him. "Dash?"

She waited for him to say something more, but he strode directly to the door without looking at her.

When he reached for the doorknob, the pain she'd felt the first time he walked away from her returned full force. "Dash, wait."

He paused, but didn't turn around.

Tears began to roll down her cheeks. "I'm sorry, Dash. I really am. This isn't the way I wanted things to work out."

He looked up at her then. "See you around, Naomi." He glanced over at Tallie one last time then he was gone.

The door clicked closed. Naomi sank to the floor, trying not to be overwhelmed by the realization that, this time, he hadn't just rejected her. He'd also rejected their daughter. Her heart hurt. She really was on her own in this. She had her mother for support, but that wouldn't be the same for Tallie. Like her, her daughter would grow up knowing her father didn't care enough about her to include her in his life.

Fifteen minutes, Naomi. You've got fifteen minutes to feel sorry for yourself. Then you need to suck it up.

She let herself cry softly for those fifteen minutes then she grabbed some tissues and cleaned her face. She walked over to the couch and lifted her daughter. She carried Tallie to her room and placed her in bed.

Adele approached as she stepped from the bedroom. "How did things go?"

"Dash is gone."

"Gone for a while or gone for good?"

Naomi closed her eyes, remembering the look in his eyes and the sound of his voice when he said, *See you around, Naomi.*

"He's gone for good, mom."

"Oh, baby." Her mother pulled her into a hug. "Are you sure?"

She squeezed her mom tightly. "I'm sure, mom. It's up to me to take care of Tallie's future." Which meant she needed to make sure she kept her job. And she knew just how she was going to do that. She had a story to get to print despite Dash's disapproval.

CHAPTER 15

Dash entered the pitch black stillness of his home. He tossed his keys onto the sideboard. They hit the top and slid to the floor with a harsh jangle that grated on his already fragile nerves.

In a daze, he wandered down his long hallway, ignoring every light fixture along the way. When he got to the end of the hallway, he turned left into a sitting room he never used. He stopped at the antique hutch he'd purchased for Naomi at Nell Hills. He'd wanted to get rid of it after their split, but he hadn't been able to give it away when push came to shove.

The piece held a lot of memories of her. He couldn't stand having it out where he could see it every time he entered the house or passed in the hallway. Unable to look at it, yet unable to part with it, he'd compromised by banishing it to this unused dungeon of sorts.

He stared at the pewter pull of the top left drawer. In

slow motion, his hand reached out and took ahold. He wasn't sure his heart was beating any more. A lethargy enshrouded him. He felt heavy.

The drawer slid open under his power, and he stared inside. Time passed. He wasn't sure how much time, but the waning dusk had turned blacker. He pulled the dangling chain on the old-fashioned hood lamp that perched on the edge of the antique. Golden light spilled across the fine oak and slashed across the open drawer like a finger pointing to the five envelopes laying loosely inside the otherwise empty drawer.

He hadn't been able to bring himself to read Naomi's correspondence, but like the hutch, he hadn't been able to simply throw them away. It had seemed fitting they be stored here with her hutch, safely out of his sight where they couldn't haunt him.

Dash gathered the envelopes. Placing them on the hutch top, he sorted them into chronological order by postmark. The earliest letter was a square, pink envelope that looked like some sort of greeting card. He flipped it over and used his finger to nudge under the flap and break open the envelope across the top. He pulled out a notecard whose front was decorated with a flying stork holding a baby in a diaper. The drawing was bordered in pink. A piece of paper slipped from the card and floated down onto the hutch counter, but he ignored it to read the front of the card: *It's a girl!*

He flipped open the card. In Naomi's elegant cursive were only the words: *I thought you'd want to know. ~ Naomi.*

The wayward paper finally caught his eye. He picked up the black and white film of a baby *in utero* and a silent sob slid up his throat. The weight of his sorrow nearly crushed him.

He stared at what was most likely the first picture of his little girl. Glancing at the labeling across the top of the sonogram he read: *Twenty-three weeks, Baby Girl Pellier.* He slumped over the hutch, catching himself with his right forearm. Small wet circles began to dot the scattered envelopes under his head. His daughter—the one who didn't know he was her father, whose development and birth he'd missed—didn't even bear his last name.

~ Ⴤ ~

The next day after practice, Dash found himself on Adele Pellier's doorstep. When she opened the door, she didn't look surprised to see him. If she was curious about how he'd found out her address, she didn't let on and she didn't ask.

"Dash, need I guess what brings you here this morning?" She gave him an amused look.

Dash blushed. "Hi, Adele. I'm sorry to drop by unannounced. I was hoping you'd let me see Tallie."

Her amused look turned serious. "And you thought I'd say no if you called before you came?"

He shrugged. "The thought crossed my mind. I can't exactly be your favorite person at the moment."

"True, but I wouldn't hold that against Tallie. It's important she gets to know you." She stepped aside and motioned him in.

Stepping into the spacious apartment, Dash made a quick visual sweep but didn't see Tallie.

Closing the door behind him, Adele put her hand on his arm. "Dash, I hope you know that neither Naomi nor I would ever keep you from Tallie. You're welcome to see her any time."

He ran a hand down his face and nodded once.

"But I will ask you to promise me one thing before I let you see little bit."

Wariness flickered through him. "What's that?"

"You must promise me that under no circumstance will you tell Tallie you're her father."

His face fell.

"Not yet, Dash. I have to let Naomi make the decision of when and how it's best to tell Tallie about you. You'll have to work that out with her. Okay? Don't put me on the spot by expecting me to get in the middle of that. I can't let you see Tallie if I think you're going to say something that may have emotional consequences for her."

"I'm not here to make trouble, Adele. I just want . . ." He couldn't finish.

She smiled softly. "To see your little girl?"

He nodded.

"Do I have your word?"

"Yeah."

"Dash?"

Adele believed if you didn't speak the words, it didn't mean anything. It stemmed from the hurtful relationship she'd weathered with Naomi's absentee father. Adele had once told them the man had a way of agreeing without actually committing himself, always leaving room to argue that he'd "never said that."

His lips turned up. "Okay. I promise I won't say anything to Tallie about who I am until I've worked it out with Naomi."

"Good. I'll go get Tallie."

"Is she asleep?"

"No. She's playing in her room."

"By herself?"

Adele smiled. "She's a great kid. She can entertain herself for quite a while." She turned towards the hallway.

"Adele." He called after her. When she turned, he said, "I didn't know. If I'd known, I would have been here for her. For both of them."

"I know that, Dash. But it's not me you have to convince."

Adele disappeared into the back of the hallway. Her voice travelled out to him in a soft murmur as she spoke to the little girl in the back. After a moment, he heard a squeal and the sound of thunderous, little feet pounding up the hallway.

Tallie came flying into the room. When she saw Dash, she grinned. The wide smile made her dimples pop in her cheeks. Dash's heart seized. He hadn't paid much attention to those last night. His daughter had his dimples—his dimples, his smile, *and* his eyes. The miracle of that tumbled over him.

"Talon!" She ran to him and lifted her arms.

He squatted, catching her as she threw herself against him. "Hey, princess. How are you today?"

"I good. You come play with me?"

"Yes, I did. As a matter of fact, I brought you something to play with."

Tallie clapped her hands. "Yay! Present."

Dash laughed. "Yeah, present." He reached into his pocket and pulled out a small Nerf football.

Tallie giggled, grabbed the football from him, and shouted, "Football!"

The little girl clutched the ball to her chest with one hand and threw her other hand up in front of her. She held her raised arm out straight and began to run around the room as if dodging tacklers.

The laughter that bubbled up from Dash echoed around the room.

Adele came from the back of the apartment at that moment and took in the scene. "Oh, my. You've done it now." She laughed.

"Future running back, I see." Dash rose and went after the toddler. Scooping up the handful of giggles, he tickled her stomach and placed kisses along her cheeks and neck. "How about you show me your room, Miss Tallie? How does that sound?"

"Okay." Her small, high-pitched voice made him smile.

Was it possible to be this happy for no apparent reason? She brought a buoyance to his spirit he hadn't realized he'd been missing. He placed the child back on the ground.

"Come on, Talon." She grabbed his hand and tugged.

Tallie showed Dash around her room at her grandmother's house. He took in the Disney Princess themed bedding, haphazardly made. Dash guessed Tallie had made the bed herself.

An odd mix of sports and truck posters graced the walls mixed in with several more Disney Princesses. Because the colors were similar or complementary, the decor worked in an odd sort of way. Tallie pulled out several toys to show him, and they played together in her room. After about an hour, Adele called them for lunch.

Dash enjoyed his time with Tallie. They visited and laughed right up to her nap time. After Tallie went down, Dash searched out Adele. She sat in the living room reading.

She pulled off her reading glasses when he came in. "Well, this was certainly the easiest afternoon I've had with my granddaughter."

Dash reached into his pocket and pulled out a folded piece of paper. He handed it to Adele.

"What's this?" She unfolded the paper as she spoke.

"Something for Tallie."

Adele read over the certified check made out for an amount in the high six figures. "Dash, this is excessive and unnecessary." She tried to hand the check back to him.

Dash stepped back. "No, it's not. She's my little girl, too. I haven't been a part of her life or her support up to this point—and I know that's my fault—but I want that to change."

"Dash, Tallie hasn't wanted for anything. Granted, she hasn't been living like a football heiress." She chuckled and looked back down at the check. "But Naomi has taken great care of her."

"I'm not doubting Naomi has been a great mother, but I need to be Tallie's dad. I don't know what that's going to look like over the long haul. Like you said, I need to work that out with Naomi. But, in the meantime, I can certainly start with financial support."

"This goes way beyond financial support. You have to know that, Dash."

He grinned, showing her the dimples that had helped her daughter fall for him. "I have more money than I can spend alone in ten lifetimes. If I can't use some of it to secure my daughter's future, exactly how do you suggest I use it?"

Her shoulders rose and fell with an internalized sigh. She recognized the signs of stubbornness that had resulted in the rift between him and Naomi in the first place. This was an argument she wouldn't win.

"Okay, fine. But you need to give this to Naomi." She offered him back the check.

He shook his head in the negative. "No way. You know she won't accept it from me. I need you to make sure she puts it in the bank for Tallie."

Dash moved to squat in front of Adele. He grabbed both her hands and held them together on her knees. "I'm sorry, Adele. I know I blew it. I should have talked to Naomi about what happened. I certainly should have understood that she wouldn't have tried to contact me so hard for something as mundane as prolonging a relationship with an idiot who didn't treat her with respect. But I need you to believe that if I had known about the baby, I would have given Naomi whatever support she needed."

She pulled a hand free and placed it on top of Dash's. "I believe that, Dash. You're as stubborn as she is. I often wondered how you two managed to last as long as you did without a major blowup." She patted his hand. "Here's the thing, *cher*. Parenting requires a commitment that doesn't allow you to run when things get hard or uncomfortable. I know the kind of childhood you had, and I understand the scars that can leave on a man. But co-parenting between two people who don't trust each other will be a recipe for disaster for that little girl." Her head tilted towards the back bedroom. "Somehow, you and Naomi have to find a bridge that puts the past in the past so that Tallie can have the great future I know you want for her."

Adele leaned in and kissed him on the cheek. "I'll take care of the check with Naomi—this time. Everything else?"

He nodded for her to continue.

"You're going to have to handle yourself."

He rose and slid his hands into his pants pockets. "Fair enough."

He'd driven Naomi to believe his little girl would be better off without him. He had no intention of letting that opinion linger. As he left Adele's, he began formulating a game plan for how to fix things with the woman who'd given him a child . . . given him the most beautiful gift he never even knew he wanted.

~ ¥ ~

Faces scrolled quickly across the computer screen as Naomi searched through the *Daily*'s story archives. She'd finally figured out from where she knew that face in the crowd at the Ibiza club. Now, she needed to verify that she had the right name to go with the face.

"Well, hello, Queenie. You're back from your island excursion." Ray Jackson cocked a hip onto the edge of her desk.

"Hello, Ray." She didn't look up. Her mouse clicked furiously as she continued to search for the photo she wanted.

Ray chuckled. "Hard at work already I see. I guess you're no worse off for wear?"

She looked up and grinned. "I'm good, Ray. Thanks."

"It appears the resort agreed with you. Nice tan."

Naomi looked down at her arms. Her light brown skin had darkened to a burnished copper. She laughed. "Tough work. All that schlepping around and investigating just steps from the beach."

Ray laughed back. "Smart-ass." He adjusted so he sat more securely on the desk with his knee bent and his thigh half on the desk. "Did you find what you were looking for?"

She glanced around, taking stock of who else was in the room.

"If you're looking for Super Spy, he's out. Working on a human interest piece related to one of the Griffins pet charities."

"Good." She pulled her smartphone from her bag, keyed in the passcode, and tapped through her picture gallery.

When she found the one she wanted, she handed the phone to Ray.

He gave the phone a casual glance then abruptly yanked it closer to his face. "Are you kidding me? This is real?"

"Yep." She swiveled side-to-side in her chair, enjoying his reaction to the selfie of her sandwiched between Dash and his twin. "Real. Above-the-fold worthy. And all mine."

He leaned in and whispered. "There are two of them?"

"Shocking, right?" She stopped swiveling. "You can imagine my reaction when I first encountered Tatum."

"Tatum?"

"The brother."

"So the kiss photo?"

"Was of the other one. He's a real estate investor. It looks like the photo was some sort of businessman's warfare. He was in the middle of a multimillion-dollar deal that fell through when his conservative investors saw the photo."

"So it had nothing to do with Dash at all?"

"Looks that way."

"So what's your angle on the story?"

"I'm thinking about sticking with the secret life theme but spinning it into a human interest multi-article spread."

Nodding, Ray looked at the photo again. "That could work. It will require multiple followups with Dash. You going to be able to swing that? You two work things out while you were gone?"

Her face tightened, and she looked away. "I'll manage."

"You'll manage . . ." Ray shifted, dropping the hand holding her phone into his lap and studying her intently. "What happened?" he asked quietly.

"Nothing, Ray. Everything's fine."

"Queenie," his voice took on an admonishing tone that

brooked no refusal, "I suggest you start talking or I'm about to walk out of here and make good on my threat to beat some quarterback ass." He leaned towards her, slipped a hand under her chin, and turned her face towards his. "What happened?"

She sighed and shook her chin loose. Her hand rubbed across her forehead a few times before she answered. "Let's just say the trip was full of highs and lows, personally and professionally. Dash went from a ball of anger to a ball of confusion when our investigation led to Tatum."

"Let me guess." His lips twisted in disgust. "He needed emotional support, and he was willing to let you give it, but now he's back to wanting nothing to do with you or—"

She jumped up and put her hand over his mouth. "Don't say it. You agreed not to mention her here."

Ray was the only one at the paper who knew about Tallie. He lowered Naomi's hand and kissed her palm. "I didn't mean to scare you. I wasn't about to say . . . you know."

She removed her hand from his. "Sorry. I know you better than that. I just . . . I'm a little jumpy I guess." She looked around again. "Dash just found out and he's angry with me. Plus, he doesn't want me to do this story. So, I have to find a way to work this without his cooperation. At least, without his willing cooperation. I can probably get DuChamps to intervene again, but under the circumstances, that might be throwing gasoline on the fire."

Ray nodded. "I'd agree. But what do you mean he just found out? He just found out what?"

"About the real reason for my leave of absence." She sat back down and rubbed a hand over her face again.

"Wait a minute." He frowned. "I'm confused. I thought you told me that you—"

"I did. Among the other things I found out this week, however, was that hardhead didn't bother to read any of them. He got a bit of a surprise when he dropped me at home from the airport. He took one look at the eyes and about threw an aneurysm."

"Damn. That's rough. I think the boy is an idiot—"

"*Ray.*"

He put his hand up. "But I wouldn't have wished that on him. Not about that." He shook his head. "I take it he didn't take it well."

"No, he didn't. I explained, but he walked out. He didn't like me much before. Now, I suspect I'm a few rungs below scum of the earth."

He stared at her.

"What?"

"You still haven't figured it out, have you?"

"Figured out what?"

"Dash doesn't hate you, Naomi. He may want to. He may behave as if he does. But his problem has always been that no matter what he does, he can't stop himself from loving you. He's just too big of a chickenshit to put aside his trust issues and accept it."

"Yeah, right." Her hand flicked in dismissal. "Cut the romanticism, Ray. It doesn't suit you." She turned back to her computer.

"Honey, a man doesn't work as hard as Janssen did to avoid an ex—won't talk to her, won't be in the same room with her, can't even read her letters—" He scoffed. "Unless that woman is so far under his skin the only way he can possible see through to eliminate the threat is to completely amputate the limb."

Her hand stalled over the keyboard. "You can't be serious?"

"I'm dead serious. Frankly, it's one of the reasons I'd just as soon throttle the boy as look at him. You deserve better."

"You're biased."

"Damn straight, I am."

Smiling, she shook her head and went back to her computer screen.

"What on earth are you searching for so diligently?"

"A face in the crowd."

His brows rose. "Huh?"

"Ha!" She swiveled her monitor towards him.

He frowned. "An old picture of the Kansas City Griffins? Okay. I'll bite. Why?"

"Him." She pointed to a man standing on the edge of the picture, wearing jersey number ten.

Ray leaned forward and squinted. "Carl Maynard, the Griffins former backup QB. What do you want with him?"

"I saw him in Ibiza."

His back straightened. "You saw Carl Maynard in Ibiza this weekend?"

"When else was I in Ibiza, Ray?" She rolled her eyes. "Yes, I saw him this weekend. We were at a club. I only caught a glimpse of him, and I couldn't put a name to the face at the time, but it's been bothering me ever since."

"Carl left—or was traded—under some questionable circumstances almost two years ago. No one ever got the full story, but my understanding was Carl wasn't happy about the trade. Felt he'd been railroaded. Is this Tatum sure the photo was a plant to ruin his business deal?"

Her shoulder lifted. "Reasonably sure. He didn't have confirmation at the time. No one had contacted him about it, but after his deal fell through, he assumed that was the motivation."

Ray turned, leaving his butt against her desk but

planting both feet firmly on the floor facing forward. "He *assumed?*" He crossed his arms over his chest and raised an eyebrow at her.

"Yes, he . . ." Her voice trailed off as she became uneasy. Journalists didn't work on assumptions. They worked on facts, hard corroboratable facts.

"And a former Griffins player, the one who used to have Dash's job, just happens to show up on the Mediterranean island from whence originated a photo that could cost Dash his job. That's quite a coincidence. Since when did you start believing in coincidences, Pellier?"

Well, duh! She snatched up her phone. "I didn't."

She needed to call Tatum. If that photo wasn't really about him then someone had been targeting Dash after all.

The question was who?

CHAPTER 16

Flustered, Dash dropped his hands to his waist. Practice wasn't going so well. The offense had been running play routes for the past forty minutes. His last pass had gone exactly where it needed to go, but Max Gordon had still dropped it. He couldn't throw the ball any more accurate than that. Max seemed to be working awfully hard *not* to catch the ball, and it was beginning to piss him off.

Thorsten James Coffey III bumped Dash's shoulder none too lightly as he walked passed.

Dash whirled. "You got a problem, Trey?"

Coffey whipped off his helmet, allowing his neatly coiled locs to fall past his shoulders. "Gordon isn't the only receiver on the field, Janssen. Try throwing the ball to someone else. You might actually get a reception." He stormed off not letting Dash get in a response.

Dash swore under his breath. Three days after discovering he had a daughter, his head still wasn't on straight. On top of that, all his receivers seemed to have a stick up their butts. He glanced over to the sideline. Although his injury kept him from practicing with the team, Shave Stephens stood in street clothes observing team play. The man had been bearish and uncongenial for weeks. A career-threatening injury could do that to a man, but Dash hadn't been happy having his grouchy butt hovering over practice with everything else Dash had going on.

Today, Shave had arrived at the stadium sporting a smile. Funny, now that Shave's disposition had improved, Dash wanted to wipe that smile off his face. The upbeat grin irritated Dash or, more accurately, the thought of what had put that smile on his face irritated Dash. He'd heard talk in the locker room that Shave had met with Naomi last night for dinner. The thought pissed him off.

Shave had contented himself with consulting with the offensive coordinator for most of the past week, but today he'd been chatting up the receiving teams. Was he stirring up trouble? It's not something Dash would have expected from him, but the starter and Gordon were tight. Maybe there was a reason Shave's favorite receiver wasn't catching the ball for his replacement. From where Dash was standing, it looked like Shave was trying to undermine his authority with the offense *and* move in on his woman.

Dash had stopped by Adele's every day after practice to play with Tallie, but he hadn't seen Naomi once. He hadn't yet figured out how to approach her about custody and childrearing issues. He expected her to be resistant. It still grated that she didn't think him man enough to be a good father to Tallie, and apparently, she'd moved on after their weekend in Ibiza and decided she preferred dating the starting quarterback after all.

Back in formation, Dash banished Naomi from his

thoughts and made the snap count. He dropped back for a long pass and let it fly. Max made the route then leapt high into the air. The route was perfect, the timing was perfect, the throw was . . .

"Shit!" Dash watched in horror as Max grazed the ball with his fingertips but failed to bring down the pass.

"Janssen! Try putting the ball in the receiver's hands why don't ya!" Coach Waterman wound a full arm rotation and slammed his clipboard to the turf. "Dammit! The goal is to move the chains, ladies. Move. The. Chains. If you two can't connect, we don't advance." He glared at the receiver and dumped his fists on his hips. "That ball was catchable, Gordon."

"The throw was off—"

"Don't give me excuses. Do your damn job." He turned back to Dash. "I don't know what's going on with you two, but ya'll better find a rhythm or our playoff chances are shot." Snatching up his clipboard, Coach stomped towards the offensive coordinator.

Dash glanced at Shave, expecting him to be gloating at the mistakes Dash was making. Instead, Shave was staring at Gordon. Stephens headed over to speak with the receiver.

"Hit the showers," Coach bellowed. "We'll pick this back up tomorrow."

Dash removed his helmet and loaded his lungs with deep breaths. His win-loss record was even. He'd won exactly as many games as he'd lost. Not the position he wanted to be in if he had any chance of keeping the starting position. He had to find a way to turn things around. As Coach had indicated, if he didn't fix the passing game, the Griffins chances of making it into the playoffs were nil.

He sauntered towards the locker room. He also had to find a way to turn things around with his "baby mamma."

He almost laughed at the thought. This was certainly not a position he ever expected to find himself in. Now that he was, life held challenges on all fronts. Well, at least there was one female Pellier in the city who liked having him around. He hit the showers and made haste to go see his little girl.

~ 4 ~

After a harsh Monday at work, Naomi arrived at her mother's apartment early. She pulled up short when she nearly collided with Dash coming out the door. She threw up her hands to keep him from smacking into her. "Dash, what are you doing here?"

He flicked his gaze behind him before he responded. "I came to visit Tallie."

"Tallie," she repeated in a breathless whisper.

He closed the apartment door. "Don't worry, Naomi. I haven't told her who I am. All I am to her right now is the guy with the football. I'd like to change that. Can we get together for dinner tonight and discuss it?"

He reached for her. When his hand moved towards her face, Naomi's brain told her she should move, but her muscles failed to respond.

Dash touched her cheek.

The heat from his fingers did odd things to her body and jumpstarted her brainwaves. She flicked her head away. "I don't know, Dash. Um . . ." She looked at the closed door. "Tonight's not a good night for me. How about I call you to set something up?"

He stared at her. "Will you?"

"Will I what?"

"Will you actually call me?"

"Of course." At his continued gaze, a flush of burgundy

crept under her lingering bronze tan. The thought of not calling him, of putting this conversation off indefinitely, *had* crossed her mind.

His smug grin warned her he'd seen her blush and understood its meaning.

She shook her head and said softly, "I'll call you, Dash. I promise. Just give me a few days. Okay?"

She needed some time to get her mind around this. She hadn't expected to see him again. She certainly hadn't expected him to want to be a part of Tallie's life.

When he'd walked away a week ago, she'd thought she'd seen the last of him—at least, in person for personal reasons. She expected to have to see him from time to time over a story about the Griffins, especially with rumors mounting that Shave Stephens might not make it back for the rest of the season. She didn't know how to handle a Dash that would become an integral part of her life, of her daughter's life. She needed a little time to regroup.

"I'm counting on that, Naomi."

She nodded and turned for the door.

"Oh, and Naomi?"

"Yes," she said over her shoulder.

"If I don't hear from you in a few days, I'll come looking for you." He turned and walked away.

Great, she mouthed to his retreating back. She pushed into her mother's apartment, closed the door, and leaned her back against it. She closed her eyes, fighting the emotional maelstrom churning inside her.

Her mother's voice broke into her introspection. "Honey, are you okay?"

Opening her eyes, she looked speculatively at her mother. "I just ran into Dash."

Her mother flinched and made a big production of

drying her hands on the tea towel she carried.

Naomi squinted at her mother. "Coming out of your apartment. What's going on, mom?"

Adele spun and headed back to the kitchen.

"Mom?"

"Nothing's going on, *mon chou*. Dash stopped by to visit Tallie."

"And you let him?" Naomi squeaked.

Adele looked at her. "Of course, I let him. He's her father."

"He hasn't been a father up 'til now."

"But he wants to change that. And he couldn't exactly be a father to a child he didn't know he had."

"That was his fault!"

"Maybe." Adele moved to the sink and continued washing the few dishes she had abandoned upon hearing the front door.

"Maybe? Mother, you can't seriously be taking his side on this."

"There's only one side I'm taking, and that's Tallie's."

"What's that supposed to mean?"

"I understand why you didn't pursue the matter with Talon when you were pregnant. Once I moved you to New Orleans, all I wanted was to make sure you carried Tallie to term. Once you moved back here, however, you had no reason to continue to hide her from him."

"I wasn't hiding her!"

"Yes, you were, and your original reasons no longer applied."

"Of course, they applied. Once people find out about Tallie, the speculation and the attempts at nabbing photographs of her will start."

"That was going to happen anyway. She's the daughter

of a professional football player, a player with a bright future ahead of him if the way he played this weekend is any indication. Any child of his will be—hopefully a brief—curiosity for the press. But, if you really intended for Dash to step up and be Tallie's father, you knew at some point you were going to have to deal with the media. So, why pretend that allowing Dash to keep his head in the sand was about saving your daughter from an unpleasant experience? It was about saving you from facing your fears."

"You're one to talk, mother."

Adele took that verbal slap in stride. "You're right. Which is exactly why I know what I'm talking about."

Naomi's mouth dropped open. "What?"

"I get that you were hurt when Dash blew you off and didn't respond to your letters." Her eyes shadowed briefly. "Boy, do I ever. When your father ignored my pregnancy and then rejected you because he couldn't see himself in your too-light—to him—infant face, I let my pride get in the way of what was best for you." She threw the tea towel on the counter. "That crap about there was no way a man with his dark skin tone could have fathered a baby who looked white was just an excuse to justify his walking away."

Adele chuckled. "You did, you know. Look white." Her mom shook her head with a light grin full of fond baby memories. "You didn't have a drop of color when you were born."

Naomi shrugged. She'd heard this story before. Her newborn pictures confirmed her mother's words, but it didn't excuse her father's asinine comment or the sting of rejection for an initial complexion over which she'd had no control.

"I could have forced a paternity test. I *should* have forced a paternity test. My failure to do so let your father pretend that I was just another gold digger making false claims."

"Another?"

"Honey, your dad attracted women like flowers attract bees. And he wasn't one to turn them away. He was a womanizer, a charming womanizer, but a womanizer nonetheless. I got wrapped up in thinking I was different because I was the one he kept coming back to, but I have to believe I wasn't the first woman who'd ever told him he was the father of her unborn child.

"I knew what I was up against, but I was in love with him. So, I ignorantly thought he'd stand by me. I didn't expect him to be happy about it necessarily. Hell, I was terrified myself. I was only nineteen at the time. It wasn't something either of us had planned. I just didn't expect him to turn on me the way he did." She placed her hands atop the back of a dinette chair, her knuckles flashing white. "I didn't pursue the matter with him. As a result, I didn't get you what you needed from him."

"I didn't need anything from him." Naomi walked away from her mother and leaned against the kitchen wall, arms crossed.

"Like hell you didn't, little girl. You needed him so bad you went looking for him in another man."

Naomi's arms flew apart. "What! You know I've always avoided professional athletes."

"How do you avoid professional athletes as a sports reporter?"

Naomi's face warmed from her throat up. Her eyes flashed with the fury of thunderstorm lightning. "You know what I mean. Until Dash, I avoided *dating* professional athletes."

"Women date men who fall within their constant circle of contact. If you pick a profession in which you are surrounded by athletes and former athletes and wannabe athletes, realistically whom do you think you're most likely to end up dating?"

Naomi scoffed. "You been getting your psychology degree by correspondence or something while watching Tallie during the day?"

"Don't smart off to me, young lady. I'm still your mother, and I'm not opposed to knocking those words back down your throat."

The fierce look in her mother's eyes gave Naomi no doubt her mom meant exactly what she said. Naomi swallowed. "Sorry."

"Maybe you didn't consciously set out to bring your life full circle, but you have. You could have dealt with this issue with Dash the moment we moved back to Kansas City. All you had to do was show up on his doorstep one day with Tallie in tow, hand her to him and say, 'I'd like you to meet your daughter.' No hiding behind voicemail messages or letters he could ignore. You took the coward's way out, and it had nothing to do with the media."

Adele put her hand up when Naomi started to protest. "Once you carried Tallie to term, the true risk was over. Wanting to shield her forever from the media is unrealistic. As the child of a professional quarterback, she may be the object of curiosity for as long as he's playing. Maybe longer. As a reporter, I know you understand what I mean."

The truth of her mother's words couldn't be denied. Dash was a public figure. By association with him, Tallie also became a public figure. Since she was a child, journalistic and legal standards would classify her more likely as a limited purpose public figure. She hadn't chosen to put herself in the public eye, but the events surrounding her birth—namely that her father was famous—meant she was fair game within reason for news reports and paparazzi. The moment Dash acknowledged her as his, people would be curious about what she looked like and what her life was like.

"I have to wonder if I had forced your dad to acknowledge you—even if all he did was pay child support—you wouldn't have tried so hard to resolve the unfinished business of that relationship via your interactions with other men."

"You're still talking that psycho mumbo jumbo."

"Oh, honey, you and Dash are so an episode of *Oprah*, or maybe Iyanla Vanzant, it's not even funny. You don't find it interesting that the woman born to a deadbeat, womanizing professional football player gets pregnant by a professional quarterback who blows her off after she finds out she's pregnant? The universe is forcing you to face your shit—as they say."

Naomi's eyes flew wide. "Mom!" Her mother rarely cursed. Hearing her do so now made this confrontation that much more of an out-of-body experience.

Adele laughed and pulled out the chair she held. "Sit."

Not in the mood for further dressing down, Naomi eased backwards toward the kitchen entry. "I need to go check on Tallie."

"She's asleep. Dash put her down." Her mom's eyes flickered with a dangerous glint before they narrowed. "*Sit!*"

Naomi stifled a tremor of inevitability and huffed out a breath as she moved towards the table to sit down.

"I'm going to make us some tea." Her mom turned the heat on under the tea kettle sitting on the stove. She gathered her special stoneware tea mugs with their individual removable tea leaf strainers and lids then pulled her tea leaf variety bin down from the cupboard. She added the tea leaf selection bin and the mugs to the table then put together a tray with honey and sugar and a crocheted trivet to await the hot tea pot.

Placing the tray on the table, Adele sat down opposite her daughter. "Put your defenses away and talk to me from your heart. Why were you really upset to see Dash here today?"

"I don't want Tallie hurt."

"Dash isn't going to hurt Tallie."

"You can't know that."

"Yes, I can. I've watched him with that little girl for a full week. He's so madly in love with her she's going to lead that man around by his nose for the rest of his life."

"A week? A *week!*" Naomi stifled the urge to leap from her seat. "Mom, Dash has been coming here for a full week and you didn't say anything to me?"

Adele looked down at the table. "He needed this time, Naomi. I didn't want to risk you doing something to prevent him from having it."

"I'm not the bad guy here, mom."

Her mom looked her directly in the eyes. "Neither is he."

The whistle of the tea kettle drew Adele's attention to the stove. She rose and poured the boiling water into a china teapot. Returning to the table, she poured hot water over the tea leaves each of them had selected.

She sat back down and placed the mug lid over her steaming brew so it could steep for three minutes. She looked up at her daughter. "I'm sorry about your dad. Like I said, I didn't do the right thing where he was concerned. And worse, I let my neuroses about men and relationships spill over onto you."

"I'm cautious about relationships, mom. Not neurotic."

"Okay, then answer my question truthfully. Aren't you really transferring your fears onto Tallie? Already feeling all the angst for her that you lived as a child whose father ignored her? Who are you more afraid he'll hurt, honey, Tallie or you?"

Elbow on the table, Naomi dropped her forehead into her palm and rubbed an eye with the heel of her hand. Her head was beginning to ache in tandem with the uncomfortable pressure in her chest around the area that housed her heart.

When she looked up at her mother, tears were forming in her eyes. "I've gotten used to this life without him. I made the mistake of letting him get close in Ibiza only to have him push me away again. I can't do this dance anymore, mom."

"Unfortunately, it's no longer just about you. You're the mother of the man's child. You are tied to him forever whether you want to be or not. You're going to have to find a way to deal with that."

Adele rose, went over to the computer nook in the kitchen. She slid open the desk drawer and pulled out a folded piece of paper. She sat back down and slid it towards Naomi.

Curious, Naomi opened it. She frowned over what she saw and slammed the cashier's check down onto the table. "So, he's trying to buy his way into our lives."

"He doesn't have to buy his way in. The law gives him the right to be in Tallie's life whether you agree or not. That's his way of showing you that he's one hundred percent in for Tallie."

A scoff rasped from Naomi's throat. "This check is obscene."

Her mother laughed. "Not for a man with his bank account. Given what they pay him, that's what? A couple hours' worth of work?"

Naomi wasn't convinced. "It's a payoff. Pure and simple."

Naomi went to tear up the check.

"Stop right there, young lady."

At the fierce tone in her mother's voice, Naomi's hands halted immediately, her brain forever programmed to respond to that authoritative sound that promised punishment for disobedience.

"Don't. You. *Dare*. Tear up that check."

Naomi looked down at her hands then back at her mother. "I'm not accepting this. I won't feel obligated to him."

"Look closely. That check's not made out to you."

A quick perusal verified that the check was made payable to Taliana Pellier. Her brow furrowed.

"It's not yours to destroy, Naomi. If you don't want to spend it, fine. But that's Tallie's money and you're going to put it in a money market account or invest it. But I won't let you throw away her gift from her father. I'll manage the money myself before I let you do that."

Naomi leapt up from the table, tossing the check down as she went.

"Get over yourself, little girl. I didn't get you what you needed from your father. You have a chance to do better. I suggest you take it."

Naomi stormed from the room and went to check on her napping child. She whipped out her mobile phone in route.

Dash wanted to talk? Fine by her. They'd talk, and she'd tell him what she thought of his multiple zero-zero-zero check.

He thought he could brainwash her mother and play the doting father behind her back. Ha. She knew that wouldn't last. As soon as the going got tough, the non-trusting blackguard would tuck his tail between his legs and disappear.

Everything stopped, including her feet. She spun the mobile phone in her hand once. Twice. A wicked grin crept across her face.

Right. She knew Dash's M.O. so she knew exactly how to bring this matter to a quick close. Dinner didn't sound like such a bad idea after all.

Her fingers tapped out his number on the touchscreen, and she placed the phone to her ear. Two could play this game. If he wanted to play daddy, she'd see just how badly he really wanted to pursue the charade.

CHAPTER 17

Dash pulled into Naomi's driveway around seven in the evening. He stepped out of his huge, black BMW and adjusted his jacket. He glanced towards the house. The porch light cast a yellow glow across the front stoop.

He stood immobile staring at her front door. Naomi had surprised him when she'd called two nights ago to accept his dinner invitation. He'd expected her to drag this out and make him wait. A mix of excitement and anxiety churned inside him. His gut warned tonight wouldn't be as easy as her carefree call had made it sound. She'd acted too agreeable on the phone. That didn't bode well. He knew her well enough not to fall for the carrot trick. The fire in her spirit would burn a man if he weren't careful. He'd best be prepared to keep a look out for the stick.

He shored himself up and walked to the door. The doorbell echoed inside the house, and Naomi called out for patience. A minute later, the locks disengaged.

Naomi pulled open the door. Bent at the waist, she slid a black high heel onto one foot. "Hi, Dash. Come on in. I just need another minute or so." She leaned the other direction and slid on the other shoe.

She scurried away leaving Dash to close the door. He watched her hips sway in the form-fitting little black dress she wore and nearly choked on his tongue. The dress left no doubts as to the nature of the curves beneath the stretchy fabric, but left enough to a man's imagination to drive him a bit crazy.

He'd planned this outing to talk about Taliana and get some parenting issues settled between them. With her looking the way she did, staying on topic would be a challenge. Right now, he'd like to order something in and see if they couldn't resolve the parenting issues and the issue growing between his legs.

He sighed and took a step towards the couch. The familiar thud of tiny feet sounded. He spun in time to block a human cannonball from crashing his shins. Snatching Taliana high into his arms, he laughed. "For such a little thing, you sure make a lot of noise."

Grinning, Tallie slipped both arms around his neck and squeezed.

"Hello, precious. I didn't expect to see you tonight. I thought you'd be with grandma."

She pulled back to look at him, raised her arms, and said, "Fly!"

He shot a furtive glance towards the hallway entrance. Naomi stood at the mouth placing diamond studs in her ears.

"We'll fly another time, little bit. Okay?" He tweaked Tallie's nose.

"No. Fly." Tallie raised her arms again. "Fly now."

Hesitation made him skirt another look at Naomi, who watched them closely. Her hands settled on her hips. She had a perplexed looked as she tried to figure out what Tallie wanted.

Without warning, Dash tossed Tallie into the air. She screamed in delight, and he caught her easily as she dropped back down.

A loud gasp sounded over her squeals. "Dash!" Naomi ran into the room. "What are you doing? Put her down."

"Fly again!" Tallie yelled over her mother.

Dash couldn't hold onto his chuckles at Tallie's enthusiasm. They played this game often at Adele's. The terrified look on Naomi's face, however, forced him to take pity on her. "No more fly right now, Tallie. We're scaring mommy. Okay?"

Tallie looked at her mom and giggled. She put her head down on Dash's shoulder, afraid she might get in trouble.

"Okay," Tallie said quietly into his neck.

Dash rubbed her back in comforting circles. Looking at Naomi, he asked, "Is your mom here?"

"No. Mom had something to do tonight. I thought we'd take Tallie with us."

Dash's lips spread slowly into a wide grin. He pulled Tallie up from his shoulder. "Okay, my girl, ready to go for a ride?"

When he looked back at Naomi, she watched him with a weird expression.

"What?"

"Nothing." She stared at him a moment longer before adding, "I'll get my keys. We'll need to take my car so Tallie has her car seat."

~ ꝑ ~

After they settled Tallie in her car seat, Naomi slid behind the wheel of her midsize SUV. They decided to cancel Dash's reservation at an upscale bistro and choose a more family-friendly establishment. As she pulled up to the restaurant they'd chosen, she began to have second thoughts about this excursion. She'd taken to heart her mom's message about not being able to keep Tallie's parentage a secret once Dash claimed her, but facing the imminent moment of going public made her insides feel like bowling balls had been tied to her intestines.

These days, practically everyone carried a mobile phone with some type of camera or recording device. Someone was bound to recognize Dash. What if people snapped pictures and figured out the resemblance between him and Tallie?

She glanced at Dash from the corner of her eye. So far, things hadn't gone as she'd expected. He hadn't missed a beat when she'd suggested they take Tallie with them. Naomi had been waiting for him to make an excuse to get her alone. She'd put on this little black dress knowing what it would do to his libido. He hadn't batted an eyelash.

Maybe the dress had been too obvious a distraction. Still, at the very least, she'd thought he'd make excuses about being seen in public with a toddler in tow or have concerns about the possible crowds or express worry about managing dinner with Tallie at the table. He hadn't.

None of those scenarios seemed to have occurred to him. He'd simply whipped out his phone to cancel his original dinner reservation and asked her to suggest a place Tallie would enjoy. He'd looked almost happier to see Tallie than he'd been to see her—even considering her strategic dress choice.

Actually, if she were honest with herself, he *had* been happier to see Tallie than her. The twinkle in his eyes when

Tallie had run up to him had been unmistakable. Every touch and every smile he gave Tallie reinforced the truth of her mother's observation. Dash was madly in love with her daughter—his daughter—*their* daughter.

A sob threatened to rise in her. She stuffed it down while Dash exited the vehicle and opened the back door on the passenger side to free Tallie from her car seat restraints.

Gathering her aplomb, Naomi quietly pulled in several deep breaths. She wouldn't let this get to her. She'd manage this somehow. Somehow, she'd learn to deal with sharing Tallie with him for the rest of her life and knowing he loved Tallie in an unrestrained way he'd never been able to love her.

She startled when Dash pulled her car door open, holding Tallie in his other arm. She stepped out.

He frowned when he saw her face. "You okay?"

She looked away. "I'm fine. Just having second thoughts."

His bent fingers lifted her chin towards him. "Naomi, we need to talk. I promise I'll make this painless."

She hesitated. "It's not you, Dash. All these people and Tallie. What if someone figures it out?"

"We can't keep her birth a secret forever. I'm going to be in Tallie's life on a regular basis. Her parentage will come out eventually. Now's as good a time as any."

He grabbed her hand and laced their fingers together. He gave her fingers a gentle squeeze before they entered the restaurant. Looking up at him, she took in the calm of his handsome face. The warmth of his fingers grounded her. He held Tallie securely in his arm. Whatever happened, Dash would protect Tallie. She had no doubts about that anymore.

She let Dash's calm filter into her. She could do this.

They walked into the restaurant. Naomi halted and

surveyed the surroundings. After a few minutes, Dash tugged at her hand to get her attention. She'd missed the approach of the hostess. Shaking off her mental reverie, she followed Dash and the hostess to their table. Time to see how things would fare with their first family outing.

Dash settled Tallie into the high chair a server brought them and tightened the safety strap. Tallie was in heaven, oblivious to her mother's anxiousness over the threesome's dinner out. The hostess offered to help with Tallie's seat, but Dash declined. The hostess lingered, offering other assistance. When Dash's attention failed to leave Tallie, she finally gave up and told them their waitress would be over shortly. Naomi thanked her, enjoying the hostess's miffed demeanor and that Dash hadn't noticed the woman had been trying to come on to him.

They ordered their meals and received their beverages without incident. No one other than assigned restaurant staff approached their table. Naomi settled into her chair and let her worries slide away.

Halfway through their meals, things changed. A young man, looking approximately ten years in age, approached. He stopped beside Dash. "Excuse me, Mr. Dash."

Dash looked into the little boy's worried face and smiled. "What can I do for you, young man?"

The boy squeezed the Griffins ball cap he held in his hand. "I'm sorry to bother you, but I was wondering . . . I was wondering . . . if you would please—"

Before the boy could finish his request, a lady came rushing to the table and grabbed him by the shoulders. "Connor, what are you doing? You shouldn't be bothering Mr. Janssen while he's at dinner."

"It's okay, ma'am." Dash turned his attention back to the little boy. "What can I do for you, Connor?"

"Well, today's my birthday. I was wondering if you'd mind signing my ball cap."

"Your birthday, huh? That's really exciting. Is that your family over there?" Dash motioned towards the table the boy had recently abandoned.

The little boy nodded. "That's my big sister and little brother with my dad."

"Cool. Tell me, Connor, who's your favorite Griffins player?"

"That's easy. You are, Mr. Dash."

Dash laughed. "Good answer."

"No really," Connor said. "All my Griffins jerseys have your number on them."

Over the little boy's head, his mother indicated he was telling the truth.

"Is that a fact?" Dash asked.

"Yeah, but my doofus sister likes Trey Coffey, the wide receiver. She says he's her favorite player."

"Your sister has great taste, Connor. Trey Coffey happens to be my favorite player as well."

The boy's eyes flew wide. "Really?"

"Really." Dash reached into his jacket pocket. "Connor, I admire a man who goes after what he wants. But, your mother's right. If I give you an autograph, then I'll have to write autographs for anyone else who wants one, which wouldn't be fair to my dinner guests." He motioned towards Naomi and Taliana. "So, I'll make you a deal." He pulled out a business card. He signed it and scribbled a number on the back. "If you present this to the ticket office, it's good for five tickets to any regular season home game of your choice."

He handed the little boy the card.

"Wow! This is so cool! Thanks, Mr. Dash." He showed the card to his mom.

Her expression blanched. She opened her mouth to say something, but Dash put a hand on her arm to stop her.

The boy ran off to show his dad.

"Let him have this moment," Dash said to the boy's mother.

"That was really nice of you, but it's too much."

"Ma'am, he said 'excuse me,' 'please,' and 'thanks.' It's rare for me to hear one of those pleasantries from a person seeking an autograph, let alone all three. It's my pleasure, really."

She glanced over her shoulder at her bubbling son, wringing her hands as she did. When she looked back at Dash, she smiled hesitantly. "Well, then. Thank you."

"You're welcome. And ma'am?"

She stopped her retreat.

"My agent's number is on the front of that card. If you give him a call and let him know what game you all have chosen, he'll make sure to set you up with a parking pass and concession vouchers."

The mom's smile relaxed and widened slowly. "Thank you." Her foot and hands moved like she wanted to hug him. She thought better of it. Settling for another, "Thank you so much," before heading back to her table.

"How did you know?" Naomi asked Dash once the mother was out of hearing range.

"How did I know what?"

"That she was concerned about the additional expense of attending a game? I've never seen you offer a parking pass or concession vouchers before."

He shrugged. "Just a lucky guess. She looked worried about something. She had a haunted face that suggested her son might be disappointed regardless of my gesture. I sort of put two and two together. It's the boy's tenth birthday.

Family of five celebrates here without additional guests. I'm thinking large amounts of discretionary income aren't included in their family budget." He adjusted his napkin in his lap. "It does me no good to give the kid tickets he can't use. What kind of birthday present would that be? You and I both know parking and concessions can run as much as, if not more than, the actual game tickets sometimes, especially for a family of that size."

The heart Naomi had been trying to keep shielded from Dash struggled against the shackles she'd placed on it. His generous spirit had always touched her, but now it threatened to expand the love she didn't want to feel.

His fork landed without sound on his plate. "I felt invisible as a foster kid. No one saw me. I felt the glazed eyes of adults glance right through me. I wasn't important. I was just a burden that had to be tolerated until I no longer became the guardian-of-the-moment's responsibility. No one thought about me. Not who I was or what I needed beyond the basics of food, shelter, and a public education. I moved like a ghost on the fringes of society biding my time until I turned eighteen. I'm not invisible anymore, and it feels good to know that for a brief moment I can make a kid feel that someone sees him."

Dash had always been attentive to his fans. It was something she'd found admirable about him when she'd first gotten to know him on a personal level. He tended not to tolerate rude fans or obnoxious groupies with a sense of entitlement to his time, his signature or his picture. When it came to the kids, however, Dash never failed to go above and beyond.

She'd never connected how much of that had to do with his upbringing. A man who took the time to make sure the children of strangers felt significant around him would do nothing less for his own flesh and blood. How could she have ever doubted that he'd make Tallie a priority?

She'd been fooling herself. He'd rejected her not Tallie. Her mother's words haunted her: *How could he be a father to a child he didn't know he had? . . . Who are you really afraid he'll hurt, Tallie or you?*

She hadn't answered her mother. She could answer to herself now though. She *had* been a coward. She'd been acting on her own fears, using Tallie as a shield and a scapegoat for why she herself couldn't face Dash. As long as he was a pariah, she'd felt justified in keeping her distance and keeping their child a secret. That way, she didn't have to face permanent rejection.

Dash wiped Tallie's messy face and hands. They looked so perfect together, father and daughter. She saw the adoration flowing openly between them and felt oddly left out, almost insignificant and invisible. She wanted some of that adoration from Dash, wanted that bond of love to flow between the three of them and not just two ways.

This idea of letting Dash play the family man so he could reveal his shortcomings had backfired on her. This wasn't a charade to him. It was real. Unfortunately, in his mind, his new family didn't include the three of them together. It only included a towheaded little girl with her daddy's eyes.

How could she live on the fringes of this unconditional love day after day for the rest of her life? It was going to tear her in two. She could feel the rend starting already.

~ Ψ ~

When they arrived back at Naomi's place, Dash insisted

on staying to put Tallie to bed.

Naomi left him alone with Tallie to do whatever bedtime ritual they wanted to create. She didn't have the stomach, or the heart, anymore tonight to observe on the fringes of their growing bond.

She busied herself in her office space checking emails, hoping *Daily* business would keep her mind off her growing misery. When that didn't work, she turned to the draft of her article.

Tatum had given her a great interview with moving comments about what it felt like to be a child of adoption and learn after all these years that he had a biological brother. She wanted to contrast Tatum's insights with commentary from Dash about his experience as a foster kid and overlay that with the thoughts on his familial discovery. Those personal touches would make her piece so much more meaningful. A reunion story laced with the story of his triumph into a successful adult and professional athlete.

She wouldn't get to make this piece what she wanted though. Dash had been adamant about his opposition to her writing the story. Since he'd learned about Tallie, she hadn't had the guts to raise the issue again. She saved her work and rubbed her eyes.

"Working hard?"

She glanced up to find Dash poised against the door frame. "More like hardly working. I think the brain is done for the night."

He pushed off the door and sauntered towards her. "How about I make us some coffee?"

He offered her his hand, which she took without thought. Pulling her from the chair, he led her from the extra bedroom she'd turned into an office and seated her at the kitchen table.

"How'd it go with Tallie?" Naomi asked him.

"It went fine." He opened several cupboards before he found what he wanted. He pulled out her coffee grinder.

Naomi's heart stuttered at the sign he remembered she liked fresh ground beans for her brew. She took a deep breath in through her nose and discreetly exhaled through her mouth, determined to keep her voice steady. "Then why do you look so troubled?"

Opening the fridge, he retrieved her half-empty bag of *Kenya* whole bean coffee then filled the coffee carafe with filtered water from the water purifying jug she kept inside. He stared into the carafe for a few seconds before he sat it aside. Slowly, he turned to look at her. "It's time, Naomi."

Unease slid down her spine. "Time for what?"

"Time to tell Tallie I'm her father."

She whirled up from her seat and left the kitchen.

He followed. "Talk to me, Naomi. Why put it off any longer? I want Tallie to know I'm her father, and I want my name added to her birth certificate."

"Just her birth certificate? I'm surprised you didn't ask me to change her last name."

"I want that, too. But I thought I'd start small and work my way up to that request."

"Small? You think this is a small matter? Why the rush, Dash? You're not ready for this."

"*Rush?* I think I've been very patient. And what's there to be ready for? I'm her father, and I want her to know. I think you're the one who isn't ready. I want Tallie to call me *Daddy* not by my first name or Mr. Dash or to think of me as some friendly uncle. Can't you understand that? How would you feel if she called you Naomi all the time?"

She crossed her arms over her chest. She felt lost and on the verge of being alone. It was an inexplicable feeling. Tallie wasn't going away once she knew Dash was her father. Yet, somehow it felt as if she were about to lose her.

Dash stepped forward and pulled her gently into his arms. "I'm not going anywhere, Mimi. If that's what you're worried about. I won't do Tallie the way your father did you. You have to trust me on that. I would never do anything to hurt my little girl." His words came out with a quiet, heartfelt fervor.

Naomi closed her eyes. Dash hadn't called her Mimi in forever. The pet name had sprang from his lips spontaneously one night while they made love. He'd been the only lover to give her a pet name; no one but him had ever called her Mimi. Her fragile heart split open and wailed for the closeness they once had.

Her hands slid around his waist, and she sank into his embrace. His arms tightened around her. He held her, allowing her the silence she needed as much as his touch at the moment.

She understood his request. What he asked was fair. What an awful thing for your child to call you by your first name. It was how she thought of her father—by his first name—not that she ever saw him or talked to him. They had no parenting relationship and the nomenclature she associated with him evidenced the lack thereof.

After a few minutes, Dash threaded his fingers through her hair and pulled her head up to kiss her forehead. "I've waited long enough. *Please.* First thing tomorrow, we need to tell her."

Naomi laid her head against his chest. A weariness settled over her that came from more than fatigue. "Okay. We'll tell her in the morning."

CHAPTER 18

Taking his victory to heart, Dash decided to push for a little more. "I want to stay here tonight so we can tell Tallie over breakfast when she first wakes up."

Naomi pulled away from him. "I'm not sleeping with you."

"That's not what I meant." He grinned at her. "Of course, I wouldn't turn you down if you changed your mind. Otherwise, I can just sleep on the couch."

Coffee forgotten, he moved out of the kitchen towards the couch and began to unbuttoned his shirt.

"You're way too big for my couch."

"I'll manage." He opened his last two shirt buttons and turned back to her.

Naomi swallowed, trying desperately to keep her eyes off the bare chest peeking through the open halves of his shirt, but failing miserably. "Dash, don't be silly. You'll be in worse shape after a night on that couch than if you'd never slept at all. You've got practice tomorrow and an important game in a few days. I won't be responsible for you playing crappy because you tried to sleep on my couch."

His muscles flexed as he strolled over to her. He pulled his shirt from his shoulders and tossed it over the arm of an oversized chair. "I'll be fine. I've managed practiced after a night much more challenging than sleeping on a small couch."

He pulled strands of her hair through his fingers. "I find your concern touching, but are you sure that's all you're worried about?"

Naomi swallowed loudly then bucked up and said in a haughty voice, "Whatever do you mean?"

The curve of his lips wound up almost in slow motion. She hadn't fooled him with her bravado. His voice dropped to a husky whisper. "Don't worry, Mimi. I'll be a good boy. I won't try to seduce you unless you ask me to. Kinda like you're doing right now with your eyes."

"Ignore my eyes. Wait for me to say the words." The order came out breathy instead of authoritative.

The chemistry between them smoldered beneath a bevy of unspoken words neither dared say. This is where things tended to go when they were alone together and within touching distance. Dash wanted her . . . like always. She wanted him. She wouldn't say the words, but her body spoke to him loud and clear.

His eyes darted to her chest. Her sprouting nipples, ragged breathing, and meadow-tinged eyes were speaking a language he knew well. Her arousal called to him. The front of his pants displayed how much he wanted to answer that call. She need only look down if she had any doubts.

She stepped back from the heat emanating from him. She didn't have any doubts.

He followed her. "Then, do us both a favor and say the words."

Interrupted by the edge of the couch, the back of her knee caved and she lost her balance.

Dash braced her with an arm around her waist. He simultaneously steadied her and sent her reeling off balance again by pulling her in for a kiss.

The simple kiss turned hungry. The gluttony ramped initially by Dash, but Naomi's attempt to devour him soon followed. Her hands went into his hair. She grabbed on while she eased her tongue along the seam of his lips. Her eager exploration continued inside his mouth and their tongues frolicked.

Dash's hand slunk down to her bottom and pressed her firmly against his swollen manhood. His other hand found one of her budded peaks and rubbed a thumb across the pearl.

Naomi moaned. The sound of her own voice shattered her aroused haze. Jerking back from him, she crossed her arms protectively over her chest. "You should go home, Dash. We'll be here when you get back."

"Naomi, don't be like that. I meant what I said. I'll keep my hands—"

"It's not just your hands I'm worried about." She gave a meaningful glance at the bulge in the front of his pants.

His head tilted towards his one-shouldered shrug. "And other body parts—to myself. Until you ask me to do otherwise."

"Until?"

He took a step towards her. She put a hand up to stop his motion even as she stepped back out of self-preservation.

"Yes, Naomi. Until. This heat between us isn't going anywhere. You know it as well as I do. But, I'll mind my manners tonight if you let me stay. It's late. It'll take me almost forty-five minutes from here to get home. It doesn't make sense for me to drive all the way home tonight and turn around in a few hours to come back here for breakfast."

From Naomi's Northland home it would be quite a drive to Dash's home in the suburbs, even with the lesser traffic of the late hour. He could see her process the logistics. Her sympathetic nature fighting her well-placed fears of seduction.

He decided to increase his odds on the sympathy side. "I'll make a deal with you. I'll even cook breakfast. You wouldn't happen to have the ingredients for a coffee cake would you?"

Her eyes lit up before she hid the sparkle. "Oooh. Now you're not playing fair. Bribery is beneath you."

He slid his hands into his pants pockets, a grin spreading wide across his face. "Nope. Actually, it's not."

Naomi had a sweet tooth. He'd learned that early in his courting of her. Dash didn't indulge much in sweets. They threw off his training regimen. He did, however, occasionally throw in a breakfast treat. He could simply add an extra workout to burn off the empty calories.

His foster sister made a mean coffee cake from scratch. He'd loved it so much that Peyton had taught him how to make it. That way he wasn't limited to the treat only the few times a year they could get together.

He'd made it for Naomi the morning after they'd made love for the first time. Her orgasmic reaction to the cake had almost sent him over the edge at the kitchen table. In fact, he'd cleared the table of breakfast leftovers and replaced it with her shortly after she'd finished her meal then proceeded to make a meal of her.

Her mouth twisted, and she bit her lower lip. "You're

really going to get up and make me a coffee cake in the morning?"

He laughed. "It will actually be for all of us. You'll have to share with me and Tallie."

She smiled a little. "I guess I could be persuaded to share. Fine. You can stay, but . . ."

"Yes."

Her smile disappeared. Her voice got soft. "You have to keep your word, Dash. You're only staying here to sleep."

His hands came out of his pockets and he gave her the Boy Scout's honor sign. She shook her head at him, which made him laugh again. He'd never been a Boy Scout, a fact she knew.

She grabbed his shirt off the couch and handed it to him. "And, I'll sleep on the couch. You take the bed."

He collected his shirt from her. "I didn't mean to displace you, Naomi. I'm fine with the couch. I just want to be on hand as early as possible."

"I get it. But I'm not letting you squeeze your six-foot-three frame onto that couch. I've got money riding on the next game." She patted his chest as she spoke. Thinking better of the move, she snatched her hand away. "Like you said. It's late. We should go to bed." After a moment's hesitation, she added, "Separately."

She pushed him towards the hallway.

Dash trudged to Naomi's room. He peeled off the rest of his clothes and sat on the edge of her bed. He glanced down at his lap. He was still aroused. Naked, aroused, and planning to sleep in Naomi's bed . . . without her. Not exactly how he'd expected this night to end, but he'd take it.

He glanced towards the master bathroom. Maybe he needed to take a cold shower. Bright and early tomorrow morning, he'd finally get to hear his little girl call him daddy. If all that took was for him to keep his hands and his penis in check, he could do that. He glanced back towards the bedroom door.

Or could he?

~ Ƴ ~

Dash tossed and turned amidst the scent of Naomi. The relief garnered from his cold shower couldn't shield him from the aromatic taunt left behind on her sheets. The smell of her favorite body gel mixed with a hint of her fragrant skin conjured memories of her body beneath his. Their recent interludes in Ibiza traipsed erotically through his semi-conscious mind until he jerked awake.

He should have taken the frigging couch. The size of the bed offered no comfort when he couldn't shut off his desire-laden mind. He grabbed the bath towel he'd tossed across the end of the bed, wrapped it around his naked hips, and padded on bare feet down the hall. When he reached the couch, he stood over Naomi to watch her sleep.

She was curled in on herself in the fetal position under a fuzzy cotton blanket. The sight made him smile. Naomi got cold easily. No matter the temperature outside, she always seemed to need covers. She'd had fuzzy blankets and throws stashed all around his house when they were together.

He'd missed seeing them after she left. He'd taken for granted such simple nuances of her. How it made him feel to walk through his door and find her on the couch hunched over her laptop wrapped in a cocoon of fuzz—or cotton or wool—hadn't registered until she was no longer around to make him feel that way.

Simple reminders of the comfort of them together plagued him. He wondered what it would be like to have the right, the privilege, to spend every night and wake every morning under the same roof as the ladies of his heart. He sighed, shutting his eyes against the ephemeral vision floating through his mind.

"Dash, is something wrong?" Her voice floated up to him.

He'd forgotten what a light sleeper she was. He hadn't meant to wake her. He'd just needed to be near her for a while. "Yes."

She jerked up. "Is something wrong with Tallie?"

His hand settled over hers on the blanket, preventing her from removing it. "No. Tallie is fine."

"Then what's wrong?"

He let the loaded question hover before telling her the truth. "Your sheets smell like you."

"Oh."

He couldn't see her face clearly, but he felt her body relax.

"Sorry about that," she whispered. "I'll get you some fresh sheets." She shook off his hand and the blanket.

"I have a better idea." He scooped her into his arms.

"Dash, put me down." She kept her voice low so as not to wake Tallie.

"In a minute." He continued his trek to the bedroom.

"Dash, this is not a good idea. Not with Tallie in the house."

Dash shoved the bedroom door partly closed until it rested ajar against the jamb. "Tallie is young enough this won't have a lasting impression on her."

"I disagree."

Climbing into bed with Naomi still in his arms, Dash dropped the towel and settle with her beneath the sheets. "Besides, tomorrow over breakfast, we're telling her I'm her father. Remember?"

Her head lifted. "That doesn't mean we should—"

"Shh." He threaded his fingers through the waves of her hair and pulled her head down to kiss her forehead. "Relax. I'm not going to break my promise. But, if I have to smell you all night, I should at least get the benefit of holding you in my arms."

As much as the smell of her skin and hair against his nose made him thick and long of manhood, he'd hold himself in check through the night. He believed Tallie would have no negative effects from seeing him sleeping with Naomi, but he'd hate for her to walk in while they were making love. That might be a whole different story.

The next morning, Dash and Naomi awoke to giggles and the tugging of the covers from the bed. Tallie was trying to pull herself up but only managed to pull most of the covers onto the floor.

Dash leaned over the bed and lifted the toddler. "Good morning, princess. How did you sleep?"

"Talon." She patted him on the cheek before hugging him tightly around the neck.

Dash looked at Naomi, a plea in his eyes.

"I guess I don't get to wait for breakfast, huh?" she said.

He smiled at her, complete with dimples. "You can if you want. But there's really no time like the present."

Naomi reached over and smoothed Tallie's wild hair. "Hey, sweetie. Can you say 'daddy'?"

"Daddy!" Tallie clapped as she said the words.

Naomi praised her. "Good job, sweetie."

Before Naomi could say anything else, Tallie dropped down against Dash's chest and said, "Daddy."

He squeezed her, his voice came out as tight as his grip. "That's right, princess. I'm your daddy, and I love you."

Over the top of Tallie's head, Dash caught Naomi's eyes. The tell-tale glistening of her emerald orbs disclosed the moment wasn't emotional only for him. Naomi jumped up from the bed and shut herself in the bathroom.

His heart ached for her. He was so full right now. Finding out about Tallie and having the connection he felt rebuilding with Naomi made him feel light enough to float. Irrationally, all he could think was now Naomi was his forever. With Tallie's existence, he would always be linked to her. How much he wanted that link to remain exclusive, without another man ever entering her life, made him absolutely giddy with the possibilities.

He hated that what should be a happy time for them turned out to be such torture for her. He had an urge to track down her loser of a dad and kick his ass. They knew where he was. He'd become a college coach after he left the pros. He currently coached at a Division I school in Nebraska, at Dash's alma mater in fact.

Looking at the bathroom door, he considered going after Naomi to see if she was alright. Thinking better of it, he decided to give her some time.

Propping Tallie against his raised knees, he bounced her. "Hey, my girl, want to help daddy make breakfast?"

Tallie clapped. "Eat!"

He laughed with her. "Eat it is." He loved his daughter's enthusiasm. Her habit of clapping when she got excited endeared him. He didn't understand how a father could ever turn his back on such wonders.

Raising up, he caught the sheets right before they slid off his naked body. Oops. He adjusted, gathering the top sheet around him and placing Tallie on the floor.

"Race you to the kitchen," he said to the toddler.

She took off running in a fit of giggles, and he quickly

negotiated on a pair of pants before running after her. Time to make a coffee cake so he could make his other girl smile as well.

And maybe, just maybe, it was time he convinced her to deal with her own daddy issues. He'd have to tread lightly, but he could no longer sit back and watch his Creole Queen suffer in silence. Could he convince her that it was time she took a road trip to Nebraska?

~ 4 ~

By the time Naomi emerged from the bathroom, Tallie was a mess and Dash had the coffee cake in the oven. She walked into the kitchen on his chuckles over Tallie's attempt to help him clean the counter. Tallie's version of cleaning included making a bigger mess, not reducing it.

Dash looked up, sensing her at the kitchen entrance. She caught his surprise when he noticed the large Griffins practice jersey she'd draped herself in. His number graced the front and his name floated across her shoulder blades in the back. The jersey flowed down to her knees. He'd left it at her place years ago. When they'd split, she'd hadn't even thought to return it. Like now, she tended to wrap herself in it when she was feeling sorry for herself. She'd wrapped herself in it and cried herself to sleep many a night after the split with Dash. When she'd found out she was pregnant with Tallie and Dash didn't care, she'd practically lived in it.

At the time, being pregnant and dumped had made her feel entitled to a week-long self-pity party. Once Tallie was born, she gave up such self-indulgent, useless habits. She had a child to raise and support. She refused to model weakness and misery to her child. She had more backbone than that.

This morning, she'd slipped a little. The scene with Dash and Tallie had hit her hard. She didn't understand how she could be so happy and so miserable at the same time. The emotions had overwhelmed her. The flood of feelings from her childhood—knowing her father didn't want her—became a deluge as she'd watched her daughter and Dash together.

What would it be like to wake up to that scene every morning? Her and Dash in each other's arms, Tallie scrambling to join them in bed. She wished for it, but knew it would never happen. She'd never even told the man she loved him. Couldn't tell him. His fear of attachment was as strong as her fear of abandonment.

She stepped the rest of the way into the kitchen. "Did you guys actually get any flour into the cake batter or is it all on my counter?"

Tallie and Dash looked at each other and grinned. The matching sets of dimples broke through Naomi's funk. She smiled, unable not to enjoy them together. She loved them both so much.

Remembering the promise she'd made to herself in the bathroom, she stashed the negative energy and decided to count this morning as a blessing. No more wasting the moment. She would allow herself to enjoy their family time together.

"What can I do to help?" She stepped up to the counter and ran a finger through a dusting of flour.

Dash picked up a flour-drenched Tallie and handed her to Naomi. "Why don't you freshen her up while I take care of the omelets?"

Dash had breakfast ready when Naomi and Tallie made it back. He'd set the table, including a child's plate and sippy cup at Tallie's highchair.

Naomi helped him move a carafe of juice and bowl of fresh cut fruit to the table and sat in the chair beside Tallie and across from Dash. When she bowed her head to say grace, Dash took her hand and Tallie's, making her look up quickly.

"Why don't you say it out loud?"

"I . . . um," she muttered, before she recovered her poise and nodded. "Okay."

Naomi blessed the food. A strange peace drifted over and around her, cocooning the trio in a normalcy that felt familiar. When Tallie began to play with her strawberry pieces, Naomi had to chastise Dash for doing more to encourage Tallie than discourage her. Almost everything Dash did seemed to make Tallie giggle. For his part, she didn't think she'd ever seen Dash laugh so much in one day, let alone one hour.

For the first time, a heavy sense of guilt washed over Naomi for having kept them from this, from each other, for so long. They'd missed out on a lot. She could already see how much her daughter would blossom into a different person than she'd be without Dash in her life, and those added facets to Tallie's personality would make her daughter sparkle more not less.

Good Lord, how could she possibly have justified denying her daughter this bond?

Startling her from her thoughts, Dash rose from his chair. He kissed Tallie on top of her head and stepped around to Naomi's chair to do the same to her. When he looked into her eyes, his expression turned concerned. "Naomi, are you alright?" he asked quietly.

She nodded. "Of course, Dash. I'm fine."

He knelt beside her chair and cupped a large hand over the fist she'd balled tightly in her lap. "Are you sure? You don't regret what we did this morning do you? Telling Tallie I'm her dad?"

"Daddy!" Tallie yelled, crumbling the fistful of omelet she held high in her hand.

Naomi and Dash looked over at her. Dash chuckled. Naomi just smiled.

Looking back at Dash, she said, "No, Dash. I don't regret it at all." She eased her other hand to his face, palming his cheek and rubbing his morning scruff lightly. "I'm so sorry. I should have found a way to tell you when we moved back. I shouldn't have—" Her voice broke.

"Shh," Dash soothed. "It's okay. I didn't make it easy for you. I'm as much to blame as you." He pressed the hand at his cheek and turned his head to kiss her palm. "Thank you."

Her brows rose in question.

"Thank you for this morning. Thank you for allowing me to be here now. I don't care about the past. I have my daughter now and for me, nothing else matters. Understand?"

She nodded, shaking loose teardrops that had been lounging against her lashes.

Dash rubbed the droplets away with his fingertips. "I have to go to practice now. I hate to eat and run, but . . ." He shrugged. "You okay with kitchen cleanup?"

Naomi cleared her throat, praying for a normal voice. "Tallie and I got this. Go to practice."

Dash eyed her intently for a moment. He hesitated, as if he wanted to say more. Finally, he leaned up, spread his fingers through the hair at her nape, and swooped in to press his lips to hers. He kissed her with an odd sense of urgency and gentleness unlike any kiss he'd ever given her before. When he pulled away, Naomi's heart raced so fast she had to wonder if the front of her—his—jersey pulsed noticeably from the pounding.

Without a word, Dash released her and shot from the room to hurry off to practice.

Naomi pressed a shaking hand to her lips. Looking over at Tallie, she said, "Taliana Marie, I think your daddy just ruined me for all other men."

Tallie clapped and burst into giggles. Naomi had to laugh with her.

CHAPTER 19

Several hours later, Dash knocked on Naomi's front door. He leaned his right forearm against the doorjamb, takeout bags in hand, listening for sounds of movement inside. Light shuffling approached the door, then silence. He suspected Naomi was checking through the peep hole.

A lock click muffled through wood before Naomi materialized in a small crease between the open door and the door frame. "Dash?"

He held up the food bags. "I hope Tallie likes Chinese food. I brought dinner."

"Um ..." She glanced behind her then down at herself. Running a lazy hand through her loose hair, she offered him a resigned smiled. "Okay. Tallie will like that. She seems to pretty much like all food."

"I see she takes after her mother in that regard." His eyes flicked over her, noticing her bare feet and long legs sticking out from under his practice shirt. His pulse stuttered with the thrill that she still wore his graphite and gold colors. He didn't even try to repress the wicked grin that spread at his discovery. He bent quickly and pecked her on the lips.

Naomi blushed, stepped back, and let him in. "Uh, we went out and ran errands after you left." She brushed a self-conscious palm over the front of his jersey. "When we got back, I decided we'd simply laze around. I didn't expect to see you again today."

His grin held while he looked her over again. "The laze-around look works."

She dropped her head, shaking it from side to side. He closed and locked the door, and she called for Tallie.

As usual, Tallie came out at a thundering run. When she saw Talon, her legs sped up. "Daddy back!"

Naomi grabbed the Chinese food from his hand, knowing he'd want to grab Tallie instead. Tallie jumped into his arms, and he used the momentum to spin her around. The sound of her laughter filled the house.

Dash carried the jubilant ball of energy into the kitchen and set her up so they could eat dinner. Dinner progressed much like breakfast had, as if they'd been doing this together for years. Dash held their hands while Naomi said grace. Tallie smeared almost as much food over her high chair table as she ate, and Dash encouraged her messy behavior. By the end of the meal, a frustrated Naomi gave up trying to discourage Dash or control the mess, making sure to warn him that he'd be the one cleaning up their daughter.

After dinner, he shooed Naomi out of the kitchen. Since he'd left her with the breakfast dishes, he insisted on full evening cleanup duty. Once he and Tallie had the kitchen in order, Dash gave Tallie a bath, then built them a magnificent fire in the living room.

He rolled around on the carpet with Tallie, deflecting Naomi's concerns that he was playing extremely rough games for a girl. Naomi finally managed to distract them by suggesting they all watch a movie together. Dash led Tallie over to the media center and allowed her to pick.

True to her football roots, Tallie selected Disney's *The Game Plan*. Dash was tickled she'd picked a movie about a football player. Naomi found it ironic Tallie had selected the story of a single football player who finds out his extremely short marriage to his ex-wife resulted in an eight-year-old child he never knew he had. As the tough bachelor quarterback with a superstar ego gears up for a big championship game, he comes to realize the biggest win he can achieve is the heart of his daughter.

Tallie didn't make it through the movie. She fell asleep in front of the fire stretched out on a Griffins stadium blanket. Dash leaned on his elbow beside her. His hands constantly touched his daughter. He rubbed her back or touched her hair while he watched the end of the movie.

As the credits rolled, he turned contemplative eyes to Naomi. "Cute movie."

"It's one of our favorites. I could look at Dwayne Johnson all night long. The man's a hunk and a half." She made an exaggerated sigh and flopped back on the couch.

"Dwayne Johnson is a wuss."

Naomi flipped onto her stomach. She mounted her chin on her folded hands. "I dare you to say that to his face."

An abrupt chuckle erupted from Dash. "Yeah, probably not."

Tallie stirred. He rubbed her back until she settled.

The quiet rolled over them, interrupted only by the crackle of the fire and Tallie's soft breathing. After a while,

Dash gathered Tallie and put her to bed. When he returned, Naomi had propped herself up on the couch, legs securely tucked beneath a fuzzy blanket. He sat down, lifting her legs and placing them across his lap, blanket and all.

His arm went along the back of the couch. He rubbed her legs through the blanket with his other hand. "You still think about your father a lot don't you?"

She stilled. Her hand began to pick at the blanket. "A lot more lately than I would like."

"Because of Tallie?"

She just looked at him.

"And me?"

She nodded.

His face turned towards the fire. "I'm sorry about that. I'd like to think my being here for Tallie makes things easier for you."

She grabbed for his hand on the back of the couch. "It does, Talon. You're not like my father. I know the difference now."

He looked at her. "Do you?" Hope laced his voice.

"Yes, I do. It's not about a high-profile profession or a charisma that attracts women like the Pied Piper or even a confirmed bachelor's inclination to flirt constantly. It's about character. Regardless of how carefree a person would like to live his life, life throws out responsibilities from time to time. A man either chooses to step up or to shirk those responsibilities. My father chose the latter."

"And that was all about him. It had nothing to do with you."

She looked away.

"Look at me, Naomi."

She looked back with sad eyes.

"You know his choice had nothing to do with you

personally, who you were or who you weren't. Right?"

"I'm beginning to."

His palm cupped her face when she tried to look away again. "If I'd never showed back up after you told me about Tallie, how much of that would you have thought was Tallie's fault."

"None of it," she burst.

"So why do you hold an infant you to a different standard?" He released her face. "Let it go, Naomi. Your father chose not to acknowledge you. It was a shitty choice, but he doesn't deserve your hurt. He's the one who missed out. Maybe it's time you let him know that. Time you confronted him so you can free yourself from this pain that isn't yours to carry. It's his. Give it back to him and move forward with your life so you can enjoy being a mother without baggage."

"We all have baggage."

"Yes, but we don't have to carry it with us indefinitely."

She gave him a strange look, and he recognized the irony of his words. He carried his baggage with him constantly and used them as weapons against all comers. He hadn't allowed himself to see what he and Naomi could be beyond this surface level of really good companions who were great together in bed. He'd resisted fully accepting his twin brother. The only person he didn't seem to constantly push away was his foster sister Peyton.

Maybe Peyton living a state away in Nebraska so that their interactions were mostly long distance made it easier to accept the familial tie, but a family tie it was. No matter his belief that he didn't need a family, he'd embraced Peyton in his heart like a true sister.

He'd also embraced Taliana. Just the thought of his little girl spread warmth from his center until it enveloped him from head to toe. "Speaking of taking responsibility, I never thanked you for Tallie."

"Thanked me?"

He nodded. "You had another choice, especially after I let you down. Thank you for having my little girl." His voice broke.

Her hand caressed his cheek. "Oh, Talon. There was never another choice for me."

"There's always a choice, Mimi."

She shook her head, but couldn't speak.

"I understand what you're saying. I understand who you are. But no matter how you look at it, you made a conscious choice. Based on your personal values, the choice was clear and maybe even easy for you. But, there's no doubt, you had another option."

He gathered her into his arms. "You also could have let your pride rule your head and stayed here during your pregnancy to force me to see the truth. Doing so would have kept you in a dangerous situation that risked our child's unborn life. I don't take lightly that you could have ended up telling me a totally different story. One where you'd gotten pregnant with my child, but the baby was gone. I can't imagine the pain of facing that."

His arms tightened around her and she snuggled into his lap. They watched the fire in silence. The heat and cadence of the flames wrapping them in a halo of comfort. Dash relaxed so much, he dozed off.

He awoke to the feel of Naomi's hand lazily stroking his upper chest. He knew the moment she recognized that his breathing had lost the evenness of sleep because her hand stuttered then stilled. Without opening his eyes, he slid a hand under her blanket to the edge of his practice shirt. His fingers whispered lightly over her thigh before they pushed further under the jersey. He moved his hand higher up her thigh.

She tilted her face up. "Dash?"

His touch started a tremble low in her abdomen that he could feel. He opened his eyes. She let her hand move to the base of his throat. She looked like she wanted to hold on yet needed to move away simultaneously.

He pressed his fingers to her core, her hips bucked. Everything she felt lay evident through the dampness beneath his touch. Pressing her onto her back, he moved his hand in slow deliberate strokes. "I want you," he whispered. "And you want me, too."

"That doesn't mean we should do this."

He slipped his hand into her panties and pressed two fingers into her. "It definitely means we should do this."

~ Ϥ ~

Naomi cried out when Dash's fingers invaded her intimately. Beginning to squirm, she panted, "Tallie might wake up."

"For one so small, Tallie sounds like a herd of elephants coming down the hall. We'll have plenty of time to cover up."

As if to shore up his words, he reached down to retrieve the blanket that had fallen off her onto the floor. Then, he released her and reached behind his head with one hand to pull off his shirt. It replaced the blanket on the floor. His eyes were darkened and heavy-lidded. Her breath caught in her throat, that earlier tingle burgeoning into a hot flash.

Dash dropped down on top of her and began to work magic through his kiss. "Make love to me, Naomi. Please. Lying beside you last night and not being able to touch you the way I wanted was the worst torture I could possibly imagine."

Despite the joy his words brought, she had her doubts about what they were doing. Making love to him and knowing this wasn't permanent was the worst torture *she* could possibly imagine.

His lips found her neck then the tip of one breast. He sucked her nipple, bare beneath his shirt, through the lithe fabric. Her hands went into his hair in an odd sort of neutralness, not quite pulling him to her but not pushing him away.

Urgency entered his moves. His hands whipped her panties from under the jersey. She gasped in surprise. The unexpected, bold move caused her heart to pound. She fought her shirt down, but he pulled her further down on the couch using her hips for leverage. The placement of his hands prevented her from covering herself. He planted himself between her legs, letting his broad hips push her legs wider. He dropped his weight on top of her, allowing his jeans-covered bulge to press against her bare core.

She arched involuntarily, groaning in frustration. "Oh my . . . Dash . . ." She pushed at his chest.

"Don't say no. You want this, too. I can tell by your scent how much you want this. Say yes."

He kissed her with abandon, moving both hands to the top of her head and working in deep with his tongue. He ground against her. His erection found her bud and he rocked until she began to pant.

She was close to a climax. Her hips pressed instinctively up into him searching for that release.

He hummed into her mouth, enjoying her participation. "Say yes, sweetheart."

She didn't respond. Her eyes were closed as she fought

what she was feeling. She wasn't winning the fight.

Dash grabbed her behind one thigh and opened her more. He gyrated, feeling her warmth against the front of his pants. Her thigh trembled beneath his hand. His look of triumph made her want to scream in frustration, but another emotion was taking over her body.

She got right to the edge and he lifted slightly, separating his hardness from her. She groaned, arching up to get completion.

"Say yes," he whispered.

Her eyes flew to his. He had stopped at that point intentionally. He knew where he'd left her. Of course, he did. He knew her body probably better than she did herself.

He placed a large hand over her heated core and pressed down. Her hips arched. A long moan eased from her throat. She barely managed to keep the sound low and controlled. Her head tilted back until her forehead touched the arm of the couch and her chin pointed to the ceiling.

Dash took advantage of her open neckline to run his tongue the length of her tiny female Adam's apple.

She shivered.

"Let me send you over. All you have to do is say yes."

"Yes," she breathed.

He reacted instantly. He leaned his shoulder into the couch and pushed one foot against the floor for leverage. He threw off his belt, undid his pants and shoved them beneath his hips. Freeing himself, he said, "I'm sorry. I can't wait."

He slid into her, seating himself all the way with one shove. Sensing the eruption rising in her, Dash covered her mouth with one hand just before a scream tore from her lips. It fell muffled beneath his hand while her internal muscles spasmed around him.

He didn't wait for her to recover. He moved steadily and

forcefully, pushing her quickly back to the edge of ecstasy. Everything became frantic in short order. He dipped his head, pressing his mouth to the crook of her neck and shoulder to muffle his own sounds of pleasure.

Naomi reached down to push his pants further down his thighs then grabbed hold of his buttocks. Pulling him tight against her, she rocked up in time with his hard thrusts. He began to tremble. He called out. Increasing his tempo, he hooked a hand over the back of her shoulder and squeezed her tighter.

He tensed. "Oh . . . hell . . ." He grunted and his grip tightened on her shoulder and her thigh. He murmured incoherently against her shoulder. A low sound, almost half whimper, sounded in her ear. At a time when she should be concentrating on the orgasm building in magnificent proportions beneath her pubic bone, she began to worry.

Dash had never reacted this way before.

"Dash?"

He didn't respond, simply made that odd sound again.

"Talon, you're scaring me. What's wrong?"

"I can't . . . I've never . . ." He tilted her hips up and drilled into her spot.

She shattered.

Dash moaned as she spasmed around him for the second time. "Ugh . . . I need to come. I can't." A deep, guttural sound of near torture tore from his throat. "Help me," he begged.

"It's alright, baby. I'm right here." She caressed the back of his head then coaxed his face around. With light strokes of her tongue, she lured him into a deep sensuous kiss. As his heart rate calmed, she slowed the tempo of her hips to the light rhythm of the kiss. "Relax for me, Talon. Nice and easy, baby. That's the way."

She reached beneath her thigh and took his sac in hand. With gentle fingers, she worked him with slow compressions. She gradually increased their pace back to a driving grind and palmed him tighter. His scrotum contracted in her grip. His release now close.

"That's it. Come on. Let go for me." Her head tilted back and she moaned, "*Now.*"

His hips jerked twice as he let go a throaty vocalization of half pleasure, half relief. He held her tight through his completion and began to tremble. He kept his head in her neck and didn't move. Didn't say anything.

Naomi stroked his back, remaining silent while he shivered in her arms.

He slowly calmed then pushed himself up. "I'm sorry. I'm squishing you."

"You're fine." She searched his eyes. "Are you alright?"

"I'm . . . I'm fine." He looked at her. His eyes looked haunted.

"Talon?"

"Marry me, Naomi."

Her heart stopped beating. Did she hear him right? She sat up, pushing him aside. "What?"

"Marry me." He pulled her into his lap. "Today has been the best day of my life. You and me and Tallie. I could get used to this family thing."

She pulled away from the hand he'd pushed into her hair. She hated to burst his bubble, but she had to clear up the illusion. "We're not a family. There's you and Tallie. There's me and Tallie. And then there's you and me sharing Tallie. That's not a family, Dash."

He dropped his voice to a caress. "We could change that."

He kissed her slow and deep. Making promises with this

press of lips and tongue that he'd never made in words.

"Marry me, Naomi, so we can give Tallie the family she needs. A family where she gets to wake up and find us together every morning."

Her heart stuttered. He wanted to make a family for Tallie, but how did he feel about her? He hadn't said he loved her. Wasn't that what a man said to the woman he asked to be his wife? Of course, if it was just a marriage of necessity—a way to get Tallie under the same roof as him every day—then he didn't actually need to love her. Did he?

She pulled away from him. "I'm not an asset for accumulating, Dash. You can't marry me just so you can wake up with Tallie every day. I deserve more than that from the man I marry. I deserve more than that from you." She stood. "I think you should go now."

Dash stood, too, and pulled up his pants. "Naomi, I didn't mean—"

"I can't marry you, Dash. Well, I guess I could. But I won't." She picked up his shirt and belt off the floor. Handing them to him, she said quietly, "I owe my daughter more than that."

"What do you mean?"

She stepped back. "Good luck this weekend."

"Naomi—"

"Please go, Dash. I really don't want to talk about this anymore." She crossed her arms over her chest and cleared her throat of the sadness lodged there.

He stared at her silently as he threaded his belt through his pants and pulled on his shirt. The hurt in his eyes mirrored that in her heart.

When he finally walked away and out the door, tears built behind her eyes. Her mind wandered through everything Dash had said about her father. She'd love to give her father back his pain. She was tired of the feelings it evoked in her. She was tired of the wimpy choices those feelings sometimes led her to make—like staying in a relationship with a man you loved, pretending you didn't love him for fear he'd abandon you if he learned the truth or like writing a kick-ass article about a pro football star raised in foster care finding his long lost twin but not turning it in.

She'd told herself she was holding on to the story so she could change Talon's mind about cooperating and giving her quotations to beef up his side of the tale. In her heart, she knew that was all self-deception. She'd been holding out on her editor—and possibly jeopardizing her career and Tallie's security—because she didn't want Dash to label her as betraying him again. She wanted him to agree voluntarily to let her tell his story.

He hadn't reached such generosity of heart. Yet, he could ask her to marry him so he could be with Tallie daily. She let go the tears she'd been holding in. Tears she cried for a proposal she wished had been real.

CHAPTER 20

Dash walked into the locker room after Sunday afternoon's game in a funk. He'd managed to pull out a win today. They'd squeaked by Denver in Mile High Stadium by a slim seventeen to fourteen victory.

It had been two days since Naomi turned down his proposal and his frustration had been messing with his game. The last two practices still had him off on his passes to Gordon, and the disconnect had continued during today's matchup. Coach had been riding his butt relentlessly. If he kept this up, they'd be putting Shave back on the field regardless of whether the starter was at one hundred percent or not. Or worse, Coach would bump him down and move up the third string QB. That would be all he needed to make his month complete.

The team had needed this win today to keep their hopes alive for getting a Wild Card berth in the playoffs. Now, they needed to wait and see if Seattle could help them out tonight by beating St. Louis. If they did, then all the Griffins had to do was win their next game and they were in.

Dash peeled off his graphite and gold jersey and headed for the showers. Behind him, he heard Gordon yell at the kicker.

"Hey, Fulton, nice work. You saved our asses out there with that last field goal. Now, if we could just find us a functioning quarterback, we might be able to ride this horse all the way."

Dash turned and glared at Gordon, his finger itching to flip him the bird. Out of the corner of his eye, he saw Coach Waterman enter the locker room so he refrained. Dash spun back around and walked into a hot shower, letting the steam from the scalding water mist up to shield the steam rising through his angry pores.

When he got home the next evening, he stripped for bed and laid on his back, one arm behind his head and the other at this waist above where the white sheet bunched across his hips. All he could think about was Naomi. How could she have turned down his marriage proposal?

He figured marriage and family would be what she wanted. She'd spent years pining for the family unit her father had refused to give her. He'd have thought with him presenting her the full family option for Tallie, she'd have been hell bent on accepting.

Foolish him. As much as he'd shown up and proved himself the doting father Tallie deserved, Naomi still didn't think he had what it took to be the man they needed. He wasn't the kind of man she expected to provide her with a white picket fence around a suburban lawn for two point five kids and a dog. He should have known better. He shouldn't have given in to the illusion that she would considered him a worthy knight in shining armor.

Who had he been kidding? He knew not to wish upon a star. He'd learned that lesson as a foster kid—don't dream too big. In fact, don't dream at all. That way, you avoided facing disappointment when you found out dreams weren't for your kind.

No Tooth Fairy. No Easter Bunny. No Santie Claus.

No white picket fence. No wife and child. No family—once again—for Talon "Dash" Janssen.

He rolled onto his belly and folded his pillow in half. Strangling the down knot beneath his chin, he thought of Peyton. She'd been the closest he'd come to a family back in the day. They'd been thrown together via circumstances: her removed from her home because her mom constantly attracted men who found the preteen daughter more tempting than the mother; him shuffled from home to home because he had some unknown defect that had allowed his twin brother to be adopted instead of him.

He wondered what Peyton would say about his current situation. He'd been Peyton's hero once upon a time, a role he hadn't sought but had embraced nonetheless. Protecting her had come as second nature to him. By that fateful day of high school, they'd become closer than most siblings.

Peyton's unfailing faith in him had scared him at first. The daunting task of being her hero had unnerved him at times. The thought of failing her when she needed him most had almost made him give up and look the other way. He'd truly considered turning a blind eye to the inappropriate looks his foster father gave her back then. Others had done so. The foster mother of the house had done so with practiced oblivion.

Then, Peyton had looked at him one day with big brown eyes that saw his knowledge. She'd seen his awareness and been embarrassed, embarrassed because she'd blamed the old man's sickness on a failing in herself. That had been the day he'd chosen not to fail.

His reward had been more than saving Peyton from abuse. His reward had come from a connection to another person in a manner he'd never had before. That feeling had made him feel larger than life. Sometimes, when he talked to Peyton, he still got that feeling. Even after all these years and from across the miles, she reminded him that where he came from had nothing to do with the man inside him.

Peyton saw him as worthy, as lovable. Why couldn't Naomi see him the same way? Why couldn't Naomi see him as the husband she needed and the father Tallie needed in her life on an everyday basis?

When Naomi had looked at him the other day with those sad emerald eyes, he'd sensed he'd failed her. Like with Peyton, he'd sensed her eyes saw something in him, a knowledge she chose not to share but decided to hold him accountable for. What was it?

He tossed and turned for several more minutes before rising and heading to the kitchen. He wasn't sleeping so no sense continuing to hang in bed. He got down the blender and pulled miscellaneous fruits and vegetables from the refrigerator crisper. He loaded two handfuls of ice into the blender, added the fruits and vegetables, and topped the pile with plain yogurt and a scoop of protein powder.

The whir of the blades spinning entertained him while he waited for his concoction to blend. He sipped out of the blender pitcher for taste. Not satisfied, he grabbed un-sweetened pineapple juice from the fridge and splashed some into the brew. He hit the pulverize button, starting the whir again.

When he felt the blending had gone on long enough, he poured the smoothie into a glass. He stood against the counter, congratulating himself on being smart enough not to keep alcohol in the house during the season. He had no doubt he'd be holding a fifth of gin instead of a fruit and veggie smoothie, and he'd probably be three sheets to the wind by now.

He managed to pour the smoothie down his throat instead of toss the glass against a wall. That's what he really had the urge to do. He didn't understand why he was so broken up by Naomi's rejection. He hadn't consciously intended to get married. Yet, when the proposal had popped from his mouth, the desire for her to say yes had overwhelmed him.

He sat the glass down. The urge to throw it hitting him harder this time.

Damn her. He wanted her under his roof, under his bedsheets, under him. And he wanted Tallie in his house with her. It made no sense for her and Tallie to live on the other side of the city in a house of their own. They belonged to him. They belonged *with* him.

But his being Tallie's father wasn't good enough for Naomi. She needed more. She needed to be the one who spread his life's tale through the media virtualsphere. He represented a story to her. She didn't see him as a man separate from the thrill and intrigue his life brought to her readers.

Maybe that's what this was all about—his refusal to sign off on her article on him and Tatum. What did it say about the status of their relationship that he couldn't rank above a byline on her priority list? Just once, he'd like to come first with her, to rate higher than a career piece.

He looked at the time and cursed. He had to be at the stadium early for the post game checkup by the team medical staff. They wouldn't have practice, but everyone had to be evaluated for injury before getting the green light to while away their Tuesday. Most of the guys would use the day to do work with their charities of choice or volunteer with various organizations. He had a scheduled appearance himself in the late afternoon at Children's Mercy Hospital on the oncology ward. He needed sleep. Yet, here he was in the wee hours of the morning pining for some woman who didn't want him.

Pathetic.

Dumping the remainder of the smoothie down the drain, he turned on the water to rinse the glass and the blender jar. Once both were stashed in the half-full dishwasher, he wandered into the living room and gathered the remnants of Naomi's letters about Tallie. He shuffled through the pictures until he found the one he wanted.

The picture showed Tallie at her first birthday party. She'd dipped her hands into the cake icing and was holding them up on display. Her face and the front of her shirt were also covered with icing. It was the most adorable snapshot he'd ever seen. He smiled to himself, not naive enough not to recognize his own bias as the girl's father.

He walked over to the fireplace and dropped the rest of the letters on the mantle in a pile. He propped the icing picture against the back of the mantle wall. Glancing up, he took in the empty wall space. Other homeowners would have filled that space by now with a family portrait. He could envision such a portrait of him, Naomi, and Tallie filling the spot, but it wasn't to be.

Not good enough. The mantra kept playing over and over in his head. He hadn't been good enough to say yes to, not good enough to pass on a story for.

Not. Good. Enough.

Dash grabbed the sonogram of Tallie off the mantle and

took it with him to the couch. He sank into the cushions. He studied the sonogram in the dim light, not motivated to do much of anything, not even sleep.

Time passed, and he lingered on the couch feeling sorry for himself. He mulled over the sad state of his life until gravity pulled his head back against the backrest. Eventually, he fell asleep in the same position into which his head had fallen. He awoke a few hours later in the same spot, and he felt every inch of it. Getting through today was going to be hell.

~ ⍦ ~

The next evening, Dash responded to his doorbell wearing baggy sweats and an old wrinkled T-shirt. They were the same clothes he'd slept in last night, again on the couch. He opened the door and looked into his own face. Well, the face of his twin.

Surprise filled him. Not exactly the person he'd expected to see. "What are you doing here?"

Tatum stared at him. "You called me."

"No, I didn't."

"Yes, you did. You just didn't use a phone."

Dash rolled his eyes. "Seriously?"

"Yeah, seriously." Tatum shouldered past him and dropped his duffle bag against the entry wall.

"Make yourself at home, why don't you?"

"Thanks," Tatum replied, intentionally ignoring Dash's sarcasm.

As he went to shut the door, Dash glanced down the drive. He frowned as a thought occurred to him. His gaze snapped to his brother. "Wait a minute. How'd you get through the gate?"

Tatum turned. "Some idiot left the gate open." His eyes travelled slowly up then down Dash's frame once, twice. "From your current state, I suspect that idiot was you. You look like crap."

Dash shut the door. "Gee, thanks." He stepped to the security panel beside the door and hit the button to close the iron gate that kept the entry to his property secure from unwanted visitors—when he remembered to close it that is.

The bottom of Tatum's jacket flared out as he pushed his hands beneath the expensive leather and dropped them on his hips in a confrontational stance. "So what's wrong?"

"There's nothing wrong."

Tatum cocked an eyebrow.

Shaking his head, Dash pushed away from the security panel and headed for the living room. He wasn't in the mood for this voodoo twin connection thing.

Tatum followed, taking in the surroundings as he went. "Nice place. Who's your decorator?"

"Naomi," Dash said without turning around.

"Ah. How is the lovely Naomi?"

Dash didn't respond. He flopped down on the couch and picked up the iced coconut water he'd abandoned to open the door. He raised his glass towards Tatum. "I'd offer you a beer, but I don't keep alcohol on the premises during the season. But I do have just about any type of water or juice you could want."

"I'm good." Not missing Dash's failure to answer his question, Tatum repeated himself. "So, how's Naomi?"

Dash took a long drink. He stared at his brother over the rim of the glass. When he lowered the glass, he said, "I don't want to talk about Naomi."

Tatum shook his head. Running his hand down his face, he swore then took the overstuffed chair opposite Dash.

"You idiot. What happened?"

"I do *not* want to talk about this, Tatum."

"Tough. When you hurt so bad I can feel it halfway across the continent, you're going to talk to me whether you want to or not." Tatum settled on the edge of the chair and rested his forearms on his spread knees.

"I think I liked it better when I didn't have a brother."

"You always had a brother. You just didn't know it."

"Okay, fine. I liked it better when I didn't *know* I had a brother."

Tatum smiled. "Like hell you did. I'm the best thing to happen to you since you learned to throw a football."

Dash's lips tilted left in a sarcastic grin. "Whatever." Strangely, he realized having Tatum here was oddly comforting.

"Actually, I take that back. I'm the second best thing to happen to you since you learned how to throw a football."

Dash considered that comment with a questioning frown.

"The best thing to happen to you, I suspect, you recently screwed up by making her leave."

Slamming his glass of coconut water on the coffee table, Dash leaned forward. "I didn't *make* her leave. We had a disagreement."

"About?"

"The two-year-old daughter she forgot to tell me I had." Tatum's eyes widened, but Dash continued. "And about a certain article I don't want her to publish."

"She had your baby and didn't tell you?"

Dash closed his eyes and sighed deeply. "Not exactly." He opened his eyes. "Turns out she tried hard to tell me, but I blew her off. She even wrote me several letters."

"Letters?"

Dash rose and grabbed the letters and baby photos from the fireplace mantel. He handed them to Tatum. Tatum looked through the correspondence, stopping at the photograph of Tallie on her first birthday.

He looked up at Dash with a bright smile. "She's adorable."

The softness in Dash's voice matched that in his heart. "She is, isn't she?"

"I don't understand. If you got the letters, how come you didn't know about the little girl?"

"I never opened them. I was so angry with Naomi when we broke up that I didn't want to hear anything from her. I stashed the letters unopened in a drawer and forgot about them."

"How did you finally find out?"

Dash told him the story and watched his brother's face as he took it all in. "Needless to say, I was a bit shocked."

"I bet. So, even knowing about the little girl, you didn't relent on the story about us?"

"The story was non-negotiable. Tallie has nothing to do with it."

"Well, I suppose you're planning to be generous with child support, but Naomi doesn't strike me as the kind of woman who would be content letting you provide for her."

"The support would be for Tallie. Naomi has her job at the *Sports Daily*."

"For how long now that you've forced her to choose between you and her job?"

"No. I forced her to choose between me and one story."

Tatum sank back into the chair. "And that one story meant her job."

Dash eyed him. "What are you talking about?"

"We talked when you guys were in Ibiza. Her editor

gave her an ultimatum. She delivered this story or she cleared out her desk."

"Naomi's a great reporter. They'd never turn her away because of one story."

"It isn't about one story. It's about stories, many of them, over the course of two years or so. Years during which she's been given crappy assignments and relegated to the broad who used to date Dash Janssen to get her stories."

Dash's jaws tightened. Naomi had said nothing to him about being effectively hazed at work. She certainly hadn't mentioned that she needed this story to save her job.

Tatum watched him. "I was curious about her after Ibiza so I went online and read through her bylines. The stuff she wrote before and during her relationship with you is extraordinary. She did this piece on Shave Stephens several years back that gave unbelievable insight into the guy's game mind. It wasn't the usual mundane sports questions.

"She has the kind of talent I could see penning *New York Times* bestselling biographies of sports legends. Hell, if she wrote one on Stephens—or you for that matter—I'd be the first in line to read it. But the stuff she's had to cover since you dumped her and trashed her in the media? Could have been covered by a high school newspaper."

"Are you trying to blame me for Naomi's career issues?"

"Not you directly, but the way you handled the blowup after the publication of the article about your life in foster care had long-term repercussions for her."

Dash just stared at Tatum.

"I read about that online, too. Are you really that self-centered that you don't understand the politics of her career?"

"Self-centered?" Dash bristled, stalking back over to the fireplace. "Right. That's me. After a lifetime of taking care of myself, I figured somebody has to make me the center of their attention."

Tatum froze. He glared at Dash. Swinging himself up from the depths of the chair, he planted his elbows on his knees and steepled his fingers together pointed down as he leaned forward. "Look, I'm sorry about the life you had as a kid, but you're not the only one who feels gypped." His voice tightened. "I love my family. I do. But there's a part of me that would trade my life with them to have had the opportunity to have grown up with my *twin* brother."

Running the fingers of his right hand through his hair, Dash sighed. He wouldn't have wanted his brother to experience the life he'd had. "No, you wouldn't."

"Yes, I would." The fingers of Tatum's left hand threaded his hair in much the same way Dash's had just done. "I know you don't understand this. But you're my brother, my blood, and I love you. I want us to be the brothers we could have been had we stayed together from birth. I realize we can't get those years back, but I think we can let them go so they don't keep us from building the relationship we're destined to have from this moment forward."

The sincerity on Tatum's face made Dash's chest ache.

"I'm here now, Dash. I'm here because I sensed you needed me. How about you drop that chip you've wedged up on your shoulder and stop roadblocking me over something I had no more control over than you did, baby brother."

Dash's brows shot up. "*Baby* brother?"

Tatum grinned. "Yes. *Baby* brother. I'm two minutes older than you."

Dash grinned back at him. "How'd you find that out?"

"Mom did."

The lighthearted expression on Dash's face soured.

"Don't. Don't blame her for this, Dash. She didn't know. In fact, she cried when I told her about you and what kind of upbringing you had."

Dash frowned. "I don't need you garnering pity for me."

"It wasn't pity. And that's not what I was doing. She wanted to know. She got angry when she realized I'd been born a twin and no one at the adoption agency or the home had told them. She went back to the agency and demanded an explanation."

Curiosity overrode Dash's simmering anger. "What did they say?"

"Most of the people involved with my adoption were no longer there, but an administrator eventually put her in contact with a woman who had worked at the agency during the same timeframe. Apparently, they had difficulty back then placing multiple children in the same permanent home. Several adoptions for children who had a sibling or two fell through the year before mine because the prospective adoptive families couldn't afford to take on more than one child. The families felt bad about splitting up siblings and backed out of the adoptions completely.

"To minimize such failed placements for infants, they decided not to discuss siblings with prospective parents unless they asked about multiples or the parents indicated during their interview that they would consider adopting more than one child. Since infants were too young to talk and reveal their family ties, adopted parents of infants left without knowing about any brothers or sisters left behind. The decision of which child to place with a family was based solely on age. The oldest child of the gender sought was the one placed. In our case, mom didn't care if she got a boy or a girl, but—"

"You were the oldest by two minutes."

Tatum nodded.

Dash shook his head in disbelief. *Two minutes.*

Only two minutes had meant the difference between life in foster care and life with a loving family. Then again, life in that loving family may not have led him to the life he had now. Tatum was a soccer guy. He didn't even follow professional football until he'd found out he had a brother in the NFL. Dash loved football, and he loved being a professional quarterback. He wouldn't want that to change. The truth of that broke a crack in the wall he'd built around his emotions.

He may not have had a family growing up, but he had one now. Here was Tatum offering him the brotherly camaraderie he would have killed for as a kid. All he had to do was accept it. That crack in his ability to form emotional attachments split wide enough for him to admit to himself how badly he wanted to do just that.

He looked at his brother. They moved at the same time, somehow understanding without words what the other was thinking. They wrapped their arms around each other in a strong embrace.

When they pulled back from each other, Dash said, "Just so you know, *big* brother. You are not to ever call me 'baby brother' in public." Dash shivered dramatically.

Tatum laughed. "I'll take that under advisement." He sat back down. "My parents want to meet you."

"Meet me? Why?"

"Because you happen to be the twin brother of their first born son. Isn't that reason enough?"

"I don't know. I'm just getting used to you. I don't know that I want to be on display for the other family."

Tatum laughed again. "The *other* family? Is that what

you call them?"

"Yeah, sometimes, in my head."

"Well, cut that crap out. They're not 'the other family.' They're my family. By extension, that makes them your family as well."

Dash sat down quietly.

Tatum decided not to push him. "Think about it. Okay? Everyone realizes you're at a critical part of your season so this isn't something that need happen right away. But when your season's over, I'd like you to come to San Diego for a visit."

"I'll think about it."

"Good. Now, what about Naomi?"

Dash sighed as he thought about Naomi and Tallie, the woman he wanted and the child she'd given him. The woman should be his wife and the child should be under his roof so he could love on her and protect her every day, but he hadn't been able to make that happen.

"I asked the woman to marry me. She turned me down."

"You told her you loved her and asked her to marry you, and she said no?" Tatum frowned as he sat back down.

Dash didn't speak for a moment.

"Dash?"

"I didn't say I loved her, but I did propose. It made perfect sense with Tallie in the picture."

Tatum threw up his hands. "You stubborn, foolish moron."

"Watch it."

"Watch it, my ass. Basically, you made her think you wanted to marry her because of the baby."

Dash sat silently again.

"Why can't you admit that you love that woman?"

All of Dash's frustration boiled to the surface. "Because I

don't know shit about love and she knows it. If I'd have claimed to love her, she'd have laughed in my face. I was being sensible. We'd get married and make a family for Tallie."

"There is no family without love, Dash. Do you love her?"

"I don't know."

"Yes, you do."

"Crap!" Dash jumped up and paced to the fireplace. "What else do you want from me?"

"I want you to admit the truth to yourself and stop sabotaging your future because of your past."

Was he doing that? Was he sabotaging what he could have with Naomi because he couldn't let go of the past?

"I don't know anything about all that love crap. All I know is that I miss her. I want her here with me. All the time. I feel like someone just played a cruel joke on me. I got used to being without her only to have her slip back into my life for a short time and remind me how much better my life was when she was with me. I want her back. And I want my daughter." Dash rubbed both hands down his face. "Ugh. I sound like some whipped punk."

Tatum picked up Dash's abandoned coconut water and tipped the glass at Dash as if in toast. "Nah, bro. You sound like a man in love." He took a sip. "With two women."

Dash gave him a puzzled look.

"One of them just happens to be pint-sized."

Dash smiled then. "I'm screwed aren't I?"

Shaking his head, Tatum replied, "Only if you're not man enough to go after what you want. I thought you professional athlete types were supposed to be single-mindedly driven and all that."

Dash tilted his head. "Why does that sound like a

challenge?"

"Maybe," Tatum grinned, "because it is."

CHAPTER 21

Naomi opened her door to a messenger. He held out an envelope and a bushel of wild flowers in a plastic sleeve. She signaled for the man to wait while she got her purse.

With a touch of his hat, he nodded. "No need, ma'am. The tip has been taken care of."

"Thank you." She closed the door. The fragrance of the wild flowers pulled at her nostrils. She pressed her face into the bushel for a long inhale. "Lovely." The soft comment echoed through the silent room.

Heading for the kitchen to fetch a vase, she flipped the envelope over several times but couldn't find a return address. She placed the envelope on the table, filled a vase, and arranged the flowers. Her fingers parted the flowers searching for a card without success.

Stepping back to the table, she centered the vase on its surface and picked up the abandoned envelope. Inside rested three tickets to the Griffins' home game this afternoon. Knowing immediately who they were from, she stared at the tickets, amazed that he had sent her three. She could only guess he intended for her to bring Tallie and her mother.

Her butt dropped into a chair. She had seats for each game, of course. The *Sports Daily* had reserved seats in the press box. Dash knew that. Nevertheless, he had sent her VIP tickets. He hadn't just made a gesture by sending her a personal ticket for a seat in some prime location. These seats were in the section reserved for the wives and families of the players. He was making a grand gesture, an outward showing that she and Tallie held a privileged place in his life.

She wondered if he'd feel the same if he knew she'd finally turned in her story about him finding his twin.

Would he still want to play family man?

She doubted it.

Tatum had called her a few days ago to let her know he was in town and intended to stay long enough to see Dash play today. She understood Tatum was giving her a heads-up that her window for exclusivity was closing. Once Tatum appeared at the stadium, that there were two of them would no longer be a secret.

A deep sigh resonated in her chest. She'd bitten the bullet and done what she thought right. She'd turned in her stories to her editor. Part one of the series had run in this morning's paper. Dash wouldn't have seen it yet. He never read the news before a game. His entire focus would center on preparation for the day and visualization of the results he wanted. By the end of today's matchup, he'd have more than score results to live with. He'd have another moment in the spotlight set off by a news article tagged with her byline. Reporters would be lining up to ask him questions.

As much as she wanted to attend today's game, and should for job purposes, Olathe Stadium was the last place she wanted to be. She tossed the tickets onto the table and turned, intent on clicking on the television so she could watch the pre-game activities.

Her mother came out of the back room before she made it out of the kitchen. "You aren't getting ready to go? You know what traffic will be like trying to get to the stadium. You better get a move on if you want time to talk to players before kickoff."

"I'm not going to the game today. I'll just watch it on the tube."

"Since when?" Her mother gave her a look that suggested she thought Naomi had developed a sudden mental defect.

Naomi continued towards the living room. "Since now." Her eyes flicked to the kitchen table as she spun.

Her mother took note and walked over to the table, causing Naomi to pause.

Adele hummed, "Mmm hmm," and held up the discarded football tickets. "These wouldn't have anything to do with you not wanting to be in the stadium on game day, would they?"

"No." Naomi turned her back on her mother and exited the kitchen.

"Why, lookie here. There are *three* tickets. I wonder who the other two are for? Hmm?" Her mother followed her and made a major production of putting her finger to her chin as if in deep thought. "Hey, Tallie! Come here."

Naomi lurched for the tickets. "Mom! *Don't.*"

Adele held the tickets aloft while the sound of stampeding toddler echoed down the hallway.

Tallie came to a stop in front of her grandmother. "Yes,

Gammie?"

Adele squatted and showed Tallie the tickets. "Look. Would you like to go to a football game?"

"Mom," Naomi groaned.

Tallie jumped up and down and clapped. Reverently, she whispered, "Football?"

"Yes." Adele smiled at the euphoric toddler.

"Yes! Football. Go. Go." Squeals joined the bounces.

Adele slid the tickets into the back pocket of her jeans and said to Naomi, "You best get dressed. We have a game to attend."

"Mom, I'm not going to that game. Those tickets are in the family section. How is that going to look?"

"Like you and Tallie are Dash's family and important enough to him that he wants everyone to know it."

"I'm—"

Adele shook her head. "Naomi, open your eyes. That man is madly in love with you. I know he hurt you with the way he proposed. That he didn't say the words you wanted—needed—to hear at that moment. But, sweetheart, he's tried to contact you repeatedly over the last few days. He's asking for another chance, and I think you ought to give it to him."

Naomi's eyes squeezed shut.

A hand landed softly on her shoulder. "Honey, he's reaching out to you. You need to meet him halfway." Naomi's eyes opened slowly, and Adele smiled. "Besides, Tallie and I really *really* want to go to this game. You're not going to rob us of the opportunity when we have such great seats, are you?"

Huffing out a breath, Naomi groused, "You're really not giving me much of a choice, are you?"

"No. I'm really not." Adele grabbed up Tallie and

headed to the bedroom to bundle her in warmer clothes.

~ ¥ ~

Olathe Stadium, home of the Kansas City Griffins, clamored with the excitement of fans on the verge of seeing their young franchise make the playoffs. A Wild Card spot was on the line, and the Griffins had strong odds in their favor. The game didn't start for another couple of hours, but tailgating activities and vendor sales were in full swing.

Tatum meandered up the winding ramp, heading for the upper level. He stopped at a concession counter. He considered a beer, thought better of it, and decided to find his seat.

The melodic groove of his favorite R&B song sounded from his pocket. He pulled out his phone and silenced the ringtone with an answering swipe. "Gentry." He skirted around the beer counter to engage in conversation with his investigator. "Michelson, what did you find out?" He frowned at the answer he received. "Are you sure? What kind of accent?" He ran a hand through his hair. "Okay. Got it. I'll need you to follow up on that right away. Bye."

Crap. He disconnected and immediately clicked through his contacts to text Naomi. An interesting twist had just been added to the saga originating in Ibiza. Without looking up, he turned and nearly stepped into the arms of a beautiful woman wearing a Griffins jersey displaying number twelve—Dash's number.

He smiled as he apologized. Her face lit up, and he knew immediately the misperception she was under. She grabbed him and pulled him into a tight hug. The large gentleman beside her didn't look too thrilled to see her arms around him.

"Dash, what are you doing out here? Since I was a little late getting to the stadium I didn't think I'd get to see you until after the game." She stepped back and eyed his attire. Frowning, she commented, "You aren't dressed for warm-ups. What's going on? Are you injured? I didn't read anything about that in the papers." Her hands went to her hips. "If you got hurt and didn't call to tell me, I'm going to beat you."

You can beat me anytime, he wanted to say, but thought better of it when he took another look at her companion. Her tirade amused Tatum. Her companion, however, was not so amused.

The man grabbed her arm and pulled her back. "Peyton, quit treating the man like a child. I'm sure he's perfectly fine."

Tatum did a double take of the woman's long dark hair, smooth walnut-brown skin, and long legs encased in a pair of body-hugging jeans. "You're Peyton?"

She disengaged herself from the gentleman. "Ha, ha. Very funny. Who else would I be?"

After a few seconds, her eyes grew big. He could almost see the imaginary light bulb go on over her head. He grinned.

"Holy cow," she breathed. She took an unconscious step towards him. "You're the twin." The awe in her voice made him want to laugh. She walked around him in a slow circle.

Her companion rolled his eyes. "You want him to bare his teeth next, Pey? Come on. Let's find our seats. I want to be settled by the time the game starts, and I want to make sure I can get reception in there," he tapped his laptop case, "if I have to do some work."

"Hold on, Marion. We can sit down in a minute."

"I don't want to miss the kick off."

Tatum tilted his wrist, unnecessarily checking the time. "I think you're pretty safe on the kickoff issue."

The glare he received communicated how unappreciative Marion was for the input.

Peyton patted the man's chest. "Fine, Marion. Go." She pulled a ticket from the right back pocket of her jeans and handed it to him. "Find our seats. I'll be along in a minute."

Marion walked off. Tatum wondered what kind of guy didn't introduce himself then walked off and left his woman with a complete stranger. He pulled his eyes away from Marion's retreating back and focused on Peyton. Dash had some explaining to do. When he'd talked about his foster sister, he'd never once mentioned what a babe she was.

She put her hand to her chest. "I'm so, so sorry if I made you feel like you were on display. But, goodness gracious, the resemblance is disturbingly uncanny."

"So, I've heard. I think it's part and parcel of the whole *identical* twin thing."

She laughed. "Right."

He extended his hand. "Pleased to meet you, Peyton. I'm Tatum Gentry."

She took his hand and placed her other over top of their joined hands. "It's so nice to meet you, Tatum." She released his hand and shook back her hair. "I apologize for my fiancé. He loves to watch the Griffins play, but he's not a big fan of Dash's. I guess by association — or maybe we should say by resemblance — those feelings now also extend to you."

Fiancé. It figured a woman as attractive as she wouldn't be unattached. "Don't worry about it. I won't hold that against you. Him? I'm not so sure about."

He wondered how Dash felt about the guy. Were the bad feelings mutual? He'd have to ask Dash after the game. Right now, he needed to get Dash a message, and perhaps he could use Miss Peyton to do it. He glanced at the laminated all-access pass around her neck. "Did I hear you say you're supposed to meet Dash before the game?"

"Yes." She glanced at her watch. "I've cut it rather close though. Dash should be headed to the field to warm up. I'm not sure they'll let me close to him now."

He took her arm. "It's important you make that happen, Peyton. I've got some information Dash needs to have before the game starts. I'll fill you in as we walk. Which way?"

~ ¥ ~

Uncharacteristically, Coach Waterman gave a pre-warmup speech before dismissing the team to the field. Dash thought the man had pulled out just about every motivational cliché except "Win one for the Gipper." Perhaps he was saving that one for right before the game.

Shaking his head, Dash turned towards the locker room exit.

"Dash, hold on a minute."

He looked back to see Shave Stephens standing by his own locker dressed in jeans, a Griffins baseball cap, and his number nineteen jersey without pads. Dash glanced at the last of his teammates heading out the door.

"This will only take a minute, kid."

Dash's lips curved up. He thought it funny to hear Shave call him "kid." You'd think the man was two to three decades his senior instead of not quite one. Dash headed back towards the lockers. "What's up, Shave?"

"I wanted to talk with you about the game."

"What about it?"

"As you know, I haven't been cleared for play yet. I'm not sure when I'll be getting back on the field with what's going on with my leg."

Dash's eyes widened.

"Don't get your hopes up too high or start any rumors yet, but you and I both know this is your shot at that starting position you want."

"I didn't want it like this."

Shave gave him a considering look. "I know you didn't. You've always been a standup guy, Janssen. I've never doubted your dedication to the team or your respect for my position. The thing is, whether I want to or not, I'm going to have to take a serious look at what's next for me when it comes to football. But, in the meantime, I've put a lot of time and effort into building this infant franchise into a serious playoff contender. I don't want to see that blown to hell because the offensive team wasn't ready to move forward with another guy in the pocket."

Dash sat down on the bench across from Shave. "What are you saying?"

"Make no mistake. I intend to fight like hell to put your ass back in the number two spot. But until I'm cleared to play, this is your team. You've got to start leading them like it is. We need to cinch that Wild Card spot today. San Francisco knows our offense well. They've used it. They've studied how we run it with me at the helm, and they've studied how we run it with you acting as if you're me. If we're going to beat these guys. I mean beat them squarely and not just squeak by like we did last week in Denver. That's not going to cut it."

"What do you suggest?"

"This is your army for the moment, Dash. It's your job to lead them to a victory. Quit trying to be a temporary me and start playing like a permanent you."

Dash frowned, remembering Naomi's similar words to

him a few weeks ago. He stared at Shave.

"What? Can't handle the truth?"

Dash toyed with his sweat towel embroidered with the Griffins logo. "It's not that. It's just that someone else told me the same thing recently."

"Oh? Who?"

"Naomi."

Shave's smile was huge. "Quite a woman that Naomi." Shave laughed at the scowl Dash shot him. "Easy, tiger. I think she's quite a woman, but she's not the woman for me. Even if I thought she was, she only has eyes for one Griffins uniform and my number ain't on it." Shave leaned back against his locker. "Look, I know your style, kid. I remember what you played like before that doofus in Chicago tried to make you over your rookie year. I think it's time you showed the Griffins fans what a collegiate All-American and two-time National Champion can really bring to the NFL.

"I'm counting on you to win this one, Dash. We need to lead this team to the Super Bowl, and you've got to keep our playoff run alive until I'm well enough to pick up the mantel again." Shave turned to leave, but stopped mid-turn. "By the way, I understand congratulations are in order."

Dash looked up.

"I heard you're a father. That you and Naomi have a daughter?"

A smile followed the nod Dash gave Shave. "Taliana."

"I hope you're planning to finally do right by that woman."

Dash frowned again.

"You know, Dash. You were lucky to get that woman the first time around. She out-classed you then, and she still out-classes you. She deserves to be more than your chick on the side."

"She doesn't act like a woman with loftier ambitions."

Shave's forehead creased, and he crossed his arms as he planted his feet hip distance apart. "What do you mean?"

"I asked her to marry me. She said no."

The surprise on Shave's face made Dash laugh. "Why do you look so surprised?"

"She's the mother of your child, she's in love with you, but she turned down your marriage proposal? I don't understand."

"First of all, you're wrong about her being in love with me. We're good together, but love me she doesn't. And second, I may have botched my proposal delivery."

"Botched?"

"I kind of gave her the impression I only asked her because of Tallie."

Shave lifted his ball cap and immediately resituated it on his head. "So you left out the part about being in love with her?"

"I hadn't quite figured that out at the time."

"Damn, Dash, I didn't realize you were so slow on the uptake. You are planning to fix things with her, right?"

"I'm sure as hell going to try."

Shave looked skyward and shook his head. "Why do I feel a *Star Wars* lesson is in order here?"

With a grimace, Dash pleaded, "Don't say it."

"Do or do not, young Skywalker. There is no try."

Dash rolled his eyes. "You just had to say it."

Chuckling, Shave dropped a hand to Dash's shoulder. "I did, and I wish you luck with that. But for now, how 'bout you get your butt in gear and post one in the *W* column? I'd like there to be some season of consequence left for me to play in, particularly some postseason, if I finally get my PT to clear me for play starting next week."

Shave made it all the way to the door before he added, "Oh, and I hope you read the defense today better than you read women. Naomi is in love with you and has been for a long time. That's evident to every man who tries to get her attention. How the hell did you miss it?"

Dash sat on the bench for ten minutes after Shave left. Shave's words about Naomi and his expectations about the game rattling around in his head. Shave wasn't asking for much. Do right by Naomi. Win today's game. Secure their playoff spot so they could keep their Super Bowl bid alive.

No pressure, right?

Right.

His entire family was here to watch him play. At least, he hoped they were. He knew Tatum was out there. And Peyton should be out there somewhere, too. She'd planned to meet him before the game, but she'd been running late and he'd had to get dressed. Still, he had no doubt she'd be here if she wasn't already.

Naomi should also be in the stadium. He'd sent her VIP tickets so she'd be seated in a spot where he could easily find her. He hadn't seen much of her this past week. He'd done all his visiting with Tallie at Adele's and had only seen Naomi on those nights when he'd "inadvertently" lost track of time and had still been at Adele's apartment when Naomi came to pick up their daughter.

Funny. He laughed to himself. She'd turned down his screwed up attempt at a proposal, and he had to use subterfuge to get to see her, but he automatically included her when he thought of family. Now that he could admit to himself that he was in love with her, the thought of her and Tallie both as his family was as natural as breathing.

Could Shave have been right? Was she in love with him, too? If that were true, no wonder she'd turned down his crappy proposal. Who'd want a marriage based on unrequited love? Tatum had called him an idiot. He now agreed with his brother.

He had to fix this. He needed to convince Naomi that his heart was healed and it beat only for her. No more walls for her to scale around. No more holding back his true feelings for her. He harbored no more fear where she was concerned, except maybe the fear that he'd never get her to give him another chance.

The first step was to get her admiration and respect back—if only part way. Football was as good a meeting ground as any. She loved football and had never missed a home game when they were together. He silently prayed she wouldn't pick today's game for her first no-show.

He stood. Time to face the music. If ever he were going to make a stand, make a stand that mattered, today would be the day. He needed a win on every level today, a professional win and a personal win.

First things first: Time to go kick some San Francisco tail.

He headed out the door and up the tunnel. He knew how to get Naomi's attention today, and he had to start with his performance on the field.

CHAPTER 22

Dash stared at the scoreboard from the sideline. The defense fought to hold San Francisco from scoring again. The Griffins were down by two touchdowns with only four minutes thirty seconds left in the third quarter. His keeping the team's playoff hopes alive wasn't looking so good.

He lifted his Griffins baseball cap and ran fingers through his hair. The passing game wasn't working. Try as he might to connect with Max Gordon, the guy's speed and timing didn't gel well with his throwing pace. He'd overshot the guy several times already tonight. He couldn't keep that up and get the team back in the game.

Shave had told him to make this team his own. Had Shave meant it? After running into Tatum and Peyton on his way out of the locker room before warmups, he had his doubts.

Tatum had learned the photographer of the kiss photo had been paid handsomely to snap that photo, and the gentleman who'd kissed Tatum had as well. According to the kissing bandit, he'd been hired to catch Tatum — who he'd been told was Dash — in a compromising position. The man who'd guaranteed payment had spoken with him on the phone and had a heavy Southern accent. Had it been Shave?

Given the conversation they'd had earlier inside, it didn't make sense that Shave would sabotage him. Then again, Shave's advice had centered on doing what was necessary to keep the team in the Wild Card hunt. That was to Shave's advantage. Until he'd been cleared for play, Shave would want Dash to keep winning. Didn't mean he wasn't planning to have Dash ousted once he was back at the helm of the team.

Dash's arms crossed over his chest. If he had a prayer to pull out a win today, he needed to take Shave's advice whatever the starter's motives. If this team was his permanently, Gordon wouldn't be his preferred option as receiver. He glanced over at number eighty-five, Trey Coffey. Coffey had great hands and great speed. Once Dash had started throwing to the guy in practice, he realized they connected well. The flow between them felt natural. Yet, the young player sat in the third option for Shave's game.

Dash glanced up at the players' family section, looking for Naomi. He wanted desperately to win this game for her. He smiled when he caught a glimpse of Tallie, clapping on her Gammie's lap, but the face he needed to see was missing. He turned back to the field, but his focus only lasted a few minutes before he was searching the seats again.

Eventually, he caught Tatum gesturing to him from the stands. Tatum pointed to the empty seat next to Adele then up at the sky box overhead. Dash watched him, opening his hands to indicate his lack of understanding. Tatum pulled his game ticket out of his shirt pocket, pointed it at the chair beside him, then at Tallie and her Gammie, then turned and pointed directly at the owner's sky box. Dash's head tilted up. His vision locked on DuChamps's box. The windows were tinted so the people inside could see out, but outsiders couldn't see in. Dash couldn't see Naomi, but he could tell from Tatum's pantomime that's from where she watched the game.

His adrenaline spiked. He'd wanted her here and she was. It figured she'd be in the owner's box with DuChamps. The man adored her. If Dash didn't know for certain the married man was vehemently appalled by adultery, he'd be jealous. As it stood, he was simply jealous that DuChamps got to spend time with her at this game, while he couldn't even see her.

He nodded to Tatum, acknowledging he'd gotten the message, then plugged back into his game. San Francisco needed to convert on a fourth and eight. Dash willed his defensive line to hold. The Griffins couldn't afford to get any further in the hole.

He glanced over his shoulder, looking up again at the owner's sky box. He'd wanted to play well for Naomi today. With the approval of the offensive coordinator, he'd tried to mix things up. Not running too many of the bread and butter plays, knowing the other team was expecting them. No matter what he tried, the running game had stalled and the passing game wasn't producing.

Shave Stephens appeared at his side. "Your game's not up there."

"Maybe it is."

"Then you need to get it back where it belongs. Out on the field. There's nothing you can do about her right now. You have a job to focus on. Get your head in the game,

Janssen, and go win this."

"That's easier said than done. Your boy seems to have a hard time catching the ball." Dash had to wonder if that was at Shave's directive.

"Then why do you keep throwing to him?" Shave fisted his hands on his hips and faced Dash squarely.

The question surprised Dash. Not what he'd expect from a guy who'd masterminded the lead receiver's recent completion problems. He studied Shave closely. "You know the routes. He's first option receiver and made the Pro Bowl for the fifth straight time last year. The last thing I need is to stir the pot by bucking the system. Besides, he whines like a two-year old when he doesn't get his way."

Shave raised an eyebrow. "Since when have you cared about bucking the system? Or whiners, for that matter?"

Dash ran a hand under his cap again. "Since DuChamps made it clear everything I do could land me in another city."

A scowl slid across Shave's face. "Look, I know DuChamps is huffing and puffing loud and strong at the moment. But, on the field, our only job is to put a win on the board. You win this game and keep us on the playoff path, DuChamps would be a fool to mess with you. The fans would have his head."

"I don't think DuChamps gives a crap about what the fans think. He's the man who dropped an expansion team in the middle of Chiefs territory when half the local population would have loved to take his scalp." Dash dropped his butt onto the bench. "Besides, putting up a win is easier said than done with Gordon having developed a chronic case of the dropsies. Nothing's clicking."

"Then change something."

"What exactly do you suggest I change?"

"I'd start with your perspective. Quit thinking about

what's not working and start thinking about what could."

Dash glanced over at number eighty-five again.

Shave noticed the look. "You've been eyeing Coffey this entire possession. What's the problem?"

"Why's he your third option?"

Shave shrugged. "I've been playing with Gordon a long time. We have a groove, a certain chemistry. Sometimes, I can find him without conscious thought. I just know where he is. Coffey's a great player, but he's young and new to the lineup. He's got a great knack for getting open when others can't, which always leaves me with a backup option."

Shave leaned his weight on his good leg. "Why do you ask?"

"Gordon and I don't work. The timing's off. First, I was overshooting him. Now, I'm hesitating every time I throw to him. It's giving the defense time to read the play. Even if I do connect with him, he can't get much yardage past the throw."

"What's your solution?"

"Normally, I'd push the running game, but San Fran's defense is shutting that down. I need to throw down field."

To Dash's surprise, Shave grinned. "You mean your solution is another receiver as first option."

"I guess so."

"Gordon is my go-to receiver. Doesn't mean he has to be yours. Do what you have to do to win. If that means Gordon drops to second or third option, then so be it. His ego will have to get over it."

Dash went quiet. His gut was telling him he could trust Shave. Someone else had to have orchestrated his press problem. He'd worry about who later. For now, he needed to get his head back in the game.

Shave joined him in his silence for several minutes then

said, "I saw Naomi in the family section earlier. She wasn't in her usual press box spot. That your doing?"

Dash nodded. He was about to turn away when a tingle went through him. He looked up. He couldn't see her, but he could feel her. Naomi watched him.

"Well, if I were trying to turn a woman's head, I'd wanna make sure I won the damn game."

A whistle drew their attention to the field. San Francisco had just scored another touchdown. *Crap!*

A few minutes later, the referee signaled a successful extra point attempt and the 49ers now led by twenty-one points. The Griffins were down three touchdowns at twenty-four to three.

The punt return team took the field. The Griffins returner made it to their own forty-eight yard line.

"We need a touchdown before the end of this quarter, Janssen." Shave snatched the baseball cap off Dash's head. "Go out and get us one."

Dash grabbed up his helmet to retake the field. He faced Shave for a moment. "Consider it done," his smirk appeared slowly, "oh Jedi Master."

The corners of Shave's eyes crinkled, but he managed to suppress his smile. "Always the smart-ass, Janssen." He motioned with his head towards the field. "Get your butt out there."

Dash slipped on his helmet and jogged to the huddle. He slid in with his guys. "Trey, I heard you hold the record at your university for the 100-meter dash."

Thorsten Coffey III's lips turned down behind his face mask. "Yeah. What of it?"

"You once told me if I could throw it, you could catch it."

The receiver tilted his helmet to the back of his head and

shrugged.

"End zone, bro. I'm throwing for the end zone. I need you there to catch the ball."

Trey's grin spread wide in his dark-chocolate face. "Now that's what I'm talking about!"

Dash grinned back. "Left side. Corner."

Trey rubbed his gloved hands together then lifted them and waggled his fingers. "I've got you. It's about time you decided to load that gun."

Dash swatted Coffey's helmet back down and called a break to the huddle.

Gordon pulled at Dash's sleeve. "What are you doing, boy? No way that grandstanding stunt is going to work. Play the game like you've got some sense and throw me the ball."

Dash disengaged his sleeve. "We're down by three touchdowns, Max. Or haven't you noticed? We've only got about two minutes left in this quarter. If we don't score this round, we'll have a massive hole to climb out of in the fourth. We need to put some points on the board."

Gordon shook his head in disgust. "Shave would never pull this Hail Mary crap this early in the game."

"I'm not Shave."

"You're damn right you're not." Gordon stomped off and fell into position.

Dash glanced over to the sideline. Shave caught his look and nodded. That was all Dash needed to set his mind at ease. He glanced up to the owner's box, feeling Naomi's eyes on him, and gave a reverent bob of his helmet as he let her words from London replay in his head. He grinned. "Yeah, damn right." He chuckled out loud as he assumed the football position. "I'm not."

"What?" His center peeked over his shoulder.

Dash patted him on the butt. "Nothing, Danny. Just hike the ball." He shoved his hands beneath Danny's ass to take the snap. "On my count . . ."

~ ϟ ~

The air in the owner's box crackled with tension. DuChamps prowled like a caged tiger, on edge and ready to pounce — on Dash's head. The score read twenty-four to three and with only two minutes three seconds left in the third quarter, Naomi felt every person in the box had to be wishing it was the even-tempered, cool-under-pressure Jonathan "Shave" Stephens headed onto the field to lead the offense instead of the impulsive, hot-headed Dash Janssen. The Griffins had been here before, but never with Dash tasked as the one to pull them out of such a significant score deficit with so little time.

Naomi held her breath as number twelve jogged to the huddle. Dash slapped down Trey Coffey's helmet and had words with Max Gordon. When he moved away to take his position, she could tell by his body language something had changed. Every prior altercation with Gordon had left Dash so uptight she could sense his tension from her perch above the field.

This time his body showed her calm and . . . *playfulness?*

He looked up towards the skybox and nodded his head. From his earlier glances this way, she'd divined he knew she was up here.

Had that gesture been directed at her?

Her woman's intuition told her it was.

She stood, a buzz of anticipation making her arm hair rise over goosebumps.

Dash positioned his hands beneath his center, looking

around to check the lineup of the defense and the Griffins offensive linemen. He took the snap, swiveled a fake to the running back, then dropped back to throw.

He pumped once towards Gordon, pulled the ball down, angled thirty degrees to his left and let the ball fly in a high arc. The leather bullet spiraled fast and sure like a torpedo with missile lock. A collective gasp went up in Olathe Stadium. Every VIP in the owner's box now stood with Naomi as did almost every Griffins fan in the stadium.

DuChamps pulled an unlit cigar from his mouth. "What the hell—?" Planting himself in front of the window, he nearly crushed the tightly-rolled stick of Cuban tobacco. "What in tarnation does that boy think he's doing?"

Naomi checked the coverage in time to see Trey Coffey spin off a defender then cut right, leaving him with an open lane. He darted through and accelerated. One defender, then two, gave chase. Coffey's feet flew like he had wings on his shoes. No one was going to catch him from behind. In an open field, the man moved like a locomotive. But would he get under the ball in time? Dash had put NASA launch power behind that throw, and the rocket looked to be headed out of Coffey's reach.

"Come on. Come on," Naomi mumbled under her breath.

Head up to watch the ball barrel forward, Coffey hit San Francisco's twenty yard line then their ten. The ball started its descent, arcing lower but with momentum destined to overshoot the end zone.

Naomi's breath caught. *No.*

Coffey leapt into the air, a gloved left hand extended high, toes pointed beneath crossed ankles like a male principal in the Kansas City ballet. The ball bounced against his glove, bobbled, and fell.

The loud gasp Naomi released would have echoed throughout the sky box if not for the matching gasps of the other VIP onlookers.

Where was the ball? In Coffey's arms?

Did he have possession before he hit the ground?

Murmurs rumbled through the stadium. No one dared react—positively or negatively—until they got a sign from the official.

When two arms clothed in black and white stripes flew straight into the air, the crowd erupted. *Touchdown!*

Coffey rolled to a crouch and aimed the ball with a dramatic one-handed point towards the Griffins fans celebrating in the stands behind the goal post.

Naomi couldn't contain her own shout of joy. Her hands flew high over her head as her eyes jerked towards the giant screen attached to the scoreboard. The replay unfolded in slow motion. The ball fell into Coffey's crossed forearms. He tucked the ball, landed on double tippy-toes with feet just inside the white lines that edged the corner of the end zone. He fell outside the lines without a jumble or other movement of his arms—perfect control.

If that catch didn't end up on every sports highlight reel tonight as one of the best plays of the week, Naomi didn't know football.

A befuddled DuChamps continued to stare at the field while the Griffins lined up for the extra point attempt. Naomi watched DuChamps. For an owner whose team had just made a play that could shift the momentum of the game their way, he didn't look very happy.

She'd never considered that DuChamps himself might be behind the kiss photo. After several texts and a phone call from Tatum, she'd been mulling over that possibility the entire game. In fact, it was why she'd accepted DuChamps's invitation to watch the game from the Griffins owners' box instead of remaining below with her mom and Tallie.

Tatum's investigator had linked the Ibiza photographer and the man with the amorous lips to a plot put in motion by a man with a Southern accent. Southern accents were a dime a dozen in the football world. Distinctive Southern accents around Griffinsland were fewer. People generally associated such an accent with the hot starting quarterback or the brash, larger-than-life owner. While several All-Pro Griffins players had similar accents, and of course others could fake it, she had an inkling her money was best placed on the owner. She just had to figure out why he'd do such a nonsensical thing.

With Shave injured, Dash represented the Griffins' best hope for making it to the playoffs. They had a third string quarterback, Kevin Wilson, who had been pulled up from the practice squad to fill a gap in the roster after DuChamps traded the old backup QB, Carl Maynard. Yet, Wilson was no more ready for primetime play than Naomi was.

Why would DuChamps risk a potential postseason on such inexperience? If the Griffins didn't secure a win today, and thereby clinch the AFC West Wild Card spot, the remaining two regular season games could each be do-or-die. Worse, if the Griffins lost today and Denver won their game, the standings could shake up enough to put the Griffins completely out of postseason running.

DuChamps had been hell bent on putting the Griffins in Kansas City. He'd ranted and postured about how the baby franchise would set NFL records by amassing the best record of any expansion team in history. What possible motive could he have for seemingly sabotaging his own team?

A referee whistle sounded. After successfully putting the extra point on the board, the Griffins punted the ball with a score of ten to San Francisco's twenty-four. The 49ers' punt returner made some progress, but was stopped at San Fran's own thirty yard line. Their offense executed the snap, and the quarterback dropped back to throw. The Griffins defense put heavy pressure on the pocket, but the opposing QB got off the throw. The pass was incomplete, defended expertly by rookie cornerback Davion Jones.

The clock ran out, ticking off the end of the third quarter. Both teams headed for the sidelines as the televised game took a commercial break.

Naomi's eyes searched the room until they found Martin DuChamps again. He looked down at his waist with a frown and pulled his cell phone off its clip. He squinted at the screen then his eyes shifted through the room as if he were about to execute some top-secret mission.

DuChamps noticed her gaze and nodded dismissively. He shuffled to the back corner of the box before he answered the phone in a hushed voice.

Naomi moved to the buffet setup, putting Oscar-worthy effort into selecting the plumpest morsels from the fruit plate. She wasn't in the mood for more food, but the position put her closer to DuChamps. Her ears strained towards his conversation while she picked slowly over sliced strawberries.

"Don't worry about it," DuChamps said in a low growl to whomever was on the phone. "They've still got a long way to go." He snorted. "I've got everything here under control. You just be ready on your end, Moretti." DuChamps ended the call, looking like he wanted to heave the phone across the room.

The crowd roared in the outer stadium. Naomi's head jerked towards the flat screen TV above the buffet. The Griffins had retaken possession of the ball on a fumble and scored another touchdown, decreasing their opponent's lead to only seven points.

Naomi ran back to the front, upset she'd missed the play. Placing her plate on her seat, she stepped outside through the open glass portal so as not to miss any additional action.

After a three and out by San Fran, the Griffins took over possession again. The team marched down field after the punt return for an additional twenty yards, until the 49ers stopped them, making it fourth down and eight just thirty-three yards from the end zone. Dash turned towards the sideline, apparently listening to something in his helmet. He shook his head. His hands hit his hips then he jogged over to the head coach to talk it out. After a few seconds, the field goal team took the field.

Naomi watched Dash remove his helmet. His face was neutral, but she could sense his frustration. He'd wanted to go for it. With ten minutes still left in the quarter, the coaching staff had opted to take the safer route. The surefooted kicker started his pre-kick routine then hammered the ball through the middle of the uprights for three points. The Griffins now only trailed by four.

From a strategic standpoint, Naomi understood the coaches' call. From a quarterback's standpoint, she sympathized with Dash's angst. It was the kind of call he used to spend the night talking about after he'd burned his post-game adrenaline between the sheets making intense, earth-shattering love to her. Except, tonight, he wouldn't be coming home to her. Granted, that was her choice not his, but the knowledge didn't prevent the wave of loss that washed over her. With it came an irrational twinge of jealousy as she wondered with whom he'd burn up the sheets after today's game to spell his leftover adrenaline and share pillow talk about his post-game frustrations.

Naomi shook off her depressing thoughts and watched San Francisco's offense retake the field. The 49ers proceeded to eat up the clock with a long drive fueled by their running game. Try as they might, the Griffins defense couldn't stop the opponent's successive string of first down runs.

Shave Stephens stood with arms crossed next to Dash. Dash dangled his helmet from the fingertips of one hand as if willing his defense to get him back on the field. The silent quarterbacks glanced simultaneously at the game clock then at each other. With just over four minutes left in the final quarter, the Griffins needed a major stop as soon as possible.

When the 49ers got within striking distance of a touchdown, just twenty yards out, the muggy weight of an oppressive silence blanketed Olathe Stadium. The offense approached the line of scrimmage with their biggest running back lined up to take a handoff from the quarterback. The Griffins formed a defensive wall at center, planning to blockade the anticipated running play.

The QB took the snap and play actioned to his star running back. Their tight end on the right swung out and dropped into the end zone wide open. The San Francisco quarterback threw a strong pass over the top that flew low towards the receiver's head.

"No!" Half the stadium screamed in denial right before they got their miracle.

Rookie Davion Jones swooped in front of the open man at the last second. Working his defensive magic one more time, he came away with an interception. Stadium despondency morphed into to euphoric bedlam as the cornerback spun from the end zone and blew past two opposing team jerseys. He got a big block from a Griffins outside linebacker and was off to the races. Jones streaked past the twenty, then the thirty, then the forty yard line. San Francisco's quarterback made a dive and got a hand on Jones's foot. The rookie shook him off, but lost his balance and tumbled to the Griffins' forty-five yard line.

Olathe Stadium erupted in pandemonium.

The rookie jumped up and refused to surrender the ball to the official. He pranced to the sideline clutching the ball from his first pro career interception. Slaps of congratulations rained against his back along the ecstatic Griffins bench.

Dash added his praise to the mix before streaking to the field. They had two minutes and fifty-three seconds to march forty-five yards to the end zone. They trailed by four points; a field goal wouldn't cut it. To win this game, Dash would have to marshal a touchdown.

Two plays got them to the two-minute warning and ten yards closer to the goal line. Once play resumed, they ate up another fifty-four seconds on two short passes that garnered another first down, but cost the team's remaining two timeouts because the receivers were stopped short of the sideline by determined defenders.

The defense lined up to blitz, determined not to give Dash any more opportunities to throw. Pressure built after the snap. Dash scrambled but couldn't find a receiver. He pulled the ball down and took off at a run. With a linebacker barreling towards him, he accelerated and was shoved out of bounds with a seven-yard gain.

The Griffins retook the line of scrimmage. San Francisco lined up for another blitz. Dash called the snap and Trey Coffey swung behind him on a jet sweep to grab the ball. Coffey made it inside the five yard line before being brought down. With no time outs, the clock kept running.

Fifty-two seconds . . . fifty-one . . . fifty . . .

Dash made frantic arm motions to get his men to the line without delay. He hiked a leg to signal his center over the noise of the crowd, took the snap, and heaved the ball at the ground to stop the clock. With lowered head and hands on hips, he paced a few steps away from the line of scrimmage. He glanced at the clock; thirty-eight seconds remained. The Griffins had time for only one more play.

A wave of lightheadedness washed over Naomi as she forgot to breathe. Sending silent prayers his way, she took a deep breath and watched Dash return to the line of scrimmage. Defenders lined up in a formation that indicated they expected Dash to run the ball. Dash motioned to Gordon and then to Coffey. Two defenders dropped back. One lined up left opposite Coffey. The other lined up opposite Gordon.

Dash took the snap. He faked a pass to Coffey who had nowhere to go, turned towards Gordon but he was covered, then danced a step or two before pulling the ball down to run himself. He stepped right and had to bob and weave to avoid defenders. Pivoting, he sprinted left.

As he approached the two yard line, the field began to close in front of him. When two San Francisco linemen lowered at full speed to jam Dash, Naomi threw her hands in front of her eyes and peeked through her fingers. Without hesitation, Dash pitched the ball backwards to Coffey a second before he got hammered into the turf. Coffey skirted around the pile and tiptoed into the end zone.

"Yes!" A quick fist pump punctuated Naomi's yell.

The Griffins had taken the lead and the victory. Thrilled like the rest of the fans, Naomi ignored the superfluous extra point attempt. Her gaze shifted inside to watch DuChamps frown at his phone. Curious behavior for a man whose franchise just clinched a Wild Card berth in the playoffs.

She thought back to his earlier call. He'd said the name Moretti. *Could he have been talking to Antonio Moretti, the music mogul?*

Antonio Moretti had been trying to buy into a NFL franchise for several years, but couldn't garner enough NFL owners' votes to get approval. Recently, he'd made waves about setting up some lucky franchise with a brand-new, state-of-the-art stadium funded one hundred percent by his entertainment holdings. Many considered it his way of bribing one foot into the NFL inner sanctum. But the Griffins didn't need a stadium.

Olathe Stadium was only a few years old. It had been built by the city and couldn't hold a candle to the bells and whistles Moretti bragged about, but she couldn't see the enticement of upgrading this soon. DuChamps had enough PR issues without aligning himself with a pro football outsider whose NFL approval rating rested somewhere beneath China.

Naomi turned back to the field and watched Dash celebrate with his team. Someone handed him the game-winning touchdown ball. He turned towards the sky box and froze when he caught sight of her standing outside. He spun the game ball in the palm of his hand then saluted her with it. She saluted him back with a gracious tilt of her head and the soft lines of a proud smile. Despite everything that had happened between them, she was truly happy for him.

Her smile blossomed into a full grin when she spied Tallie standing on her grandmother's lap and cheering like a crazy kid. What fun this must be for her. Her dad had come through.

Looking back at DuChamps, who furiously texted on his phone, Naomi remained perplexed by the owner's stern continence. Given the look on his face, somehow she didn't think winning this game had managed to get Dash's head off the chopping block. She needed to figure out why.

CHAPTER 23

Two days after the narrow victory over San Francisco, Dash walked into the *Sports Daily* newsroom carrying a large gift bag. He zeroed in on Naomi's empty desk and paused for a minute to look around the room. His eyes fell on Ray Jackson.

Ray looked up from his own desk as Dash approached. "Well, well, well. The prodigal quarterback appears."

Overlooking the sarcastic tone, Dash extended a hand. "Ray."

Crossing his arms, Ray ignored the hand. "Come to complain about Naomi's latest article?"

"No." Dash continued to extend his hand.

The newspaper man glanced at the proffered palm. "No?"

When he looked back up at Dash, Dash gave him a pointed look. Grudgingly, Ray stood and shook his hand.

"I don't have any complaints about the article, Jackson.

It was a good piece."

"Really? Naomi didn't seem to think you'd be that generous. What changed?"

"It took me some . . . time . . . to realize I didn't really have a problem with the content of the piece she wanted to write. Someone would have written it. It might as well have been her since she was the one who discovered I had a twin. It was more about . . ."

"Power?" Ray supplied. "Control?"

Dash shook his head. "Trust."

Ray frowned. "You didn't trust her to do a good job? Come on—"

"Of course, I did." He didn't trust that he was as important to her as getting the story, but he wasn't admitting that to Ray. "It's a little more complicated than that."

"Uh-huh."

Dash ignored Ray's caustic tone and looked around the office.

"She's not here at the moment."

Taking a few steps over to Naomi's desk, Dash nodded. He placed the gold foil bag on top of her large, black desk blotter and tucked a sealed envelope precisely between the tissue paper peeking from the top of the bag. His eyes went back to Ray's. "Make sure only she gets that note, would you?"

Ray's forehead creased and he tilted his head.

"I understand her coworker likes to stick his nose where it doesn't belong."

The expression on Ray's face made it clear Dash didn't need to elaborate on which coworker he was talking about. Ray nodded his assent.

"Thanks." Dash ran a hand through his hair and turned

to leave. He stopped for several seconds with his back to Ray then turned back. "About that previous article—"

Ray walked away from him. "You're about three years too late, Janssen," he said over his shoulder.

"So I hear," Dash mumbled under his breath. Louder, he said, "I was wrong."

Ray stopped, spun abruptly. "Excuse me?"

Dash stifled a grimace. "You heard me." He wasn't repeating that admission. "Naomi told me what really happened. I understand it could have gone much worse, and I owe your fast thinking for why it didn't. I appreciate that."

Skepticism shadowed Ray's face. "Is that so?" He clearly wasn't going to make this easy for Dash.

"Look, I'm not proud of how I behaved. I made a mistake. A mistake I'm trying to correct."

Ray walked back towards him. "You know, I've always thought she deserved better than you."

"You'll get no argument from me on that. But I love her. I'm not going anywhere."

Ray's eyebrow rose.

"This time." The heat of chagrin crept up Dash's neck.

Satisfied that Dash recognized his shortcomings, Ray nodded towards the package on Naomi's desk. "Expensive gifts aren't the way to that woman's heart. She's not that shallow."

The bow that smirked Dash's lips couldn't be contained. "I may be slow, Jackson, but I'm not stupid."

The newspaper man chuckled.

"Besides, I wouldn't exactly call that expensive . . ." His eyes skirted to Naomi's desk. ". . . or even really a gift. She'll understand when she reads the note."

Doubt must have clouded his expression because Ray asked, "You hope?"

Dash shrugged nonchalantly.

"I'll admit, son," Ray stashed his fingers in the front pockets of his jeans, hooking his thumbs through the front belt loops, "you've got the kind of swagger I can see attracting a sister. But keeping one as fine — and as fierce — as Naomi?"

Dash's eyes narrowed at the way Ray said *fine*. He'd always wondered if the guy had a thing for Naomi. She'd told him more than once that wasn't the nature of their relationship, or Ray's feelings for her, but he made a mental note not to be complacent where her mentor was concerned. Clamping down on the percolating jealousy, Dash motioned for the man to continue.

"Well, that requires taking swag to a whole other level." Ray leaned his butt against Naomi's desk and crossed his arms. "So, the question is: Do you really think you have enough to keep the one you hooked?"

Dash grinned. "Just watch me, old man."

~ ₩ ~

Dash strolled into his agent's office building across town an hour. Pete had set up a meeting with DuChamps and his representatives. As Dash had expected, even with Naomi's information clarifying the mixup between him and his twin, DuChamps had taken a hard-ass position about Dash's less than favorable bounty of headlines.

A large, plushly-carpeted elevator opened on the eighteenth floor of Pete's office building and released Dash. The fading sweetness of Prada *Candy* perfume drifted across his nose as he stepped from the lift. The hydraulic swish of the closing metal doors of another elevator drew his attention. Intuition fired his reflexes, and he whipped around, shooting his hand into the disappearing slit of the elevator next to his. The doors snagged on his hand then reversed on hidden pulleys to return to their open position. The scent of *Candy* intensified.

Inside the arrested elevator, wide green eyes stared at him. "Hey." Her voice floated out on a low timbre.

"Hey, yourself." He stepped into the elevator facing her.

The elevator doors closed, and the box began to descend.

He shifted to stand beside her. "What are you doing here?"

She fidgeted before answering. "I had to drop something off for Pete."

Dash frowned. "Pete?"

"Yes." Her right hand tugged on a loose curl from the waterfall ponytail gathered, as usual, at the top of her head. "A little ammunition he needed for a client."

"I see." His head bobbed absently, and he hauled in a fortifying breath. "Could we —"

"Shouldn't you —"

They spoke over each other.

She made no effort to continue so he did. "Could we have dinner together? Tonight? Just the two of us? I'd like to talk to you about something."

"I don't think so Dash. I'm all talked out at the moment."

"Naomi . . ." His hand reached for her elbow, but she dodged his touch. He diverted the hand through his shaggy hair. "Please. Give me a chance to clear the air."

"The air is clear, Dash. You've been *very* clear about what you want and how you feel. I get it. We don't need to have dinner to rehash old news."

"Yes, we do. That's just it. I haven't been clear. Give me another chance."

The elevator dinged its arrival on the ground floor.

"I can't do this dance anymore, Dash." She rushed from the elevator. After only a few feet, she turned, sadness and regret filling her eyes. "Congratulations on the game. You were . . . phenomenal. It was nice to see the old Dash on the field."

"Thanks. And congratulations on the article. You did a great job. It was a nice piece."

She stared at him blankly, suspiciously. "Really?"

"Really. I wish I hadn't given you such a hard time about it. I—" He cleared his throat. What he needed to say challenging him on the way out. "I'm sorry." His hands dropped into the pockets of his coat and popped right back out. "If you're still interested on input—um, quotes—or something from me for the future installments, just let me know."

Her head tilted. She observed him quietly for several seconds. "You know, I don't think I've ever heard you apologize before." A small smile edged the side of her mouth. "It sounds good on you."

"I—"

She cut him off by raising a hand, her long fingers splayed in an arresting motion. "Don't ruin the moment for me. There's nothing else you could say that would make my day any better." She dropped her hand. "I'll contact Pete to set something up if you're serious."

His hands found his coat pockets again. "I am."

"Good." For the first time in a long time, she gave him a genuine—though no less sad—smile. "Bye, Dash. And thanks."

At the exit, she stopped to greet a gentlemen wearing a long coat similar to his. She hugged the guy, giving Dash a glimpse of his doppelganger over her shoulder. Tatum said something that made her laugh. It burned that his brother could make her laugh and shine when he couldn't anymore.

Dash stood with hands still in his pockets when his brother approached. Tatum stopped in front of him. He glanced at the front door and then back at him. "Still haven't rebuilt that bridge?"

"I'm working on it." Dash hit the *Up* button.

As one, they turned and stepped into the waiting elevator.

"What the hell are you doing here? And don't give me that 'I called you' crap again."

A laugh burst from Tatum. "Nope. Not this time, little brother."

Dash raised an eyebrow at the little brother comment.

Tatum just laughed louder. "A little birdie told me you could use some moral support today. Thought I'd swing by and see what's going on."

"A little birdie, huh?" Dash glanced at Tatum, one side of his mouth tilted. "About five foot seven, reddish brown hair, green eyes?"

Tatum leaned back against the elevator wall with a grin. "That would be the one."

Dash shook his head. *What was Naomi up to?* First, she'd dropped something off for Pete. Now, she'd rallied his brother into the mix. Whatever he was about to walk into, when he was done, he intended to hunt down a certain reporter and have that conversation he wanted whether she was ready to do this dance again or not.

~ ዛ ~

Waves rolled and crashed against the surf. Poised on a ragged stone spit out eons ago by an angry sea, Naomi rocked slowly in the perfect dusk. She stared at the strip of beach where Dash had chased her a few short weeks ago on their foray to Ibiza, remembering what it had felt like to be with him without pain, without regrets, and without doubts.

Her phone dinged. Tilting on a hip, she pulled the phone from the pocket of her sundress. A notification for a video message from her mother appeared on the screen. Her eyebrows rose. Her mother was one of the most non-tech-savvy people she knew. The high-tech achievement of her having managed to send a video message intrigued Naomi. She'd been out of touch with everyone, blocking their calls and allowing voicemail to answer, everyone except her mother, who had Tallie and needed to be able to reach her at all times.

Her mom's text read: *Hit play. Don't call me. Don't ask questions. Just hit play.*

A hard laugh coughed from Naomi's throat. "Yes, ma'am," she said aloud.

She hit the play button. As she stared at her phone, the dulcet sounds of a piano solo began somewhere down the beach. Highlights of the game between the Griffins and San Francisco flitted across the screen, starting with Dash's sixty-eight-yard touchdown pass to Trey Coffey.

Dash had played like a man possessed—or more like he had a magic gridiron charm in his pocket—to achieve the three-point victory that secured the Griffins' Wild Card spot in the playoffs. In a post-game interview, he'd dedicated the game to her. He'd told the viewing public she was responsible for helping him regain his on-field mojo by reminding him how to play like his old self.

When Naomi had left Dash at Pete's office the other day and returned to the newsroom, she'd melted upon finding the game ball for the final Griffins touchdown waiting for her with a note from Dash telling her it belonged to her as did he. Despite the overwhelming emotions inspired by the note, Naomi hadn't been able to put aside the skepticism that the gesture was more about claiming Tallie than claiming her. She'd boarded a flight for Ibiza the next day.

Focused back on the slideshow, Naomi marveled at the pictures of her and Dash that progressed in well-produced spirals and fades. Snapshots from their trip to Nell Hills floated by in a sentimental haze. In the backdrop, the haunting song from down the beach seemed to draw closer as the sultry vocals of John Legend joined the weeping piano. Legend balladeered about a love that consumed him even as it uplifted. It was the slow song she and Dash had danced to at the club Tatum had taken them to. The beautiful love anthem, penned by the singer, touted how much all of him loved all of his beloved, including all her "perfect imperfections."

As the lyrics of *All of Me* moved her to tears, the pictures of her and Dash as a couple slowly changed to pictures of her pregnant then to pictures of Naomi with a baby Tallie. By the time the screen changed to pictures of Tallie alone then pictures of Tallie with Dash, the sounds of the song were unmistakably approaching. She looked up to find Dash strolling towards her.

Her hands began to shake. He reached her and dropped his mega-sized phone on top of her smaller one. The same slideshow played, but the images on his screen were accompanied by the love song, their love song. A tear dropped on his touch screen.

"Good thing that's waterproof." Removing a small box from his pocket, he placed it in her other hand. "I think this might be a better fit for those small fingers."

She looked up weepy-eyed.

He knelt in front of her. "I love you, Mimi. I'm not good at saying the words. Hell, I'm not good at understanding the words. Until you that is. If I were poetic or eloquent, I'd write you a song as beautiful as John Legend's or know how to recite romantic words that would make you swoon, but that's not me." He reached up with his right hand and wiped her left cheek with a swipe of his thumb. "I'm the guy from the hood. The scrappy loner with an attitude problem. The guy so screwed up by a childhood that had him convinced no one wanted him that he overlooked the one person who really did. And the guy who's hoping you still love him, despite all my imperfections."

Her chin lifted. "Still?"

He chuckled. "Yes. Still. I have it on good authority—several good authorities actually—that you've been in love with me for some time. I had my doubts. Then I sat in that meeting with DuChamps trying to end my career with the Griffins and listened to Pete shut him down with some pretty impressive intel, and I knew."

He removed their phones from her hand and placed them in his pocket. Taking the now empty hand, he squeezed. "I knew you were the one who dug up the information Pete had. The evidence that revealed DuChamps planned to let me go to undermine the Griffins' chances for a winning season and intentionally drive down the value of the franchise so Moretti could bank roll him in acquiring a larger stake in the team. That's what you dropped off at Pete's office that day, right?"

She nodded, weeping quietly.

"I knew you had to love me to put that much effort into helping me keep the job I love in the city I want to be in. After everything I put you through, only love could drive you to do that for me when your Creole blood would probably just as soon have handed me my family jewels on a platter."

She grinned despite her tears.

"I may be a little slow on the uptake, but now that I've figured out what's really going on between you and me, I'm not wasting any more time." He turned her other hand palm up, the small box displayed in its center. "Marry me, Naomi. Not so I can see Tallie every morning for breakfast. Not so we can make a family for Tallie—or at least, not *just* so we can make a family for Tallie—but because I end and begin with you. You are my heart as much as that little girl. Actually, more so because I've loved you longer. I was just too stupid not to fight it. It took three people to convince my head what my heart already knew. I have no life without you. I felt this way before I found out about Tallie. I'd planned to ask you back the morning after we were together here, but I screwed that up. I'm done screwing up, and I'm done letting you hide away from me."

He opened the box.

She ignored the contents and threw her hands around his neck. "Oh, Dash. I do love you."

"Enough to marry me?"

She held him tighter and wetness coated his neck, but she didn't say anything.

He placed his hands on her shoulders and leaned her away from him. He looked deep into her eyes. "It's okay. I know my past behavior has given you a justifiable doubt about my motives." He swallowed. "At least tell me you're ready to be my girl again."

She nodded.

His eyes closed. "Good," he breathed on a deep sigh. He closed the lid of the ring box and wrapped her fingers around it. "You hold on to that, and let me know when you're ready to put it on. I'm not going anywhere, and I'm not giving up until I convince you to do just that."

He kissed her slowly, until she couldn't think straight, until her insides melted, until she believed him in every cell of her body.

When their lips parted, she pushed into his arms, causing him to fall back onto the sand. She stretched out on top of him and whispered, "I'm going to hold you to that."

Epilogue

Six *months later . . .*

Naomi walked slowly across the field of the University of Nebraska-Lincoln, her sight focused squarely on the back of the man sporting a team windbreaker and holding a clipboard.

"Coach?" One of his athlete's gestured to her over the man's shoulder.

The coach turned towards her. "This is a closed practice, miss. If you need to talk to me, please make an appointment with the athletic office." He turned back to his players, abruptly dismissing her.

Naomi stood silently behind him. She refused to walk away this time. He'd only looked away for a few brief seconds when his head whipped back around and his body soon followed. He stared at her face, recognition plain in his eyes.

"You know who I am." Her voice made a statement, not a question.

Without turning back to his team, he said, "Boys, excuse me for a few minutes."

His players moved away to the other side of the field.

Coach Jeremiah Marshall continued to stare at her quietly for a bit. "You look almost exactly like her."

Naomi nodded, knowing he was referring to her mother. "I hear that a lot. Now that I'm close to you, I realize I also look a bit like you—in features if not in color."

His dark-brown face pinched. She almost thought she saw a bit of pain in his expression, but she didn't let herself feel any sympathy for this man who had walked away from her without even caring—without having the strength of character—to find out the truth. That made him lacking, not her. Dash had taught her that much.

No matter her mother's belief that her being rejected by her father was the result of Adele's failure to provide the man with proof of paternity, Naomi had come to realize that real men took responsibility for their actions. The man had slept with a woman who had gotten pregnant in a timeframe that made him the potential father. Any responsible man would have demanded a paternity test himself if he had doubts. He wouldn't have risked abandoning his own flesh and blood.

"What do you want from me?"

She handed him an envelope.

He accepted it and flipped it over to see it was sealed. "What's this?"

"It's the name and address of a lab on the other side of the city. I've made arrangements for us to have a paternity test."

The look of panic in his eyes almost made her laugh.

"Don't worry. The med tech is a friend of mine. He's agreed to put the test specimens in under assumed names. The results will only be provided to you and me. I won't share them with anyone else. What you do with your copy will be up to you."

He flipped the envelope back over. He looked to be considering her request.

"I don't want anything from you, Jeremiah, except your acknowledgement to me that I'm your daughter. I don't want—or need—your money or your time or public disclosure. If you show up at that appointment, it will be the last you ever see of me. I'll disappear into the fog and you can go on pretending that I don't exist."

"And if I don't show up?"

"Then I won't disappear and your pretending will be over . . . for everyone." She turned her back on him and started to walk away. She stopped, hesitated, then reached into her crossbody bag for her wallet. She pulled out a wallet-sized photograph, turned and handed it to him. "In case you're curious, you're a grandfather. That's Taliana Adele Janssen. My daughter."

"Janssen? You actually married Dash Janssen?"

Naomi's eyes widened.

He cleared his throat. "Don't look so surprised. I'm a college football coach, I follow what goes on in the pros, particularly when the players are alums of my school. That business with his long lost twin was pretty hard to miss in the press."

Of course, he would have heard about that. Foolish of her to think for a moment he'd been keeping tabs on her. "I haven't married him yet. He claimed Taliana as his right away. He insisted on giving her his last name and putting his name on her birth certificate. Some men do the right thing by their daughters. See you tomorrow."

Under the curious glances of the offensive line and another young man dressed in non-team attire, she began to walk away again.

The young man approached and stopped next to Jeremiah. "Who was that, Dad?"

The question pulled at her. She stopped and glanced over her shoulder at her father, curious as to what he'd say. He held her gaze steadily, but didn't respond to the guy who appeared to be in his late twenties.

Naomi eyed the young man who she recognized from media clippings as one of the three half-brothers she'd never met and would probably never be introduced to. He was an attractive young man. He stood tall and fit and had a strong resemblance to his father. She suspected that's what her father had looked like when her mother had fallen for him.

Her father stood with eyes heavy on her, curious no doubt as to what she'd say. She quirked a brow, letting him know she was leaving the answer to him. As she suspected, he didn't come up with a response. She was fine with that. She'd delivered her message. She didn't need anything else from him but for him to show up at the lab tomorrow. Then, she'd be free of this burden she'd been carrying for over three decades.

She walked away without looking back this time. She was done looking back, done pining for the love of a man who didn't deserve that much emotional expenditure. She had all the man she needed waiting for her back home, a man who'd taught her what it meant to stay, and it was time to give him an answer.

~ 🙙 ~

A manila envelope smacked against the low table beside the bed where Dash lounged perusing a back issue of *Sports Illustrated*. "What's that?" he asked, looking up at Naomi.

"The results of the paternity test."

He noticed they hadn't been opened. "Aren't you curious as to what they say?"

"I already know what they say."

Dash's eyebrows rose in question.

"I knew the moment he looked at me. I could see it in his eyes. He may not have seen himself in me when I was a baby, but he saw it that day on the field. It's what made him show up for the test. He needed to free himself from the prison he'd trapped himself in by denying me all those decades ago. He may not want to be my father in relationship, but he needed to get rid of the ghost of possibility that's been haunting him all these years."

"And what about you? How do you feel?"

Naomi's shoes clunked to the floor. She slid under the covers fully dressed and snuggled against him. "I feel the only family I need is right here in my arms and asleep on the couch in the other room."

Dash chuckled. "They're napping?"

She nodded.

"I guess Tallie finally wore out her Gammie."

"I guess so." Naomi put a hand on the magazine he held and flipped the front down so she could see the cover. "Don't you ever get tired of reading that piece?"

"I never get tired of seeing my woman's byline in a national magazine. I love that you were able to turn what started out as cheap gossip into a hard-hitting piece on bigotry and bribery in professional sports."

She laughed. "And all it took to land me in the big leagues was a crooked owner who railroaded a gay player off his team and that player's desire for revenge."

He shook his head. "I still can't believe Carl Maynard was tossed off the team simply because DuChamps stumbled on him making out with his partner after a game. How many times have players' wives come down to the locker area to give them a congratulatory kiss? It's not like they were guilty of indecent exposure or anything. They both had all their clothes on."

She rolled over, pulled her sweater off under the covers, and tossed it out onto a nearby chair. "I kind of feel sorry for him."

"Maynard?"

"Yes. He probably could have petitioned for reinstatement if he'd spoken up. Now that everyone knows he conspired to set you up—or who he thought was you—his treachery has forever ruined his chances of getting back in a Griffins uniform. And I heard the team that picked him up as a backup after DuChamps released him recently dropped him down to the practice squad."

"That's unfortunate, but I kinda understand." The postseason hadn't worked out exactly how Dash had envisioned, but from his conversations with Shave Stephens and his recent experiences on the field, he'd learned a thing or two about what it took to lead a franchise to success. "Trust plays an important role in a quarter-back's success. If your team can't trust you off the field, they're unlikely to trust you on the field."

He closed the magazine and tossed it on top of her envelope. "To think Maynard saw Tatum in Ibiza and thought it was me. I guess when Tatum ignored him, he assumed I was intentionally blowing him off because I was on the down-low and didn't want to be outed. So, he made sure DuChamps found out about my supposed stomping ground. I could see how it would bother the guy that he'd lost his position for being gay only to be replaced by a guy still in the closet."

Dash hadn't been named starting quarterback for the Griffins . . . yet. Thanks to Naomi and Pete, he continued to wear the number twelve on a Griffins jersey so he still had a shot.

"He should have said something. Gotten a lawyer. Approached you—or Tatum—in Ibiza. Something." Her voice took on that scolding tone she used when she was trying to teach Tallie a lesson. "Attempting to take down another player wasn't the way. That makes him as bad as DuChamps."

"Maybe." He slid down and wrapped his arms around her. "It's kind of ironic. For all his talk about being a one-woman man, DuChamps was a lousy husband. With Francine DuChamps planning to divorce him and take her greater than forty-percent interest in the team out of his control, I guess the guy panicked."

She nodded. "Since he only had twelve percent of the team in his own name, he was intent on building a backing to finagle majority control of the franchise from Mrs. DuChamps by the time the divorce was final."

Laughing, Dash stroked her back. "DuChamps about fell out of his chair when she walked into that meeting. Who knew she was the one with the old-money, Texas-oil deep pockets that could buy the DuChamps family holdings several times over? Well, I guess you did." He kissed her. "You never told me how you got her to show up."

Her fingers played along his bottom lip. "I didn't have to do anything. Turns out, you happen to be her favorite Griffins player." She leaned back to get a better view of his face. "Hmm. I wonder how *that* came about?"

Dash chuckled without response.

"When I told her DuChamps's plans for you, she gave a harsh laugh and said, *'We'll just see about that.'*" Naomi channeled Francine DuChamps's southern accent. "*'Someone's leaving alright, but it's not going to be my Dash.'*"

He grinned. "Who knew dancing with the ladies and offering an occasional shoulder to cry on would leave me so well connected." His hands slowly mapped her torso. When he found she still wore a bra and pants, all thoughts of Francine and Martin's marital issues fled his mind. "Baby, you have on way too many clothes."

"Do I?" Her grin held an edge of deviltry.

He reached for the button on her pants. "Yes, and I hope you locked the door."

She nodded but swatted at his hands. "Wait a minute. Not so fast. I'm not done talking yet."

"I am." He tugged her zipper down.

Grabbing his wrists, she squeezed hard. "Too bad. Humor me. Because you don't get to take these off me until—" She rolled to pull something out of the drawer of the bedside table. "You put this on me." She placed his ring box in his hand.

He blinked a few times; he couldn't breathe or speak.

Her bottom lip tucked into her teeth. "Unless you've changed your mind," she said quietly.

He grabbed her face and kissed her hard and deep. He released her mouth, but not her face. His eyes bored into hers. "No way." He looked down at the box. "I was beginning to think you'd pawned this thing."

"Never. To get top dollar, I would have sold it on eBay."

He swatted her hip. "Very funny, you." He popped the spring-loaded lid and pulled out a large, marquis-cut diamond solitaire. He sat the box aside and lifted her left hand. "Naomi Marie Pellier, will you finally, *finally* agree to marry me?"

"Yes. Yes. Oh, yes!" She watched as he slid the ring on her finger then looked up with tears in her eyes. "Let's elope to Vegas and do it this weekend."

"No can do. I want all the frills and flowers and fuss. Besides, your mother would kill us, and I want to see Tallie walk down the aisle in a flower girl dress."

She frowned. "Are you marrying me or Tallie?"

He rolled her beneath him. "I'm marrying both of you. You're both my girls." He turned serious and his voice softened. "You're both my heart." Slowly, he communicated those words with lips and tongue.

Naomi melted under the intimate conversation. When he finally released her lips, he gave her a big grin, knowing his dimples were showing and she couldn't resist those dimples.

"Fine." She pouted. "I'll marry you the old-fashion way. You better be glad I love you."

"I am glad. Very, very glad." He tapped her pouting lips. "But Miss Pellier?"

"Hmm?"

"You still have on *way* too many clothes."

She laughed as he proceeded, with eager hands and a devilish leer, to remedy the problem.

~ ~ Ч ~ ~

AUTHOR'S NOTE

Once again, I offer my gratitude to the ladies of STCC Book Club (www.stccbookclub.com), who served as beta readers for this novel and dedicated an entire meeting to offering invaluable feedback on the storyline and characters of the book.

I am also beholden to the 2015 Kansas City Chiefs, whose stellar season with an eleven-game winning streak (and AFC Wild Card victory in the playoffs) helped fuel my creativity when the football scenes wouldn't flow.

And of course, to my readers, I'm happy you took the time to read Dash and Naomi's story. If you're curious to see what's next for the Griffins or whether Dash takes that trip to San Diego, look for Shave Stephens's and Tatum Gentry's stories, coming soon to the *Kansas City Griffins* series. I've included a preview of *Sideline Serenade* (Shave's story) on the pages that follow.

Please consider letting me and others know what you think of *Quarterback Casanova* by leaving a review (or just a star rating if you're pressed for time) on *Goodreads* and *Amazon* (scroll down to the Customer Reviews section of the Amazon book page and click on "Write a customer review"). **Even if only a few sentences, good or bad, reviews help increase the visibility for a book and can help other readers decide whether to purchase a book.**

Till next time,

Lisa Rayne

Sideline Serenade
(A *Kansas City Griffins* Novel)

by Lisa Rayne

Starting quarterback JONATHAN "SHAVE" STEPHENS has been sidelined with a career-threatening injury. When his struggle to walk again tanks his attitude and his hope of staying off the injured reserve list, physical therapist VANESSA THOMPSON steps in to give him an attitude adjustment. Shave butts heads with the headstrong PT until she issues him a challenge he can't refuse.

Vanessa's the only female supervisor in the sports medicine practice serving Shave's team, and she's not about to let the brash football legend destroy her promotion chances by sabotaging his own recovery. A former athlete herself, she's intentionally foregone marriage and family to pursue the highest sports medicine position in the career of her dreams. So, she's not opposed to exploiting Shave's competitive nature to get him to follow her program.

Vanessa may get more than she bargained for, however. Intrigued by the confirmed bachelorette, Shave's issuing a challenge of his own. Now that's she's got him back on his game, the next pass he's making is aimed straight for her heart.

AVAILABLE SOON

SEE NEXT PAGE FOR A PREVIEW

Preview:

SIDELINE SERENADE

Shave Stephens fell hard on his ass . . . again. Sharp pain shot up his hip, making him bite off a string of curses that would make his roughneck, ranch hand buddies back home proud, but wouldn't gel well with the straight-laced role model he'd become. He let his head drop down onto the cold, sterile tile floor—not hard enough to do any damage, just hard enough to knock some sense into his previously in-denial mind.

His career in the NFL was over. He felt it. No matter what the doctors said to keep his spirits up, his gut told him otherwise.

Washed up as a starting quarterback at the age of thirty-four. A guttural groan clawed from his throat. With one hand, he gave a hard shove to the wooden walking cane that had failed him. The cane skittered along the white tiles and clanged against the gray metal leg of the parallel walking bars his physical therapist intended he use next.

The uncharacteristic fit came from deep inside, but he

felt as frustrated by the immature act as by his current physical limitations. His usual easygoing disposition had abandoned him. He didn't know where it had gone and doubted it would return anytime soon. He'd felt it sneaking away little by little, day after day, week after week, as regular season play moved on without him.

He was known for keeping his cool—on the gridiron and off—no matter the pressure or situation, but he didn't feel like going through the motions anymore. He'd lost the drive to pretend any of this made a difference. It didn't. He threw an elbow over his eyes but didn't close them.

Through the slit between his arm and face, a mahogany, monster of a hand appeared, hovering in the vicinity of his middle chest. "Come on, Shave. We're not done yet."

Shave dropped his elbow and pushed away the PT's hand. "Leave me alone, Derrick." His usually understated Lone-Star-State accent thickened with the tension in his voice. "I'm through wasting my time. The leg feels as weak as it did the day I injured it."

Derrick, a former offensive lineman for Chicago, ignored Shave's dismissal and grabbed him under the arms. He yanked Shave off the floor as if he were lifting a child instead of a two-hundred-twenty-five-pound male comprised of solid muscle. "Give it some time, Shave. We're good at what we do, but we're not miracle workers. It's only been a few weeks."

In his younger days, a few weeks would have been all it took to get Shave's body back on the mend. He'd never had this type of injury before though, so in truth, he didn't have a real-world, personal comparison from which to draw. Nevertheless, he knew his odds. At thirty-four, he couldn't expect his body to heal itself as quickly as when he was in his twenties. He'd worried about whether the injury would completely heal at all. He'd suspected that even if it did heal, his leg would never be the same. Boy, what an understated, negative prognosis that had turned out to be.

Shave wanted to believe he'd be as good as new, ready to take on the strongest and baddest of his division competitors in no time, but he found it hard to conjure up his usual optimism. His backup quarterback had looked pretty good in the pocket the other day. Now that the kid had loosened up a bit, he had all the makings of a future Hall of Famer. Give the guy another few game starts, and he'd be in full swing. If Shave took too long to get back on the field, he'd find himself out of a job even if he got back to one hundred percent.

He wasn't ready to be sidelined. He wanted to take the Kansas City Griffins to the Super Bowl . . . and win. He already had a Super Bowl ring, but he'd won it as a backup quarterback for another team. He'd only played the last quarter of that game. He'd added two touchdowns to the final score, but the record books credit the win to the starter. He wanted a ring he'd earned—from the start to the finish of the game.

"Derrick if you keep picking the man up, he's never going to make any progress."

Shave glanced over Derrick's shoulder to find the source of the husky female voice chastising the PT. He encountered caramel-colored eyes so light they almost glowed. The feline-like irises stood out against the rich color of the woman's skin, a flawless, warm walnut-brown. She'd pulled her long, dark hair into a high ponytail. Her makeup was understated with subtle mascara and liner that made her already dramatic eyes stand out even more. Tall and fit, the lady wore running shoes with black athletic leggings and a gray three-quarter zip, lightweight athletic pullover. She looked like she'd just come from a run.

"Next time, leave him on the floor until he gets up himself," the husky-voiced intruder said, dropping a hand to her hip.

Shave had seen the woman a few times in the hallways when leaving or entering the building. He'd never seen her in a white coat so he hadn't realized she was part of the PT staff. Even now, she stood without the white coat indicative of members of the sports medicine crew, and no coat meant no name tag. He wondered who she was.

Derrick led Shave to the parallel bars and released him. "I've got this, Vanessa. Mr. Stephens just had a rough morning."

Vanessa. So that was her name.

She propped her remaining hand on her other shapely hip and gave Derrick a look that left no doubt she considered his explanation a total pile of bull. She glanced at Shave, allowing her caramel eyes to flit down his body and linger on his bad leg. She assessed his posture. He'd been favoring the leg a lot the last few days despite being advised to start putting his full weight on it. As much as he wanted to heed the advice, something didn't feel right when he tried.

Vanessa walked over to the PT desk and picked up his file. The pullover fell to her hips, but didn't completely cover her bottom. The firm, tight shape of her glutes displayed nicely under the form-fitting leggings. The lady's body was toned and looked near body fat free. He hadn't hung around female athletes since college. He'd forgotten how sexy a woman with serious muscle tone could be. Sculpted thighs, cut biceps, and full perky breasts made him think of intimate calisthenics—not physical therapy. The woman apparently lived exercise science and didn't just consider it a career.

"Yes, you've got this all right, Derrick. You're coddling him. Maybe you're a little too sympathetic to handle this case." Vanessa's frank admonishment of the retired lineman almost three times her size drew Shave out of his distracted testosterone moment.

Shave had lived in the Greater Kansas City area for three years now, but still hadn't gotten use to the way vowels rolled smooth and round off the Midwestern tongue. The lady's Heartland dialect, and take-charge attitude, affected him. The deep alto of her odd vowel sounds skittered across his nerve endings, and her in-control demeanor sent an unexpected rush of blood to the southerly body part between his thighs. Despite his foul mood, the effect was the exact opposite of irritating, which irritated him. At this critical juncture in his recuperation, women had been the last thing on his mind . . . until now. The lady was a distraction—a distraction he couldn't afford and *definitely* didn't need.

The pages of his file whispered gently as she flipped them one by one with the long fingers of a perfectly manicured, French-tipped hand. She looked up from the file. "Mr. Stephens, how many hours a day have you been putting your full weight on the leg?"

He didn't answer. He looked at Derrick. "What's the deal? Is she handling my case or are you?"

Her eyes narrowed. He'd apparently insulted her by questioning Derrick instead of answering her question. He suspected if she could throw fireballs with those large, cat-like eyes of hers, he'd be a pile of smoldering ash about now. He didn't care. His bad mood made him less than solicitous. Facing the end of his professional career tended to do that to a man. He didn't feel like playing nicey-nice with a new physical therapist who likely had delusions of grandeur, no matter how great her butt looked under spandex. He wasn't making progress and putting more weight on his leg wasn't going to change that.

"Do you have a problem answering my question, Mr. Stephens?"

"No, Ms. . . . ?"

"Thompson."

"No, Ms. Thompson, I don't have a problem answering your question. I have a problem with wasting my time. The therapy isn't working and putting more weight on my leg isn't going to make any difference."

"How do you know that if you don't follow instructions, Mr. Stephens?"

Shave gripped the parallel bar beside him tightly with one hand and turned so he could face her squarely. His annoyance made him move quicker than he should have, and he had to lock his knee when he felt it start to buckle beneath him. It was the same snafu that had occurred earlier, the reason he'd ended up on his backside ten minutes ago.

Vanessa watched his movements closely. She squinted when he corrected himself.

Great. Just what he needed: to lose control and end up on the floor again, and this time, in front of the workout princess.

She put down his file and took a step towards him. "Mr. Stephens how about you show me the walking drills you've been working on with Derrick."

"How about I not."

To his surprise, her lips curved up. "That wasn't a request." She titled her head to the side. "I can rephrase if you need me to."

His eyebrows rose in challenge.

"Show me the walking exercises you've been working

on." Her hands went to her hips again, and she lifted an eyebrow of her own. "*Now.*"

He stared at her, taking her measure more closely. He'd been right about her height. She was tall for a woman. He stood six-foot-three, and she could almost look him in the eye without wearing heels.

She stared back at him, holding her position without flinching. He had to work at hiding his amusement. So, Ms. Vanessa Thompson had grit. Fine. He'd do things her way for the moment.

Stepping between the parallel bars, he gripped each side with one hand. The task required him to use the bars only to steady his movement and to place as much weight as possible on his legs. He took two steps. Pain shot up his bad leg and over his kneecap when he put his weight on that side.

Derrick took a step towards him, but Vanessa stopped him. "Keep going, Mr. Stephens."

Shave ground down on his molars. Her calling him Mr. Stephens ratcheted up his already prickly mood. While she'd probably initially used his surname out of respect, her current tone gave him the impression she found him somehow unworthy of that respect. The thought bothered him more than a little.

Trying to block Vanessa out of his mind, he focused on taking one step after another. He'd gone about ten additional steps when the knee gave out and he went down. He tried to hold on to both bars to prevent hard contact with the floor, but he wasn't able to break his fall enough to avoid the intense pain that shot up his leg and through his groin.

He groaned and his hand shot to the tendon above his knee. The sharp movement unbalanced him and caused his other hand to slip off the opposite bar. He twisted to prevent himself from face-planting and landed with a thud on his back.

Thrice in one day, sent sprawling on his ass. This time, to make things extra special, he'd done it in front of this Amazon of a woman. He glanced up to see her staring down at him—arms still akimbo, ponytail draped in front of her shoulder, full breasts and curvy hips outlined appealingly in athletic wear. Correction, he'd done it in front of this *sexy*— albeit overbearing—Amazon of a woman. *Humiliating.*

He rolled to lever himself up, but the action caused pain to shoot through his kneecap again. He flopped down on the ground and went still.

* * *

Vanessa stood staring down at Jonathan "Shave" Stephens. He'd closed his eyes. She could feel the frustration radiating from him and a part of her understood. The other part of her, the part tasked with making sure her team got him back on the gridiron, needed him to stop feeling sorry for himself.

Her year-end evaluation score would determine whether or not she remained on track for advancement within the practice. She wanted to eventually make Department Director. With the current Director up for retirement in two years, competition and lobbying for the position had begun in earnest. Her fiercest competition, and the two top contenders to succeed the Director, were both male. In the twenty-year history of the practice, a women had never held the position. Given the practice's focus on professional sports, particularly professional football, current company gossips bet a woman never would. She intended to prove them wrong.

If her team failed to get Shave Stephens back in action within the standard timeframe for his documented injury, however, she'd be shredded in her evaluation. That alone would put her out of contention for the promotion. She couldn't let that happen. "Get up, Mr. Stephens."

"Stop calling me that," he snapped without opening his eyes.

Her own eyes widened at his tone and the tingle his rich, southern accent sent down her spine. "It's your name."

"You've just watched me fall flat on my ass." His eyelids lifted. His eyes were an intense blue, almost navy. They pierced her. "I feel our relationship has progressed enough that you can call me Shave. Or Jonathan, if you prefer."

His striking irises telegraphed his dislike of her along with a slight haze of discomfort. She couldn't do anything about the dislike. She wasn't here to be his friend.

The thought came with a bit of regret. She admired Shave Stephens. At least, she had in the past. She'd been a fan since his college days at Texas Fullerton University. He was currently her favorite quarterback in the league. He'd earned his nickname because he could shave more points off an opponent's lead, in the least amount of time, than any other quarterback in the history of the game and do it with a lazy, even-tempered finesse that made it look as easy as walking across the street.

He played with more heart and more determination than any other player in the country. She understood this injury challenged him, but she hadn't expected him to be one of those self-indulgent, everything-comes-easy-for-me whiney boys. It didn't mesh with the gutsy, roll-with-the-punches personality she'd followed through the years.

Right now, she needed him to find his determination and never-say-die drive and apply it to his rehabilitation.

"Fine. *Shave*, please get up."

Derrick stepped around her. "Vanessa, cut the guy some slack. The way that knee buckled, something else is going on."

Vanessa put her arm straight out, parallel to the floor, across the front of Derrick's chest to bar his progress. "I agree, but I think he can get up." She looked back down at Shave. "What's going to happen if this occurs when you're at home? You just going to lie on the floor waiting for someone to stop by? The mailman perhaps? A girlfriend? Or are you going to hope you have your cell phone on you so you can call Derrick to come over and pick you up off the carpet?"

Those blue eyes turned Artic. She shored herself up to show no outward sign of the shiver that ran through her at his cold glare.

Shave rolled onto his chest, the movement placing him directly under one of the bars. He did a pushup to raise himself, using only the foot of his good leg for leverage. Then, he balanced himself on one arm and reached for the bar over his head. His arm muscles flexed with the movement. Once he had a strong grip on the bar, he pulled himself up, pushing against the floor with his foot to get more height. It was an exceptional show of upper body strength. He stood, leaning heavily on the bar and keeping all his weight on his good leg.

He pulled a breath in and out. That's all it took for him to regain even respiration. The effort hadn't even taxed him.

Her eyes skimmed over the muscles of his arms and chest, readily discernible under his moisture-wicking Under Armour long-sleeved tee. He might have a bum leg, but there was nothing wrong with his core or upper body. Engrossed in her appreciation of his build, she took a few too many seconds to acknowledge him.

"Okay, I'm up. What's next on your torture agenda?"

His sarcastic quip brought her attention to his face. When her eyes met his, he purposefully allowed his gaze to drop and roam over her physique. He didn't ogle. Simply took in her build as if taking inventory of her assets. She interpreted the action as his way of letting her know he'd caught her checking him out. Her eyes narrowed.

His lips slanted slightly sideways in an understated smirk. She'd take that as a sign he had some of his fight back. Fine by her. *This* Shave she could handle.

~ *END PREVIEW* ~

Counselor Undone

by Lisa Rayne

The most passionate kiss of his life . . .

Kansas City attorney MICHAEL REMINGTON is in the middle of a corporate case he can't afford to lose. The jaded workaholic has laser focus until he's blindsided by an unsettling distraction—an anonymous encounter that ends with the most passionate kiss of his life. When his search for the sexy mystery woman gets sidetracked by his unexpected attraction to an ambitious new associate, his life goes from merely unsettled to downright complicated.

The biggest case of her career . . .

JORDIS MORGAN has one goal at her new firm: make partner at all costs... well, almost any cost. She's determined to earn the firm's coveted case assignment—as Michael's co-counsel on the most high-profile patent case in the country—without having an illicit affair with her boss. More interested in career advancement than romance, Jordis does everything in her power to resist the explosive chemistry brewing between her and the man who's not used to being told no.

Leads to their greatest adversarial challenge . . . each other

Amidst evidence of case sabotage and high-stakes litigation he can't risk for an unethical liaison, Michael must make a life-altering choice—fight for the woman he can't live without or hold on to the patent case of the century. In a world where he'd like to have it all, the staid attorney soon finds himself faced with his greatest adversarial challenge—the one to win Jordis's heart.

AVAILABLE NOW

SEE NEXT PAGE FOR AN EXCERPT

COUNSELOR UNDONE

CHAPTER 1

Michael Remington had never had to work so hard for a one-night stand in his life.

It went against his grain and his ego.

He'd long ago become jaded about love and all things Cupid, but he generally had no problem finding a casual bedmate when he wanted. As a named partner in a prestigious law firm with political connections and ties to the social elite of Kansas City, women practically threw themselves at him. Yet, here he stood at the local bar association's annual New Year's Eve masked ball—at five minutes till midnight—looking for a woman who had made herself scarce. If he hadn't been the one to walk away from his elusive prey earlier, he'd think he'd lost his touch.

"What are you doing standing here all alone?" Michael's best friend and law partner, Chase Hager, snuck up behind him and slapped him on the shoulder. "The whole point of my convincing you to come was so you could meet someone new."

Michael grunted. "I must have been out of my mind. And I can't believe I let you talk me into this ridiculous costume. I feel like a piece of meat on display."

Chase laughed. His eyes scanned the costume that made Michael look like an ancient gladiator *sans* breastplate. "How do you expect to attract quality prospects if you don't show off the merchandise?"

Michael rolled his eyes, finding the comment ironic coming from a guy whose costume kept all his significant body parts covered. "You know I'm not in the market for quality prospects. I'm not in the market for *any* prospects."

"Oh really?" Chase eyed the two champagne glasses in Michael's hand. "It looks like you're in the market for something. Didn't mean to interrupt. Carry on." Chase walked away, loud chuckles accompanying his self-satisfied grin.

Tuning out the annoying sound of his friend's retreating mirth, Michael resumed the search for his evening entertainment. She wore a Juliet costume. Other than that, he didn't know much about her. He hadn't bothered to ask her any questions or even get her real name. It hadn't mattered. The moment she'd spotted him, she'd turned on a flirt that promised more than good conversation.

Not one, usually, to go for the vampy come-on, he'd humored her. He may be jaded, but he wasn't rude. She'd made a pouty complaint about her Romeo having gone off "roaming" and suggested Michael play her knight in shining armor. He'd laughed and responded, "Wrong costume."

When she'd looked at him with a blank stare, he'd realized she couldn't make the distinction between a Roman gladiator and a knight of the realm. He'd wondered if her

Elizabethan-styled wig covered a natural blond. Then he'd chastised himself for the insensitive stereotyping. A woman certainly didn't have to be blond to be intellectually challenged. He'd met enough female cerebral lightweights to know.

Categorizing Juliet as good for an easy lay, but never one to rise above an occasional late night tryst, he'd politely excused himself. He hadn't originally felt like playing the game tonight. He'd recognized her type and the hunger in her eyes immediately. He avoided—or fought off—women like her all the time, women set on attaching themselves permanently to a rich professional with a strong reputation in the community.

He didn't make himself available for that kind of liaison. At thirty-eight, he'd seen enough of his buddies take the plunge only to end up doing the sap two-step when romantic bliss turned into an episode of reality TV divorce court. He'd almost made that mistake once, with a firm colleague no less, and his engagement had ended in disaster. He'd learned his lesson. He didn't believe in forever-after, and he didn't think this masked ball would net him a Cinderella. He had one use for women currently—a physical use, which is exactly where his one-night stand came in, if he could find her.

He glanced at the two flutes of champagne in his hand, tempted to down them both. He abstained. He'd probably had one too many drinks already. After he'd escaped Juliet, he'd had a few to take the edge off his boredom. That had been a mistake. He'd only managed to slide his boredom into frustration.

His gladiator costume had brought out the predator in otherwise reserved ladies. After being groped and propositioned relentlessly by women he knew—despite their masks and costumes — and a few he didn't, he'd decided to go with it. Maybe getting laid for the first time in four months would improve his disposition. Unfortunately, now that he'd decided to give in to dimwitted Juliet's offer of a sure thing, she'd disappeared.

He should have stayed home and watched the ball drop over Times Square. Better yet, he should have gone to the office to figure out how a box of discovery documents had gone missing in his multimillion dollar patent infringement case. He planned to build the firm founded by his late father and his grandfather into a national powerhouse. He wouldn't succeed if he dropped the ball on the intellectual property case of the year, a case journalists predicted would change the legal landscape for pharmaceutical patents.

He sighed. He'd deal with his case issues tomorrow. Banishing work from his mind, he stepped onto the balcony of the penthouse condo. A smile spread across his lips. A lovely vision stood staring out over the railing.

He'd found her.

❧ ❧ | ❧ ❧

Mask still in place, a costumed Juliet stood on the balcony wondering why she hadn't left this party. The couple she'd planned to meet, her first cousin plus one, hadn't shown and she didn't know anyone else here. She planned to give her mysteriously absent cousin a scathing piece of her mind for pressuring her to attend this party then leaving her high and dry.

She hated New Year's Eve parties. She didn't need to wax nostalgic about the past year. Betrayal and heartbreak had haunted most of the last three hundred and sixty-five days. She'd left the unpleasant memories behind in Los

Angeles six months ago, and she never wanted to revisit them. As for New Year's resolutions, the only resolution that mattered mandated letting nothing—and no one—distract her from making partner by the end of the year at the KC law firm to which she'd recently transferred.

She'd only come to this midnight-fest foray—against her better judgment—to appease her cousin. Then she'd compounded the mistake by letting her cousin arrange for her costume. She'd wanted Cleopatra, but a mix-up at the costume shop had led to the delivery of this Juliet getup instead. By the time she'd realized the mistake, the shop had closed and she couldn't make an exchange.

The sound of the balcony door sliding open drew her attention. She turned towards a walking piece of art wearing a gladiator costume.

Four . . . Three . . .

"Juliet! There you are!" the masked gladiator cooed, his baritone voice slightly singsong from one too many glasses of wine . . . or something. "I wondered where you'd gone."

He placed a strong hand around her arm.

Two . . . One . . . Happy New Year!

Despite the two flutes of champagne he held in his other hand, the gladiator turned her deftly into his embrace. The shawl she'd wrapped around her shoulders fell to the ground as plastic horn toots erupted inside amidst cheers. He slid his occupied fist behind her back, gripped the base of her neck with his free hand, and kissed her thoroughly.

She pushed hard against his chest. When she opened her mouth to tell him he'd made a mistake, he took the liberty of sliding his tongue inside to play wickedly with hers. She moaned softly, which caused him to chuckle.

She didn't know who this man was or why he thought he had an open invitation to make love to her mouth, but her ability to think straight slowly evaporated. She'd never been kissed like this—like the last beautiful woman on earth. Her libido sparked, making her excited and appalled at the same time. She'd been unattached for fourteen long months, and this hunk's skill with his tongue sent hot flashes to an area of her body she'd almost forgotten existed.

Without removing his lips from hers, the gladiator backed her into a corner alcove west of the sliding glass door, not stopping until her back nearly touched the stone wall. With a bit of apprehension, she noticed darkness covered the alcove he'd selected, the few existing patio sconces not aggressive enough to throw their light around the turn in the wall. Her mind began to whirl. She shouldn't be here—not at this party and definitely not in this man's arms.

The thought made her push harder against his chest. *"Please."*

"Honey, there's no need to beg. Whatever you want, I plan to give it to you *all night long.*" Pulling back slightly, he handed her a glass of champagne.

She accepted the glass on reflex. "You don't under-stand—"

"Here's to the New Year," he interrupted and lifted his glass dramatically. He paused, as if searching for a more mindful toast, but simply added with a wicked grin, "It's suddenly looking very promising." He downed his champagne in one gulp then tossed the flute onto a cushion-covered wrought iron chair not far away.

"Drink up, Juliet." He wrapped his fingers around hers on the stem of the glass she held and assisted it to her lips. "Don't you know it's bad luck not to drink to a toast made on New Year's Eve?"

She took a sip while pressing persistently against his

chest with her other hand. He budged a smidge. Her breathing came easier with the space she'd created between them until she realized his stingy costume left most of his chest bare. Her hand rested against the wall of his smooth pectorals, and what a wall it was. He sported the physique of a Calvin Klein underwear model, all planes and bulges and six-pack. Those reawakened body parts began to liquefy.

"Y-You've made a mistake," she murmured, flustered by her unexpected female response to him.

Though she could count the number of lovers she'd had on half of one hand, she didn't lack sexual experience. Still, none of her lovers, even the man to whom she'd once been engaged, had stirred in her with a simple kiss a fraction of the heat currently rising inside her. "I think you're looking for someone else." *And that's a shame*, she thought, surprising herself.

The gladiator smiled down at her. She stood approx.-imately five feet ten in the flat leather sandals she wore, but he still stretched several inches above her. He had to be well over six feet tall.

She'd gotten a brief look at his face before he embraced her and noted odd colored eyes in a rugged face. He wore his hair a little long. The back brushed the top of his epaulettes, and a wavy wisp fell across his forehead, touching the top of a dark brow. Given the paucity of the starlight, she couldn't quite discern the color of the tresses — black or maybe a deep brown. He qualified as objectively handsome by any woman's standards, but she didn't understand this intense attraction. Even with his olive-toned skin, he didn't fit her usual type.

Removing her champagne glass with one hand, he pressed his other over the hand she rested on his chest. "No, milady, there's no mistaking you. How about we get better acquainted, like you suggested earlier?"

He tucked his face into the curve of her neck. "Mmm, you smell good. All flowers, and sweetness, and woman." His lips trailed kisses along her neckline while he showered her with words of seduction. The sound of his voice, two parts sexy and one part awe, stirred her. She became enraptured by the risqué words he whispered. When he got to the part about what he wanted to do with his tongue, she shivered.

He took her mouth in another rousing kiss. His tongue sliding warm across her lips, then along the length of her own, evoked sheer bliss. Wrapped in the feel of him, she didn't notice the hand he slid to the split at the side of her costume until that hand invaded the fabric and moved up her thigh.

Through a haze, she became conscious of his fingers caressing the side of her bare bottom, the stringy thong she wore giving him full access. His fingers massaged the firm muscles of her buttock. He still held her half-full champagne flute in his other hand, but the burden didn't slow him down. He pressed at her back until she leaned flush against him from hip to shoulder. The long hardness of his arousal met her abdomen, and her hips swayed in a manner that made him groan aloud.

When that old R. Kelly song about a little bump and grind began to play in her head, she decided she'd lost her mind. What was she doing in a darkened corner — outside no less — with a stranger, making out like a horny teenager?

Something in her consciousness chided she needed to stop him, but she couldn't muster the will to resist. She felt as if he'd put a spell on her. Maybe he should have come dressed like a warlock. He'd been looking for another Juliet, but he'd magically homed in on the one so deprived of a man's touch she'd let him have his way with her outside on an open balcony.

Everything happens for a reason, her grandmother always said. Taking grandmamma at her word, she wondered if there was a reason she'd ended up dressed like Juliet on this particular balcony at midnight so Mr. Gladiator could kiss her until she turned into a shameless hussy. At the moment, a reason escaped her, but perhaps she needed to accept the serendipity of the evening to truly appreciate the divine order.

What would happen if she completely surrendered to the moment? Why not enjoy her first real New Year's Eve kiss — not counting the kisses from her godchildren last year — in three years? She was long overdue for a serious, grownup New Year's Eve kiss so surrender to the moment she did, with gusto.

The act marked a defining moment in her life. Her nature didn't include spontaneous or frivolous. She was the intellectual in her group of friends, the deep thinker, the analytical one. Known as a FranklinCovey planner junkie, she couldn't get through her day without a prioritized daily task list. She didn't take uncalculated risks, and she didn't even kiss on the first date. Despite those deep-set character traits, she slowly raised her hand, pushed her fingers into his long, silky hair, and kissed him back as if he were the love of her life.

~ END EXCERPT ~

FIND OUT WHAT'S NEXT FROM

LISA RAYNE

VISIT

www.lisarayne.com

ABOUT THE AUTHOR

LISA RAYNE is an award-winning author who loves sports,  movies, music, and books. An avid reader, the only thing she likes more than curling up with a good book is writing one. She won a Top 10 Finalist berth in the prestigious, global Harlequin® "So You Think You Can Write" Contest with her first manuscript and is a 2016 Emma Award Winner. As a former practicing attorney, naturally, she loves to write about lawyers, but the athlete in her ensures she also infuses her love of sports into her works.

Lisa earned a bachelor's degree in Comparative Literature from Princeton and her law degree from Stanford. Her passion for the creative arts led her to practice intellectual property, entertainment, and media law for many years before she decided to start producing her own creative works instead of simply representing others who did. She currently lives in the Midwest and has two daughters.

For all the latest news on Lisa Rayne books, giveaways, and appearances follow her online at:

Twitter: @AuthorRayne;
facebook.com/authorlisarayne;
lisarayne.com.